THE 1976 ANNUAL WORLD'S BEST SF

Edited by

DONALD A. WOLLHEIM

with Arthur W. Saha

DAW BOOKS, INC.
DONALD A. WOLLHEIM, PUBLISHER

1301 Avenue of the Americas
New York, N. Y. 10019

Cover art by Jack Gaughan.

FIRST PRINTING, MAY 1976

1 2 3 4 5 6 7 8 9

PRINTED IN U.S.A.

Table of Contents

INTRODUCTION

In our introduction to last year's selections we pointed out that as the world of the present changes so does the world of the future. In the case of utopian writings, for instance, we pointed out that the period of the uninhibited squandering of the Earth's resources had come to an end and that the matter of facing the real economic and ecological problems of the final quarter of this century was forcing itself to society's attention.

This was reflected by a trend to thinking about utopias as they might be conceived by alien minds for alien worlds.

Transition is still the order of the day for the real world and it is very much in evidence in the realm of science fiction and fantasy. The past year has reflected this trend which is still going on. There has been no stable conclusions reached and the year's crop of fiction reflects this element of whither and why and where. . . .

The most obvious evidence for this transition in the field of science fiction writing have been the announcements of three well-known writers of their plans to leave the field. Robert Silverberg has stated that his next novel, due for 1976 publication, will also be his last novel. He may still do anthologies—he has done many in the last few years—but he himself, once amazingly prolific, will write no more science fiction.

Harlan Ellison, whose long-delayed *Last Dangerous Visions*, is expected to see print finally in 1976, announced that he will be turning his talents to "making it" in the mainstream, determined to force the Literary Establishment to take notice with a "bestseller." Ellison has spoken before of his dissatisfaction with the—to him—limited sphere of science fiction. But he has given himself the challenge publicly and we may expect therefore that he will carry it through.

Barry Malzberg, a law unto himself and first winner of the John W. Campbell Memorial Award, has also announced that he will leave the field, after having hundreds of short stories and a dozen or more books to his credit.

All three of these have been associated with what was once called the New Wave but which is more or less working out as the introduction of new styles and experimental techniques into the writing of sf. All three have done this with skill and their innovations will surely linger in the work of the many who have learned from them.

Transition is also the term for what is going on in science fiction publishing. *Galaxy,* once one of the two great leader sf magazines, is skipping issues and showing other signs of publishing weakness. *Vertex,* the unusual magazine from the West Coast, has ceased publication. *Analog* and *Fantasy and Science Fiction* continue to hold up strongly. Rumors of two or three new periodicals to come abound. In England the astonishing *Science Fiction Monthly*—more color posters than text—appears to be thriving and it is hard to know what to make of that. *New Worlds,* struggling along as a paperback periodical, has changed publishers again. Reports of weakness in *Amazing* and *Fantastic* continue with the possibility that these old established titles may change hands. In Europe the field appears strong and increases.

In books, sf is definitely booming with many paperback companies increasing their output and new imprints showing up. This seems to us to have the status of a "boom" based on emulation rather than real evidence of an enlarged market and we are concerned as to the consequences should the hopes of high profits not materialize. But meanwhile the field is emerging from obscurity and gaining public notice in such journals as *Time* and *Newsweek* as well as major newspapers. Conventions continue to increase in number and profitable attendance.

This 1976 selection may display some of this transitional mood. Some of the big names have not been doing much in the way of shorter material, allowing thereby newer and younger writers to blossom. New names are forcing their way into the front ranks. Quality holds up with a noticeable increase in the thoughtful consideration of time and the risks of the future. Nothing that we would call utopian this time—rather a pause to reflect.

But a "good read" as we like to say. Enjoy it.

—DONALD A. WOLLHEIM

CATCH THAT ZEPPELIN!

by Fritz Leiber

Sometimes we think that history has made some turns which it need not have made. Whether there are indeed alternate worlds where things came out differently we cannot know, though lately sf writers have been speculating on this. The current nostalgia for zeppelins, for instance, is almost inexplicable—most of our readers could not possibly ever have seen them and their period of existence was really quite short. Still, it is something of a delight when a wonder-spinner like Leiber turns his hand to reweaving the structure of society.

This year on a trip to New York City to visit my son, who is a social historian at a leading municipal university there, I had a very unsettling experience. At black moments, of which at my age I have quite a few, it still makes me distrust profoundly those absolute boundaries in Space and Time which are our sole protection against Chaos, and fear that my mind—no, my entire individual existence—may at any moment at all and without any warning whatsoever be blown by a sudden gust of Cosmic Wind to an entirely different spot in a Universe of Infinite Possibilities. Or, rather, into another Universe altogether. And that my mind and individuality will be changed to fit.

But at other moments, which are still in the majority, I believe that my unsettling experience was only one of those remarkably vivid waking dreams to which old people become increasingly susceptible, generally waking dreams about the past, and especially waking dreams about a past in which at some crucial point one made an entirely different and braver choice than one actually did, or in which the whole world made such a decision, with a completely different future resulting. Golden glowing might-have-beens nag increasingly at the minds of some older people.

In line with this interpretation I must admit that my whole unsettling experience was structured very much like a dream. It began with startling flashes of a changed world. It continued into a longer period when I completely accepted the changed world and delighted in it and, despite fleeting quivers of uneasiness, wished I could bask in its glow forever. And it ended in horrors, or nightmares, which I hate to mention, let alone discuss, until I must.

Opposing this dream notion, there are times when I am completely convinced that what happened to me in Manhattan and in a certain famous building there was no dream at all, but absolutely real, and that I did indeed visit another Time Stream.

Finally, I must point out that what I am about to tell you I am necessarily describing in retrospect, highly aware of several transitions involved and, whether I want to or not, commenting on them and making deductions that never once occurred to me at the time.

No, at the time it happened to me—and now at this moment of writing I am convinced that it did happen and was absolutely real—one instant simply succeeded another in the most natural way possible. I questioned nothing.

As to why it all happened to me, and what particular mechanism was involved, well, I am convinced that every man or woman has rare brief moments of extreme sensitivity, or rather vulnerability, when his mind and entire being may be blown by the Change Winds to Somewhere Else. And then, by what I call the Law of the Conservation of Reality, blown back again.

I was walking down Broadway somewhere near 34th Street. It was a chilly day, sunny despite the smog—a bracing day—and I suddenly began to stride along more briskly than is my cautious habit, throwing my feet ahead of me with a faint suggestion of the goose step. I also threw back my shoulders and took deep breaths, ignoring the fumes which tickled my nostrils. Beside me, traffic growled and snarled, rising at times to a machine-gun rata-tat-tat. While pedestrians were scuttling about with that desperate ratlike urgency characteristic of all big American cities, but which reaches its ultimate in New York. I cheerfully ignored that too. I even smiled at the sight of a ragged bum and a fur-coated gray-haired society lady both independently dodging across the street through the hurtling traffic with a cool practiced skill one sees only in America's biggest metropolis.

Just then I noticed a dark, wide shadow athwart the street ahead of me. It could not be that of a cloud, for it did not move. I craned my neck sharply and looked straight up like the veriest yokel, a regular *Hans-Kopf-in-die-Luft* (Hans-Head-in-the-Air, a German figure of comedy).

My gaze had to climb up the giddy 102 stories of the tallest building in the world, the Empire State. My gaze was strangely accompanied by the vision of a gigantic, long-fanged ape making the same ascent with a beautiful girl in one paw—oh, yes, I was recollecting the charming American fantasy-film *King Kong,* or as they name it in Sweden, *Kong King.*

And then my gaze clambered higher still up the 222-foot sturdy tower, to the top of which was moored the nose of the vast, breath-takingly beautiful, streamlined, silvery shape which was making the shadow.

Now here is a most important point. I was not at the time in the least startled by what I saw. I knew at once that it was simply the bow section of the German Zeppelin *Ostwald,* named for the great German pioneer of physical chemistry and electrochemistry, and queen of the mighty passenger and light-freight fleet of luxury airliners, working out of Berlin, Baden-Baden, and Bremerhaven. That matchless Armada of Peace, each titanic airship named for a world-famous German scientist—the *Mach,* the *Nernst,* the *Humboldt,* the *Fritz Haber,* the French-named *Antoine Henri Becquerel,* the American-named *Edison,* the Polish-named *Sklodowska,* the American-Polish *T. Sklodowska Edison,* and even the Jewish-named *Einstein!* The great humanitarian navy in which I held a not unimportant position as international sales consultant and *Fachman*—I mean expert. My chest swelled with justified pride at this *edel*—noble—achievement of *der Vaterland.*

I knew also without any mind-searching or surprise that the length of the *Ostwald* was more than one half the 1,472-foot height of the Empire State Building plus its mooring tower, thick enough to hold an elevator. And my heart swelled again with the thought that the Berlin *Zeppelinturm* (dirigible tower) was only a few meters less high. Germany, I told myself, need not strain for mere numerical records—

her sweeping scientific and technical achievements speak for themselves to the entire planet.

All this literally took little more than a second, and I never broke my snappy stride. As my gaze descended, I cheerfully hummed under my breath *Deutschland, Deutschland uber Alles.*

The Broadway I saw was utterly transformed, though at the time this seemed every bit as natural as the serene presence of the *Ostwald* high overhead, vast ellipsoid held aloft by helium. Silvery electric trucks and buses and private cars innumerable purred along far more evenly and quietly, and almost as swiftly, as had the noisy, stenchful, jerky gasoline-powered vehicles only moments before, though to me now the latter were completely forgotten. About two blocks ahead, an occasional gleaming electric car smoothly swung into the wide silver arch of a quick-battery-change station, while others emerged from under the arch to rejoin the almost dreamlike stream of traffic.

The air I gratefully inhaled was fresh and clean, without trace of smog.

The somewhat fewer pedestrians around me still moved quite swiftly, but with a dignity and courtesy largely absent before, with the numerous blackamoors among them quite as well dressed and exuding the same quiet confidence as the Caucasians.

The only slightly jarring note was struck by a tall, pale, rather emaciated man in black dress and with unmistakably Hebraic features. His somber clothing was somewhat shabby, though well kept, and his thin shoulders were hunched. I got the impression he had been looking closely at me, and then instantly glancing away as my eyes sought his. For some reason I recalled what my son had told me about the City College of New York—CCNY—being referred to surreptitiously and jokingly as Christian College Now Yiddish. I couldn't help chuckling a bit at that witticism, though I am glad to say it was a genial little guffaw rather than a malicious snicker. Germany in her well-known tolerance and noblemindedness has completely outgrown her old, disfiguring anti-Semitism—after all, we must admit in all fairness that perhaps a third of our great men are Jews or carry Jewish genes, Haber and Einstein among them—despite what dark and, yes, wicked memories may lurk in the subconscious minds of oldsters like myself and occasionally briefly surface into awareness like submarines bent on ship murder.

My happily self-satisfied mood immediately reasserted itself, and with a smart, almost military gesture I brushed to either side with a thumbnail the short, horizontal black mustache which decorates my upper lip, and I automatically swept back into place the thick comma of black hair (I confess I dye it) which tends to fall down across my forehead.

I stole another glance up at the *Ostwald,* which made me think of the matchless amenities of that wondrous deluxe airliner: the softly purring motors that powered its propellers—electric motors, naturally, energized by banks of lightweight TSE batteries and as safe as its helium; the Grand Corridor running the length of the passenger deck from the Bow Observatory to the stern's like-windowed Games Room, which becomes the Grand Ballroom at night; the other peerless rooms letting off that corridor—the *Gesellschaftsraum der Kapitan* (Captain's Lounge) with its dark woodwork, manly cigar smoke and *Damentische* (Tables for Ladies), the Premier Dining Room with its linen napery and silver-plated aluminum dining service, the Ladies' Retiring Room always set out profusely with fresh flowers, the Schwartzwald bar, the gambling casino with its roulette, baccarat, chemmy, blackjack (*vingt-et-un*), its tables for skat and bridge and dominoes and sixty-six, its chess tables presided over by the delightfully eccentric world's champion Nimzowitch, who would defeat you blindfold, but always brilliantly, simultaneously or one at a time, in charmingly baroque brief games for only two gold pieces per person per game (one gold piece to nutsy Nimzy, one to the DLG), and the supremely luxurious staterooms with costly veneers of mahogany over balsa; the hosts of attentive stewards, either as short and skinny as jockeys or else actual dwarfs, both types chosen to save weight; and the titanium elevator rising through the countless bags of helium to the two-decked Zenith Observatory, the sun deck wind-screened but roofless to let in the ever-changing clouds, the mysterious fog, the rays of the stars and good old Sol, and all the heavens. Ah, where else on land or sea could you buy such high living?

I called to mind in detail the single cabin which was always mine when I sailed on the *Ostwald—meine Stammkabine.* I visualized the Grand Corridor thronged with wealthy passengers in evening dress, the handsome officers, the unobtrusive ever-attentive stewards, the gleam of white shirt fronts, the glow of bare shoulders, the muted dazzle of jewels, the music of conversations like string quartets, the lilting low laughter that traveled along.

Exactly on time I did a neat *"Links, marschieren!"* ("To the left, march!") and passed through the impressive portals of the Empire State and across its towering lobby to the mutedly silver-glowing date: 6 May 1937 and the time of day: 1:07 P.M. Good!—since the *Ostwald* did not cast off until the tick of three P.M., I would be left plenty of time for a leisurely lunch and good talk with my son, if he had remembered to meet me—and there was actually no doubt of that, since he is the most considerate and orderly minded of sons, a real German mentality, though I say it myself.

I headed for the express bank, enjoying my passage through the clusters of high-class people who thronged the lobby without any unseemly crowding, and placed myself before the doors designated "Dirigible Departure Lounge" and in briefer German *"Zum Zeppelin."*

The elevator hostess was an attractive Japanese girl in skirt of dull silver with the DLG, Double Eagle and Dirigible insignia of the German Airship Union emblazoned in small on the left breast of her mutedly silver jacket. I noted with unvoiced approval that she appeared to have an excellent command of both German and English and was uniformly courteous to the passengers in her smiling but unemotional Nipponese fashion, which is so like our German scientific precision of speech, though without the latter's warm underlying passion. How good that our two federations, at opposite sides of the globe, have strong commercial and behavioral ties!

My fellow passengers in the lift, chiefly Americans and Germans, were of the finest type, very well dressed—except that just as the doors were about to close, there pressed in my doleful Jew in black. He seemed ill at ease, perhaps because of his shabby clothing. I was surprised, but made a point of being particularly polite towards him, giving him a slight bow and brief but friendly smile, while flashing my eyes. Jews have as much right to the acme of luxury travel as any other people on the planet, if they have the money—and most of them do.

During our uninterrupted and infinitely smooth passage upward, I touched my outside left breast pocket to reassure myself that my ticket—first class on the *Ostwald!*—and my papers were there. But actually I got far more reassurance and even secret joy from the feel and thought of the documents in my tightly zippered inside left breast pocket: the signed preliminary agreements that would launch America herself into the manufacture of passenger zeppelins. Modern Germany is always generous in sharing her great technical achievements with responsible sister nations, supremely confident that the genius of her scientists and engineers will continue to keep her well ahead of all other lands; and after all, the genius of two Americans, father and son, had made vital though indirect contributions to the development of safe airship travel (and not forgetting the part played by the Polish-born wife of the one and mother of the other).

The obtaining of those documents had been the chief and official reason for my trip to New York City, though I had been able to combine it most pleasurably with a long overdue visit with my son, the social historian, and with his charming wife.

These happy reflections were cut short by the jarless arrival of our elevator at its lofty terminus on the 100th floor. The journey old love-smitten King Kong had made only after exhausting exertion we had accomplished effortlessly. The silvery doors spread wide. My fellow passengers hung back for a moment in awe and perhaps a little trepidation at the thought of the awesome journey ahead of them, and I—seasoned airship traveler that I am—was the first to step out, favoring with a smile and nod of approval my pert yet cool Japanese fellow employee of the lower echelons.

Hardly sparing a glance toward the great, fleckless window confronting the doors and showing a matchless view of Manhattan from an elevation of 1,250 feet minus two stories, I briskly turned, not right to the portals of the Departure Lounge and tower elevator, but left to those of the superb German restaurant *Krahenest* (Crow's Nest).

I passed between the flanking three-foot-high bronze statuettes of Thomas Edison and Marie Sklodowska Edison niched in one wall and those of Count von Zeppelin and Thomas Sklodowska Edison facing them from the other, and entered the select precincts of the finest German dining place outside the Fatherland. I paused while my eyes traveled searchingly around the room with its restful, dark wood paneling deeply carved with beautiful representations of the Black Forest and its grotesque supernatural denizens—kobolds, elves, gnomes, dryads (tastefully sexy) and the like. They interested me since I am what Americans call a Sunday painter, though almost my sole subject matter is zeppelins seen against blue sky and airy, soaring clouds.

The *Oberkellner* came hurrying toward me with menu tucked under his left elbow and saying, "*Mein Herr!* Charmed to see you once more! I have a perfect table-for-one with porthole looking out across the Hudson."

But just then a youthful figure rose springily from behind a table set against the far wall, and a dear and familiar voice rang out to me with "*Hier, Papa!*"

"*Nein, Herr Ober,*" I smilingly told the head waiter as I walked past him, "*heute hab ich ein Gesellschafter. Mein Sohn.*"

I confidently made my way between tables occupied by well-dressed folk, both white and black.

My son wrung my hand with fierce family affection, though we had last parted only that morning. He insisted that I take the wide, dark, leather-upholstered seat against the wall, which gave me a fine view of the entire restaurant, while he took the facing chair.

"Because during this meal I wish to look only on you, Papa," he assured me with manly tenderness. "And we have at least an hour and a half together, Papa—I have checked your luggage through, and it is likely already aboard the *Ostwald*." Thoughtful, dependable boy!

"And now, Papa, what shall it be?" he continued after we had settled ourselves. "I see that today's special is *Sauerbraten mit Spatzel* and sweet-sour red cabbage. But there is also *Paprikahuhn* and—"

"Leave the chicken to flaunt her paprika in lonely red splendor today," I interrupted him. "*Sauerbraten* sounds fine."

Ordered by my Herr Ober, the aged wine waiter had already approached our table. I was about to give him directions when my son took upon himself that task with an authority and a hostfulness that warmed my heart. He scanned the wine menu rapidly but thoroughly.

"The Zinfandel 1933," he ordered with decision, though glancing my way to see if I concurred with his judgment. I smiled and nodded.

"And perhaps *ein Tropfchen Schnapps* to begin with?" He suggested.

"A brandy?—yes!" I replied. "And not just a drop, either. Make it a double. It is not every day I lunch with that distinguished scholar, my son."

"Oh, Papa," he protested, dropping his eyes and almost blushing. Then firmly to the bent-backed, white-haired wine waiter, *"Schnapps also. Doppel."* The old waiter nodded his approval and hurried off.

We gazed fondly at each other for a few blissful seconds. Then I said, "Now tell me more fully about your achievements as a social historian on an exchange professorship in the New World. I know we have spoken about this several times, but only rather briefly and generally when various of your friends were present, or at least your lovely wife. Now I would like a more leisurely man-to-man account of your great work. Incidentally, do you find the scholarly apparatus—books, *und so weiter* (et cetera)—of the Municipal Universities of New York City adequate to your needs after having enjoyed those of Baden-Baden University and the institutions of high learning in the German Federation?"

"In some respects they are lacking," he admitted. "However, for my purposes they have proved completely adequate." Then once more he dropped his eyes and almost blushed. "But, Papa, you praise my small efforts far too highly." He lowered his voice. "They do not compare with the victory for international industrial relations you yourself have won in a fortnight."

"All in a day's work for the DLG," I said self-deprecatingly, though once again lightly touching my left chest to establish contact with those most important documents safely stowed in my inside left breast pocket. "But now, no more polite fencing!" I went on briskly. "Tell me all about those 'small efforts,' as you modestly refer to them."

His eyes met mine. "Well, Papa," he began in suddenly matter-of-fact fashion, "all my work these last two years has been increasingly dominated by a firm awareness of the fragility of the underpinnings of the good world-society we enjoy today. If certain historically minute key-events, or cusps, in only the past one hundred years had been decided differently—if another course had been chosen than the one that was—then the whole world might now be plunged in wars and worse horrors then we ever dream of. It is a chilling insight, but it bulks continually larger in my entire work, my every paper."

I felt the thrilling touch of inspiration. At that moment the wine waiter arrived with our double brandies in small goblets of cut glass. I wove the interruption into the fabric of my inspiration. "Let us drink then to what you name your chilling insight," I said. *"Prosit!"*

The bite and spreading warmth of the excellent *schnapps*

quickened my inspiration further. "I believe I understand exactly what you're getting at . . ." I told my son. I set down my half-emptied goblet and pointed at something over my son's shoulder.

He turned his head around, and after one glance back at my pointing finger, which intentionally waggled a tiny bit from side to side, he realized that I was not indicating the entry of the *Krahenest,* but the four sizable bronze statuettes flanking it.

"For instance," I said, "if Thomas Edison and Marie Sklodowska had not married, and especially if they had not had their supergenius son, then Edison's knowledge of electricity and hers of radium and other radioactives might never have been joined. There might never have been developed the fabulous T.S. Edison battery, which is the prime mover of all today's surface and air traffic. Those pioneering electric trucks introduced by the *Saturday Evening Post* in Philadelphia might have remained an expensive freak. And the gas helium might never have been produced industrially to supplement earth's meager subterranean supply."

My son's eyes brightened with the flame of pure scholarship. "Papa," he said eagerly, "you are a genius yourself! You have precisely hit on what is perhaps the most important of those cusp-events I referred to. I am at this moment finishing the necessary research for a long paper on it. Do you know, Papa, that I have firmly established by researching Parisian records that there was in 1894 a close personal relationship between Marie Sklodowska and her fellow radium researcher Pierre Curie, and that she might well have become Madame Curie—or perhaps Madame Becquerel, for he too was in that work—if the dashing and brilliant Edison had not most opportunely arrived in Paris in December, 1894, to sweep her off her feet and carry her off to the New World to even greater achievements?

"And just think, Papa," he went on, his eyes aflame, "what might have happened if their son's battery had not been invented—the most difficult technical achievement, hedged by all sorts of seemingly scientific impossibilities, in the entire millennium-long history of industry. Why, Henry Ford might have manufactured automobiles powered by steam or by exploding natural gas or conceivably even vaporized liquid gasoline, rather than the mass-produced electric cars which have been such a boon to mankind everywhere—not our smokeless cars, but cars spouting all sorts of noxious fumes to pollute the environment."

Cars powered by the danger-fraught combustion of vaporized liquid gasoline!—it almost made me shudder and certainly it was a fantastic thought, yet not altogether beyond the bounds of possibility, I had to admit.

Just then I noticed my gloomy, black-clad Jew sitting only two tables away from us, though how he had got himself into the exclusive *Krahenest* was a wonder. Strange that I had missed his entry—probably immediately after my own, while I had eyes only for my son. His presence somehow threw a dark though only momentary shadow over my bright mood. Let him get some good German food inside him and some fine German wine, I thought generously—it will fill that empty belly of his and even put a bit of a good German smile into those sunken Yiddish cheeks! I combed my little mustache with my thumbnail and swept the errant lock of hair off my forehead.

Meanwhile my son was saying, "Also, Father, if electric transport had not been developed, and if during the last decade relations between Germany and the United States had not been so good, then we might never have gotten from the wells in Texas the supply of natural helium our Zeppelins desperately needed during the brief but vital period before we had put the artificial creation of helium onto an industrial footing. My researchers at Washington have revealed that there was a strong movement in the U.S. military to ban the sale of helium to any other nation, Germany in particular. Only the powerful influence of Edison, Ford, and a few other key Americans, instantly brought to bear, prevented that stupid injunction. Yet if it had gone through, Germany might have been forced to use hydrogen instead of helium to float her passenger dirigibles. That was another crucial cusp."

"A hydrogen-supported Zeppelin!—ridiculous! Such an airship would be a floating bomb, ready to be touched off by the slightest spark," I protested.

"Not ridiculous, Father," my son calmly contradicted me, shaking his head. "Pardon me for trespassing in your field, but there is an inescapable imperative about certain industrial developments. If there is not a safe road of advance, then a dangerous one will invariably be taken. You must admit, Father, that the development of commercial airships was in its early stages a most perilous venture. During the 1920's there were the dreadful wrecks of the American dirigibles *Roma*,

Shenandoah, which broke in two, *Akron,* and *Macon,* the British *R-38,* which also broke apart in the air, and *R-101,* the French *Dixmude,* which disappeared in the Mediterranean, Mussolini's *Italia,* which crashed trying to reach the North Pole, and the Russian *Maxim Gorky,* struck down by a plane, with a total loss of no fewer than 340 crew members for the nine accidents. If that had been followed by the explosions of two or three hydrogen Zeppelins, world industry might well have abandoned forever the attempts to create passenger airships and turned instead to the development of large propeller-driven, heavier-than-air craft."

Monster airplanes, in danger every moment of crash from engine failure, competing with good old unsinkable Zeppelins?—impossible, at least at first thought. I shook my head, but not with as much conviction as I might have wished. My son's suggestion was really a valid one.

Besides, he had all his facts at his fingertips and was complete master of his subject, as I also had to allow. Those nine fearful airship disasters he mentioned had indeed occurred, as I knew well, and might have tipped the scale in favor of long-distance passenger and troop-carrying airplanes, had it not been for helium, the T.S. Edison battery, and German genius.

Fortunately I was able to dump from my mind these uncomfortable speculations and immerse myself in admiration of my son's multisided scholarship. That boy was a wonder!—a real chip off the old block, and, yes, a bit more.

"And now, Dolfy," he went on, using my nickname (I did not mind), "may I turn to an entirely different topic? Or rather to a very different example of my hypothesis of historical cusps?"

I nodded mutely. My mouth was busily full with fine *Sauerbraten* and those lovely, tiny German dumplings, while my nostrils enjoyed the unique aroma of sweet-sour red cabbage. I had been so engrossed in my son's revelations that I had not consciously noted our luncheon being served. I swallowed, took a slug of the good, red Zinfandel, and said, "Please go on."

"It's about the consequences of the American Civil War, Father," he said surprisingly. "Did you know that in the decade after that bloody conflict, there was a very real danger that the whole cause of Negro freedom and rights—for which the war was fought, whatever they say—might well have been completely smashed? The fine work of Abraham Lincoln,

Thaddeus Stevens, Charles Sumner, the Freedmen's Bureau, and the Union League Clubs put to naught? And even the Ku Klux Klan underground allowed free reign rather than being sternly repressed? Yes, Father, my thoroughgoing researchings have convinced me such things might easily have happened, resulting in some sort of re-enslavement of the Blacks, with the whole war to be refought at an indefinite future date, or at any rate Reconstruction brought to a dead halt for many decades—with what disastrous effects on the American character, turning its deep simple faith in freedom to hypocrisy, it is impossible to exaggerate. I have published a sizable paper on this subject in the *Journal of Civil War Studies.*"

I nodded somberly. Quite a bit of this new subject matter of his was *terra incognita* to me; yet I knew enough of American history to realizc he had made a cogent point. More than ever before, I was impressed by his multifaceted learning—he was indubitably a figure in the great tradition of German scholarship, a profound thinker, broad and deep. How fortunate to be his father. Not for the first time, but perhaps with the greatest sincerity yet, I thanked God and the Laws of Nature that I had early moved my family from Braunau, Austria, where I had been born in 1899, to Baden-Baden, where he had grown up in the ambience of the great new university on the edge of the Black Forest and only 150 kilometers from Count Zeppelin's dirigible factory in Wurttemberg, at Friedrichshafen on Lake Constance.

I raised my glass of *Kirschwasser* to him in a solemn, silent toast—we had somehow got to that stage in our meal—and downed a sip of the potent, fiery, white, cherry brandy.

He leaned toward me and said, "I might as well tell you, Dolf, that my big book, at once popular and scholarly, my *Meisterwerk,* to be titled *If Things Had Gone Wrong*, or perhaps *If Things Had Turned for the Worse,* will deal solely—though illuminated by dozens of diverse examples—with my theory of historical cusps, a highly speculative concept but firmly footed in fact." He glanced at his wristwatch, muttered, "Yes, there's still time for it. So now—" His face grew grave, his voice clear though small—"I will venture to tell you about one more cusp, the most disputable and yet most crucial of them all." He paused. "I warn you, dear Dolf, that this cusp may cause you pain."

"I doubt that," I told him indulgently. "Anyhow, go ahead."

"Very well. In November of 1918, when the British had broken the Hindenburg Line and the weary German army was defiantly dug in along the Rhine, and just before the Allies, under Marshal Foch, launched the final crushing drive which would cut a bloody swath across the heartland to Berlin—"

I understood his warning at once. Memories flamed in my mind like the sudden blinding flares of the battlefield with their deafening thunder. The company I had commanded had been among the most desperately defiant of those he mentioned, heroically nerved for a last-ditch resistance. And then Foch had delivered that last vast blow, and we had fallen back and back and back before the overwhelming numbers of our enemies with their field guns and tanks and armored cars innumerable and above all their huge aerial armadas of De Haviland and Handley-Page and other big bombers escorted by insect-buzzing fleets of Spads and other fighters shooting to bits our last Fokkers and Pfalzes and visiting on Germany a destruction greater far than our Zeps had worked on England. Back, back, back, endlessly reeling and regrouping, across the devastated German countryside, a dozen times decimated yet still defiant until the end came at last amid the ruins of Berlin, and the most bold among us had to admit we were beaten and we surrendered unconditionally—

These vivid, fiery recollections came to me almost instantaneously.

I heard my son continuing, "At that cusp moment in November, 1918, Dolf, there existed a very strong possibility—I have established this beyond question—that an immediate armistice would be offered and signed, and the war ended inconclusively. President Wilson was wavering, the French were very tired, and so on.

"And if that had happened in actuality—harken closely to me now, Dolf—then the German temper entering the decade of the 1920's would have been entirely different. She would have felt she had not been really licked, and there would inevitably have been a secret recrudescence of pan-German militarism. German scientific humanism would not have won its total victory over the Germany of the—yes!—Huns.

"As for the Allies, self-tricked out of the complete victory which lay within their grasp, they would in the long run have treated Germany far less generously than they did after their lust for revenge had been sated by that last drive to Berlin. The League of Nations would not have become the strong instrument for world peace that it is today; it might well have been repudiated by America and certainly secretly detested by Germany. Old wounds would not have healed because, paradoxically, they would not have been deep enough.

"There, I've said my say. I hope it hasn't bothered you too badly, Dolf."

I let out a gusty sigh. Then my wincing frown was replaced by a brow serene. I said very deliberately, "Not one bit, my son, though you have certainly touched my own old wounds to the quick. Yet I feel in my bones that your interpretation is completely valid. Rumors of an armistice were indeed running like wildfire through our troops in that black autumn of 1918. And I know only too well that if there had been an armistice at that time, then officers like myself would have believed that the German soldier had never really been defeated, only betrayed by his leaders and by red incendiaries, and we would have begun to conspire endlessly for a resumption of the war under happier circumstances. My son, let us drink to our amazing cusps."

Our tiny glasses touched with a delicate ting, and the last drops went down of biting, faintly bitter *Kirschwasser*. I buttered a thin slice of pumpernickel and nibbled it—always good to finish off a meal with bread. I was suddenly filled with an immeasurable content. It was a golden moment, which I would have been happy to have go on forever, while I listened to my son's wise words and fed my satisfaction in him. Yes, indeed, it was a golden nugget of pause in the terrible rush of time—the enriching conversation, the peerless food and drink, the darkly pleasant surroundings—

At that moment I chanced to look at my discordant Jew two tables away. For some weird reason he was glaring at me with naked hate, though he instantly dropped his gaze—

But even that strange and disquieting event did not disrupt my mood of golden tranquillity, which I sought to prolong by saying in summation, "My dear son, this has been the most exciting though eerie lunch I have ever enjoyed. Your remarkable cusps have opened to me a fabulous world in which I can nevertheless utterly believe. A horridly fascinating world of sizzling hydrogen Zeppelins, of countless evil-smelling gasoline cars built by Ford instead of his electrics, of re-enslaved American blackamoors, of Madame Becquerels or Curies, a world without the T.S. Edison battery and even T.S. himself, a world in which German scientists are sinister pariahs instead of tolerant, humanitarian, great-souled leaders of world thought, a world in which a mateless old Edison tinkers forever at a powerful storage battery he cannot perfect, a world in which Woodrow Wilson doesn't insist on Germany being admitted at once to the League of Nations, a world of festering hatreds reeling toward a second and worse world war. Oh, altogether an incredible world, yet one in which you have momentarily made me believe, to the extent that I do actually have the fear that time will suddenly shift gears and we will be plunged into that bad dream world, and our real world will become a dream—"

I suddenly chanced to see the face of my watch—

At the same time my son looked at his own left wrist—

"Dolf," he said, springing up in agitation, "I do hope that with my stupid chatter I haven't made you miss—"

I had sprung up too—

"No, no, my son," I heard myself say in a fluttering voice, "but it's true I have little time in which to catch the *Ostwald. Auf Wiedersehn, mein Sohn, auf Wiedersehn!*"

And with that I was hastening, indeed almost running, or else sweeping through the air like a ghost—leaving him behind to settle our reckoning—across a room that seemed to waver with my feverish agitation, alternately darkening and brightening like an electric bulb with its fine tungsten filament about to fly to powder and wink out forever—

Inside my head a voice was saying in calm yet death-knell tones. "The lights of Europe are going out. I do not think they will be rekindled in my generation—"

Suddenly the only important thing in the world for me was to catch the *Ostwald*, get aboard her before she unmoored. That and only that would reassure me that I was in my rightful world. I would touch and feel the *Ostwald*, not just talk about her—

As I dashed between the four bronze figures, they seemed to hunch down and become deformed, while their faces became those of grotesque, aged witches—four evil kobolds leering up at me with a horrid knowledge bright in their eyes—

While behind me I glimpsed in pursuit a tall, black, white-faced figure, skeletally lean—

The strangely short corridor ahead of me had a blank end—the Departure Lounge wasn't there—

I instantly jerked open the narrow door to the stairs and darted nimbly up them as if I were a young man again and not 48 years old—

On the third sharp turn I risked a glance behind and down—

Hardly a flight behind me, taking great pursuing leaps, was my dreadful Jew—

I tore open the door to the 102nd floor. There at last, only a few feet away, was the silver door I sought of the final elevator and softly glowing above it the words, *"Zum Zeppelin."* At last I would be shot aloft to the *Ostwald* and reality.

But the sign began to blink as the *Krahenest* had, while across the door was pasted askew a white cardboard sign which read "Out of Order."

I threw myself at the door and scrabbled at it, squeezing my eyes several times to make my vision come clear. When I finally fully opened them, the cardboard sign was gone.

But the silver door was gone too, and the words above it forever. I was scrabbling at seamless pale plaster.

There was a touch on my elbow. I spun around.

"Excuse me, sir, but you seem troubled," my Jew said solicitously. "Is there anything I can do?"

I shook my head, but whether in negation or rejection or to clear it, I don't know. "I'm looking for the *Ostwald,*" I gasped, only now realizing I'd winded myself on the stairs. "For the zeppelin," I explained when he looked puzzled.

I may be wrong, but it seemed to me that a look of secret glee flashed deep in his eyes, though his general sympathetic expression remained unchanged.

"Oh, the zeppelin," he said in a voice that seemed to me to have become sugary in its solicitude. "You must mean the *Hindenburg.*"

Hindenburg?—I asked myself. There was no zeppelin named *Hindenburg.* Or was there? Could it be that I was mistaken about such a simple and, one would think, immutable matter? My mind had been getting very foggy the last minute or two. Desperately I tried to assure myself that I was indeed myself and in my right world. My lips worked and I muttered to myself, *Bin Adolf Hitler, Zeppelin Fachman . . .*

"But the *Hindenburg* doesn't land here, in any case," my Jew was telling me, "though I think some vague intention once was voiced about topping the Empire State with a mooring mast for dirigibles. Perhaps you saw some news story and assumed—"

His face fell, or he made it seem to fall. The sugary solicitude in his voice became unendurable as he told me, "But apparently you can't have heard today's tragic news. Oh, I do hope you weren't seeking the *Hindenburg* so as to meet some beloved family member or close friend. Brace yourself, sir. Only hours ago, coming in for her landing at Lakehurst, New Jersey, the *Hindenburg* caught fire and burned up entire in a matter of seconds. Thirty or forty at least of her passengers and crew were burned alive. Oh, steady yourself, sir."

"But the *Hindenburg*—I mean the *Ostwald!*—couldn't burn like that," I protested. "She's a helium zeppelin."

He shook his head. "Oh, no. I'm no scientist, but I know the *Hindenburg* was filled with hydrogen—a wholly typical bit of reckless German risk-running. At least we've never sold helium to the Nazis, thank God."

I stared at him, wavering my face from side to side in feeble denial.

While he stared back at me with obviously a new thought in mind.

"Excuse me once again," he said, "but I believe I heard you start to say something about Adolf Hitler. I suppose you know that you bear a certain resemblance to that execrable dictator. If I were you, sir, I'd shave my mustache."

I felt a wave of fury at this inexplicable remark with all its baffling references, yet withal a remark delivered in the unmistakable tones of an insult. And then all my surroundings momentarily reddened and flickered, and I felt a tremendous wrench in the inmost core of my being, the sort of wrench one might experience in transiting timelessly from one universe into another parallel to it. Briefly I became a man still named Adolf Hitler, same as the Nazi dictator and almost the same age, a German-American born in Chicago, who had never visited Germany or spoke German, whose friends teased him about his chance resemblance to the other Hitler, and who used stubbornly to say, "No, I won't change my name! Let that *Fuehrer* bastard across the Atlantic change his! Ever hear about the British Winston Churchill writing the American Winston Churchill, who wrote *The Crisis* and other novels, and suggesting he change his name to avoid confusion, since the Englishman had done some writing too? The American wrote back it was a good idea, but since he was three years older, he was senior and so the Britisher should change *his* name. That's exactly how I feel about that son of a bitch Hitler."

The Jew still stared at me sneeringly. I started to tell him off, but then I was lost in a second weird, wrenching transition. The first had been directly from one parallel universe to another. The second was also in time—I aged 14 or 15 years in a single infinite instant while transiting from 1937 (where I had been born in 1889 and was 48) to 1973 (where I had been born in 1910 and and was 63). My name changed back to my truly own (but what is that?), and I no longer looked one bit like Adolf Hitler the Nazi dictator (or dirigible expert?), and I had a married son who was a sort of social historian in a New York City municipal university, and he had many brilliant theories, but none of historical cusps.

And the Jew—I mean the tall, thin man in black with possibly Semitic features—was gone. I looked around and around but there was no one there.

I touched my outside left breast pocket, then my hand darted tremblingly underneath. There was no zipper on the pocket inside and no precious documents, only a couple of grimy envelopes with notes I'd scribbled on them in pencil.

I don't know how I got out of the Empire State Building. Presumably by elevator. Though all my memory holds for that period is a persistent image of King Kong tumbling down from its top like a ridiculous yet poignantly pitiable giant teddy bear.

I do recollect walking in a sort of trance for what seemed hours through a Manhattan stinking with monoxide and carcinogens innumerable, half waking from time to time (usually while crossing streets that snarled, not purred) and then relapsing into trance. There were big dogs.

When I at last fully came to myself, I was walking down a twilit Hudson Street at the north end of Greenwich Village. My gaze was fixed on a distant and unremarkable pale-gray square of building top. I guessed it must be that of the World Trade Center, 1,350 feet tall.

And then it was blotted out by the grinning face of my son, the professor.

"Justin!" I said.

"Fritz!" he said. "We'd begun to worry a bit. Where did you get off to, anyhow? Not that it's a damn bit of my business. If you had an assignation with a go-go girl, you needn't tell me."

"Thanks," I said. "I do feel tired. I must admit, and somewhat cold. But no, I was just looking at some of my old stamping grounds," I told him, "and taking longer than I realized. Manhattan's changed during my years on the West Coast, but not all that much."

"It's getting chilly," he said. "Let's stop in at that place ahead with the black front. It's the White Horse. Dylan Thomas used to drink there. He's supposed to have scribbled a poem on the wall of the can, only they painted it over. But it has the authentic sawdust."

"Good," I said, "only we'll make mine coffee, not ale. Or if I can't get coffee, then cola."

I am not really a *Prosit!*-type person.

THE PEDDLER'S APPRENTICE

by Joan D. Vinge and Vernor Vinge

Once again to the problem of restructuring society, there is always the possibility, not of reversing history or finding alternate worlds, but of correcting mistakes, of putting time back on the right track. Here is an example of how some future era might handle that.

Lord Buckry I of Fyffe lounged on his throne, watching his two youngest sons engaged in mock battle in the empty Audience Hall. The daggers were wooden but the rivalry was real, and the smaller boy was at a disadvantage. Lord Buckry tugged on a heavy gold earring; thin, brown-haired Hanaban was his private favorite, the boy took after his father both in appearance and turn of mind.

The lord of the Flatlands was a tall man, his own unkempt brown hair graying now at the temples. The blue eyes in his lean, foxlike face still perceived with disconcerting sharpness, though years of experience kept his own thoughts hidden. More than twenty years had passed since he had won control of his lands; he had not kept his precarious place as lord so long without good reason.

Now his eyes flashed rare approval as Hanaban cried, "Trace, look there!" and, as his brother turned, distracted, whacked him soundly on the chest.

"Gotcha!" Hanaban shrieked delightedly. Trace grimaced with disgust.

Their father chuckled, but his face changed suddenly as the sound of a commotion outside the chamber reached him. The heavy, windowed doors at the far end of the room burst open; the Flatlander courier shook off guards, crossed the high-ceilinged, echoing chamber and flung himself into a bow, his rifle clattering on the floor. "Your Lordship!"

Lord Buckry snapped his fingers; his gaping children silently fled the room. "Get up," he said impatiently. "What in tarnation is this?"

"Your Lordship." The courier raised a dusty face, wincing mentally at his lord's Highland drawl. "There's word the sea kingdoms have raised another army. They're crossing the coast mountains, and—"

"That ain't possible. We cleaned them out not half a year since."

"They've a lot of folk along the coast, Your Lordship." The horseman stood apologetically. "And Jayley Sharkstooth's made a pact this time with the Southlands."

Lord Buckry stiffened. "They've been at each other's throats long as I can remember." He frowned, pulling at his earring. "Only thing they've got in common is—me. Damn!"

He listened distractedly to the rider's report, then stood abruptly, dismissing the man as an afterthought. As the heavy doors of the hall slid shut he was already striding toward the elevator, past the shaft of the ballistic vehicle exit, unused for more than thirty years. His soft-soled Highlander boots made no sound on the cold polished floor.

From the parapet of his castle he could survey a wide stretch of his domain, the rich, utterly flat farmlands of the hundred-mile-wide valley—the lands the South and West were hungry for. The fields were dark now with turned earth, ready for the spring planting; it was no time to be calling up an army. He was sure his enemies were aware of that. The day was exceptionally clear, and at the eastern reaches of his sight he could make out the grayed purple wall of the mountains: the Highlands, that held his birthplace—and something more important to him now.

The dry wind ruffled his hair as he looked back across thirty years; his sunburned hands tightened on the seamless, ancient green-blackness of the parapet. "Damn you, Mr. Jagged," he said to the wind. "Where's your magic when I *need* it?"

The peddler came to Darkwood Corners from the east, on Wim Buckry's seventeenth birthday. It was early summer, and Wim could still see sun flashing on snow up the pine-wooded hill that towered above the Corners; the snowpack in the higher hills was melting at last, sluicing down gullies that stood dry through most of the year, changing Littlebig Creek into a cold, singing torrent tearing at the earth below the cabins on the north side of the road. Even a week ago the East Pass had lain under more than thirty feet of snow.

Something like silence came over the townspeople as they saw the peddler dragging his cart down the east road toward the Corners. His wagon was nearly ten feet tall and fifteen long, with carved, bright-painted wooden sides that bent sharply out over the wheels to meet a gabled roof. Wim gaped in wonder as he saw those wheels, spindly as willow wood yet over five feet across. Under the cart's weight they sank half a foot and more into the mud of the road, but cut through the mud without resistance, without leaving a rut.

Even so, the peddler was bent nearly double with the effort of pulling his load. The fellow was short and heavy, with skin a good deal darker than Wim had ever seen. His pointed black beard jutted at a determined angle as he staggered along the rutted track, up to his ankles in mud. Above his calves the tooled leather of his leggings gleamed black and clean. Several scrofulous dogs nosed warily around him as he plodded down the center of the road; he ignored them as he ignored the staring townsfolk.

Wim shoved his empty mug back at Ounze Rumpster, sitting nearest the tavern door. "More," he said. Ounze swore, got up from the steps, and disappeared into the tavern.

Wim's attention never left the peddler for an instant. As the dark man reached the widening in the road at the center of town, he pulled his wagon into the muddy morass where the Widow Henley's house had stood until the Littlebig Creek dragged it to destruction. The stranger had everyone's attention now. Even the town's smith had left his fire, and stood in his doorway gazing down the street at the peddler.

The peddler turned his back on them as he kicked an arresting gear down from the rear of the painted wagon and let it settle into the mud. He returned to the front of the cart and moved a small wheel set in the wood paneling: a narrow blue pennant sprouted from the peak of the gable and fluttered briskly; crisp and metallic, a pinging melody came from the wagon. That sound emptied the tavern and brought the remainder of the Corners' population onto the street. Ounze Rumpster nearly fell down the wooden steps in his haste to see the source of the music; he sat down heavily, handing the refilled mug to Wim. Wim ignored him.

As the peddler turned back to the crowd the eerie music

stopped, and the creek sounded loud in the silence. Then the little man's surprising bass voice rumbled out at them, "Jagit Katchetooriantz is my name, and fine wrought goods is my trade. Needles, adze-heads, blades—you need 'em?" He pulled a latch on the wagon's wall and a panel swung out from its side, revealing rows of shining knife-blades and needles so fine Wim could see only glitter where they caught the sunlight. "Step right on up, folks. Take a look, take a feel. Tell me what they might be worth to you." There was no need to repeat the invitation—in seconds he was surrounded. As the townspeople closed around him, he mounted a small step set in the side of the wagon, so that he could still be seen over the crowd.

Wim's boys were on their feet; but he sat motionless, his sharp face intent. "Set down," he said, just loudly enough. "Your eyes is near busting out of your heads. They'd skin us right fast if we try anything here. There's too many. Set!" He gave the nearest of them, Bathecar Henley, a sideways kick in the shin; they all sat. "Gimme that big ring of yours, Sothead."

Ounze Rumpster's younger brother glared at him, then extended his jeweled fist from a filthy woolen cuff. "How come you're so feisty of a sudden, Wim?" He dropped the ring peevishly into the other's hand. Wim turned away without comment, passing the massive chunk of gold to Bathecar's plump, fair girlfriend.

"All right, Emmy, you just take yourself over to that wagon and see about buying us some knife-blades—not too long, say about so." He stretched his fingers. "And find out how they're fastened on the rack."

"Sure, Wim." She rose from the steps and minced away across the muddy road toward the crowd at the peddler's wagon. Wim grimaced, reflecting that the red knit dress Bathecar had brought her was perhaps too small.

The peddler's spiel continued, all but drowning out the sound of Littlebig Creek: "Just try your blades 'gin mine, friends. Go ahead. Nary a scratch you've made on mine, see? Now how much is it worth, friends? I'll take gold, silver. Or craft items. And I need a horse—lost my own, coming down those blamed trails." He waved toward the East Pass. The townspeople were packed tightly together now as each of them tried for a chance to test the gleaming metal, and to make some bid that would catch the peddler's fancy. Emmy wriggled expertly into the mass; in seconds Wim could see her red dress right at the front of the crowd. She was happily fondling the merchandise, competing with the rest for the stranger's attention.

Hanaban Kroy shifted his bulk on the hard wooden step. "Three gold pigs says that outlander is from down west. He just come in from the east to set us all to talking. Nobody makes knives like them east of the pass."

Wim nodded slightly. "Could be." He watched the peddler and fingered the thick gold earring half-hidden in his shaggy brown hair.

Across the road, the merchant was engaged in a four-way bidding session. Many of the townsfolk wanted to trade furs, or crossbows, but Jagit Katchetooriantz wasn't interested. This narrowed his potential clientele considerably. Even as he argued avidly with those below him, his quick dark eyes flickered up and down the street, took in the gang by the tavern, impaled Wim for a long, cold instant.

The peddler lifted several blades off the rack and handed them down, apparently receiving metal in return. Emmy got at least two. Then he raised his arms for quiet. "Folks, I'm real sorry for dropping in so sudden, when you all wasn't ready for me. Let's us quit now and try again tomorrow; when you can bring what you have to trade. I might even take on some furs. And bring horses, too, if you want to. Seein' as how I'm in need of one, I'll give two, maybe three adze-heads for a good horse or mule. All right?"

It wasn't. Several frustrated townsfolk tried to pry merchandise off the rack. Wim noticed that they were unsuccessful. The merchant pulled the lanyard at the front of the cart and the rack turned inward, returning carved wood paneling to the outside. As the crowd thinned, Wim saw Emmy, clutching two knives and a piece of print cloth, still talking earnestly to the peddler.

The peddler took a silvery chain from around his waist, passed it through the wheels of his cart and then around a nearby tree. Then he followed Emmy back across the road.

Ounze Rumpster snorted. "That sure is a teensy ketter. Betcha we could bust it right easy."

"Could be . . ." Wim nodded again, not listening. Anger turned his eyes to blue ice as Emmy led the peddler right to the tavern steps.

"Oh, Bathecar, just lookit the fine needles Mr. Ketchatoor sold me—"

Sothead struggled to his feet. "You stupid little—little—

We told you to buy knives. Knives! And you used my ring to buy needles!" He grabbed the cloth from Emmy's hands and began ripping it up.

"Hey—!" Emmy began to pound him in useless fury, clawing after her prize. "Bathecar, make him stop!" Bathecar and Ounze pulled Sothead down, retrieved needles and cloth. Emmy pouted, "Big lout."

Wim frowned and drank, his attention fixed on the peddler. The dark man stood looking from one gang member to another, hands loosely at his sides, smiling faintly; the calm black eyes missed nothing. Eyes like that didn't belong in the face of a fat peddler. Wim shifted uncomfortably, gnawed by sudden uncertainty. He shook it off. How many chances did you get up here, to try a contest where the outcome wasn't sure— He stood and thrust out his hand. "Wim Buckry's the name, Mr. Ketchatoor. Sorry about Sothead; he's drunk all the time, 'truth."

The peddler had to reach up slightly to shake his hand. "Folks mostly call me Jagit. Pleased to meet you. Miss Emmy here tells me you and your men sometimes hire out to protect folks such as me."

Behind him, Bathecar Henley was open-mouthed. Emmy simpered; every so often, she proved that she was not as stupid as she looked. Wim nodded judiciously. "We do, and it's surely worth it to have our service. There's a sight of thieves in these hills, but most of them will back down from six good bows." He glanced at Sothead. "Five good bows."

"Well then." The pudgy little man smiled blandly, and for a moment Wim wondered how he could ever have seen anything deadly in that face. "I'd like to give you some of my business."

And so they came down out of the high hills. It was early summer, but in the Highlands more like a boisterous spring: Under the brilliant blue sky, green spread everywhere over the ground, nudging the dingy hummocks of melting snow and outcropping shelves of ancient granite. Full leaping streams sang down the alpine valleys, plunged over falls and rapids that smashed the water to white foam and spread it in glinting veils scarcely an inch deep over bedrock. The ragged peaks skirted with glacier fell further and further behind, yet the day grew no warmer; everywhere the chill water kept the air cool.

The peddler and his six "protectors" followed a winding

course through deep soughing pine forest, broken by alpine meadows where bright star-like flowers bloomed and the short hummocky grass made their ankles ache with fatigue. They passed by marshes that even in the coolness swarmed with eager mosquitoes, and Wim's high moccasins squelched on the soft dank earth.

But by late afternoon the party had reached Witch Hollow Trail, and the way grew easier for the horse pulling the merchant's wagon. Somewhere ahead of them Ounze Rumpster kept the point position; off to the side were fat Hanaban, Bathecar, and Shorty, while Sothead Rumpster, now nearly sober, brought up the rear. In the Highlands even the robbers—particularly the robbers—journeyed with caution.

For most of the day Wim traveled silently, listening to the streaming water, the wind, the twittering birds among the pines—listening for sounds of human treachery. But it seemed they were alone. He had seen one farmer about four miles outside of Darkwood Corners and since then, no one.

Yesterday the peddler had questioned him about the area, and how many folk were in the vicinity of the Corners, what they did for a living. He'd seemed disappointed when he'd heard they were mostly poor, scattered farmers and trappers, saying his goods were more the kind to interest rich city folk. Wim had promptly allowed as how he was one of the few Highlanders who had ever been down into the Great Valley, all the way to the grand city of Fyffe; and that they'd be more than glad to guide him down into the Flatlands—for a price. If a little greed would conceal their real intentions, so much the better. And the peddler's partial payment, of strange, jewel-studded silver balls, had only added to the sincerity of their interest in his future plans.

Wim glanced over at the peddler, walking beside him near the dappled cart horse. Up close, the stranger seemed even more peculiar than at a distance. His straight black hair was cut with unbelievable precision at the base of his neck; Wim wondered if he'd set a bowl on his head and cut around it. And he smelled odd; not unpleasant, but more like old pine-needles than man. The silver thread stitched into the peddler's soft leather shirt was finer than Wim had ever seen. That would be a nice shirt to have— Wim tugged absently at the loops of bead and polished metal hanging against his own worn linen shirt.

Though short and heavy, the stranger walked briskly and didn't seem to tire; in fact, became friendlier and more talkative as the afternoon passed. But when they reached Witch Hollow he fell silent again, looking first at the unusual smoothness of the path, then up at the naked bedrock wall that jutted up at the side of the narrow trail.

They had walked for about half a mile when Wim volunteered, "This here's called Witch Hollow. There's a story, how once folk had magic to fly through the air in strange contraptions. One of them lost his magic hereabouts—up till twenty years ago, there was still a place you could see the bones, and pieces of steel, they say, all rusted up. Some say this trail through the holler ain't natural, either."

Jagit made no reply, but walked with his head down, his pointy black beard tucked into his chest. For the first time since they had begun the journey he seemed to lose interest in the scenery. At last he said, "How long you figure it's been since this flying contraption crashed here?"

Wim shrugged. "My granther heard the story from his own granther."

"Hmm. And that's all the . . . magic you've heard tell of?"

Wim decided not to tell the peddler what he knew about Fyffe. That might scare the little man into turning back, and force a premature confrontation. "Well, we have witches in these hills, like Widow Henley's cousin, but they're most of them fakes—least the ones I seen. Outside of them and the bad luck that folks claim follows sin"—a grin twitched his mouth—"well, I don't know of no magic. What was you expecting?"

Jagit shook his head. "Something more than a piddling failed witch, that's sure. The more I see of this country, the more I know it ain't the place I started out for."

They walked the next mile in silence. The trail pierced a granite ridge; Wim glimpsed Hanaban high up on their left, paralleling the wagon. Red-faced with exertion, he waved briefly down at them, indicating no problems. Wim returned the signal, and returned to his thoughts about the peculiar little man who walked at his side. Somehow he kept remembering yesterday, Hanaban whining, "Wim, that there little man smells rotten to me. I say we should drop him," and the unease that had crept back into his own mind. Angry at himself as much as anything, he'd snapped, "You going yellow, Han? Just because a feller's strange don't mean he's got an evil eye." And known it hadn't convinced either of them . . .

Perhaps sensing the drift of his silence, or perhaps for some other reason, the peddler began to talk again. This time it was not of where he was going, however, but rather about himself, and where he had come from—a place called Sharn, a land of such incredible wonders that if Wim had heard the tale from someone else he would have laughed.

For Sharn was a land where true magicians ruled, where a flying contraption of steel would be remarkable only for its commonness. Sharn was an immense land—but a city also, a city without streets, a single gleaming sentient crystal that challenged the sky with spears of light. And the people of Sharn by their magic had become like gods; they wore clothing like gossamer, threw themselves across the sky in lightning while thunder followed, spoke to one another over miles. They settled beneath the warm seas of their borders, the weather obeyed them, and they remained young as long as they lived. And their magic made them dreadful warriors and mighty conquerors, for they could kill with scarcely more than a thought and a nod. If a mountain offended them they could destroy it in an instant. Wim thought of his Highlands, and shuddered, touching the bone hilt of the knife strapped to his leg.

Jagit had come to Sharn from a land still further east, and much more primitive. He had stayed and learned what he could of Sharn's magic. The goods he brought to Sharn were popular and had brought high prices; during the time he had spent in the enchanted land he had acquired a small collection of the weaker Sharnish spells. Then he left, to seek a market for these acquisitions—some land where magic was known, but not so deeply as in Sharn.

As the peddler finished his tale, Wim saw that the sun had nearly reached the ridge of the hills to the west before them. He walked on for several minutes, squinting into the sunset for traces of lost Sharn.

The trail curved through ninety degrees, headed down across a small valley. Half-hidden in the deepening shadow that now spread over the land, a precarious wooden bridge crossed a stream. Beyond the bridge the pines climbed the darkened hillside into sudden sunlight. Along the far ridgeline, not more than a mile away, ten or twelve immense, solitary trees caught the light, towering over the forest.

"Mr. Jagged, you're the best liar I ever met." Stubbornly Wim swallowed his awe, felt the peddler's unnerving eyes on his face as he pointed across the valley. "Just beyond that ridgeline's where we figure on putting up tonight. A place called Grandfather Grove. Could be you never seen trees that big even in Sharn!"

The peddler peered into the leveling sunlight. "Could be," he said. "I'd surely like to see such trees, anyhow."

They descended from the sunlight into rising darkness. Wim glimpsed Ounze's high felt hat as he walked out of the shadow on the other side of the valley, but none of the other gang members were visible. Wim and the peddler were forced to leave Witch Hollow Trail, and the going became more difficult for horse and wagon; but they reached the edge of the Grandfather Grove in less than half an hour, passing one of the soaring trees, and then two, and three. The dwarfed, spindly pines thinned and finally were gone. Ahead of them were only grandfather trees, their shaggy striated trunks russet and gold in the dying light. The breeze that had crossed the valley with them, the roaring of the stream behind them, all sounds faded into cathedral silence, leaving only the cool, still air and the golden trees. Wim stopped and bent his head back to catch even a glimpse of the lowest branches, needled with pungent golden-green. This was their land, and he knew more than one tale that told of how the trees guarded it, kept pestiferous creatures away, kept the air cool and the soil fragrant and faintly moist throughout the summer.

"Over here." Hanaban's voice came muted from their left. They rounded the twenty-foot base of a tree, and found Hanaban and Bathecar, setting a small fire with kindling they had carried into the grove—Wim knew the bark of the grandfather trees was almost unburnable. The struggling blaze illuminated an immense pit of darkness behind them: the gutted trunk of an ancient grandfather tree, that formed a living cave-shelter for the night's camp.

By the time they had eaten and rotated lookouts, the sun had set. Wim smothered the fire, and the only light was from the sickle moon following the sun down into the west.

The peddler made no move to bed down, Wim noticed with growing irritation. He sat with legs crossed under him in the shadow of his wagon; motionless and wearing a dark coat against the chill, he was all but invisible, but Wim thought the little man was looking up into the sky. His silence stretched on, until Wim thought he would have to pretend to sleep himself before the peddler would. Finally Jagit stood and walked to the rear of his wagon. He opened a tiny hatch and removed two objects.

"What's them?" Wim asked, both curious and suspicious.

"Just a bit of harmless magic." He set one of the contraptions down on the ground, what seemed to be a long rod with a grip at one end. Wim came up to him, as he put the second object against his eye. The second contraption looked much more complex. It glinted, almost sparkled in the dim moonlight, and Wim thought he saw mirrors and strange rulings on its side. A tiny bubble floated along the side in a tube. The peddler stared through the gadget at the scattering of pale stars visible between the trees. At last he set the device back inside the wagon, and picked up the rod. Wim watched him cautiously as the other walked toward the cave tree; the rod looked too much like a weapon.

Jagit fiddled at the grip of the rod, and an eerie whine spread through the grove. The screaming faded into silence again, but Wim was sure that now the front of the rod was spinning. Jagit set it against the moon-silvered bark of the cave tree, and the tip of the rod began to bore effortlessly into the massive trunk.

Wim's voice quavered faintly. "That . . . that there some of your Sharnish magic, Mr. Jagged?"

The peddler chuckled softly, finishing his experiment. "It ain't hardly that. A Sharnish enchantment is a lot craftier, a lot simpler *looking*. This here's just a simple spell for reading the Signs."

"Um." Wim wavered almost visibly, his curiosity doing battle with his fear. There was a deep, precise hole in the cave tree. *Just because a fellow's strange, Han, don't mean he's got an evil eye . . .* instinctively Wim's fingers crossed. Because it looked like the peddler might not be the world's biggest liar; and that meant— "Maybe I better check how the boys is settled."

When the peddler didn't answer, Wim turned and walked briskly away. At least he hoped that was how it looked; he felt like running. He passed Ounze, half-hidden behind a gigantic stump; Wim said nothing, but motioned for him to continue his surveillance of the peddler and his wagon. The rest stood waiting at a medium-sized grandfather tree nearly a hundred yards from the cave tree, the spot they had agreed on last night in Darkwood Corners. Wim moved silently across the springy ground, rounding the ruins of what must once have been one of the largest trees in the grove: a four-hundred-foot giant that disease and the years had brought crashing down. The great disc of its shattered root system rose more than thirty feet into the air, dwarfing him as he dropped down heavily beside Hanaban.

Bathecar Henley whispered, "Ounze and Sothead I left out as guards."

Wim nodded. "It don't hardly matter. We're not going to touch that peddler."

"What!" Bathecar's exclamation was loud with surprise. He lowered his voice only slightly as he continued, "One man? You're ascared of one man?"

Wim motioned threateningly for silence. "You heard me. Hanaban here was right—that Jagged is just too damn dangerous. He's a warlock, he's got an evil eye. And he's got some kind of knife back there that can cut clean through a grandfather tree! And the way he talks, that's just the least . . ."

The others' muttered curses cut him off. Only Hanaban Kroy kept silent.

"You're crazy, Wim," the hulking shadow of Shorty said. "We've walked fifteen miles today. And you're telling us it was for nothing! It'd be easier to farm for a living!"

"We'll still get something, but it looks like we'll have to go honest for a while. I figure on guiding him down, say to where the leaf forests start, and then asking pretty please for half of what he promised us back at the Corners."

"I sure as hell ain't going to follow nobody that far down toward the Valley." Bathecar frowned.

"Well, then, you can just turn around and head back. I'm running this here gang, Bathecar, don't you forget it. We already got something out of this deal, them silver balls he give us as first payment—"

Something went *hisss* and then *thuk:* Hanaban sprawled forward, collapsed on the moonlit ground beyond the tree's shadow. A crossbow bolt protruded from his throat.

As Wim and Bathecar scrabbled for the cover of the rotting root system, Shorty rose and snarled, "That damn peddler!" It cost him his life; three arrows smashed into him where he stood, and he collapsed across Hanaban.

Wim heard their attackers closing in on them, noisily confident. From what he could see, he realized they were all armed with crossbows; his boys didn't stand a chance against odds like that. He burrowed his way deeper into the clawing roots, felt a string of beads snap and shower over his hand. Behind him Bathecar unslung his own crossbow and cocked it.

Wim looked over his shoulder, and then, for the length of a heartbeat, he saw the silvery white of the moon-painted landscape blaze with harshly shadowed blue brilliance. He shook his head, dazzled and wondering; until amazement was driven from his mind by sudden screams. He began to curse and pray at the same time.

But then their assailants had reached the fallen tree. Wim heard them thrusting into the roots, shrank back further out of reach of their knives. Another scream echoed close and a voice remarked, "Hey, Rufe, I got the bastard as shot Rocker last fall."

A different voice answered, "That makes five then. Everybody excepting the peddler and Wim Buckry."

Wim held his breath, sweating. He recognized the second voice—Axl Bork, the oldest of the Bork brothers. For the last two years Wim's gang had cut into the Bork clan's habitual thievery, and up until tonight his quick-wittedness had kept them safe from the Borks' revenge. But tonight— how had he gone so wrong tonight? Damn that peddler!

He heard hands thrusting again among the roots, closer now. Then abruptly fingers caught in his hair. He pulled away, but another pair of hands joined the first, catching him by the hair and then the collar of his leather jerkin. He was hauled roughly from the tangle of roots and thrown down. He scrambled to his feet, was kicked in the stomach before he could run off. He fell gasping back onto the ground, felt his knife jerked from the sheath; three shadowy figures loomed over him. The nearest placed a heavy foot on his middle and said, "Well, Wim Buckry. You just lie still, boy. It's been a good night, even if we don't catch that peddler. You just got a little crazy with greed, boy. My cousins done killed every last one of your gang." Their laughter raked him. "Fifteen minutes and we done what we couldn't do the last two years.

"Lew, you take Wim here over to that cave tree. Once we find that peddler we're going to have us a little fun with the both of them."

Wim was pulled to his feet and then kicked, sprawling over the bodies of Hanaban and Shorty. He struggled to his feet and ran, only to be tripped and booted by another Bork. By the time he reached the cave tree his right arm hung useless at his side, and one eye was blind with warm sticky blood.

The Borks had tried to rekindle the campfire. Three of them stood around him in the wavering light; he listened to the rest searching among the trees. He wondered dismally why they couldn't find one wagon on open ground, when they'd found every one of his boys.

One of the younger cousins—scarcely more than fifteen—amused himself halfheartedly by thrusting glowing twigs at Wim's face. Wim slapped at him, missed, and at last one of the other Borks knocked the burning wood from the boy's hand; Wim remembered that Axl Bork claimed first rights against anyone who ran afoul of the gang. He squirmed back away from the fire and propped himself against the dry resilient trunk of the cave tree, stunned with pain and despair. Through one eye he could see the other Borks returning empty-handed from their search. He counted six Borks altogether, but by the feeble flame-cast light he couldn't make out their features. The only one he could have recognized for sure was Axl Bork, and his runty silhouette was missing. Two of the clansmen moved past him into the blackness of the cave tree's heart, he heard them get down on their hands and knees to crawl around the bend at the end of the passage. The peddler could have hidden back there, but his wagon would have filled the cave's entrance. Wim wondered again why the Borks couldn't find that wagon; and wished again that he'd never seen it at all.

The two men emerged from the tree just as Axl limped into the shrinking circle of firelight. The stubby bandit was at least forty years old, but through those forty years he had lost his share of fights, and walked slightly bent-over; Wim knew that his drooping hat covered a hairless skull marred with scars and even one dent. The eldest Bork cut close by the fire, heedlessly sending dust and unburnable bark into the guttering flames. "Awright, where in the motherdevil blazes you toad-gets been keeping your eyes? You was standing ever' whichway from this tree, you skewered every one of that damn Buckry gang excepting Wim here. Why ain't you found that peddler?"

"He's gone, Ax', gone." The boy who had been playing with Wim seemed to think that was a revelation. But Axl was not impressed, his backhand sent the boy up against the side of the tree.

One of the other silhouetted figures spoke hesitantly. "Don't go misbelieving me when I tell you this, Axl . . . but I was looking straight at this here cave tree when you went after them others. I could see that peddler clear as I see you now, standing right beside his wagon and his horse. Then all of a sudden there was this blue flash—I tell you, Ax', it was *bright*—and for a minute I couldn't see nothing, and then when I could again, why there wasn't hide nor hair of that outlander."

"Hmm." The elder Bork took this story without apparent anger. He scratched under his left armpit and began to shuffle around the dying fire toward where Wim lay. "Gone, eh? Just like that. He sounds like a right good prize . . ." He reached suddenly and caught Wim by the collar, dragged him toward the fire. Stopping just inside the ring of light, he pulled Wim up close to his face. The wide, sagging brim of his hat threw his face into a hollow blackness that was somehow more terrible than any reality.

Seeing Wim's expression, he laughed raspingly, and did not turn his face toward the fire. "It's been a long time, Wim, that I been wanting to learn you a lesson. But now I can mix business and pleasure. We're just gonna burn you an inch at a time until you tell us where your friend lit out to."

Wim barely stifled the whimper he felt growing in his throat; Axl Bork began to force his good hand inch by inch into the fire. All he wanted to do was to scream the truth, to tell them the peddler had never made him party to his magic. But he knew the truth would no more be accepted than his cries for mercy; the only way out was to lie—to lie better than he ever had before. The tales the peddler had told him during the day rose from his mind to shape his words, "Just go ahead, Ax! Get your fun. I know I'm good as dead. But so's all of you—" The grip stayed firm on his shoulders and neck, but the knotted hand stopped forcing him toward the fire. He felt his own hand scorching in the super-heated air above the embers. Desperately he forced the pain into the same place with his fear and ignored it, "Why d'you think me and my boys didn't lay a hand on that peddler all day long? Just so's we could get ambushed by you?" His laughter was slightly hysterical. "The truth is we was scared clean out of our wits! That foreigner's a warlock, he's too dangerous to go after. He can reach straight into your head, cloud your mind, make you see what just plain isn't. He can kill you, just by looking at you kinda mean-like. Why"—and true inspiration struck him—"why, he could even have killed one of your perty cousins, and be standing here right now pretending to be a Bork, and you'd never know it till he struck *you* dead . . ."

Axl swore and ground Wim's hand into the embers. Even

expecting it, Wim couldn't help himself; his scream was loud and shrill. After an instant as long as forever Axl pulled his hand from the heat. The motion stirred the embers, sending a final spurt of evil reddish flame up from the coals before the fire guttered out, leaving only dim ruby points to compete with the moonlight. For a long moment no one spoke; Wim bit his tongue to keep from moaning. The only sounds were a faint rustling breeze, hundreds of feet up among the leafy crowns of the grandfather trees—and the snort of a horse somewhere close by.

"Hey, we ain't got no horses," someone said uneasily.

Seven human figures stood in the immense spreading shadow of the cave tree, lined in faint silver by the setting moon. The Borks stood very still, watching one another—and then Wim realized what they must just have noticed themselves: there should have been eight Bork kinsmen. Somehow the peddler had eliminated one of the Borks during the attack, so silently, so quickly, that his loss had gone unnoticed. Wim shuddered, suddenly remembering a flare of unreal blue-white light, and the claims he had just made for the peddler. If one Bork could be killed so easily, why not two? In which case—

"He's here, pretending to be one of you!" Wim cried, his voice cracking.

And he could almost feel their terror echoing back and forth, from one to another, growing—until one of the shortest of the silhouettes broke and ran out into the moonlight. He got only about twenty feet, before he was brought down by a crossbow quarrel in the back. Even as the fugitive crumpled onto the soft, silver dirt a second crossbow thunked and another of the brothers fell dead across Win's feet.

"That was Clyne, you . . . warlock!" More bows lowered around the circle.

"Hold on now!" shouted Axl. There were five Borks left standing; two bodies sprawled unmoving on the ground. "The peddler got us in his spell. We got to keep our sense and figure out which of us he's pretendin' to be."

"But Ax', he ain't just in disguise, we woulda seen which one he is ... he—he can trick us into believing he's anybody!"

Trapped beneath the corpse, all Wim could see were five shadows against the night. Their faces were hidden from the light, and bulky clothing disguised any differences. He bit his lips against the least sound of pain; now was no time to remind the remaining Borks of Wim Buckry— But the agony of his hand pulsed up his arm until he felt a terrible dizziness wrench the blurring world away and his head drooped . . .

He opened his eyes again and saw that only three men stood now in the glade. Two more had died; the newest corpse still twitched on the ground.

Axl's voice was shrill with rage. "You . . . monster! You done tricked all of us into killing each other!"

"No, Ax', I had to shoot him. It was the peddler, I swear. Turn him over. Look! He shot Jan after you told us to hold off—"

"Warlock!" a third voice cried. "All of them dead—!" Two crossbows came down and fired simultaneously. Two men fell.

Axl stood silent and alone among the dead for a long moment. The moon had set at last, and the starlight was rare and faint through the shifting branches of the grandfather tree far overhead. Wim lay still as death, aware of the smell of blood and sweat and burned flesh. And the sound of footsteps, approaching. Sick with fear he looked up at the dark stubby form of Axl Bork.

"Still here? Good." A black-booted foot rolled the dead body from his legs. "Well, boy, you better leave me look at that hand." The voice belonged to Jagit Katchetooriantz.

"Uh." Wim began to tremble. "Uh. Mr. Jagged . . . is that . . . you?"

A light appeared in the hand of the peddler who had come from Sharn.

Wim fainted.

Early morning filled the Grandfather Grove with dusty shafts of light. Wim Buckry sat propped against the cave tree's entrance, sipping awkwardly at a cup of something hot and bitter held in a bandaged hand. His other hand was tucked through his belt, to protect a sprained right shoulder. Silently he watched the peddler grooming the dappled cart horse; glanced for the tenth time around the sunlit grove, where no sign of the last night's events marred the quiet tranquillity of the day. Like a bad dream the memory of his terror seemed unreal to him now, and he wondered if that was more witchery, like the drink that had eased the pains of his body. He looked down, where dried blood stained his pants. *He'd took care of the remains,* the peddler had said. It was real, all right—all of the Borks. And all of his boys. He thought wistfully for a moment of the jewelry that had gone into the ground with them; shied away from a deeper sense of loss beneath it.

The peddler returned to the campfire, kicked dirt over the blaze. He had had no trouble in getting a fire to burn. Wim drew his feet up; the dark eyes looked questioningly at his sullen face.

"Mr. Jagged"—there was no trace of mockery in that title now—"just what do you want from me?"

Jagit dusted off his leather shirt. "Well, Wim—I was thinking if you was up to it, maybe you'd want to go on with our agreement."

Wim raised his bandaged hand. "Wouldn't be much pertection, one cripple."

"But I don't know the way down through that there Valley, which you do."

Wim laughed incredulously. "I reckon you could fly over the moon on a broomstick and you wouldn't need no map. And you sure as hell don't need pertecting! Why'd you ever take us on, Mr. Jagged?" Grief sobered him suddenly, and realization— "You knew all along, didn't you? What we were fixing to do. You took us along so's you could watch us, and maybe scare us off. Well, you needn't be watching me no more. I—we already changed our minds, even before what happened with them Borks. We was fixing to take you on down like we said, all honest."

"I know that." The peddler nodded. "You ever hear an old saying, Wim: 'Two heads are better than one'? You can't never tell; you might just come in handy."

Wim shrugged ruefully, and wondered where the peddler ever heard that "old saying." "Well . . . ain't heard no better offers this morning."

They left the grandfather trees and continued the descent toward the Great Valley. Throughout the early morning the pine woods continued to surround them, but as the morning wore on Wim noticed that the evergreens had given way to oak and sycamore, as the air lost its chill and much of its moistness. By late in the day he could catch glimpses between the trees of the green and amber vastness that was the valley floor, and pointed it out to the peddler. Jagit nodded, seeming pleased, and returned to the aimless humming that Wim suspected covered diabolical thoughts. He glanced again at the round, stubby merchant, the last man in the world a body'd suspect of magical powers. Which was perhaps what made them so convincing . . . "Mr. Jagged? How'd you do it? Hex them Borks, I mean."

Jagit smiled and shook his head. "A good magician never tells how. What, maybe, but never how. You have to watch, and figure how for yourself. That's how you get to *be* a good magician."

Wim sighed, shifted his hand under his belt. "Reckon I don't want to know, then."

The peddler chuckled. "Fair enough."

Surreptitiously, Wim watched his every move for the rest of the day.

After the evening meal the peddler again spent time at his wagon in the dark. Wim, sprawled exhausted by the campfire, saw the gleam of a warlock's wand but this time made no move to investigate, only crossing his fingers as a precautionary gesture. Inactivity had left him with too much else to consider. He stared fixedly into the flames, his hand smarting.

"Reckon we should be down to the valley floor in about an hour's travel, tomorrow. Then you say we head northwest, till we come to Fyffe?"

Wim started at the sound of the peddler's voice. "Oh . . . yeah, I reckon. Cut north and any road'll get you there; they all go to Fyffe."

" 'All roads lead to Fyffe'?" The peddler laughed unexpectedly, squatted by the fire.

Wim wondered what was funny. "Anybody can tell you the way from here, Mr. Jagged. I think come morning I'll be heading back; I . . . we never figured to come this far. Us hill folk don't much like going down into the Flatlands."

"Hm. I'm sorry to hear that, Wim." Jagit pushed another branch into the fire. "But somehow I'd figured it you'd really been to Fyffe?"

"Well, yeah, I was . . . almost." He looked up, surprised. "Three, four years ago, when I was hardly more'n a young'un, with my pa and some other men. See, my granther was the smith at Darkwood Corners, and he got hold of a gun—" And he found himself telling a peddler-man things everyone knew, and things he'd never told to anyone: How his grandfather had discovered gunpowder, how the Highlanders had plotted to overthrow the lords of Fyffe and take the rich valley farmlands for themselves. And how horsemen had come out from the city to meet them, with guns and magic, how the amber fields were torn and reddened and his pa had died when his homemade gun blew up in his face. How a bloody, tight-lipped boy returning alone to Darkwood Corners had filled its citizens with the fear of the Lord, and of the lords of Fyffe . . . He sat twisting painfully at a golden earring. "And—I heard tell as how they got dark magics down there that we never even saw, so's to keep all the Flatlanders under a spell . . . Maybe you oughta think again 'bout going down there too, Mr. Jagged."

"I thank you for the warning, Wim." Jagit nodded. "But I'll tell you—I'm a merchant by trade, and by inclination. If I can't sell my wares, I got no point in being, and I can't sell my wares in these hills."

"You ain't afraid they'll try to stop you?"

He smiled. "Well, now, I didn't say that. Their magic ain't up to Sharn, I'm pretty sure. But it is an unknown . . . Who knows—they may turn out to be my best customers; lords are like to be free with their money." He looked at Wim with something like respect. "But like I say, two heads are better than one. I'm right sorry you won't be along. Mayhap in the morning we can settle accounts—"

In the morning the peddler hitched up his wagon and started down toward the Great Valley. And not really understanding why, Wim Buckry went with him.

Early in the day they left the welcome shelter of the last oak forest, started across the open rolling hills of ripening wild grasses, until they struck a rutted track heading north. Win stripped off his jerkin and loosened his shirt, his pale Highland skin turning red under the climbing sun of the Valley. The dark-skinned peddler in his leather shirt smiled at him, and Wim figured, annoyed, that he must enjoy the heat. By noon they reached the endless green corduroy fringe of the cultivated Flatlands, and with a jolt they found themselves on paved road. Jagit knelt and prodded the resilient surface before they continued on their way. Wim vaguely remembered the soft pavement, a bizarre luxury to Highland feet, stretching all the way to Fyffe; this time he noticed that in places the pavement was eaten away by time, and neatly patched with smooth-cut stone.

The peddler spoke little to him, only humming, apparently intent on searching out signs of Flatlander magic. *A good magician watches* . . . Wim forced himself to study the half-remembered landscape. The ripening fields and pasturelands blanketed the Valley to the limit of his sight, like an immense, living crazy-quilt in greens and gold, spread over the rich dark earth. In the distance he could see pale mist hovering over the fields, wondered if it was a trick of witchery or only the heat of the day. And he saw the Flatlanders at work in the fields by the road, well-fed and roughly dressed; tanned, placid faces that regarded their passage with the resigned disinterest that he would have expected of a plowmule. Wim frowned.

"A rather curious lack of curiosity, I'd say, wouldn't you?" The peddler glanced at him. "They're going to make bad customers."

"Look at 'em!" Wim burst out angrily. "How could they do all of this? They ain't no better farmers 'n Highlanders; in the hills you work your hands to the bone to farm, and you get nothing, stones— And look at them, they're fat. How, Mr. Jagged?"

"How do *you* think they do it, Wim?"

"I—" He stopped. *Good magicians figure it out . . .* "Well—they got better land."

"True."

"And . . . there's magic."

"Is there now?"

"You saw it—them smooth-bedded streams, this here road; it ain't natural. But . . . they all look as how they're bewitched, themselves, just like I heard. Mayhap it's only the lords of Fyffe as have all the magic—it's them we got to watch for?" He crossed his fingers.

"Maybe so. It looks like they may be the only customers I'll have, too, if this doesn't change." The peddler's face was devoid of expression. "Quit crossing your fingers, Wim; the only thing that'll ever save you from is the respect of educated men."

Wim uncrossed his fingers. He walked on for several minutes before he realized the peddler spoke like a Flatlander now, as perfectly as he'd spoken the Highland talk before.

Late in the afternoon they came to a well, at one of the farm villages that centered like a hub in a great wheel of fields. The peddler dipped a cup into the dripping container, and then Wim took a gulp straight from the bucket. A taste of bitter metal filled his mouth, and he spat in dismay, looking back at the merchant. Jagit was passing his hand over—no, dropping something *into* the cup—and as Wim watched the water began to foam, and suddenly turned bright red. The peddler's black brows rose with interest, and he poured the water slowly out onto the ground. Wim blanched and wiped his mouth hard on his sleeve. "It *tastes* like poison!"

Jagit shook his head. "That's not poison you taste: I'd say farming's just polluted the water table some. But it is drugged." He watched the villagers standing with desultory murmurs around his wagon.

"Sheep," Wim's face twisted with disgust.

The peddler shrugged. "But all of them healthy, wealthy, and wise . . . well, healthy and wise, anyway . . . healthy—?" He moved away to offer his wares. There were few takers. As Wim returned to the wagon, taking a drink of stale mountain water from the barrel on the back, he heard the little man muttering again, like an incantation, "Fyffe . . . Fyffe . . . Dyston-Fyffe, they call it here . . . *District Town Five?* . . . Couldn't be." He frowned, oblivious. "But then again, why couldn't it—?"

For the rest of that day the peddler kept his thoughts to himself, looking strangely grim, only pronouncing an occasional curse in some incomprehensible language. And that night, as they camped, as Wim's weary mind unwillingly relived the loss of the only friends he had, he wondered if the dark silent stranger across the fire shared his loneliness; a peddler was always a stranger, even if he was a magician. "Mr. Jagged, you ever feel like going home?"

"Home?" Jagit glanced up. "Sometimes. Tonight, maybe. But I've come so far, I guess that would be impossible. When I got back, it'd all be gone." Suddenly through the flames his face looked very old. "What made it home was gone before I left . . . But maybe I'll find it again, somewhere else, as I go."

"Yeah . . ." Wim nodded, understanding both more and less than he realized. He curled down into his blanket, oddly comforted, and went soundly to sleep.

Minor wonders continued to assail him on their journey, and also the question, "Why?"; until gradually Jagit's prodding transformed his superstitious awe into a cocky curiosity that sometimes made the peddler frown, though he made no comment.

Until the third morning, when Wim finally declared, "Everything's a trick, if'n you can see behind it, just like with them witches in the hills. Everything's got a—reason. I think there ain't no such thing as magic!"

Jagit fixed him with a long mild look, and the specter of

the night in the Grandfather Grove seemed to flicker in the dark eyes. "You think not, eh?"

Wim looked down nervously.

"There's magic, all right, Wim; all around you here. Only now you're seeing it with a magician's eyes: Because there's a reason behind everything that happens; you may not know what it is, but it's there. And knowing that doesn't make the thing less magic, or strange, or terrible—it just makes it easier to deal with. That's something to keep in mind, wherever you are . . . Also keep in mind that a *little* knowledge is a dangerous thing."

Wim nodded, chastened, felt his ears grow red as the peddler muttered, "So's a little ignorance . . ."

The afternoon of the third day showed them Fyffe, still a vague blot wavering against the horizon. Wim looked back over endless green toward the mountains, but they were hidden from him now by the yellow Flatland haze. Peering ahead again toward the city, he was aware that the fear that had come with him into the Great Valley had grown less instead of greater as they followed the familiar-strange road to Fyffe. The dappled cart horse snorted loudly in the hot, dusty silence, and he realized it was the peddler with his wagon full of magics that gave him his newfound courage.

He smiled, flexing his burned hand. Jagit had never made any apology for what he'd done, but Wim was not such a hypocrite that he really expected one, under the circumstances. And the peddler had treated his wounds with potions, so that bruises began to fade and skin to heal almost while he watched. It was almost—

Wim's thoughts were interrupted as he stumbled on a rough patch in the road. The city, much closer now, lay stolidly among the fields in the lengthening shadows of the hot afternoon. He wondered in which field his father—abruptly turned his thoughts ahead again, noticing that the city was without walls or other visible signs of defense. *Why?* Mayhap because they had nothing to fear— He felt his body tighten with old terrors. But Jagit's former grim mood had seemingly dropped away as his goal drew near, as though he had reached some resolution. If the peddler was confident, then Wim would be, too. He looked on the city with magician's eyes; and it struck him that a more outlandish challenge had most likely never visited the lords of Fyffe.

They entered Fyffe, and though the peddler seemed almost disappointed, Wim tried to conceal his gaping with little success. The heavy stone and timber buildings crowded the cobble-patched street, rising up two and three stories to cut off his view of the fields. The street's edge was lined with shop fronts; windows of bulls-eyed glass and peeling painted signs advertised their trade. The levels above the shops, he supposed, were where the people lived. The weathered stone of the curbs had been worn to hollows from the tread of countless feet, and the idea of so many people—5,000, the peddler had guessed—in so little area made him shudder.

They made their way past dully-dressed, well-fed townsfolk and farmers finishing the day's commerce in the cooling afternoon. Wim caught snatches of sometimes heated bargaining, but he noticed that the town showed little more interest in the bizarre spectacle of himself and the peddler than had the folk they dealt with on their journey. Children at least ought to follow the bright wagon—he was vaguely disturbed to realize he'd scarcely seen any, here or anywhere, and those he saw were kept close by parents. It seemed the peddler's business would be no better here than in the hills after all. *Like hogs in a pen . . .* He glanced down the street, back over his shoulder. "Where's all the hogs?"

"What?" The peddler looked at him.

"It's clean. All them folk living here and there ain't any garbage. How can that be, less'n they keep hogs to eat it? But I don't see any hogs. Nor—hardly any young'uns."

"Hmm." The peddler shrugged, smiling. "Good questions. Maybe we should ask the lords of Fyffe."

Wim shook his head. Yet he had to admit that the city so far, for all its strangeness, had shown him no signs of any magic more powerful or grim than that he'd seen in the fields. Perhaps the lords of Fyffe weren't so fearsome as the tales claimed; their warriors weren't bewitched, but only better armed.

The street curved sharply, and ahead the clustered buildings gave way on an open square, filled with the covered stalls of a public marketplace. And beyond it—Wim stopped, staring. Beyond it, he knew, stood the dwelling of the lords of Fyffe. Twice as massive as any building he had seen, its pilastered green-black walls reflected the square like a dark, malevolent mirror. The building had the solidity of a thing that had grown from the earth, a permanence that made the town itself seem ephemeral. Now, he knew, he looked on the house for magic that might match the peddler and Sharn.

Beside him, Jagit's smile was genuine and unreadable.

"Pardon me, ma'm," the peddler stopped a passing woman and child, "but we're strangers. What's that building there called?"

"Why, that's Government House." The woman looked only mildly surprised. Wim admired her stocking-covered ankles.

"I see. And what do they do there?"

She pulled her little girl absently back from the wagon. "That's where the governors are. Folks go there with petitions and such. They—govern, I suppose. Lissy, keep away from that dusty beast."

"Thank you, ma'm. And could I show you—"

"Not today. Come on, child, we'll be late."

The peddler bowed in congenial exasperation as she moved on. Wim sighed, and he shook his head. "Hardly a market for Sharnish wonders here, either, I begin to think. I may have outfoxed myself for once. Looks like my only choice is to pay a call on your lords of Fyffe over there; I might still have a thing or two to interest them." His eyes narrowed in appraisal as he looked across the square.

At a grunt of disapproval from Wim, Jagit glanced back, gestured at the lengthening shadows, "Too late to start selling now, anyway. What do you say we just take a look—" Suddenly he fell silent.

Wim turned. A group of half a dozen dour-faced men were approaching them; the leader bore a crest on his stiff-brimmed hat that Wim remembered. They were unslinging guns from their shoulders. Wim's question choked off as they quietly circled the wagon, cut him off from the peddler. The militiaman addressed Jagit, faintly disdainful. "The Governors—"

Wim seized the barrel of the nearest rifle, slinging its owner into the man standing next to him. He wrenched the gun free and brought it down on the head of a third gaping guard.

"Wim!" He froze at the sound of the peddler's voice, turned back. "Drop the gun." The peddler stood unresisting beside his wagon. And three remaining guns were pointing at Wim Buckry. Face filled with angry betrayal, he threw down the rifle.

"Tie the hillbilly up . . . The Governors require a few words with you two, peddler, as I was saying. You'll come with us." The militia leader stood back, unperturbed, as his townsman guards got to their feet.

Wim winced as his hands were bound roughly before him,

but there was no vindictiveness on the guard's bruised face. Pushed forward to walk with the peddler, he muttered bitterly, "Whyn't you use your magic!"

Jagit shook his head. "Would've been bad for business. After all, the lords of Fyffe have come to *me*."

Wim crossed his fingers, deliberately, as they climbed the green-black steps of Government House.

The hours stretched interminably in the windowless, featureless room where they were left to wait, and Wim soon tired of staring at the evenness of the walls and the smokeless lamps. The peddler sat fiddling with small items left in his pockets; but Wim had begun to doze in spite of himself by the time guards returned at last, to take them to their long-delayed audience with the lords of Fyffe.

The guards left them to the lone man who rose, smiling, from behind a tawny expanse of desk as they entered the green-walled room. "Well, at last!" He was in his late fifties and plainly dressed like the townsmen, about Wim's height but heavier, with graying hair. Wim saw that the smiling face held none of the dullness of their captors' faces. "I'm Charl Aydricks, representative of the World Government. My apologies for keeping you waiting, but I was—out of town. We've been following your progress with some interest."

Wim wondered what in tarnation this poor-man governor took himself for, claiming the Flatlands was the whole world. He glanced past Aydricks into the unimpressive, lamplit room. On the governor's desk he noticed the only sign of a lord's riches he'd yet seen—a curious ball of inlaid metals, mostly blue but blotched with brown and green, fixed on a golden stand. He wondered with more interest where the other lords of Fyffe might be; Aydricks was alone, without even guards . . . Wim suddenly remembered that whatever this man wasn't, he was a magician, no less than the peddler.

Jagit made a polite bow. "Jagit Katchetooriantz, at your service. Merchant by trade, and flattered by the interest. This is my apprentice—"

"—Wim Buckry." The governor's appraising glance moved unexpectedly to Wim. "Yes, we remember you, Wim. I must say I'm surprised to see you here again. But pleased—we've been wanting to get ahold of you." A look of too much interest crossed Aydricks' face.

Wim eyed the closed door with longing.

"Please be seated." The governor returned to his desk. "We rarely get such . . . unique visitors—"

Jagit took a seat calmly, and Wim dropped into the second chair, knees suddenly weak. As he settled into the softness he felt a sourceless pressure bearing down on him, lunged upward like a frightened colt only to be forced back into the seat. Panting, he felt the pressure ease as he collapsed in defeat.

Jagit looked at him with sympathy before glancing back at the governor; Wim saw the peddler's fingers twitch impotently on the chair-arm. "Surely you don't consider us a threat?" His voice was faintly mocking.

The governor's congeniality stopped short of his eyes. "We know about the forces you were using in the Grandfather Grove."

"Do you now! That's what I'd hoped." Jagit met the gaze and held it. "Then I'm obviously in the presence of some technological sophistication, at last. I have some items of trade that might interest you . . ."

"You may be sure they'll receive our attention. But let's just be honest with each other, shall we? You're no more a peddler than I am; not with what we've seen you do. And if you'd really come from the east—from anywhere—I'd know about it; our communications network is excellent. You simply appeared from nowhere, in the Highlands Preserve. And it really was nowhere on this earth, wasn't it?"

Jagit said nothing, looking expectant. Wim stared fixedly at the textured green of the wall, trying to forget that he was witness to a debate of warlocks.

Aydricks stirred impatiently. "From nowhere on this earth. Our moon colony is long gone; that means no planet in this system. Which leaves the Lost Colonies—you've come from one of the empire's colony worlds, from another star system, Jagit; and if you expected that to surprise us after all this time, you're mistaken."

Jagit attempted a shrug. "No—I didn't expect that, frankly. But I didn't expect any of the rest of this, either; things haven't turned out as I'd planned at all . . ."

Wim listened in spite of himself, in silent wonder. Were there worlds beyond his own, that were no more than sparks in the black vastness of earth's night? Was that where Sharn was, then, with its wonders; beyond the sky, where folks said was heaven—?

". . . Obviously," the governor was saying, "you're a precedent-shattering threat to the World Government. Because this is a *world* government, and it has maintained peace and stability over millennia. Our space defense system sees to it that—outsiders don't upset that peace. At least it always has until now; you're the first person to penetrate our system, and we don't even know how you did it. That's what we want to know—*must* know, Jagit, not who you represent, or where, or even why, so much as *how*. We can't allow anything to disrupt our stability." Aydricks leaned forward across his desk; his hand tightened protectively over the stand of the strange metal globe. His affability had disappeared entirely, and Wim felt his own hopes sink, realizing the governor somehow knew the peddler's every secret. Jagit wasn't infallible, and this time he had let himself be trapped.

But Jagit seemed undismayed. "If you value your stability that much, then I'd say it's time somebody did disturb it."

"That's to be expected." Aydricks sat back, his expression relaxing into contempt. "But you won't be the one. We've had ten thousand years to perfect our system, and in that time no one else has succeeded in upsetting it. We've put an end at last to all the millennia of destructive waste on this world . . ."

Ten thousand years—? As Aydricks spoke, Wim groped to understand a second truth that tore at the very roots of his comprehension:

For the history of mankind stretched back wonder on wonder for unimaginable thousands of years, through tremendous cycles filled with lesser cycles. Civilization reached highs where every dream was made a reality and humanity sent offshoots to the stars, only to fall back, through its own folly, into abysses of loss when men forgot their humanity and reality became a nightmare. Then slowly the cycle would change again, and in time mankind would reach new heights, that paradoxically it could never maintain. Always men seemed unable in the midst of their creation to resist the urge to destroy, and always they found the means to destroy utterly.

Until the end of the last great cyclical empire, when a group among the ruling class saw that a new decline was imminent, and acted to prevent it. They had forced the world into a new order, one of patternless stability at a low level, and had stopped it there. ". . . And because of us that state, free from strife and suffering, the world has continued for ten thousand years, unchanged. Literally unchanged. I am one of the original founders of the World Government."

Wim looked unbelievingly into the smiling, unremarkable face; found the eyes of a fanatic and incredible age.

"You're well preserved," Jagit said.

The governor burst into honest laughter. "This isn't my original body. By using our computer network we're able to transfer our memories intact into the body of an 'heir': someone from the general population, young and full of potential. As long as the individual's personality is compatible, it's absorbed into the greater whole, and he becomes a revitalizing part of us. That's why I've been keeping track of Wim, here; he has traits that should make him an excellent governor." The too-interested smile showed on the governor's face again.

Wim's bound hands tightened into fists—the invisible pressure forced him back down into the seat, his face stricken.

Aydricks watched him, amused. "Technological initiative and personal aggressiveness are key factors that lead to an unstable society. Since, to keep stability, we have to suppress those factors in the population, we keep control groups free from interference—like the hill folk, the Highlanders—to give us a dependable source of the personality types we need ourselves.

"But the system as a whole really is very well designed. Our computer network provides us with our continuity, with the technology, communications, and—sources of power we need to maintain stability. We in turn ensure the computer's continuity, since we preserve the knowledge to keep it functioning. There's no reason why the system can't go on forever."

Wim looked toward the peddler for some sign of reassurance; but found a grimness that made him look away again as Jagit said, "And you think that's a feat I should appreciate: that you've manipulated the fate of every being on this planet for ten thousand years, to your own ends, and that you plan to go on doing it indefinitely?"

"But it's for their own good, can't you see that? We ask nothing from this, no profit for ourselves, no reward other than knowing that humanity will never be able to throw itself into barbarism again, that the cycle of destructive waste, of rise and fall, has finally been stopped on earth. The people are secure, their world is stable, they know it will be safe for future generations. Could your own world claim as much? Think of the years that must have passed on your journey here—would you even have a civilization to return to by now?"

Wim saw Jagit forcibly relax; the peddler's smile reappeared, full of irony. "But the fact remains that a cycle of rise and fall is the natural order of things—life and death, if you want to call it that. It gives humanity a chance to reach new heights, and gives an old order a clean death. Stasis is a coma—no lows, but no highs either, no *choice*. Somehow I think that Sharn would have preferred a clean death to this—"

"Sharn? What do you know about the old empire?" The governor leaned forward, complaisance lost.

"Sharn—?" Wim's bewilderment was lost on the air.

"They knew everything about Sharn, where I come from. The crystal city with rot at its heart, the Games of Three. They were even seeing the trends that would lead to this, though they had no idea it would prove so eminently successful."

"Well, this gets more and more interesting." The governor's voice hardened. "Considering that there should be no way someone from outside could have known of the last years of the empire. But I suspect we'll only continue to raise more questions this way. I think it's time we got some answers."

Wim slumped in his seat, visions of torture leaping into his mind. But the governor only left his desk, passing Wim with a glance that suggested hunger, and placed a shining band of filigreed metal on Jagit's head.

"You may be surprised at what you get," Jagit's expression remained calm, but Wim thought strain tightened his voice.

The governor returned to his chair. "Oh, I don't think so. I've just linked you into our computer net—"

Abruptly Jagit went rigid with surprise, settled back into a half-smile; but not before Aydricks had seen the change. "Once it gets into your mind you'll have considerable difficulty concealing anything at all. It's quick and always effective; though unfortunately I can't guarantee that it won't drive you crazy."

The peddler's smile faded. "How civilized," he said quietly. He met Wim's questioning eyes. "Well, Wim, you remember what I showed you. And crossing your fingers didn't help, did it?"

Wim shook his head. "Whatever you say, Mr. Jagged . . ." He suspected he'd never have an opportunity to remember anything.

Suddenly the peddler gasped, and his eyes closed, his body went limp in the seat. "Mr. Jagged—?" But there was no response. Alone, Wim wondered numbly what sort of terrible enchantment the metal crown held, and whether it would hurt when the computer—whatever that was—swallowed his own soul.

"Are you monitoring? All districts? Direct hookup, yes." The governor seemed to be speaking to his desk. He hesitated as though listening, then stared into space.

Wim sagged fatalistically against his chair, past horror now, ignoring—and ignored by—the two entranced men. Silence stretched in the green room. Then the light in the room flickered and dimmed momentarily. Wim's eyes widened as he felt the unseen pressure that held him down weaken slightly, then return with the lighting. The governor frowned at nothing, still staring into space. Wim began ineffectually to twist at his bound hands. However the magic worked in this room, it had just stopped working; if it stopped again he'd be ready . . . He glanced at Jagit. Was there a smile—?

"District Eighteen here. Aydricks, what is this?"

Wim shuddered. The live disembodied head of a red-haired youth had just appeared in a patch of sudden brightness by the wall. The governor turned blinking toward thc ghost.

"Our reception's getting garbled. This data can't be right, it says he's . . ." The ghostly face wavered and the voice was drowned in a sound like water rushing. ". . . it, what's wrong with the transmission? Is he linked up directly? We aren't getting anything now—"

Two more faces—one old, with skin even darker than the peddler's, and one a middle-aged woman—appeared in the wall, protesting. And Wim realized then that he saw the other lords of Fyffe—and truly of the world—here and yet not here, transported by their magic from the far ends of the earth. The red-haired ghost peered at Wim, who shrank away from the angry, young-old eyes, then looked past to Jagit. The frown grew fixed and then puzzled, was transformed into incredulity. "No, that's impossible!"

"What is?" Aydricks looked harassed.

"I know that man."

The black-haired woman turned as though she could see him. "What do you mean you—"

"I know that man too!" Another dark face appeared. "From Sharn, from the empire. But . . . after ten thousand years, how can he be the *same* . . . Aydricks! Remember the Primitive Arts man, he was famous, he spent . . ." the voice blurred, ". . . got to get him out of the comm system! He knows the comm-sat codes, he can—" The ghostly face dematerialized entirely.

Aydricks looked wildly at the unmoving peddler, back at the remaining governors.

Wim saw more faces appear, and another face flicker out; *the same man . . .*

"Stop him, Aydricks!" The woman's voice rose. "He'll ruin us. He's altering the comm codes, killing the tie-up!"

"I can't cut him off!"

"He's into my link now, I'm losing con—" The red-haired ghost disappeared.

"Stop him, Aydricks, or we'll burn out Fyffe!"

"Jagged! Look out!" Wim struggled against his invisible bonds as he saw the governor reach with grim resolution for the colored metal globe on his desk. He knew Aydricks meant to bash in the peddler's skull, and the helpless body in the chair couldn't stop him. "Mr. Jagged, wake up!" Desperately Wim stuck out his feet as Aydricks passed; the governor stumbled. Another face disappeared from the wall, and the lights went out. Wim slid from the chair, free and groping awkwardly for a knife he no longer had. Under the faltering gaze of the ghosts in the wall, Aydricks fumbled toward Jagit.

Wim grabbed at Aydricks' feet just as the light returned, catching an ankle. The governor turned back, cursing, to kick at him, but Wim was already up, leaping away from a blow with the heavy statue.

"Aydricks, stop the peddler!"

Full of sudden fury, Wim gasped, "Damn you, you won't stop it this time!" As the governor turned away Wim flung himself against the other's back, staggering him, and hooked his bound hands over Aydricks' head. Aydricks fought to pull him loose, dropping the globe as he threw himself backward to slam his attacker against the desk. Wim groaned as his backbone grated against the desk edge, and lost his balance. He brought his knee up as he fell; there was a sharp *crack* as the governor landed beside him, and lay still. Wim got to his knees; the ancient eyes stabbed him with accusation and fear. "No, Oh, *no*." The eyes glazed.

A week after his seventeenth birthday, Wim Buckry had killed a ten-thousand-year-old-man. And, unknowingly, helped to destroy an empire. The room was quiet; the last of the governors had faded from the wall. Wim got slowly to his feet, his mouth pulled back in a grin of revulsion. All the magic in the world hadn't done this warlock any good. He moved to where Jagit still sat entranced, lifted his hands to pull the metal crown off and break the spell. And hesitated, suddenly unsure of himself. Would breaking the spell wake the peddler, or kill him? They had to get out of here: but Jagit was somehow fighting the bewitchment, that much he understood, and if he stopped him now— His hands dropped, he stood irresolutely, waiting. And waiting.

His hands reached again for the metal band, twitching with indecision; jerked back as Jagit suddenly smiled at him. The dark eyes opened and the peddler sat forward, taking the metal band gently from his own head with a sigh. "I'm glad you waited. You'll probably never know how glad." Wim's grin became real, and relieved.

Jagit got unsteadily to his feet, glanced at Aydricks' body and shook his head; his face was haggard. "Said you might be a help, didn't I?" Wim stood phlegmatically while the peddler who was as old as Sharn itself unfastened the cords on his raw wrists. "I'd say our business is finished. You ready to get out of here? We don't have much time."

Wim started for the door in response, opened it, and came face to face with the unsummoned guard standing in the hall. His fist connected with the gaping jaw; the guard's knees buckled and he dropped to the floor, unconscious. Wim picked up the guard's rifle as Jagit appeared beside him, motioning him down the dim hallway.

"Where is everybody?"

"Let's hope they're home in bed; it's four-thirty in the morning. There shouldn't be any alarms."

Wim laughed giddily. "This's a sight easier than getting away from the Borks!"

"We're not away yet; we may be too late already. Those faces on the wall were trying to drop a—piece of sun on Fyffe. I think I stopped them, but I don't know for sure. If it wasn't a total success, I don't want to find out the hard way." He led Wim back down the wide stairway, into the empty hall where petitioners had gathered during the day. Wim started across the echoing floor but Jagit called him back, peering at something on the wall; they went down another flight into a well of darkness, guided by the peddler's magic light. At the foot of the stairs the way was blocked by a door, solidly shut. Jagit looked chagrined, then suddenly the beam of his light shone blue; he flashed it against a metal plate set in the door. The door slid back and he went through it.

Wim followed him, into a cramped, softly glowing cubicle nearly filled by three heavily padded seats around a peculiar table. Wim noticed they seemed to be bolted to the floor, and suddenly felt claustrophobic.

"Get into a seat, Wim. Thank God I was right about this tower being a ballistic exit. Strap in, because we're about to use it." He began to push lighted buttons on the table before him.

Wim fumbled with the restraining straps, afraid to wonder what the peddler thought they were doing, as a heavy inner door shut the room off from the outside. Why weren't they out of the building, running? How could this— Something pressed him down into the seat cushions like a gentle, insistent hand. His first thought was of another trap; but as the pressure continued, he realized this was something new. And then, glancing up past Jagit's intent face, he saw that instead of blank walls, they were now surrounded by the starry sky of night. He leaned forward—and below his feet was the town of Fyffe, shrinking away with every heartbeat, disappearing into the greater darkness. He saw what the eagle saw . . . he was flying. He sat back again, feeling for the reassuring hardness of the invisible floor, only to discover suddenly that his feet no longer touched it. There was no pressure bearing him down now, there was nothing at all. His body drifted against the restraining straps, lighter than a bird. A small sound of incredulous wonder escaped him as he stared out at the unexpected stars.

And saw a brightness begin to grow at the opaque line of the horizon, spreading and creeping upward second by second, blotting out the stars with the fragile hues of dawn. The sun's flaming face thrust itself up past the edge of the world, making him squint, rising with arcane speed and uncanny brilliance into a sky that remained stubbornly black with night. At last the whole sphere of the sun was revealed, and continued to climb in the midnight sky while now Wim could see a thin streak of sky-blue stretched along the horizon, left behind with the citron glow of dawn still lighting its center. Above the line in darkness the sun wore the pointed crown of a star that dimmed all others, and below it he could see the world at the horizon's edge moving into day. And the horizon did not lie absolutely flat, but was bowing gently downward now at the sides . . . Below his feet was still the utter darkness that had swallowed Fyffe. He sighed.

"Quite a view." Jagit sat back from the glowing table, drifting slightly above his seat, a tired smile on his face.

"You see it too?" Wim said hoarsely.

The peddler nodded. "I felt the same way, the first time. I guess everyone always has. Every time civilization has gained space flight, it's been rewarded again by that sight."

Wim said nothing, unable to find the words. His view of the bowed horizon had changed subtly, and now as he watched there came a further change—the sun began, slowly but perceptibly, to move backward down its track, sinking once more toward the point of dawn that had given it birth. Or, he suddenly saw, it was they who were slipping, back down from the heights of glory into his world's darkness once more. Wim waited while the sun sank from the black and alien sky, setting where it had risen, its afterglow reabsorbed into night as the edge of the world blocked his vision again. He dropped to the seat of his chair, as though the world had reclaimed him, and the stars reappeared. A heavy lurch, like a blow, shook the cubicle, and then all motion stopped.

He sat still, not understanding, as the door slid back in darkness and a breath of cold, sharp air filled the tiny room. Beyond the doorway was darkness again, but he knew it was not the night of a building hallway.

Jagit fumbled wearily with the restraining straps on his seat. "Home the same day . . ."

Wim didn't wait, but driven by instinct freed himself and went to the doorway. And jerked to a stop as he discovered they were no longer at ground level. His feet found the ladder, and as he stepped down from its bottom rung he heard and felt the gritty shifting of gravel. The only other sounds were the sigh of the icy wind, and water lapping. As his eyes adjusted they told him what his other senses already knew—that he was home. Not Darkwood Corners, but somewhere in his own cruelly beautiful Highlands. Fanged shadow peaks rose up on either hand, blotting out the stars, but more stars shone in the smooth waters of the lake; they shivered slightly, as he shivered in the cold breeze, clammy with sweat under his thin shirt. He stood on the rubble of a mountain pass somewhere above the treeline, and in the east the gash between the peaks showed pinkish-gray with returning day.

Behind him he heard Jagit, and turned to see the peddler climbing slowly down the few steps to the ground. From outside, the magician's chamber was the shape of a truncated rifle bullet. Jagit carried the guard's stolen rifle, leaning on it now like a walking stick. "Well, my navigation hasn't failed me yet." He rubbed his eyes, stretched.

Wim recalled making a certain comment about flying over the moon on a broomstick, too long ago, and looked again at the dawn, this time progressing formally and peacefully up a lightening sky. "We flew here. Didn't we, Mr. Jagged?" His teeth chattered. "Like a bird. Only . . . we f-flew right off the world." He stopped, awed by his own revelation. For a moment a lifetime of superstitious dread cried that he had no right to know of the things he had seen, or to believe— The words burst out in a defiant rush. "That's it. Right off the world. And . . . and it's all true: I heard how the world's round like a stone. It must be true, how there's other worlds, that's what you said back there, with people just like here; I seen it, the sun's like all them other stars, only it's bigger . . ." He frowned. "It's—closer? I—"

Jagit was grinning, his teeth showed white in his beard. "Magician, first-class."

Wim looked back up into the sky. "If that don't beat all—" he said softly. Then, struck by more practical matters, he said, "What about them ghosts? Are they going to come after us?"

Jagit shook his head. "No. I think I laid those ghosts to rest pretty permanently. I changed the code words in their communications system, a good part of it is totally unusable now. Their computer net is broken up, and their space defense system must be out for good, because they didn't destroy Fyffe, I'd say the World Government is finished; they don't know it yet, and they may not go for a few hundred years, but they'll go in the end. Their grand 'stability' machine has a monkey wrench in its works at last . . . They won't be around to use their magic in these parts any more, I expect."

Wim considered, and then looked hopeful. "You going to take over back there, Mr. Jagged? Use your magic on them Flatlanders? We could—"

But the peddler shook his head. "No, I'm afraid that just doesn't interest me, Wim. All I really wanted was to break the hold those other magician sorts had on this world; and I've done that already."

"Then . . . you mean you really did all that, you risked our necks, for nothing? Like you said, because it just wasn't right, for them to use their magic on folks who couldn't stop them? You did it for us—and you didn't want *any*thing? You must be crazy."

Jagit laughed. "Well, I wouldn't say that. I told you before: All I want is to be able to see new sights, and sell my wares. And the World Government was bad for my business."

Wim met the peddler's gaze, glanced away undecided. "Where you going to go now?" He half expected the answer to be, Back beyond the sky.

"Back to bed." Jagit left the ballistic vehicle, and began to climb the rubbly slope up from the lake; he gestured for Wim to follow.

Wim followed, breathing hard in the thin air, until they reached a large fall of boulders before a sheer granite wall. Only when he was directly before it did he realize they had come on the entrance to a cave hidden by the rocks. He noticed that the opening was oddly symmetrical; and there seemed to be a rainbow shimmering across the darkness like mist. He stared at it uncomprehendingly, rubbing his chilled hands.

"This is where I came from, Wim. Not from the East, as you figured, or from space as the governor thought." The peddler nodded toward the dark entrance. "You see, the World Government had me entirely misplaced—they assumed I could only have come from somewhere outside their control. But actually I've been here on earth all the time; this cave has been my home for fifty-seven thousand years. There's a kind of magic in there that puts me into an 'enchanted' sleep for five or ten thousand years at a time here. And meanwhile the world changes. When it's changed enough, I wake up again and go out to see it. That's what I was doing in Sharn, ten thousand years ago: I brought art works from an earlier, primitive era; they were popular, and I got to be something of a celebrity. That way I got access to my new items of trade—my Sharnish magics—to take somewhere else, when things changed again.

"That was the problem with the World Government—they interrupted the natural cycles of history that I depend on, and it threw me out of synch. They'd made stability such a science they might have kept things static for fifty or a hundred thousand years. Ten or fifteen thousand, and I could have come back here and outwaited them, but fifty thousand was just too long. I had to get things moving again, or I'd have been out of business."

Wim's imagination faltered at the prospect of the centuries that separated him from the peddler, that separated the peddler from everything that had ever been a part of the man, or ever could be. What kind of belief did it take, what sort of a man, to face that alone? And what losses or rewards to drive him to it? There must be something, that made it all worthwhile—

"There have been more things *done,* Wim, than the descendants of Sharn have *dreamed.* I am surprised at each new peak I attend . . . I'll be leaving you now. You were a better guide than I expected; I thank you for it. I'd say Darkwood Corners is two or three days' journey northwest from here."

Wim hesitated, half afraid, half longing. "Let me go with you—?"

Jagit shook his head. "There's only room for one, from here on. But you've seen a few more wonders than most people already; and I think you've learned a few things, too. There are going to be a lot of opportunities for putting it all to use right here, I'd say. You helped change your world, Wim—what are you going to do for an encore?"

Wim stood silent with indecision; Jagit lifted the rifle, tossed it to him.

Wim caught the gun, and a slow smile, filled with possibilities, grew on his face.

"Good-bye, Wim."

"Good-bye, Mr. Jagged." Wim watched the peddler move away toward his cave.

As he reached the entrance, Jagit hesitated, looking back. "And Wim—there are more wonders in this cave than you've ever dreamed of. I haven't been around this long because I'm an easy mark. Don't be tempted to grave-rob." He was outlined momentarily by a rainbow as he passed into the darkness.

Wim lingered at the entrance, until at last the cold forced him to move and he picked his way back down the sterile gray detritus of the slope. He stopped again by the mirror lake, peering back past the magician's bullet-shaped vehicle at the cliff face. The rising sun washed it in golden light, but now somehow he really wasn't even sure where the cave had been.

He sighed, slinging his rifle over his shoulder, and began the long walk home.

Lord Buckry sighed as memories receded, and with them the gnawing desire to seek out the peddler's cave again; the desire that had been with him for thirty years. There lay the solutions to every problem he had ever faced, but he had never tested Jagged's warning. It wasn't simply the risk, though the risk was both deadly and sufficient—it was the knowledge that however much he gained in this life, it was ephemeral, less than nothing, held up to a man whose life spanned half that of humanity itself. Within the peddler's cave lay the impossible, and that was why he would never try to take it for his own.

Instead he had turned to the possible and made it fact, depending on himself, and on the strangely clear view of things the peddler had left him. He had solved every problem alone, because he had had to, and now he would just have to solve this one alone too.

He stared down with sudden possessive pride over the townsfolk in the square, his city of Fyffe now ringed by a sturdy wall . . . So the West and the South were together, for one reason, and one alone. It balanced the scales precariously against plenty of old hatreds, and if something were to tip them back again— A few rumors, well-placed, and they'd be at each other's throats. Perhaps he wouldn't even need to raise an army. They'd solve that problem for him. And afterward—

Lord Buckry began to smile. He'd always had a hankering to visit the sea.

THE BEES OF KNOWLEDGE

by Barrington J. Bayley

Many have pondered the apparent resemblances between the complex social order of bees, termites and ants, and the civilizations and cities of humanity. The tendency to consider these social organizations in anthropomorphic terms is almost irresistible, but in all truth the programmed constructs of social insects cannot be equated with the learned constructs of brain-toting mammals. And while the bees of Barrington Bayley are not exactly those of Earth, there is enough resemblance to make this point.

It scarcely seems necessary to relate how I first came to be cast on to Handrea, like a man thrown up on a strange shore. To the Bees of Handrea these details, though possibly known to them, are of negligible interest since in their regard I rate as no more than an unremarkable piece of flotsam that chanced to drift into their domain. Let it suffice, then, that I had paused to say a prayer at the shrine of Saint Hysastum, the patron saint of interstellar travellers, when an explosion in the region of the engine room wrecked the entire liner. The cause of the catastrophe remains a mystery to me. Such accidents are far from common aboard passenger ships, though when they do occur subsequent rescue is an uncertain hope, owing to the great choice of routes open to interstellar navigators and their habit of changing course in mid-flight to provide additional sightseeing.

My timely devotions saved my life, though reserving me for a weirder fate. Within seconds I was able to gain a lifeboat, which was stationed thoughtfully adjacent to the shrine, and amid flame and buckling metal I was ejected into space.

After the explosion, picking my way through the scattered debris, I learned that no one but myself had escaped.

The crushing sense of desolation that comes over one at such a moment cannot adequately be described. Nothing brings one so thoroughly face to face with blind, uncaring Nature as this sudden, utter remoteness from one's fellow human beings. Here I was, surrounded by vast light years of space, with probably not another human soul within hundreds of parsecs, totally alone and very nearly helpless.

My feeling of isolation mounted to a state of terror when I discovered that the rescue beacon was not operating. Once again I had recourse to prayer, which calmed me a little and brought me to a more hopeful appraisal of my situation. The lifeboat, I reminded myself, could keep me alive for up to a year if all went well. There would have been little point in activating the beacon immediately in any case. The star liner would not be reported missing for several weeks, and taking into account the delay before a search was organised, and the dozens of possible routes to be surveyed, a sweep within range of the beacon might not occur for months, if at all. During that time its repair seemed a feasible project, or at any rate not a hopeless one.

But it could not be done conveniently in space, and I peered again through the lifeboat's portholes. On one side glimmered a reddish-yellow sun. Close by on the other side hung a big murky globe resembling an overripe fruit—the planet Handrea, to provide a view of which the star liner had been slowing down at the time of the explosion. It had received its name but an hour previously from one of the passengers (the privilege of naming newly sighted worlds being another of the minor perquisites of interstellar travel) and had already been ascertained as being tolerable as regards chemistry and geology. So, heartened by having at least some course of action to pursue, I turned my small lifeboat towards it.

As I passed through them I made a careful recording of the bands of magnetism and radiation that planets of this type usually possess, noting as I did so that they were uncommonly strong and complicated. I was perturbed to find that the atmosphere was a deep one, descending nearly seven hundred miles. Upon my entering its outer fringes the sky turned from jet black to dark brown and the stars quickly vanished from sight. A hundred miles further down I entered a sphere of electrical storms and was buffeted about by powerful gusts. It had been my intention, had Handrea looked unduly inhospitable, to fly straight out again, but before long it was all I could do to keep on an even keel, not being an expert pilot. Eventually, much relieved after a harrowing passage, I entered the layer of calm air that lies close to the surface and accomplished a landing amid large tufts of a plant which, though maroon in colour, could fairly be described as grasslike.

I peered at the landscape. Vision was limited to about a hundred yards, and within this span I saw only the mild undulations of the ground, the drab coloration of the vegetation, the dull grey air. Instruments told me that the air was dense, but not of the intolerable pressure suggested by the depth of the atmosphere, consisting of light inert gases and about five per cent oxygen. The temperature, at twenty degrees, was comfortable enough to require no special protective clothing.

After a while I put on an oxygen mask—not trusting myself to the outside's natural mix—and equalised pressures before opening the hatch. Taking with me the lifeboat's tool kit, I stepped outside to remove the beacon's service plate.

Underfoot the maroon grass had a thick-piled springy texture. As I moved the air felt thick, almost like water, and perfect silence prevailed. I tried to close my mind to the fact that I stood on an alien and unknown planet, and concentrated on the task in hand.

I worked thus for perhaps twenty minutes before becoming aware of a low-pitched droning or burring sound, which, almost before I could react to it, swelled in volume until it made the air vibrate all about me. Like the parting of a curtain the opaque atmosphere suddenly disgorged two huge flying shapes. And so I saw them for the first time: the Bees of Handrea.

Describing them offers no particular difficulties, since unlike many alien forms of life they can be compared with a terrestrial species. They are, of course, vast if measured alongside our Earthly bees, and the resemblance is in some respects a superficial one. The body, in two segments, is nearly twice the size of a man, the thorax being very large and round so as to make the creature closest in appearance, perhaps, to our bumble bee. As in the terrestrial bee the fur is striped but only slightly so—a relic, I would guess, from some previous evolutionary period the Bees have passed through—the stripes being fuzzy fawn and soft gold, so that the Bees seemed almost to shine in their monotonous environment.

On Earth this great mass could never take to the air at all, but the density of Handrea's atmosphere enables such a creature to be supported by two pairs of surprisingly small wings which vibrate rapidly, giving off the pronounced drone I had first noticed. The Bees move, moreover, with all the speed and agility of their Earthly counterparts. Their arrival occasioned me some alarm, naturally, and I attempted to make a hasty retreat into the lifeboat, but I had time to take only a couple of steps before one of the huge creatures had darted to me and lifted me up with its frontward limbs which ended in tangles of hooks and pincers.

The desperation of my initial struggles may be imagined. From acquaintance with Earthly insects I had expected instantly to receive some dreadful sting which would paralyse me or kill me outright, and I fought with all my might to free myself from the monster. In the struggle my oxygen mask was torn loose and fell to the ground, so that for the first time, with a cold shock, I drew Handrea's air into my lungs. All my efforts were to no avail; no sting was forthcoming, but the Bee merely modified its powerful grip so as to leave me completely helpless, and I was borne off into the mists, leaving the lifeboat far behind.

The two Bees flew, as near as I could tell, in a straight line, keeping abreast of one another. The narrow patch of landscape in my view at any one time presented no change of aspect, but we travelled through the foggy, impenetrable air at what seemed to me a prodigious speed. Unhindered now by my oxygen mask, the world of Handrea met my senses with a new immediacy. The breath that coursed through my nostrils smelled damp, bearing hints of dank vegetable fragrance. Quite separate from this, I was aware of the much stronger smell of the Bee that carried me—a sharp, oddly sweet smell that could not be ignored.

Reminding myself of insect habits, I was fearful now of a much worse fate than being stung to death. My imagination worked apace: these Bees would hardly have seized me for nothing, I told myself, and in all probability their intention was to use me as a body in which to lay eggs, so that the larvae could feed off my flesh. In my despair I even contemplated the sin of suicide, wondering how I might kill myself before the worst happened. When I remember these fears now, my present circumstances seem relatively good.

On and on we droned, the increasing distance between myself and the lifeboat, and the virtual impossibility of my ever returning to it, causing me no small agony of mind. At least an hour, and possibly several, passed in this fashion before the Bees' destination came looming out of the fog.

At first I took the shape ahead to be an oddly-formed mountain until its artificial nature became apparent. Then it emerged as an uneven, elongated dome whose limits passed entirely out of sight in the dimness: a stupendous beehive. I now know its height to attain several thousand feet, with nearly the same proportions at the base. As we came closer a generalised humming could be heard emanating from the huge edifice. At the same time I saw giant Bees flitting hither and thither, coming and going from the great hive.

We approached an entrance set about a hundred feet from ground level and without pause passed through to the interior. I observed a number of Bees stationed just within the opening, some apparently standing guard, others vibrating their wings rapidly, presumably to ventilate the hive as Bees do on Earth. Indeed, their work set up such a wind that the clothes were nearly torn from my back as my captors alighted on the floor of the vestibule. From this chamber several passages radiated—that, at least, was my first impression. As my captors set off down one of these I realised that in fact the openings all connected with one another; the internal structure of the hive was largely an open one, the space of any level being divided by the pillars which supported the next.

I will not dwell on how fully I appreciated the horror of my apparent situation as I was dragged into this den. Bees swarmed everywhere, and their pungent-sweet smell was overpowering. To think that I, a human being bearing a spark of the divinity, was reduced to the role of some smaller insect for these beasts, as if I were a caterpillar or a grub, affected me almost as strongly as the thought of the physical horror which I had no doubt was to come. Deeper and deeper I was carried into the hive, descending and ascending I did not know how many levels. It was like a vast city, filled with the rustling, buzzing and chittering of its inhabitants. Once my captors (they remained together) were accosted by a group of their fellows and performed a kind of waggling dance, at the same time emitting loud noises which sounded like the wailing of a whole team of buzz-saws. Finally our journey came to an end: the two Bees halted in a bowl-shaped depression some tens of feet across, and the hold on my aching body was at last released.

I tumbled, rolled over, and steeled myself to take my first good look at the Bee's head: the faceted eyes glinting with myriad colours, the rolled proboscis, the tufted cheeks and the swollen cranium, all of which are now so familiar to me. Unable to bear the suspense any longer I squeezed my eyes shut and tried not to exist. Now it would come—the deep-thrusting sting, mortal as any sword, or the cruel insertion of the ovipositor.

The muscular limbs turned me over and over, bristly fur scratching my skin. When, after some time, nothing else transpired I opened my eyes a little. The two Bees were huddled over me, holding me almost in a double embrace, and fondling me with their forelegs. Their wings trembled; their droning buzz-saw voices, with no articulation that I could discern, rose and fell in harmony. The movements of the forelegs became light and caressing, so that I wondered what kind of insect ritual I was being subjected to. Then, to my surprise, the manipulatory claws began clumsily to strip me of my clothing. Shortly I lay naked, while my garments were lifted one by one, inspected and tossed aside.

The Bees' attention returned to my naked body, probing it with a feather-like touch, examining orifices, holding me upside down or in whatever fashion was convenient, as though I were an inanimate object. I experienced a moment of supreme terror when a stiff digit entered my anus and slid up my rectum. The organ withdrew in a second or two, but I was left in little uncertainty of mind as to what had taken place.

At length the Bees seemed to have finished. One wandered off, while the other lifted me up and took to the air again. I observed that we were in a spacious vault, allowing the Bees ample room for flight and somewhat dimly lit (unlike much of the hive I had passed through). We swooped low to pass under a barrier, swam up a sort of gully, and emerged in yet another vault even larger, whose far side was not clearly visible but which contained great indistinct piles. On one of these the Bee unceremoniously dropped me, and I sprawled and slithered down a slope composed of loose objects, like a rubbish heap.

After the Bee had flown away my urgent concern was with the eggs I felt sure it had deposited in my rectum. I felt up with my finger as far as I could, but encountered nothing. I decided it was imperative to sweep out the passage straight away. After a great deal of frantic straining I managed to pass an amount of fecal matter and examined it anxiously for sign of the eggs. There was none, and eventually I concluded with immense relief that the Bee's intrusion had been exploratory, nothing more.

Finding myself unexpectedly alive and unharmed, I was able to take a more leisurely interest in my surroundings. The first question to pique my curiosity was how the interior of the hive came to be lighted, when it should have been in complete darkness. Some parts of it, in fact, were bathed in a fairly bright haze. Peering at the near-by wall of the vault, I saw that the material out of which the hive was constructed was itself fluorescent, thus explaining the mystery. I pondered a little further on the nature of this material. Being phosphorescent it was very likely organic in origin, I reflected. Possibly the Bees used their own excrement as a building material, as termites do on Earth.

Perhaps the luminosity was an accidental by-product and extraneous to the Bees' needs. But if it formed part of their economy then it was a wonderful example of the ingenuity of Nature, which had evolved phosphorescent excrement for such a purpose.

I pulled myself upright on the unsteady pile where I was precariously perched and took a closer survey of my immediate environs. I stood on a jumble of objects of various shapes and sizes, all indistinct in the gloom. Bending, I picked one up.

The thing was made of a substance indistinguishable from wood. And it was a carving of some kind of animal, perhaps another giant insect, with a peculiar flowering snout. I was not sure whether the representation was meant to be a naturalistic one or whether it was fanciful; what was in no doubt was that it was the product of art.

I dropped it and selected another object. This turned out to be something whose purpose I could not decipher: a black rod about three feet in length with a hemispherical bowl attached to one end. But again, I judged it to be artificial.

In a state of fresh excitement I extended my explorations. The heap proved to be varied in its composition; much of it consisted of decayed vegetable matter. But buried in it, strewn on top of it, piled here and there, was a treasure house of alien artefacts too diverse to describe. Many of them were rotted, broken and crushed, but others seemed intact and even new.

What was the reason for this rubbish heap? Who had manufactured the artefacts? Not the Bees—somehow that did not strike me as a likely proposition, and the impression was confirmed when I found what I could only call, from its shape and size, a drinking cup.

Bees would not use drinking cups.

Somewhere on this planet, then, was an intelligent race. While I was mulling this over there came a loud droning noise and another Bee entered the vault, dropped an article on the heap and departed. I scrambled towards the discarded object and discovered it to be a mysterious instrument consisting of hinged and interlocking boxes.

I recalled the manner in which I had been snatched from the ground while attempting to repair my rescue beacon, and all seemed to become clear to me. The Bees had a magpie instinct: they were collectors of any object they came across that attracted their attention. I, just like anything else, had been added to their mindless hoard.

For some time that remained the total of my understanding of the Bees of Handrea.

A length I clambered down from the pile and began to explore beyond the vault. By now hunger was beginning to affect me, and while I still could not speculate as to what my future might be, I wondered as to the possibility of obtaining food.

My needs were answered much sooner than I had expected. Half an hour of probing (trying always to keep track of my movements) brought me to a wall which exuded a heavy, sweet aroma. This wall was made of a golden bread-like substance which crumbled and broke easily in the hand to yield chunks from which seeped a light yellow syrup. It had every appearance of being edible, and though afraid of poisoning myself I sampled a morsel, recalling that though the protein structure of alien life may differ from our own, that protein is everywhere constructed out of the same small group of amino acids, into which the digestive system decomposes it. I was soon reassured: the bread was delicious, sweet without being nauseous, and of a texture like honeycake. As a food it proved completely satisfying. I ate a quantity of it, reasoning as I did so that in all probability this was a corner of the Bees' food store, or at any rate of one of a number of such stores.

My meal was interrupted by a rustling sound. I was alarmed to see the approach of an insect-like creature, smaller than the Bees and indeed somewhat smaller than myself, but nevertheless of horrifying appearance. I was put in mind of a fly—not the common housefly, but something closer to a mosquito, with small folded wings and spike-like proboscis. I ran for my life, but on rounding a corner of the passageway, and hearing no sound of pursuit, I stopped and cautiously peeped back. The Fly had inserted its proboscis into the honeybread and was presumably sucking out the liqueur.

I decided to risk no further confrontation but made my way back to the vault where lay the junkheaps. There I discovered some pools of brackish water and further refreshed myself. Then I set about finding a weapon in case I should need to defend myself against monsters such as I had just witnessed—or, for that matter, against the Bees, though I fervently hoped I should not be called upon to fight such prodigious creatures. After some searching I found a long metal pole with a pointed end which would serve tolerably well as a spear.

The vault seemed empty, lonely, silent and echoing. From afar came the continual murmur of the business of the hive, like the ceaseless activity of a city, but it barely broke the silence. Already I had begun to think of the place as a refuge, and eventually I found a spot for myself where, wearied and strained by my experiences, I settled down to sleep.

On waking I drank more water and made the short trip to obtain more honeybread. Then, naked though I was, and armed with my spear, I set out to explore the hive in earnest.

Thus began a fairly long period in which I acquainted myself with the life of the great bee-city, though in what I now know to be a superficial way. Slowly and tentatively I explored the passages and galleries, making sure all the time that I could find my way back to the familiar territory of the junkheaps where I was at least assured of water and food, and to which I periodically returned to rest. Always I made my way upwards, searching for the entrance by which I had been brought into the hive.

The Bees, who busied themselves everywhere, consistently ignored me. I discovered that the hive was host to numerous other parasites like myself, species of insects and giant worms who had made their home here and were apparently tolerated, if they were noticed at all. Usually (but not invariably) they were smaller than the Bees, and either stole honeybread or stalked one another for food. Thus for any but the Bees themselves (who of course were never attacked) the hive was a jungle in which every ecological niche was filled.

The dangers to myself were considerable, and I soon found that I had been lucky in my choice of weapon, for the spear enabled me to keep most predators at bay. Nevertheless my early experiences were horrifying. On my first reconnoitre I was attacked three times: twice by grub-like beasts with hideous scissor-type jaws, and once by something resembling a giant mite whose habit it is to drop a net on passers-by from above. I could not free myself from this trap for some time, during which I was obliged to fight for my life while still enmeshed, wielding the spear through the holes and finally killing my adversary.

I quickly learned which species were harmless and which to beware. I learned to recognise the kind of corners and approaches the predators were apt to lurk in, and so these bouts of deadly combat became much less frequent.

My third sortie brought me at last to the entrance. I hesitated on the approach to the vestibule, seeing ahead of me the humped shapes of the guards, and bracing myself against the wind set up by the whirring wings of the ventilator Bees. So powerful was this dense current that when I finally went forward I was obliged to edge myself across the floor with the help of my spear. I stopped close to the broad slot-like opening and looked out into the free air of Handrea.

A fog-like cold smote my skin, in contrast to the warmth of the hive. I could see only thick misty air which eddied and swirled as more Bees came to alight inside the entrance. The ground was quite out of sight.

I believe the guards would not have prevented me from leaving the hive. I could have scrambled down its rough surface to the ground. But where to then? I had no means of achieving the goal which had been uppermost in my mind: that of returning to the lifeboat and completing the repair of the beacon. Not only had I no idea of which direction to take, but I had no way of holding to that direction if I found it. Once away from the hive I would be unlikely to locate it again, and would die of hunger or thirst or else fall victim to larger predators than I had yet seen.

But could I accept the corollary: that I must live out my remaining years in the hive with the status of a parasitic worm? A curiously forlorn, deserted feeling came over me: I had been treated badly during the explosion on the passenger liner; my companions had all died and been spared any further problems, but I had been excluded from the common fate and left alone, abandoned by death.

This odd and sinful feeling lasted but a minute or two. With heavy heart I made my way back down below, wondering if I could pluck up the courage for the near-suicidal attempt to retrace the course of the Bees who had brought me here. When I arrived at the junkheaps an extraordinary sight met my eyes. There, flung at a lurching angle atop the nearest pile, was the lifeboat!

I scrambled up the heap towards it with a cry of joy. On reaching the small spacecraft, however, I was in for a crushing disappointment. It had been gutted. Everything had been stripped from it, inside and out, leaving only an empty shell.

Strewn over a fairly wide area round about was all the equipment with which the lifeboat had been stocked. To my astonishment every item had been torn to pieces: the Bees seemed to exhibit a destructive animal curiosity over everything they touched. I found the beacon after searching for some minutes. Like everything else it was completely wrecked, practically disintegrated component by component. Any kind of repair was absolutely out of the question, and after staring at the remains for some while in a state of shock, I sat down and buried my face in my hands, sobbing to think what life was to mean to me from now on.

For some time afterwards wild schemes were apt to enter my head. It occurred to me that perhaps I was not necessarily doomed to remain indefinitely in the hive. Judging by the contents of the junkheaps intelligence existed somewhere on the planet, and the Bees visited the scene of that intelligence. I entertained the notion of clinging to a Bee's back, possibly attaching myself there by means of a harness, and flying with it to where life might be more agreeable, even though I still would not be among my own kind. It was even possible, I conjectured (remembering that some of the artefacts I had seen denoted a fairly advanced technology) that once learning of my plight the creatures I met would be kind enough to set up a beacon of their own to signal the rescue ship, if I could explain its mode of operation clearly enough.

These plans served chiefly to ward off my despair, for common sense told me how unlikely they were to succeed. My faith also came under great strain at this time, but I am glad to say I retained it, though with some difficulty at first, and prayer was, as ever, my solace.

But as the days succeeded one another my mood turned to one of apathy, although I tried to rouse myself to action and to remind myself that the time remaining before a search expedition arrived within signalling distance was not unlimited. Thinking that I should fashion a harness with which to carry out my project of riding on a Bee, I began to sort through the junkheaps. The detritus of alien industry was fascinating to browse through. I presumed at first that the artefacts were all the product of the same civilisation, but later I realised that I had no verification of this. Indeed I could construct no picture of a single culture out of the objects I perused; rather they suggested a number of different, quite unconnected civilisations, or even species.

I was also struck by the number of artefacts which were clearly not tools or ornaments and whose use could not easily be discerned. At length I discovered some of the more curiously shaped of them to bear close-packed markings, and I surmised that these and others, including some I believed to be electronic in operation, were books or records of some kind, though I could not explain why they made up such a large percentage of the junkheaps.

My desultory efforts to escape the hive were all brought to an end when an extraordinary event occurred. I had gone on another exploratory foray with the intention of making some rough assessment of Bee anatomy when the usual bumbling activity of the hive turned to a state of agitation. I heard sounds of rending and general destruction, and on investigating perceived that numbers of the Bees were engaged in tearing down parts of the hive. The reason for this soon became apparent: they were clearing a passage for a great ship, too large to enter the hive by any of its entrances or to negotiate its interior spaces.

The ship was clearly built to ride on water. Of a wood-like material, it had a sweeping profile at least a hundred and fifty feet long, with an elegant pattern of raised decks at intervals, stepped slightly higher forward and aft. In its general lines the closest resemblance would be, I suppose, to a Greek galley, a resemblance heightened by the carving which adorned the fore and aft railings and the protruding wales which swept from stem to stern. The brute force by which the Bees moved this ship was a sight to behold. They must have flown it here an unknown distance by the concerted power of their wings alone—a feat which even in Handrea's thickened atmosphere was astonishing—and now they nudged, heaved and strained at it in their hundreds, wings buzzing in a deafening clamour (for it appeared to be their wings they mostly used to gain traction). The ship lurched forward foot by foot, grinding and crushing everything in its path, shouldering aside masses of building material where the cleared pathway was not wide enough, and causing yet more to come crashing down behind it. When it had passed Bees set to work immediately to repair the damage, a task which I knew they could accomplish with unbelievable rapidity.

Steadily the ship was being edged into the heart of the hive. I crept forward, dodged past Bee bodies, and found myself able to clamber up the side of the vessel. Briefly I found myself standing on the deck, which, I was interested to see, was inlaid with silvery designs. I could see no sign of any crew. A moment later I heard an impatient buzz behind me and a bristly limb knocked me over the side. I fell to the ground, winded and badly bruised.

Slowly the ship jerked from view amid clouds of dust and a rain of rubble, swaying cumbersomely. Limping, I followed, still curious and wondering how the Bees were regarded by the intelligent race or races from whom they filched so many valuable artefacts.

It occurred to me that for all my wanderings I had remained in the peripheral region of the hive, my mind obsessed by the idea of escape. Vaguely I had imagined the hive to present the same aspect wherever one stood in it, but venturing deeper into the interior in pursuit of the ship I saw my mistake. The light strengthened to become a golden ambience in which the golden fur of the Bees shone. The architecture of the hive also changed. The monotonous tiered floors gave way to a more complex structure in which there were spiral ramps, great halls, and linked chambers of various shapes, sometimes comprising whole banks of huge polyhedra of perfect geometrical regularity, so that the hive came to resemble more and more the 'golden palace' beloved of the more sentimental naturalists when writing of Earthly Bees. And the sharp-sweet odour of these Bees, to which I thought I had become accustomed, became so strong that I was almost stifled.

All these wonders, like everything else about the Bees, I understood up to this moment to be the product of instinct. I had almost caught up with the lurching ship when I saw something which gave me pause for thought.

A number of artefacts had apparently fallen from the ship in the course of its progress and lay about in the rubble. One Bee lingered and was playing with a device of a shiny brown material, in shape somewhere between a sphere and a cube and numbering among its features several protuberances and a circular plate of dull silver. The Bee touched a protuberance with a foreleg, and the plate came abruptly to life.

I edged closer to spy on what was taking place. The plate showed a full-colour motion picture that at first was of no recognisable object or scene. After some moments I realised that it was displaying a series of geometrical figures arranged in a logical series. A mathematics lesson!

To my bemusement the huge insect's gaze seemed intent on the picture plate. Shortly it again touched the protuberance, which was a control of the sliding sort, and the picture changed to a text in some kind of writing or ideograms, illustrated by enigmatic symbols. Again the Bee followed the lesson with every appearance of understanding it, but even when this was succeeded by the Bee's manipulating various knobs in seemingly skilful fashion, eliciting information at will, I still could not grasp what the evidence of my eyes suggested.

The Bee turned to another pastime. It turned the device over and in a few moments had removed the outer casing. A mass of close-packed parts was revealed, which the Bee took to pieces with surprisingly delicate pincers. I thought I was seeing the usual destructiveness I already had cause to complain of on the part of these insects, but was astonished by what followed. With the machine in fragments, the Bee suddenly set to work to put it all together again. In a minute or two it was again functioning perfectly.

Along came a second Bee. A buzz-saw exchange took place between them. Wings trembled. The first Bee again stripped down the machine. Together they played with the components, assembling and disassembling them several times over, their droning voices rising and falling, until finally they tired of the game and the pieces were flung carelessly to the ground.

There could be no doubt of it. The Bees were intelligent! And they understood technology!

Saint Hysastum, I thought, you have answered my prayers!

How foolish I had been to give practically no thought to this possibility! How ridiculous to plan journeys across Handrea when the answer lay right here under my nose!

But why had the Bees behaved towards me like brute beasts? I recalled that I had been outside the lifeboat when they arrived. Possibly I had been taken for a denizen of their own planet. They had mistaken my nature, just as I had mistaken theirs.

But it was imperative that I enlighten them without delay. I dashed forward, right under the gaze of those huge mosaic eyes, and began scratching diagrams in the dust with my spear. A circle, a triangle, a square, a pentagon—surely a sentient creature familiar with mathematics (as my recent observations showed the Bee to be) would recognise these as signs of intelligence on my part? The Bee did not seem to notice and made to move off, but I skipped forward again, placing myself impetuously in its path, and again began my eager scribbling. I made three dots, then another three, followed by six dots—a clear demonstration that I could count! For good measure I scribbled out the diagram that accompanies Pythagoras' theorem, even though it is perhaps too elaborate for a first contact between species. The Bee seemed nonplussed for a moment. But then it brushed me aside and passed on, followed by its companion.

My frantic efforts as I sought to make contact with the Bees during the next hour or two approached the level of hysteria. All was to no avail. I remained a nonentity as far as they were concerned: I spoke to them, gesticulated, drew, showed them my spear and play-acted its use, but was simply ignored. From their conduct, which to all appearances exemplified insect mindlessness, it was hard to believe that they really possessed intelligence.

At last, disheartened and perplexed, I returned to my quiet refuge in the vault of the junkheaps. I was not completely alone there: the Fly, the mosquito-like creature I had first encountered at the honeybread bank, was pottering about among the rubbish. I often met this creature on my trips to the honeybread, and occasionally it ventured into the vault and roamed aimlessly among the heaps of artefacts. Never having received any threat from it, I had come to accept its presence.

Sighing and despairing, I fell at length into a light sleep. And as I slept I dreamed.

We came between a defile in the hills and ahead of us, with mist rising and falling about it like steam, lay the Hive. Bees came hither and thither in ceaseless streams. Otwun, my Handreatic companion, a member of one of the mammalian species of the planet, laid a hand on my shoulder.

'There it is,' he said. 'The Hive of the Bees of Knowledge, where is made the Honey of Experience.'

I glanced into his opal eyes. From the cast of his face I knew he was feeling a certain kind of emotion. 'You seem afraid of these creatures,' I remarked. 'Are they dangerous?'

'They are voracious and implacable,' he answered. 'They know everything old and discover everything new. They range over the whole world in search of knowledge, which is their food, taking it wherever they find it. Yet no man can communicate with them.'

'An aloof intelligence then? No pacts or alliances are made with the Bees? No wars or quarrels?'

'Such is out of the question. The Bees are not beings such as the warm-blooded races. They belong in the class of creeping, crawling and flying things. Come, we must pass by the Hive if we are to be about our business.'

We went forward, the fine rain laying a mantle about our shoulders and casting the Hive in a lush setting. We skirted the Hive to the east, but suddenly a huge Bee loomed out of the mist and hovered before us, giving off a loud buzzing sound that wavered up and down the scale. Although Otwun had told me it was impossible to communicate with the Bees the buzzing penetrated my brain like bright light through glass and seemed somehow to bypass the speech centre to impart information directly to my consciousness. A terrifying flood of knowledge of the most dazzling and intellectual kind overwhelmed me and caused me almost to faint . . .

I awoke with the dream vivid in my mind. It was the kind of dream that leaves behind it a mingling of hopeful emotions, seeming to convey a message more real than waking reality itself. I strove to recover the tacit details of the dream—what, for instance was the important business on which I and Otwun were engaged? But these were gone, as they often are in dreams, and I was left with only the central theme: the nature of the Bees of Handrea. Of this I had received a direct and compelling impression, much more comprehensive than was implied by Otwun's few remarks.

Every sentient creature's intelligence is modified by its ancestral nature. Bees are honey gatherers. Hence when intellectual curiosity developed in the Bees of Handrea it took just this form. The Bees liked to forage into their world seeking to satisfy their avid thirst for knowledge and to bring back their findings into the hive. The physical objects they brought back were of cursory interest only: their main diet was of intellectual ideas and observations, which they were adept at stealing from surrounding civilisations.

This interpretation of the Bees made such an impression on me that, irrationally perhaps, I accepted it as literally true. I believed I had been vouchsafed a minor vision by Saint Hysastum to help me. Then I recalled a passage by the philosopher Nietzsche who lived some centuries ago. Although a heathen in his outlook Nietzsche had many insights. Here he depicted man's mind as a beehive. We are honey gatherers, bringing in little loads of knowledge and ideas—exactly like the Bees of Handrea.

Nietzsche was also the inventor of the doctrine of eternal recurrence, which posits that since the universe is infinite and eternal everything in it, including the Earth and all its inhabitants, must somewhere, sometime, be repeated. If one follows this argument further then it means that every product of man's imagination must somewhere be a reality—and here was Nietzsche's mental beehive, not as the analogy he had conceived, but a literal reality! What a strange confirmation of Nietzsche's beliefs!

There was a slurping sound. The Fly was sucking up water from one of the tepid pools.

Elsewhere on Handrea, the dream had reminded me, were other races, less alien than the Bees and more amenable to contact. Should I perhaps stock up with honeybread and strike out on foot in the hope of finding them? But no—the message of the dream clearly indicated that it was with the Bees that my salvation lay. It would be wrong to reject Saint Hysastum's advice.

Accordingly I turned my mind again to the problem of making my nature and my requirements known. To advertise myself as a calculating, tool-making creature seemed to me the best approach. I conceived a plan, and rummaging through the junk and scrap I gathered together the material I needed and set to work.

In an hour or two I had made my Arithmetical Demonstrator. It consisted of a circular board around whose circumference I had marked, with a soft chalk-like substance I found, the numbers One to Twenty-Five in dot notation, so that any sighted intelligent creature anywhere in creation could have recognised them. Pinned to the centre of the board were two pointers each of a different shape, so that the whole affair looked much like a clock.

The Demonstrator was simple to operate. With the first hand I would point to two numbers successively, and then point to their sum with the second hand. Once I had caught the attention of the Bees in this way I would write the addition sign on the board, then write the multiplication sign and perform a few simple multiplications. In the same manner I would also be able to demonstrate subtraction and division and leave the Bees in no doubt as to my rationality.

Sitting halfway up the junkheap, I practised with the completed board for a short while. Suddenly the sound of dislodged rubbish close behind me made me jump. Turning, I saw that the Fly had descended furtively on me from the top of the heap and its head was craned forward in what I took to be a menacing manner.

In my alarm I half-rolled, half-scrambled down the heap, forgetting all about the demonstration board and trying to think where I had left my spear. The Fly made no attempt to follow me, however. When I next saw it, about ten minutes later, it had climbed down the far side of the heap and was squatting on the ground as if preoccupied. To my exasperation I saw that it was in the possession of my Arithmetical Demonstrator.

Having found my spear I decided to use the Fly's own tactic against it to recover the board. Carefully, making as little noise as possible, I skirted round the heap and climbed up it on all fours so as to bring myself above and behind the Fly. Then I began a stealthy descent, reasoning that a noisy attack at close quarters would be enough to scare the insect into abandoning the board just as I had done.

Less deftly than the Fly I climbed to within a few feet of it. Its hearing did not seem particularly acute: it took no notice of my less than silent approach. But before I launched an onslaught I noticed something purposeful about the movement of its foreleg and stayed my hand.

The Fly was playing with the Demonstrator, displaying computations on it exactly as I had intended.

On each occasion it moved the first pointer twice and the second pointer once.

Five and Eight equals Thirteen. Addition.

Four and Six equals Twenty-Four. Multiplication.

Then it struck me. Two to the *power* Three equals Eight!

The fourth or fifth manipulation I observed made me think at first that these results were coincidental. Two and Three equals Eight. Incorrect.

My amazement, not to say bewilderment, was so great that the spear dropped from my hand. I could not doubt but that the Fly, too, possessed intellectual power.

Here was my introduction to the Bees!

But why was the Fly, if it belonged to an intelligent species, living the life of a scavenger? Was it perhaps trapped in the Hive, as I was? Or was *every* insect species on Handrea intelligent, as a matter of course?

I slithered to the ground and stood near the Fly, forcing myself to disregard its powerful stench. It moved back but a few feet when I reached out my hand to pick up the demonstration board and regarded me intently as I spelled out the initial steps of our dialogue.

So began an incredible period of learning and interchange between my friend the Fly and myself. To be honest the learning was mostly on his part, for I could never have absorbed information as he did.

The Fly's memory was as rapid and unfaltering as a computer's. Everything I showed him he knew instantly. First I introduced him to the Arabic decimal notation and then, though he seemed content to rush into an orgy of abstruse calculation, I induced him to learn alphabetical writing. He mastered words and concepts with machine-like ease, and in the space of a few weeks we were able to converse on almost any subject, using an alphabetical version I made of the demonstration board.

My new friend's curiosity was prodigious. He asked me where I came from, and what was the size and distance of my home planet. He then asked how the spaceship that had brought me here had been propelled, and I explained it to him as best as I was able. I also managed to elicit from him one or two scraps of information about Handrea, though his answers were vague.

The Fly's chief obsession, however, lay in the mathematics of numbers. In this he was a wizard, possessing the type of brain that the human race produces perhaps once in a couple of centuries. I was never able to understand a fraction of what the Fly knew about numbers. It would have taken a Fermat or a Poincaré to keep up with him.

There was much wonderment in the thought of what strange vessels God chooses to imbue with his divine spark. I had little enthusiasm, however, for exploring the more recondite properties of Fibonacci numbers, prime numbers and the like, and as soon as was practicable I broached the subject that was the aim of the entire operation as far as I was concerned: would the Fly help me to establish relations with the Bees, so that I might persuade them to construct a rescue beacon for me?

While I posed this question on the alphabet board the Fly was hunched over the much improved number board. Although I was sure he read my request as I presented it to him he gave no sign of understanding it and continued playing with his own board.

Annoyed, I snatched the number board away from him and repeated my demand. The Fly squatted there, unmoving. As I was coming near the end of my letter-pointing he casually shuffled to the number board again and continued his rapid calculations, which I believed concerned number curios of a high order but which I was in no position to follow without textual explanations.

I asked:

'Why will you not answer me?'

And was ignored.

I made increasingly desperate attempts at a closer accord and similarly was rebuffed, while the Fly continued his mathematical orgy in what looked increasingly like a frantic ecstasy. It suddenly occurred to me that up until my request for help none of our exchanges had been in the nature of true conversation but had consisted purely of an exchange of dry knowledge. Otherwise the Fly was behaving like someone who had not quite realised I existed—indeed, except for his obvious intelligence, like an idiot. Or a witless animal.

My failure to create a true relationship with the Fly was extremely disappointing. It taught me yet again how different was the intelligence of the Handreatic insects from my own. I concluded, after taking to the board for further attempts at a more personal contact, that I had been mistaken in thinking that the Fly was speaking to me when using the boards. Except for his initial enquiries into my origins he had been talking to himself, using the boards as a new toy or tool of thought.

So depressing was this reversal to my hopes that I felt unutterably weary. I reflected that I had wasted several weeks on what had proved to be a blind alley, and that if the Fly had rejected me as a fellow sentient being then so, probably, would the Bees. I dragged myself away from the busy insect, and flung myself down to sleep.

Otwun caught my arm and dragged me past the hovering Bee, whereupon normal perception returned to me. The Bee flew away and left us standing in the rain-sodden grass.

'What—what happened?' I asked dully.

'By accident you touched the mind of the Bee with your mind. It happens sometimes. Come, we must make haste if we are to arrive in time to take part in the assault against Totcune. Our Kessene allies will not wait indefinitely.'

I looked down at the arm he held. Unlike his arm, which was pale green, mine was a dark brown. Understanding for the first time that I also was a Handreatic I looked down at the whole of myself. My race was different from Otwun's. I was smaller, squat, like a goblin beside his lankness.

'Come.'

He noticed me gazing at the Hive. 'Men have sometimes entered the Hive to taste the Bees' honey,' he said. 'None have come out again, to my knowledge.'

'It would be a great adventure.'

'Only for a fool who no longer wishes to live.'

'Perhaps. Give my greetings to the Kessene.'

I moved away from him, walking slowly towards the Hive.

I had slept but a few minutes, and on waking found my mind buzzing with new energy.

The dream. I was sure the dream was telling me what to do. I had taken the Bees too much for granted, not pondering enough as to their true nature. And yet all I had to do was to think about terrestrial bees.

The gathering of nectar was not the end of the bees' food-making process. That nectar was taken into the hive and made into honey. The same must be true, I reasoned, of the Bees of Handrea and their gathering of knowledge. That knowledge was further refined in the depths of the Hive. But what was the honey that resulted from this refining?

Men have sometimes entered the Hive to taste the Bees' honey.

The Bees of Knowledge; the Honey of Experience. The phrase came into my mind, I did not know from where.

Of course! The answer came to me in a flash. It explained everything—why the Bees ignored me, why they pulled artefacts to pieces and abandoned them, apparently fashioning nothing similar themselves.

Social insects, as individuals, are not complete. They live only to serve the hive, or colony. Usually they are biologically specialised to perform specific functions and are oblivious of any other. Workers do not know sex. Drones do not know anything else.

The individual Bees I had encountered were not, by themselves, intelligent. What *was* intelligent was the *Hive Mind,* the collectivity of all the Bees, existing as some sort of separate entity. This Mind sent out its golden insects to bring back items of interest from the surrounding world. The Bees collected ideas and observations which were then mulled over by the Mind to provide itself with experience. Because the Hive Mind itself had no direct perception; everything had to come through the Bees.

Experience was the honey that was made from this dry, arid knowledge. It was the Hive Mind's food.

And it was the Hive Mind, not the individual Bees, that would understand my needs!

Could it have been the Hive Mind and not Saint Hysastum, I wondered, that had been calling to me through my dreams? At any rate my course of action seemed clear. I must descend deep into the Hive in search of the Mind, hoping that I could contact it somehow.

The Fly was still fiddling with the number board when, for the last time, I left the dim vault of the junkheaps. How close I was to the truth—and yet how far! Armed as usual with my spear I set off, heading for the very centre of the Hive where I imagined the Mind to manifest itself.

The damage caused by dragging the alien ship into the interior had all been repaired. The ceaselessly busy and largely inconsequential-looking activity of the giant insects went on all around me. The Bees rushed to and fro, buzz-saw voices rising and falling and wings trembling on meeting, or performed their odd waggling dance before one another. Except for their size and some physical differences it could have been any beehive on Earth.

I journeyed through the golden chambers I have already described. Beyond these lay a labyrinth of worm-like tunnels in which were interspersed empty egg-shaped chambers or nests. I discovered this to appertain to the Hive's reproductive arrangements, for eventually I entered a part of the labyrinth that was not empty. Here larvae crawled about the chambers, tended by worker Bees. Then I suddenly broke through the labyrinth and was confronted by an enormous honeycombed wall extending far overhead. Each cell of this honeycomb evidently contained an egg, for newly-hatched larvae were emerging here and there and crawling down the surface.

Somewhere, conceivably, was a huge bloated queen, mother to the whole Hive. Could this queen constitute the intelligence I sought? I rejected the idea. As among Earthly insects, she would be totally overburdened with her egg-laying role and unfit for anything else.

A longitudinal slit, about eight foot in height, separated the honeycomb from the ground. Since my destination lay in this direction I passed through it and walked, in semi-darkness, for a time with the bulk of the honeycomb pressing down above me.

Then the space seemed to open up abruptly and at the same time I was in the midst of a golden haze which intensified with each step I took, so that the limits of the place I was in were indistinct. Vague shapes looked at me as if in a dream. Among them was the alien ship I had seen carried into the Hive, sliding past me as if into a mist.

My foot caught against something. The floor was littered with objects of all kinds so as to resemble the floor of the vault of the junkheaps, except that here they were bathed in the golden ambience covering everything. I went on, picking my way among them. Presently I heard a familiar buzzing sound. Ahead of me were a number of Bees that appeared to be in an ecstatic trance. Their legs were rigid, their wings were open and vibrating tremulously, their antennae quivered, while the droning they gave off had an almost hypnotic effect.

During the course of my journey I had gradually become aware of an oppressive feeling in my head and an aching sensation at the bridge of my nose. These feelings became unbearably strong in the golden haze. I looked at the gathered Bees and understood that this was the place where their honey was processed, or perhaps where it was stored. With that thought the aching in my head became like a migraine and then suddenly vanished. Something pushed its way into my brain.

I tasted the Bees' honey. I experienced as the Bees experience.

The dream had been a precursor. But it could not have prepared me for such total immersion. What is experience? It comes through the senses, is processed by the mind and presented to the consciousness. The Bees' honey bypasses all these, except perhaps the last. It is raw experience, predigested, intensified, blotting out everything else.

This honey has an actual physical basis. It is magnetism. Handrea's magnetic field, as I have mentioned earlier, is unusually strong and intricate. The Bees have incorporated this magnetic intricacy into their evolution. By means of it they are able to perform a kind of telepathy on the creatures they borrow their knowledge from, using magnetic currents of great delicacy to read the memory banks of living minds. By tuning in to Handrea's magnetic field they know a great deal about what is taking place across the planet, and by the same means they can extend their knowledge into space within the limits of the field. Thus they knew of the accident aboard the passenger liner, and perhaps had learned much of mankind before I ever set foot on Handrea.

Sometimes magnetic strains from this golden interior store sweep through the Hive in wayward currents. Twice these currents had impinged on my mind to create dreams, giving me the information that had led me into this trap.

I do not know how long my first trance lasted. When it ended I found myself lying on the floor and understood that I must have been overwhelmed by the rush of impressions and passed out. Clarity of the senses lasted only a few minutes, however. The magnetic furore swept through my brain again, and once more I was subjected to amazing experiences.

One does not lose consciousness during these trances. It is rather that one's normal perceptions are blotted out by a stronger force, as the light of a candle is annihilated by the light of the sun.

And what are these stronger experiences?

How am I to describe the contents of alien minds?

At first my experiences were almost wholly abstract, but possessing a baroque quality quite different from what one normally thinks of as abstract. When I try to recall them I am left with a sense of something golden and ornate, of sweetish-musk aromas and of depth within depth.

Like my friend the Fly the Bees are much interested in mathematics, but theirs is of a type that not even he would be able to understand (any more than I could, except intuitively when I was in the grip of the trance). What would he have made, with his obsession with numbers, of the Bees' theorem that there is a highest positive integer! To human mathematicians this would make no sense. The Bees accomplish it by arranging all numbers radially on six spokes, centred about the number One. They then place on the spokes of this great wheel certain number series which are claimed to contain the essence of numbers and which go spiralling through it, diverging and converging in a winding dance. All these series meet at last in a single immense number. This, according to the theorem, is the opposite pole of the system of positive integers, of which One is the other pole, and is referred to as Hyper-One. This is the end of numbers as we know them. Hyper-One then serves as One for a number system of a higher order.

But, to show the hypothetical nature of the Bees' deliberations there is a quite contrary doctrine which portrays all numbers as emanating from a number Plenum, so that every number is potentially zero.

These are items, scraps, crumbs from the feast of the Bees' honey. The raw material of this honey is the knowledge and ideas that the individual Bees forage from all over Handrea. In the safety of their Hive the Bees get busy with this knowledge, converting it into direct experience. With the tirelessness of all insects they use it to create innumerable hypothetical worlds, testing them, as it were, with their prodigious intellects to see how they serve as vehicles for experience. I have lived in these worlds. When I am in them they are as real as my own. I have tasted intellectual abstractions of such a rarified nature that it is useless for me to try to think about them.

But as my brain began to accommodate itself to the honey my experiences became more concrete. Instead of finding myself in a realm of vast theoretical calculation I would find myself sailing the seas of Handrea in a big ship, walking cities that lay somewhere on the other side of the globe, or participating in historical events, many of which had taken place thousands of years previously. Yet even here the Bees' intellectual preoccupations asserted themselves. Nearly always the adventures I met ended in the studies of philosophers and mathematicians, where lengthy debate took place, sometimes followed by translation into a world of pure ideas.

There was a third stage. My experiences began to include

material that could only have come from my own brain. I was back in my home city on my home planet. I was with my friends and loved ones. I relived events from the past. None of this was as it has actually happened, but restructured and mixed together and always with mingled emotions of joy, regret and nostalgia, as happens in dreams. In addition I lived fantastic scenes from fiction; even comic-strip caricatures came to life, as if the Bees did not know the difference between them and reality.

My own world came, perhaps, to be my own private corner of the honey-store, for it was certainly only a minor item in the Bees' vast hoard. Yet what a sense of desolation I feel on coming out of it, in the periods when for some reason the magnetic currents no longer inflame my brain, and realise that it is only hallucination! Then I find myself in this arid, lonely place, with Bees buzzing and trembling all around me, and crawl from the chamber for near-by food and water, knowing that I shall never, in reality, see home again.

I have been here many years. My hair and beard are long and shaggy now that I no longer trim them. Often at the beginning I tried to break away from this addiction to the Bees' honey, but without it the reality of my position is simply too unbearable. Once I even dragged myself halfway back to the vault of the junkheaps again, but I knew all the time that I would be forced to return, so great is the pull of those waking dreams.

The time is long past, of course, when a rescue beacon could do anything to help me. Not that there was ever any chance of constructing one. Because the Bees are not intelligent.

Incredibly, but truly, they are not intelligent. They have intellect merely, pure intellect, but not intelligence, for this requires the exertion both of the intellect and of the feelings—and of the soul. The Bees have no feelings, any more than any insect has, and—of this I am convinced—God has not endowed them with souls.

They are insects, merely. Their intellectual powers, their avid thirst for knowledge, are but instincts with them, like the instinct that prompts them to feats of engineering and which, in the past, has also misled men into thinking the ants, termites and bees of Earth to be intelligent. No rational mind, able to respond to and communicate with other rational minds, lies behind their voracious appetite.

It seems fitting that if by some accident or quirk of nature intellectual brains should evolve in that class of creature roughly corresponding to our terrestrial arthropods (and Handrea offers the only case of this as far as I know, even though insect-like fauna are abundant throughout the universe) they should do so in this bizarre fashion. One does not expect insects to be intelligent, and indeed they are not, even when endowed with analytical powers greater than our own.

But how long it took me to grasp this fact when I strove so desperately to convey messages to the Hive Mind! For there *is* a Hive Mind; but it has no qualities or intelligence that an individual Bee does not have. It is merely an insect collectivised, a single Bee writ large, and would not be worth mentioning were it not for one curious power it has, or that I think it has.

It seems able by some means I cannot explain to congeal objects out of thought. Perhaps they are imprinted on matter by magnetism. At any rate several times I have found in the chamber small artefacts which earlier I had encountered in visions, and which I do not think could have been obtained on Handrea. Once, for instance, I found a copy of a newspaper, including in its pages the adventures of the Amazing Human Spider.

For all the abstract knowledge available to me my grip on concrete reality has steadily deteriorated. I can no longer say with certainty which of the experiences given me by the honey really happened in my former life and which are alterations, interpolations or fantasies. For instance, was I really a companion of the Amazing Human Spider, a crime-fighter who leaps from skyscraper to skyscraper by means of his gravity-defying web?

Recently I discovered a small bound book in which was written all the events I have outlined in this account.

I do not know whether I have copied my story from this book or whether the book was copied by the Bees from my mind.

What does it matter? I do not know for certain if the book, or any of the other objects I found in the chamber, really existed.

And so here I remain and must remain, more a parasite upon these monsters than I ever had imagined I could be. For monsters they are—monsters in the Satanic sense. How else can one describe creatures of such prodigious knowledge and such negligible understanding? And for my enjoyment I have this honey—this all-spanning knowledge. Mad knowledge, too great for human encompassing and fit only for these manic Bees and the work of their ceaseless insect intellects. It is knowledge that has no meaning, nothing to check or illuminate it, and which produces no practical end.

Only one true solace is left to me: I know that even here, amid the unseeing Bees of Handrea, far from the temples and comforts of my religion, God is present.

THE STORMS OF WINDHAVEN

by Lisa Tuttle and George R. R. Martin

Would that we could fly! Somehow airplanes and balloons do not fulfill this deep-rooted fantasy, this desire from earliest childhood that surely must permeate every observant human being. Gliding comes closest, yes . . . but on Windhaven, that world of islands and gales and atmospheric density, gliding is not the final solution; instead it is the beginning.

Maris rode the storm ten feet above the sea, taming the winds on wide cloth-of-metal wings. She flew fiercely, recklessly, delighting in the danger and the feel of the spray, not bothered by the cold. The sky was an ominous cobalt blue, the winds were building, and she had wings; that was enough. She could die now, and die happy, flying.

She flew better than she ever had before, twisting and gliding between the air currents without thought, catching each time the updraft or downwind which would carry her farther or faster. She made no wrong choices, was forced into no hasty scrambles above the leaping ocean; the tacking she did was all for joy. It would have been safer to fly high, like a child; up above the waves as far as she could climb, safe from her own mistakes. But Maris skimmed the sea, like a *flyer*, where a single dip, a brush of wing against water, meant a clumsy tumble from the sky. And death; you don't swim far when your wingspan is twenty feet.

Maris was daring, but she knew the winds.

Ahead she spied the neck of a scylla, a sinuous rope dark against the horizon. Almost without thinking, she responded. Her arms, outspread and strapped to the underside of the forward wing strut, shifted slightly. The great silver wings—tissue thin and almost weightless, but immensely strong—shifted with her. One wingtip all but grazed the whitecaps snapping below, the other lifted; and Maris caught the rising winds more fully, and began to climb.

Death, sky death, had been on her mind, but she would not end like that; snapped from the air like an unwary gull, lunch for a hungry monster.

Minutes later she caught up to the scylla, and paused for a taunting circle just beyond its reach. From above she could see its body, barely beneath the waves, the rows of slick black flippers beating rhythmically. The tiny head, swaying slowly from side to side atop the long neck, ignored her. Perhaps it has known flyers, she thought then, and it does not like the taste.

The winds were colder now, and heavy with salt. The storm was gathering strength; she could feel a trembling in the air. Maris, exhilarated, soon left the scylla far behind. Then she was alone again, flying effortlessly, through an empty, darkening world of sea and sky where the only sound was the wind upon her wings.

In a time, the island reared out of the sea: her destination. Sighing, sorry for the journey's end, Maris let herself descend.

Gina and Tor, two of the local land-bound—Maris didn't know what they did when they weren't caring for visiting flyers—were on duty out on the landing spit. She circled once above them to catch their attention, and they rose from the soft sand and waved at her. The second time she came around they were ready. Maris dipped lower and lower, until her feet were just inches above the ground; Gina and Tor ran across the sand parallel to her, each beside a wing. When her toes brushed surface and she began to slow in a shower of sand, they each caught a wingtip and held.

Maris dragged them several feet, and the three of them left a triple gouge down the landing spit. But finally she was stopped, lying facedown on the cool, dry sand. She felt silly. A downed flyer is like a turtle on its back; she could get on her feet if she had to, but it was a difficult, undignified process. Still, it had been a good landing.

Gina and Tor rose, brushing themselves off. As Maris struggled to stand, they began to fold up her wings, joint by foot-long joint. As each strut unlocked and folded back on the next segment, the tissue fabric between them went limp. When all the extensors were pulled in, the wings hung in two loose folds of drooping metal from the central axis strapped to Maris' back.

"We'd expected Coll," said Gina, as she folded back the final strut. Her short dark hair stood out in spikes around her face.

Maris shook her head. It should have been Coll's journey perhaps, but she had been desperate, longing for the air. She'd taken the wings—still *her* wings—and gone before he was out of bed.

"He'll have flying enough after next week, I expect," Tor said cheerfully. There was still sand in his lank blond hair and he was shivering a little from the sea winds, but he smiled as he spoke. "All the flying he'll want." He stepped in front of Maris to help her unstrap the wings.

"I'll wear them," Maris snapped at him, impatient, angered by his casual words. How could he understand? How could *any* of them understand? They were land-bound.

She started up the spit toward the lodge, Gina and Tor falling in beside her. There she took the usual refreshments and, standing before a huge open fire, allowed herself to be dried and warmed. The friendly questions she answered curtly, trying to be silent, trying not to think: this may be the last time. Because she was a flyer, they all respected her silence, although with disappointment. For most of the land-bound the flyers were the only source of contact with the other islands. The seas, infested with scyllas and seacats and other predators and daily storm-lashed, were too dangerous for regular ship travel except among islands within the same local group. The flyers were the links, and the others looked to them for news, gossip, songs, stories, romance.

"The Landsman will be ready whenever you are rested," Gina said, touching Maris tentatively on the shoulder. Maris pulled away, thinking, yes, to you it is enough to serve the flyers. You'd like a flyer husband, Coll perhaps when he's grown—and you don't know what it means to me that Coll should be the flyer, and not I. But she said only, "I'm ready now. It was an easy flight. The winds did all the work."

Gina led her to another room, where the Landsman was waiting for her message. Like the first, it was long and sparsely furnished, with a blazing fire crackling in a great stone hearth. The Landsman sat in a cushioned chair near the flames, and rose when Maris entered. Flyers were always greeted as equals, even on islands where the Landsmen were worshipped as gods and held godlike powers.

After the ritual greetings had been exchanged Maris closed her eyes and let the message flow. She didn't know or care what she said. The words used her voice without troubling her conscious thought. Probably politics, she knew. Lately it had all been politics.

When the message ended, Maris opened her eyes and smiled at the Landsman—perversely, on purpose, because he looked worried by her words. But he recovered quickly and returned her smile. "Thank you," he said, a little weakly. "You've done well."

She was invited to stay the night, but she refused. The storm might die by morning; besides, she liked night flying. Tor and Gina accompanied her outside, and up the rocky path to the flyers' cliff. There were lanterns set in the stone every few feet, to make the twisting ascent safer at night.

At the top of the climb there was a natural ledge, made deeper and wider by human hands. Beyond it, a forty-foot drop, and breakers crashing on a rocky beach. There Gina and Tor unfolded her wings, and locked the struts in place, and the tissue metal stretched tight and taut and silvery. And Maris jumped.

The wind caught her, lifted. She was flying again, dark sea below and rumbling storm above. Once launched she never looked back at the two wistful land-bound following her with their eyes. Too soon she would be one of them.

She did not turn toward home. Instead she flew with the storm winds, blowing violently now, westerly. Soon the thunder would come, and rain, and then Maris would be forced up, above the clouds, where the lightning was less likely to burn her from the sky. At home it would be calm; the storm past. People would be out beachcombing to see what the winds had brought, and a few small dories might be casting off in the hope that a day's fishing might not be entirely lost.

The wind sang in her ears and pushed at her, and she swam in the sky-stream gracefully. Then, oddly, she thought of Coll. And suddenly she lost the feel. She wavered, dipped, then pulled herself up sharply, tacking, searching for it. And cursing herself. It had been so good before—did it have to end this way? This might be her last flight ever, and it had to be her best. But it was no use; she'd lost the certainty. The wind and she were no longer lovers.

She began to fly at cross-purposes to the storm, battling grimly, fighting until her muscles were strained and aching. She gained altitude now; once the wind-feel left you, it was not safe to fly so near the water.

She was exhausted, tired of fighting, when she caught sight

of the rocky face of the Eyrie and realized how far she had come.

The Eyrie was nothing but a huge rock thrust up from the sea, a crumbling tower of stones surrounded by an angry froth where the waters broke against its tall, sheer walls. It was not an island; nothing would grow here but pockets of touch lichen. Birds made their nests in the few protected crevices and ledges, though, and atop the rock the flyers had built their nest. Here, where no ship could moor, here where no one but flyers—bird and human—could roost, here stood their dark stone lodge.

"Maris!"

She looked up at the sound of her name, and saw Dorrel diving on her, laughing, his wings dark against the clouds. At the last possible moment she turned from him, banking sharply, and slipped out from under his dive. He chased her around the Eyrie, and Maris forgot that she was tired and aching, and lost herself in the sheer joy of flying.

When at last they landed, the rains had just begun, howling suddenly from the east, stinging their faces and slapping hard against their wings. Maris realized that she was nearly numb with cold. They came down in a soft earth landing pit carved in the solid rock, without help, and Maris slid ten feet in sudden mud before coming to a stop. Then it took her five minutes to find her feet, and fumble with the triple straps that wrapped around her body. She tied the wings carefully to a tether rope, then walked out to a wingtip and began to fold them up.

By the time she was finished, her teeth were chattering convulsively, and she could feel the soreness in her arms. Dorrel frowned as he watched her work; his own wings, neatly folded, were slung over his shoulder. "Had you been out long?" he asked. "I should have let you land. I'm sorry. I didn't realize. You must have been with the storm all the way, just in front of it. Difficult weather. I got some of the crosswinds myself. Are you all right?"

"Oh, yes. I was tired—but not really, not now. I'm glad you were there to meet me. That was good flying, and I needed it. The last part of the trip was rough—I thought I would drop. But good flying's better than rest."

Dorrel laughed and put his arm around her. She felt how warm he was after the flight and, by contrast, how cold she was. He felt it too and squeezed her more tightly. "Come inside before you freeze. Garth brought some bottles of *kivas* from the Shotans, and one of them should be hot by now. Between us and the *kivas* we'll get you warm again."

The common room of the lodge was warm and cheerful, as always, but almost empty. Garth, a short well-muscled flyer ten years her senior, was the only one there. He looked up from his place by the fire and called them by name. Maris wanted to answer, but her throat was tight with longing, and her teeth were clenched together. Dorrel led her to the fireplace.

"Like a woodwinged idiot I kept her out in the cold," Dorrel said. "Is the *kivas* hot? Pour us some." He stripped off his wet, muddy clothes quickly and efficiently, and pulled two large towels from a pile near the fire.

"Why should I waste my *kivas* on you?" Garth rumbled. "For Maris, of course, for she is very beautiful and a superb flyer." He made a mock bow in her direction.

"You should waste your *kivas* on me," Dorrel said, rubbing himself briskly with the big towel, "unless you would care to waste it all over the floor."

Garth replied, and they traded insults and threats in laconic voices. Maris didn't listen—she had heard it all before. She squeezed the water from her long hair, watching the patterns the wetness made on the hearth stones and how quickly they faded. She looked at Dorrel, trying to memorize his lean, muscular body—a good flyer's body—and the quick changes of his face as he teased Garth. But he turned when he felt Maris watching him, and his eyes gentled. Garth's final witticism fell limply into silence. Dorrel touched Maris softly, tracing the line of her jaw.

"You're still shivering." He took the towel from her hands and wrapped it around her. "Garth, take this bottle off the fire before it explodes and let us all get warm."

The *kivas* was served in great stone mugs, a hot spice wine flavored with raisins and nuts. The first sip sent thin lines of fire down her veins, and the shivering stopped.

Garth smiled at her. "Good, isn't it? Not that Dorrel will appreciate it. I tricked a slimy old fisherman out of a dozen bottles. He found it in a shipwreck, didn't know what he had, and his wife didn't want it in the house. I gave him some trinkets for it, some metal beads I'd picked up for my sister."

"And what does your sister get?" Maris asked, between sips of *kivas*.

Garth shrugged. "Her? Oh, it was a surprise, anyway. I'll

bring something from Poweet the next time I go. Some painted eggs."

"If he doesn't see something else he can trade them for on his way back," Dorrel said. "If your sister ever gets her surprise, Garth, the shock will kill all pleasure. You were born a trader. I think you'd swap your wings if the deal was good enough."

Garth snorted indignantly. "Close your mouth when you say that, bird." He turned to Maris. "How is your brother? I never see him."

Maris took another sip of her drink, holding on to calm with both hands. "He'll be of age next week," she said carefully. "The wings will be his, then. I wouldn't know about his comings and goings. Maybe he doesn't like your company."

"Huh," said Garth. "Why shouldn't he?" He sounded wounded. Maris waved a hand, and forced herself to smile. She had meant it lightly. "I like him well enough." Garth went on. "We all like him, don't we, Dorrel? He's young, quiet, maybe a bit too cautious, but he should improve. He's different somehow—oh, but he can tell some stories! And sing! The land-bound will learn to love the sight of his wings." Garth shook his head in wonder. "Where does he learn them all? I've done more traveling than him, but . . ."

"He makes them up," said Maris.

"Himself?" Garth was impressed. "He'll be our singer, then. We'll take the prize away from Eastern at the next competition. Western always has the best flyers," he said loyally, "but our singers have never been worthy of the title."

"I sang for Western at the last meet," Dorrel objected.

"That's what I mean."

"*You* shriek like a seacat."

"Yes," said Garth, "but I have no delusions about my ability."

Maris missed Dorrel's reply. Her mind had drifted away from their dialogue, and she was watching the flames, thinking, nursing her still-warm drink. She felt peaceful here in the Eyrie, even now, even after Garth had mentioned Coll. And strangely comfortable. No one lived on the flyers' rock, but it was a home of sorts. Her home. It was hard to think of not coming here any more.

She remembered the first time she'd seen the Eyrie, a good six years ago, just after her coming-of-age day. She'd been a girl of thirteen, proud of having flown so far alone, but scared too, and shy. Inside the lodge she'd found a good dozen flyers, sitting around a fire, drinking, laughing. A party was in progress. But they'd stopped and smiled at her. Garth had been a quiet youth then, Dorrel a skinny boy just barely older than she was. She hadn't known either of them. But Helmer, a middle-aged flyer from the island closest to hers, had been among the company, and he made the introductions. Even now she remembered the faces, the names; red-headed Anni from Culhall, Foster who later grew too fat to fly, Jamis the Senior, and especially the one nicknamed Raven, an arrogant youth who dressed in black fur and metal and had won awards for Eastern in three straight competitions. There was another too, a lanky blonde from the Outer Islands. The party was in her honor; it was seldom any of the Outers flew so very, very far.

They'd all welcomed Maris, and soon it seemed almost as if she'd replaced the tall blonde as the guest of honor. They gave her wine, despite her age, and they made her sing with them, and told her stories about flying, most of which she'd heard before, but never from such as these. Finally, when she felt very much part of the group, they let their attentions wander from her, and the festivities resumed their normal course.

It had been a strange, unforgettable party, and one incident in particular was burned golden in her memory. Raven, the only Eastern wing in the group, had been taking a lot of needling. Finally, a little drunk, he rebelled. "You call yourselves flyers," he'd said, in a whiplash voice that Maris would always recall. "Come with me, I'll show you flying."

And the whole party had gone outside, to the flyers' cliff of Eyrie, the highest cliff of all. Two hundred feet straight down it plunged, to where the rocks stared up like teeth and the water churned furiously against them. Raven, wearing folded wings, walked up to the brink. He unfolded the first three joints of his wing struts carefully, and strapped them on his arms. But he did not lock them; the hinges still moved, and the struts bent back and forth with his arms, flexible. The other struts he held, folded, in his hands.

Maris had wondered what he was up to. She soon found out.

He ran and jumped, out as far as he could, off the flyers' cliff. With his wings still folded.

She'd gasped, run to the edge. The others followed, some looking pale, a few grinning. Dorrel had stood beside her.

Raven was falling straight down, a rock, his hands at his

sides, his wing cloth flapping like a cape. Head first he flew, and the plunge seemed to last forever.

Then, at the very last moment, when he was almost on the rocks, when Maris could almost feel the impact—silver wings, suddenly, flashing in the sunlight. Wings from nowhere. And Raven caught the winds, and flew.

Maris had been awed. But Jamis the Senior, the oldest flyer Western had, only laughed. "Raven's trick," he growled. "I've seen him do it twice before. He oils his wing struts. After he's fallen far enough, he flings them away as hard as he can. As each one locks in place, the snap flings loose the next one. Pretty, yes. You can bet he practiced it plenty before he tried it out in front of anyone. One of these days, though, a hinge is going to jam, and we won't have to listen to Raven any more."

But even his words hadn't tarnished the magic. Maris often had seen flyers, impatient with their land-bound help, draw their almost-open wings up over their heads and shake out the last joint or two with a sharp snap. But never anything like this.

Raven had been smirking when he met them at the landing pit. "When you can do *that*," he told the company, "then you can call yourselves flyers." He'd been a conceited, reckless sort, yes, but right at that moment and for years afterwards, Maris had thought herself in love with him.

She shook her head sadly, and finished her *kivas*. It all seemed silly now. Raven had died less than two years after that party, vanished at sea without a trace. A dozen flyers died each year, and their wings usually were lost with them; clumsy flying would down and drown them, long-necked scyllas had been known to attack unwary skimmers, storms could blow them from the sky, lightning hunted out the metal of their wings—yes, there were many ways a flyer could die. Most of them, Maris suspected, just lost their way, and missed their destination, flying on blindly till exhaustion pulled them down. A few perhaps hit that rarest and most feared menace of the sky: still air. But Maris knew now that Raven had been a more likely candidate for death than most; a foolish flashy flyer with no sky sense.

Dorrel's voice jarred her from her memories. "Maris," he said, "hey, don't go to sleep on us."

Maris set down her empty cup, her hand curved around

the rough stone, still seeking the warmth it had held. With an effort, she pulled her head away and picked up her sweater.

"It's not dry," Garth protested.

"Are you cold?" asked Dorrel.

"No. I must get back."

"You're too tired," Dorrel said. "Stay the night."

Maris drew her eyes away from his. "I mustn't. They'll worry."

Dorrel sighed. "Then take dry clothes." He stood, went to the far end of the common room, and pulled open the doors of a carved wooden wardrobe. "Come here and pick out something that fits."

Maris did not move. "I'd better take my own clothes. I won't be coming back."

Dorrel swore softly. "Maris. Don't make things—you know that—oh, come, take the clothes. You're welcome to them, you know that. Leave yours in exchange if you like. I won't let you go out in wet clothes."

"I'm sorry," Maris said. Garth smiled at her while Dorrel stood waiting. She got up slowly, pulling the towel more closely around her as she moved away from the heat of the fire. With Dorrel she searched through the piles of clothes until she found trousers and sweater that fit. Dorrel watched her dress, then quickly found clothes for himself. Then they went to the rack near the door, and took down their wings. Maris briefly checked the struts for weakness or damage; the wings seldom failed, but when they did, the trouble was nearly always in the joints. The fabric itself shone as soft and strong as it had when the star sailors rode it to this world. Satisfied, Maris strapped on the wings. They were in good shape; Coll would wear them for years, and his children for generations after him.

Garth had come to stand beside her; she looked at him.

"I'm not so good at words as Coll is, or Dorrel," he started. "I . . . well. Good-bye, Maris." He blushed, looking miserable. Flyers did not say good-bye to each other. But I am not a flyer, she thought, and so she hugged Garth, and kissed him, and said good-bye, the word of the land-bound.

Dorrel walked outside with her. The winds were strong, as always around the Eyrie, but the storm had passed. The only water in the air was the faint mist of sea-spray. But the stars were out.

"At least stay till moon-rise," Dorrel said. "We could have

dinner—Garth and I would fight for the pleasure of serving you."

Maris shook her head. She shouldn't have come; she should have flown straight home and never said good-bye to Garth or Dorrel. Easier not to make the ending, easier to pretend that things would always be the same and then to vanish at the end. When they reached the high flyers' cliff, the same from where Raven once leapt so long ago, she reached for Dorrel's hand and they stood a while longer in silence.

"Maris," he said finally, hesitantly. He looked straight out to sea, standing by her side, holding her hand. "Maris, you could marry me. I would share my wings with you—you needn't give up flying entirely."

Maris dropped his hand, and felt herself go hot all over with shame. He had no right; it was cruel to pretend. "Don't," she said in a whisper. "The wings aren't yours to share."

"Tradition," he said, sounding desperate. She could tell he was embarrassed also. He wanted to help her, not to make things worse. "We could try it. The wings are mine, but you could use them . . ."

"Oh, Dorrel, don't. The Landsmen, your Landsmen, would never allow it. It's more than tradition, it's law. They might take your wings away and give them to someone with more respect, like they did to Lind the smuggler. Besides, even if we ran away, to a place without law or Landsmen, to a place by ourselves—how long could you bear to share your wings? With me, with *anyone?* Don't you see? We'd come to hate one another. I'm not a child who can practice when you're resting. I can't live like that, flying on sufferance, knowing the wings could never be mine. And you would grow tired of the way I would watch you—we would—oh." She broke off, fumbling for words.

Dorrel was silent for a moment. "I'm sorry," he said. "I wanted to do something—to help you, Maris. It hurts unbearably knowing what is about to happen to you. I wanted to give you something. I can't bear to think of you going away and becoming . . ."

She took his hand again and held it tightly. "Yes, yes. Shh."

"You do know I love you, Maris. You do, don't you?"

"And I love you, Dorrel. But—I'll never marry a flyer. Not now. I couldn't. I'd murder him for his wings." She looked at him, trying to lighten the bleak truth of her words. And failing.

They clung to each other, balanced on the edge of the moment of parting, trying to say everything they might ever want to say to each other now, with the pressure of their bodies. Then they pulled away, and looked at each other through tears.

Maris fumbled with her wings, shaking, suddenly cold again. Dorrel tried to help, but his fingers collided with hers, and they laughed, haltingly, at their clumsiness. She let him unfold her wings for her. When one of them was fully extended, and the second nearly so, she suddenly thought of Raven, and waved Dorrel away. Puzzled, he watched. Maris lifted the wing like an air-weary elder, and threw the final joint into lock with a clean strong snap. And then shc was ready to leave.

"Go well," he said, finally.

Maris opened her mouth, then closed it, nodding foolishly. "And you," she said at last. "Take care, until . . ." But she could not add the final lie, any more than she could say good-bye to him. She turned and ran from him, and launched herself away from the Eyrie, out on the nightwinds into a cold dark sky.

It was a long and lonely flight over a starlit sea where nothing stirred. The winds were steady from the west, forcing Maris to tack all the way, losing time and speed. By the time she spotted the light tower of Lesser Amberly, her home island, midnight was past.

There was another light below, turning on their landing beach. She saw it as she coasted in, smooth and easy, and thought it must be the lodge men. But they should have gone off duty long ago; few flyers were aloft this late. She frowned in puzzlement just as she hit the ground with a jarring shock.

Maris groaned, hurried to get up, and set to work on the wing straps. She should know enough not to be distracted at the moment of landing. The light advanced on her.

"So you decided to come back," the voice said, harsh and angry. It was Russ, her father—stepfather, really—coming toward her with a lantern in his good hand, his right arm hanging dead and useless at his side.

"I stopped by Eyrie first," she said, defensively. "You weren't worried?"

"Coll was to go, not you." The lines of his face were set hard.

"He was in bed," Maris said. "He was too slow—I knew he'd miss the best of the storm winds. He would have caught nothing but rain, and it would have taken him forever to get there. If he did. He's not good in rain yet."

"Then he must learn to be better. The boy must make his own mistakes now. You were his teacher, but soon the wings will be his. He's the flyer, not you."

Maris winced as if struck. This was the man who had taught her to fly, who had been so proud of her and the way she seemed to know instinctively what to do. The wings would be hers, he'd told her more than once, though she was not of his blood. He and his wife had taken her in when it seemed that he would never father a child of his own to inherit the wings. He'd had an accident and lost the sky, and it was important to find a flyer to replace him—if not someone of his blood, then someone he loved. His wife had refused to learn; she had lived thirty-five years as a land-bound, and she did not intend to jump off any cliffs, wings or no. Besides, it was too late; flyers had to be taught young. So it was Maris he had taught, adopted, and come to love—Maris the fisherman's daughter, who would rather watch from flyers' cliff than play with the other children.

And then, against all probability, Coll had been born. His mother had died after the prolonged and difficult labor—Maris, very much a child, remembered a dark night full of people running, and later her stepfather crying alone in a corner—but Coll had lived on. Maris, suddenly a child-mother, came to care for him, love him. At first they didn't expect him to live. She was happy when he did; and for three years she had loved him as both brother and son, while she practiced with the wings under her father's watchful eyes.

Until the night when the same father told her that Coll, baby Coll, must be given *her* wings.

"I am a far better flyer than he will ever be," Maris told him now, on the beach, her voice trembling.

"I do not dispute that. It makes no difference. He is my son."

"It's not fair!" she cried, letting out the protest that had been lodged inside her since that first time he had told her, on the day before she was to come of age and claim the wings as her own. By then Coll had been strong, healthy; still too small to bear the wings, but they would be his on his coming-of-age day. Maris had no claim, no right at all. That was the law of the flyers, stretching back through generations to the star sailors themselves, the legendary wing-forgers. The first-born child of each of the flying families would inherit the wings of the parent. Skill counted for nothing; this was a law of inheritance, and Maris came from a fishing family who had nothing to leave her but the scattered wreckage of a wooden boat.

"Fair or no, it is the law, Maris. You've known it for a long time, even if you chose to ignore it. For six years you've played at being a flyer, and I've let you, because you loved it, and because Coll needed a teacher, a skilled one, and because this island is too big to rely on only two flyers. But you knew all the while this day would come."

He could be more kind, she thought wildly. He must know what it means, to give up the sky.

"Now come with me," he said. "You'll not fly again."

Her wings were still fully extended; only one strap was undone. "I'll run away," she said madly. "You'll never see me again. I'll go to some island where they don't have a flyer of their own. They'll be glad to have me, no matter how I got my wings."

"Never," her father said, sadly. "The other flyers would shun the island, like the Easterns did after the mad Landsman of Kennehut executed the Flyer-Who-Brought-Bad-News. You would be stripped of your stolen wings no matter where you went. No Landsman would take the risk."

"I'll break them, then!" Maris said, riding the edge of hysteria. "Then he'll never fly either, any more than . . . than . . ."

Glass shattered on rock and the light went out as her father dropped the lantern. Maris felt his grip on her hands. "You couldn't even if you wanted to. And you wouldn't do that to Coll. But give me the wings."

"I wouldn't . . ."

"I don't know what you wouldn't do. I thought you'd gone out to kill yourself this morning, to die flying in the storm. I know the feelings, Maris. That's why I was so frightened, and so angry. You mustn't blame Coll."

"I don't. And I would not keep him from flying—but I want to fly so badly myself—Father, please." Tears ran down her face in the dark, and she moved closer reaching for comfort.

"Yes, Maris," he said. He could not put his arm about her; the wings got in the way. "There is nothing I can do. This is the way of things. You must learn to live without wings, as I have. At least you've had them for a time—you know what it is like to fly."

"It's not enough!" she said, tearful, stubborn. "I used to think it would be, when I was a little girl, not even yours yet, just a stranger, and you were Amberly's greatest flyer. I watched you and the others from the cliff and I used to think—if I could have wings, even for a moment, that would be life enough. But it isn't, it *isn't*. I can't give them up."

The hard lines were all gone now in her father's face. He touched her face gently, brushing away tears. "Perhaps you're right," he said, in a slow heavy voice. "Perhaps it was not a good thing. I thought—if I could let you fly for a while, a little bit—that would be better than nothing, it would be a fine bright gift indeed. But it wasn't, was it? Now you can never be happy. You can never be a land-bound, really, for you've flown, and you'll always know how you are imprisoned." His words stopped abruptly and Maris realized that he was talking of himself as much as her.

He helped her unstrap and fold the wings and they walked back home together.

Their house was a simple wood frame, surrounded by trees and land. A creek ran through the back. Flyers could live well and easy. Russ said good-night just inside the door and took the wings upstairs with him. Has he really lost all trust? Maris thought. What have I done? And she felt like crying again.

Instead she wandered into the kitchen, found cheese and cold meat and tea, and took them back into the dining room. A bowl-shaped sand candle sat in the center of the table. She lit it, ate, and watched the flame dance.

Coll entered just as she finished, and stood awkwardly in the doorway. " 'Lo, Maris," he said uncertainly. "I'm glad you're back. I was waiting." He was tall for a thirteen-year-old, with a soft slender body, long red-blond hair, and the wispy beginnings of a mustache.

" 'Lo, Coll," Maris said. "Don't just stand there. I'm sorry I took the wings."

He sat down. "I don't mind, you know that. You fly a lot better than me, and—well—you know. Was Father mad?"

Maris nodded.

Coll looked grim and frightened. "It's only one week away now, Maris. What are we going to do?" He was looking straight down at the candle, not at her.

Maris sighed, and put a gentle hand on his arm. "We'll do

what we must, Coll. We have no choice." They had talked before, she and Coll, and she knew his agony as much as her own. She was his sister, almost his mother, and the boy had shared with her his shame and his secret. That was the ultimate irony.

He looked up at her now, looking to her again as the child to the mother; although he knew now that she was as helpless as he, still he hoped. "Why don't we have a choice? I don't understand."

Maris sighed. "It's law, Coll. We don't go against tradition here, you know that. We all have duties put upon us. If we had a choice I would keep the wings, I would be a flyer. And you could be a singer. We'd both be proud, and know we were good at what we did. Life will be hard as a land-bound. I want the wings so much. I've had them, and it doesn't seem right that they should be taken from me, but maybe—maybe the rightness in it is something I just don't see. People wiser than we decided that things should be the way they are, and maybe I'm just being a child about it, wanting everything my own way."

Coll wet his lips, nervous. "No."

She looked a question at him.

He shook his head stubbornly. "It's not right, Maris, it just isn't. I don't want to fly, I don't want to take your wings. It's all so stupid. I'm hurting you and I don't want to, but I don't want to hurt Father either. How can I tell him? I'm his son and all that—I'm *supposed* to take the wings. He'd hate me. The songs don't say anything about flyers who were scared of the sky like I am. Flyers *aren't* afraid—I'm not meant for a flyer." His hands were shaking visibly.

"Coll, don't worry. It will be all right, really it will. Everyone is frightened at first. I was too." She wasn't thinking about the lie, only saying words to reassure him.

"But it's not fair," he cried. "I don't want to give up my singing, and if I fly I can't sing, not like Barrion, not like I'd like to. So why are they going to make me? Maris, why can't *you* be the flyer, like you want to be? *Why?*"

She looked at him, so close to crying, and felt like joining him in tears. She didn't have an answer, not for him or for herself. "I don't know," she said, her voice hollow. "I don't know, little one. That is the way things have always been done, though, and that is the way they must be."

They stared at each other, both trapped, caught together by a law older than both and a tradition neither understood.

Helpless and hurt, they talked long in the candlelight, saying the same things over and over again until, late, they parted for bed, nothing resolved.

But once in bed alone, the resentment came flooding back to Maris, the sense of loss, and with it, shame. She cried herself to sleep that night, and dreamed of purple storm-skies that she would never fly.

The week went on forever.

A dozen times during those endless days Maris walked up to flyers' cliff, to stand helplessly with her hands in her pockets looking out over the sea. Fishing boats she saw, and gulls, and once a hunting pack of sleek gray seacats far, far off. It made her hurt the more, the sudden closing of the world she knew, the way the horizons seemed to shrink about her. So she stood there, lusting for the wind, but the only thing that flew was her hair.

Once she caught Coll watching her from a distance. Afterward neither of them mentioned it.

Russ had the wings now, *his* wings, as they had always been, as they would be until Coll took them. When Lesser Amberly needed a flyer, Corm answered the call from the far side of the island, or gay Shalli who had flown guard when Maris was a child first learning simple sky sense. As far as her father was concerned, the island had no third flyer, and would have none until Coll claimed his birthright.

His attitude toward Maris had changed too. Sometimes he raged at her when he found her brooding, sometimes he put his good arm around her and all but wept. He could not find a middle ground between anger and pity; so, helpless, he tried to avoid her. Instead he spent his time with Coll, acting excited and enthusiastic. The boy, a dutiful son, tried to catch and echo the mood. But Maris knew that he too went for long walks, and spent a lot of time alone with his guitar.

On the day before Coll was to come of age, Maris sat high on flyers' cliff, her legs dangling over the edge, watching Shalli wheel in silver arcs across the noonday sky. Spotting seacats for the fishermen, Shalli had said, but Maris knew better. She'd been a flyer long enough to recognize a joy-flight when she saw one. Even now, as she sat trapped, she could feel a distant echo of that joy; something soared within her whenever Shalli banked, and a shaft of silvered sunlight blazed briefly from a wing.

Is this the way it ends? Maris asked herself. It can't be. No, this is the way it began. I remember.

And she did remember. Sometimes she thought she had watched the flyers even before she could walk, though her mother, her real mother, said that wasn't so. Maris did have vivid memories of the cliff, though; she'd run away and come here almost weekly when she was four and five and six. There—*here*—she'd sit, watching the flyers come and go. Her mother would always find her, and she would always be furious.

"You are land-bound, Maris," she'd say, after she had administered a spanking. "Don't waste your time with foolish dreams. I won't have my daughter be a Woodwings."

That was an old folk tale; her mother told it to her anew each time she caught her on the cliff. Woodwings was a carpenter's son who wanted to be a flyer. But, of course, he wasn't in a flying family. He did not care, the story said; he did not listen to friends or family, he wanted nothing but sky. Finally, in his father's shop, he built himself a beautiful pair of wings; great butterfly wings of carved and polished wood. And everyone said they were beautiful, everyone but the flyers; the flyers only shook their heads silently. Finally Woodwings climbed to flyers' cliff. They were waiting for him up there, wordless, circling and banking bright and quiet in the dawn light. Woodwings ran to meet them, and fell tumbling to his death.

"And the moral," Maris' mother would always say, "is that you shouldn't try to be something you're not."

But *was* that the moral? The child Maris didn't worry about it; she just dismissed Woodwings as an oaf. But when she was older, the story came back to her often. At times she thought her mother had gotten it all wrong. Woodwings had won, Maris thought. He *had* flown, if only for an instant, and that made it all worthwhile, even his death. It was a flyer's death. And the others, the flyers, they had not come out to mock him, or warn him off—no, they flew guard for him, because he was just a beginner, and because they understood. The land-bound often laughed at Woodwings; the name had become a synonym for fool. But how could a flyer hear the story and do anything but cry?

Maris thought of Woodwings then, as she sat in the cold watching Shalli fly, and the old questions came back. Was it worth it, Woodwings? she thought. An instant of flight, then death forever? And for me, was it worth it? A dozen years of stormwinds, and now a life without?

When Russ had first begun to notice her on the cliff, she was the happiest child in the world. A few years later, when he adopted her and pushed her proudly into the sky, she thought she would die from joy. Her real father was dead, gone with his boat, killed by an angry scylla after a storm had blown him far off course; her mother was gladly rid of her. She leapt at the new life, at the sky; it seemed that all her dreams were coming true. Woodwings had the right idea, she thought then. Dream anything hard enough, and it can be yours.

Her faith had left when Coll came, and she was told.

Coll. Everything came back to Coll.

So, lost, Maris brushed all thought aside, and watched in melancholy peace.

The day came, as Maris knew it must.

It was a small party, though the Landsman himself was the host. He was a portly, genial man, with a kind face hidden by a full beard that he hoped would make him fierce. When he met them at the door, his clothes dripped wealth; rich embroidered fabrics, rings of copper and brass, and a heavy necklace of real wrought iron. But the welcome was warm.

Inside the lodge was a great party room. Bare wooden beams above, torches flaming bright along the walls, a scarlet carpet underneath. And a table, groaning under its burden; *kivas* from the Shotans and Amberly's own wines, cheeses flown in from Culhall, fruit from the Outer Islands, great bowls of green salad. In the hearth, a seacat turned on a spit.

Their land-bound friends were all there, and they clustered around Coll, offering congratulations. Some of them even felt compelled to talk to Maris, to tell her how lucky she was to have a flyer for a brother, to have been a flyer herself. Have been, have been, have been. She wanted to scream.

But the flyers were worse. They were there in force, of course. Corm, handsome as ever, dripping charm, held court in one corner, telling stories of far-off places to starry-eyed land-bound girls. Shalli was dancing: before the evening had run its course she would burn out a half-dozen men with her frantic energy. Other flyers had come from other islands. Anni of Culhall, the boy Jamis the Younger, fast-aging Helmer whose own daughter would claim his wings in less than a year, a half-dozen others from the West, three cliquish Easterners. Her friends, her brothers, her comrades in the Eyrie.

But now they avoided her. Anni smiled politely and looked the other way. Jamis delivered his father's greetings, then lapsed into an uncomfortable silence, shifting from foot to foot until Maris let him go. His sigh of relief was almost audible. Even Corm, who said he was never nervous, seemed ill at ease with her. He brought her a cup of hot *kivas*, then saw a friend across the room that he simply *had* to talk to.

Feeling cut off and shunned, Maris found a leather chair by the window. There she sat and sipped her *kivas* and listened to the rising wind pull at the shutters. She didn't blame them. How can you talk to a wingless flyer?

She was glad that Garth and Dorrel had not come, nor any of the others she had come to love especially. And she was ashamed of being glad.

Then there was a stir by the door, and her mood lifted slightly. Barrion had arrived.

Maris smiled despite herself. Although Russ thought him a bad influence on Coll, she liked Barrion, tall and gray and serious, with his guitar sewn to his hand and his rumbly deep voice. He was Amberly's best singer, so it was said. At least Coll said it, and Barrion himself, of course. But then he also said that he'd been to a dozen islands, unthinkable for a wingless man. And he claimed that his guitar had arrived generations ago from Earth, and the star sailors themselves. His family had handed it down, he said, all serious, as if he expected Coll and Maris to believe him. But the idea was nonsense—treating a guitar as if it were a pair of wings.

Still, liar or no, lanky Barrion was entertaining enough, and romantic enough, and he sang like the very wind. Coll had studied under him, and now they were great friends.

The Landsman clapped him roundly on the back, and Barrion laughed, sat down, and prepared to sing. The room grew quiet; even Corm stopped in mid-story.

He began with the "Song of the Star Sailors."

It was the oldest ballad, the first of those that they could rightly call their own. Barrion sang it simply, with easy loving familiarity, and Maris softened to the sound of his deep voice. How often she used to hear Coll staying up late at night, plucking his own instrument and singing the same song. His voice had been changing then; it made him furious. Every third stanza would be interrupted by a hideous cracked note and a minute of swearing. Maris used to lie in bed and giggle helplessly at the noises from down the hall.

Now she listened to the words, as Barrion sang sweetly of

the star sailors and their great ship, with its silver sails that stretched a hundred miles to catch the wild starwinds. The whole story was there. The mysterious storm, the crippled ship, the coffins where they died a while; then, driven off course, they came *here*, to a world of endless ocean and raging storms, a world where the only land was a thousand scattered rocky islands, and the winds blew constantly. The song told of the landing, in a ship not meant to land, of the death of thousands in their coffins, and the way the sail—barely heavier than air—had floated atop the sea, turning the waters silver all around the Shotans. Barrion sang of the star sailors' magic, and their dream of repairing the ship, and the slow agonizing dying of that dream. He lingered melancholy over the fading powers of their magic machines, the fading that ended in darkness. Finally came the battle, just off Big Shotan, when the Old Captain and his loyalists went down defending the precious metal sails against their sons. Then, with the last magic, the sons of the star sailors, the first children of Windhaven, cut the sails into pieces, light, flexible, immensely strong. And, with whatever metal they could salvage from the ship, they forged the wings.

For the scattered people of Windhaven needed communication. Without fuel, without metal, faced by oceans full of storms and predators, given nothing free but the powerful winds: the choice was easy.

The last chords faded from the air. The poor sailors, Maris thought, as always. The Old Captain and his crew, they were flyers too, though their wings were starwings. But their way of flying had to die so a new way could be born.

Barrion grinned at someone's request, and began a new tune. He did a half-dozen songs from ancient Earth, then looked around sheepishly and offered up a composition of his own, a bawdy drinking song about a horny scylla who mistook a fishing ship for its mate. Maris hardly listened. Her mind was on the star sailors still. In a way, they were like Woodwings, she thought; they couldn't give up their dream: And it meant they had to die. I wonder if they thought it was worth it?

"Barrion," Russ called from the floor. "This is a flyer's age-day. Give us some flying songs!"

The singer grinned, and nodded. Maris looked over at Russ. He stood by the table, a wine glass in his good hand, a smile on his face. He is proud, she thought. His son is soon to be a flyer, and he has forgotten me. She felt sick and beaten.

Barrion sang flying songs; ballads from the Outer Islands, from Shotan, from Culhall and Amberly and Poweet. He sang of the ghost flyers, lost forever over the seas when they obeyed the Landsman-Captain and took swords into the sky. In still air you can see them yet, wandering hopelessly through the storms on phantom wings. Or so the legends go. But flyers who hit still air seldom return to talk of it, so no one could say for sure.

He did the song of white-haired Royn, who was past eighty when he found his flyer grandson dead in a lover's quarrel, and took the wings to chase and kill the culprit.

He did the ballad of Aron and Jeni, the saddest song of all. Jeni had been a land-born, and worse, crippled: unable to walk, she had lived with her mother, a washerwoman, and daily she sat by the window to watch the flyers' cliff on Little Shotan. There she fell in love with Aron, a graceful laughing flyer, and in her dreams he loved her too. But one day, alone in her house, she saw him play in the sky with another flyer, a fire-haired woman, and when they landed they kissed each other. When her mother came home, Jeni was dead. Aron, when they told him, would not let them bury the woman he had never known. He took her in his arms and carried her up to the cliff; then, slinging her beneath him, he rode the winds far out to sea and gave her a flyer's death.

Woodwings had a song too, though not a very good one; it made him a comical fool. Barrion sang it, though, and the one about the Flyer-Who-Brought-Bad-News, and Winddance, the flyers' wedding song, and a dozen others. Maris could hardly move, so caught was she. The *kivas* was rain cold in her hand, forgotten in the face of the words. It was a good feeling, a restless disturbing glorious sadness, and it brought back her memories of the winds.

"Your brother is a flyer born," a soft voice whispered by her side, and she saw that Corm was resting on the arm of her chair. He gestured gracefully with his wine glass, to where Coll sat at Barrion's feet. The youth had his hands folded tightly around his knees, and his look was one of rapture.

"See how the songs touch him," Corm said, easily. "Only songs to a land-bound, but more, much more, to a flyer. You and I know that, Maris, and your brother too. I can tell by watching. I know how it must be for you, but think of him, girl. He loves it as much as you."

Maris looked up at him, and all but laughed at his wisdom.

Yes, Coll looked entranced, and she knew why and he did not. It was singing he loved, not flying; the songs, not the subject. But how could Corm know that, smiling handsome Corm who was so sure of himself and knew so little. "Do you think that only flyers dream, Corm?" she asked him in a whisper, then quickly glanced away to where Barrion was finishing a song.

"There are more flying songs," Barrion said. "If I sang them all, we would be here all night, and I'd never get to eat." He looked at Coll. "Wait. You'll learn more than I'll ever know when you reach the Eyrie. I've only been to a dozen islands, your flyers have seen hundreds." Corm, by Maris' side, raised his glass in salute.

Coll stood up. "I want to do one."

Barrion smiled. "I think I can trust you with my guitar. Nobody else, maybe, but you, yes." He got up, relinquishing his seat to the quiet, pale-faced youth.

Coll sat down, strummed nervously, biting his lip. He blinked at the torches, looked over at Maris, blinked again. "I want to do a new song, about a flyer. I—well, I wrote it. I wasn't there, you understand, but I heard the story, and well, it's all true. It *ought* to be a song, and it hasn't been, till now."

"Well, sing it then, boy," the Landsman boomed.

Coll smiled, glanced at Maris again. "I call this 'Raven's Fall.' "

And he sang it.

Clear and pure, with a beautiful voice, just the way it happened. Maris watched him with wide eyes, listened with awe. He got it all right. He even caught the feeling, the lump that twisted in her when Raven's folded wings bloomed mirror-bright in the sun, and he climbed away from death. All of the school-girl love she had felt for him was in Coll's song; the Raven that he sang of was a glorious winged knight, dark and daring and defiant. As Maris once had thought.

He has a gift, Maris thought, and Corm looked down at her and said, "What?" and suddenly she realized that she'd whispered it aloud.

"Coll," she said, in a low voice. The last notes of the song rang in her ears. "He could be better than Barrion, if he had a chance. I told him that story, Corm. I was there, and a dozen others, when Raven did his trick. But none of us could have made it beautiful, as Coll did. He has a very special gift."

Corm smiled at her complacently. "True. Next year we'll wipe out Eastern in the singing competition."

And Maris looked at him, suddenly furious. It was all so wrong, she thought. Across the room, Coll was watching her, a question in his eyes. Maris nodded to him, and he grinned proudly. He had done it right.

And she had decided.

But then, before Coll could start another song, Russ came forward. "Now," he said, "now we must get serious. We've had singing and talk, good eating and good drink here in the warmth. But outside are the winds."

They all listened gravely, as was expected, and the sound of the winds, forgotten background for so long, now seemed to fill the room. Maris heard, and shivered.

"The wings," her father said. The Landsman came forward, holding them in his hands like the trust they were. He spoke his ritual words. "Long have these wings served Amberly, linking us to all the folk of Windhaven, for generations, back unto the days of the star sailors. Marion flew them, daughter of a star sailor, and *her* daughter Jeri, and her son Jon, and Anni, and Flan, and Denis" . . . the geneology went on a long time . . . "and last Russ and his daughter Maris." There was a slight ripple in the crowd; the Landsman had broken tradition slightly. Maris had not been a true flyer; she ought not to have been named. "And now young Coll will take them, and now, as other Landsmen have done for generations, I hold them for a brief while, to bring them luck with my touch. And through me all the folk of Lesser Amberly touch these wings, and with my voice they say, 'Fly well, Coll!' "

The Landsman handed the folded wings to Russ, and her father took them and turned to Coll. He was standing then, the guitar at his feet, and he looked very small and very pale. "It is time for someone to become a flyer," Russ said. "It is time for me to pass on the wings, and for Coll to accept them, and it would be folly to strap on wings in a house. Let us go to flyers' cliff and watch a boy become a man."

The torch-bearers, flyers all, were ready. They left the lodge, Coll in a place of honor between his father and the Landsman, the flyers close behind with the torches. Maris and the rest of the party followed further back.

It was a ten-minute walk, slow step in other-worldly silence, before they stood in a rough semi-circle on the stage of the cliff. Alone by the edge, Russ, one-handed and disdaining help, strapped the wings onto his son. Coll's face was chalk white. He stood very still indeed while Russ unfolded the wings, and looked straight down at the abyss before him, where dark waves clawed against the beach.

Finally, it was done. "My son, you are a flyer," Russ said, and then he stepped back with the rest of them, close to Maris. Coll stood alone beneath the stars, perched on the brink, his immense silvery wings making him look smaller than ever before. Maris wanted to shout, to interrupt, to do something; she could feel the tears on her cheek. But she could not move. Like all the rest, she waited for the traditional first flight.

And Coll at last, with a sharp indrawn breath, kicked off from the cliff.

His last running step was a stumble, and he plunged down out of sight. The crowd rushed forward. By the time the party-goers reached the edge, he had recovered and was climbing slowly up. He made a wide circle out over the ocean, then glided in close to the cliff, then back out again. Sometimes young flyers gave their friends a show, but Coll was no showman. A winged silver wraith, he wandered awkward and a little lost in a sky that was not his home.

Other wings were being broken out; Corm and Shalli and the others prepared to fly. Shortly now they would join Coll in the sky, make a few passes in formation, then leave the land-bound behind and fly off to the Eyrie to spend the rest of the night in celebration of their newest member.

Before any of them could leap, though, the wind changed; Maris felt it with a flyer's perception. And she heard it, a gale of cold that screeched forlorn over the rocky edges of the peak, and most of all she saw it, for out above the waves Coll faltered visibly. He dipped slightly, fought to save himself, went into a sudden spin. Someone gasped. Then, quickly again, he was back in control, and headed back to them. But struggling, struggling. It was a rough wind, angry, pushing him down; the sort of wind a flyer had to coax and soothe and tame. Coll wrestled with it, and it was beating him.

"He's in trouble," Corm said, and the handsome flyer flung out his last wing struts with a snap. "I'll fly guard." With that, he was suddenly aloft.

Too late to be of much help, though. Coll, his wings swaying back and forth as he was buffeted by the sudden turbulence, was headed toward the landing beach. A wordless decision was made, and the party moved as one to meet him, Maris and her father in the lead.

Coll came down fast, too fast. He was not riding the wind, no, he was being pushed. His wings shook as he dropped, and he tilted, so one wingtip brushed the ground while the other pointed up toward the sky. Wrong, wrong, all wrong. Even as they rushed onto the beach, there was a great spraying shower of dry sand and then the sudden horrible sound of metal snapping and Coll was down, lying safe in the sand.

But his left wing was limp and broken.

Russ reached him first, knelt over him, started to work on the straps. The others gathered around. Then Coll rose a little, and they saw that he was shaking, and his eyes were full of tears.

"Don't worry," Russ said, in a mock-hearty voice. "It was only a strut, son, they break all the time. We'll fix it easy. You were a little shaky, but all of us are the first time up, Next time will be better."

"Next time, next time, next time!" Coll said. "I can't do it, I can't do it, Father. I don't *want* a next time! I don't *want* your wings!" He was crying openly now, and his body shook with his sobs.

The guests stood in mute shock, and his father's face grew stern. "You are my son, and a flyer. There will be a next time. And you will learn."

Coll continued to shake and sob, the wings off now, lying unstrapped at his feet, broken and useless at least for now. There would be no flight to the Eyrie tonight.

The father reached out his good arm and took his son by the shoulder, shaking him. "You hear? You *hear?* I won't listen to such nonsense. You fly, or you are no son of mine."

Coll's sudden defiance was all gone now. He nodded, biting back the tears, looked up. "Yes, Father," he said. "I'm sorry. I just got scared out there. I didn't mean to say it." He was only thirteen, Maris remembered as she watched from among the guests. Thirteen and scared and not at all a flyer. "I don't know why I said it. I didn't mean it, really."

And Maris found her voice. "Yes, you did," she said loudly, remembering the way Coll had sung of Raven, remembering the decision she had made. The others turned to look at her with shock, and Shalli put a restraining hand on her arm. But Maris shrugged it off and pushed forward to stand between Coll and his father.

"He did mean it," she said quietly, her voice steady and

sure while her heart trembled. "Couldn't you see, Father? He's not a flyer. He's a good son, and you should be proud of him, but he will never love the wind. I don't care what the law says."

"Maris," Russ said, and there was nothing warm in his voice, only despair and hurt. "You would take the wings from your own brother? I thought you loved him."

A week ago she would have cried, but now her tears were all used up. "I do love him, and I want him to have a long and happy life. He will not be happy as a flyer; he does it just to make *you* proud. Coll is a singer, a good one. Why must you take from him the life he loves?"

"I take nothing," Russ said coldly. "Tradition . . ."

"A stupid tradition," a new voice interjected. Maris looked for her ally, and saw Barrion pushing through the crowd. "Maris is right. Coll sings like an angel, and we all saw how he flies." He glanced around contemptuously at the flyers in the crowd. "You flyers are such creatures of habit that you have forgotten how to think. You follow tradition blindly no matter who is hurt."

Almost unnoticed, Corm had landed and folded up his wings. Now he stood before them, his smooth dark face flushed with anger. "The flyers and their traditions have made Amberly great, have shaped the very history of Windhaven a thousand times over. I don't care how well you sing, Barrion, you are not beyond the law." He looked at Russ, and continued. "Don't worry, friend. We'll make your son a flyer such as Amberly has never seen."

But then Coll looked up, and though the tears flowed still, suddenly there was anger in his face too, and decision. *"No!"* he shouted, and his glance at Corm was defiant. "You won't make me anything I don't want to be, I don't care who you are. I'm not a coward, I'm not a baby, but I don't want to fly, I don't, *I DON'T!*" His words were a torrent, all but screamed into the wind, as his secret came pouring out and all the barriers fell at once. "You flyers think you're so good, that everybody else is beneath you, but you're not, you know, you're not. Barrion has been to a dozen islands, and he knows more songs than a dozen flyers, I don't care what you think, Corm. He's not land-bound, he takes ships when everybody else is too scared. You flyers stay clear of scyllas, but Barrion killed one once with a harpoon, from a little wooden boat. I bet you didn't know that.

"I can be like him, too. I have a talent. He's going to the

Outer Islands, and he wants me to come with him, and he told me once that he'd give me his guitar one day. He can take flying and make it beautiful with his words, but he can do the same thing with fishing or hunting or *anything*. Flyers can't do that, but he can. He's *Barrion!* He's a *singer*, and that's just as good as being a flyer. And I can do it too, like I did tonight with Raven." He glared at Corm with hate. "Take your old wings, give them to Maris, she's the flyer," he shouted, kicking at the limp fabric on the ground. "I want to go with Barrion."

There was an awful silence. Russ stood mute for a long time, then looked at his son with a face that was older than it had ever been. "They are not his wings to take, Coll," he said. "They were my wings, and my father's, and his mother's before him, and I wanted—I wanted—" His voice broke.

"You are responsible for this," Corm said angrily, with a glance at Barrion. "And you, yes *you*, his own sister," he added, shifting his gaze to Maris.

"All right, Corm," she said. "We are responsible, Barrion and I, because we love Coll and we want to see him happy—and alive. The flyers have followed tradition too long. Barrion is right, don't you see? Every year bad flyers take the wings of their fathers and die with them, and Windhaven is poorer, for wings cannot be replaced. How many flyers were there in the days of the star sailors? How many are there today? Can't you see what tradition is doing to us? The wings are a trust; they should be worn by those who love the sky, who will fly best and keep them best. Instead, birth is our only measure for awarding wings. Birth, not skill, but a flyer's skill is all that saves him from death, all that binds Windhaven together."

Corm snorted. "This is a disgrace. You are no flyer, Maris, and you have no right to speak of these matters. Your words disgrace the sky and you violate all tradition. If your brother chooses to give up his birthright, very well, then. But he won't make a mockery of our law and give them to anyone he chooses." He looked around, at the shock-still crowd. "Where is the Landsman? Tell us the law!"

The Landsman's voice was slow, troubled. "The law—the tradition—but this case is so special, Corm. Maris has served Amberly well, and we all know how she flies. I—"

"The *law*," Corm insisted.

The Landsman shook his head. "Yes, that is my duty,

but—the law says that—that if a flyer renounces his wings then they shall be taken by another flyer from the island, the senior, and he and the Landsman shall hold them until a new wing-bearer is chosen. But Corm, no flyer has ever renounced his wings—the law is only used when a flyer dies without an heir, and here, in this case, Maris is—"

"The law is the law," Corm said.

"And you will follow it blindly," Barrion put in.

Corm ignored him. "I am Amberly's senior flyer, since Russ has passed on the wings. I will take custody, until we find someone worthy of being a flyer, someone who will recognize the honor and keep the traditions."

"No!" Coll shouted. "I want *Maris* to have the wings."

"You have no say in the matter," Corm told him. "You are a land-bound." So saying, he stooped and picked up the discarded, broken wings. Methodically he began to fold them.

Maris looked around for help, but it was hopeless. Barrion spread his hands, Shalli and Helmer would not meet her gaze, and her father stood broken and weeping, a flyer no more, not even in name, only an old cripple. The party-goers, one by one, began to drift away.

The Landsman came to her. "Maris," he started. "I am sorry, I would give the wings to you if I could. The law is not meant for this—not as punishment, but only as a guide. But it's flyers' law, and I cannot go against the flyers. If I deny Corm, Amberly will become like Kennehut and the songs will call me mad."

She nodded. "I understand," she said. Corm, wings under either arm, was stalking off the beach.

The Landsman turned and left, and Maris went across the sand to Russ. "Father—" she began.

He looked up. "You are no daughter of mine," he said, and turned away from her deliberately. She watched the old man moving stiffly away, walking with difficulty, going inland to hide his shame.

Finally the three of them stood alone on the landing beach, wordless and beaten. Maris went to Coll and put her arms around him and hugged him. They held on to each other, both for the moment children seeking comfort they could not give.

"I have a place," Barrion said at last, his voice waking them. They parted groggily, watched as the singer slung his guitar across his shoulders, and followed him home.

For Maris, the days that followed were dark and troubled.

Barrion lived in a small cabin by the harbor, just off a deserted, rotting wharf, and it was there they stayed. Coll was happier than Maris had ever seen him; each day he sang with Barrion, and he knew that he would be a singer after all. Only the fact that Russ refused to see him bothered the boy, and even that was often forgotten. He was young, and he had discovered that many his own age looked on him with guilty admiration, like a rebel, and he gloried in the feeling.

But for Maris, things were not as easy. She seldom left the cabin, except to wander out on the wharf at sunset and watch the fishing boats come in. She could think only of her loss. She was trapped and helpless. She had tried as hard as she could, she had done the right thing, but still her wings were gone. Tradition, like a mad cruel Landsman, had ruled, and now kept her prisoner.

Two weeks after the incident on the beach, Barrion returned to the cabin after a day on the docks, where he went daily to gather new songs from the fishermen of Amberly and sing at wharfside inns. As they ate bowls of hot, meaty stew, he looked at Maris and the boy and said, "I have arranged for a boat. In a month I will sail for the Outer Islands."

Coll smiled eagerly. "Us too?"

Barrion nodded. "You, yes, certainly. And Maris?"

She shook her head. "No."

The singer sighed. "You can gain nothing by staying here. Things will be hard for you on Amberly. Even for me, times are getting difficult. The Landsman moves against me, prompted by Corm, and respectable folk are starting to avoid me. Besides, there is a lot of world to see. Come with us." He smiled. "Maybe I can even teach *you* to sing."

Maris played idly with her stew. "I sing worse than my brother flies, Barrion. No, I can't go. I'm a flyer. I must stay, and win my wings again."

"I admire you, Maris," he said, "but your fight is hopeless. What can you do?"

"I don't know. Something. The Landsman, perhaps. I can go to him. The Landsman makes the law, and he sympathizes. If he sees that it is best for the people of Amberly, then . . ."

"He can't defy Corm. Besides, this is a matter of flyers' law, and he has no control over that. Besides . . ." he hesitated.

"What?"

"There is news. It's all over the docks. They've found a new flyer, or an old one, actually. Devin of Gavora is en route here by boat to take up residence and wear your wings." He watched her carefully, concern written across his face.

"Devin!" She slammed down her fork, and stood. "Have their laws blinded them to common sense?" She paced back and forth across the room. "Devin is a worse flyer than Coll ever was. He lost his own wings when he swooped too low and grazed water. If it hadn't been for a ship passing by, he would be dead. So Corm wants to give him another pair?"

Barrion grinned bitterly. "He's a flyer, and he keeps the old traditions."

"How long ago did he leave?"

"A few days, the word says."

"It's a two-week voyage, easily," Maris said. "If I'm going to act, it must be before he gets here. Once he has worn the wings, they'll be his, and lost to me."

"But Maris," Coll said, "what can you do?"

"Nothing," Barrion said. "Oh, we could steal the wings, of course. Corm has had them repaired, good as new. But where would you go? You'd never find a welcome. Give it up, girl. You can't change flyers' law."

"No?" she said. Suddenly her voice was animated. She stopped pacing and leaned against the table. "Are you sure? Have the traditions *never* been changed? Where did they come from?"

Barrion looked puzzled. "Well, there was the council, just after the Old Captain was killed, when the Landsman-Captain of Big Shotan passed out the new-forged wings. That was when it was decided that no flyer would ever bear a weapon in the sky. They remembered the battle, and the way the old star sailors used the last two sky sleds to rain fire from above."

"Yes," said Maris, "and remember, there were two other councils as well. Generations after that, when another Landsman-Captain wanted to bend the other Landsmen to his will and bring all of Windhaven under his control, he sent the flyers of Big Shotan into the sky with swords to strike at Little Shotan. And the flyers of the other islands met in council and condemned him, after his ghost flyers had vanished. So he was the last Landsman-Captain, and now Big Shotan is just another island."

"Yes," Coll said, "and the third council was when all the

flyers voted not to land on Kennehut, after the Mad Landsman killed the Flyer-Who-Brought-Bad News."

Barrion was nodding. "All right. But no council has been called since then. Are you sure they would assemble?"

"Of course," said Maris. "It is an unwritten law, one of Corm's precious traditions. Any flyer can call a council. And I could present my case there, to all the flyers of Windhaven, and . . ."

She stopped. Barrion looked at her and she looked back, the same thought on their minds.

"Any flyer," he said, the emphasis unvoiced.

"But I am not a flyer," Maris said. She slumped into her chair. "And Coll has renounced his wings, and Russ—even if he would see us—has passed them on. Corm would not honor our request. The word would not go out."

"You could ask Shalli," Coll suggested. "Or wait up on flyers' cliff, or . . ."

"Shalli is too much junior to Corm, and too frightened," Barrion said. "I hear the stories. She's sad for you, like the Landsman, but she won't break tradition. Corm might try to take her wings as well. And the others—who could you count on? And how long could you wait? Helmer visits most often, but he's as hidebound as Corm. Jamis is too young, and so on. You'd be asking them to take quite a risk." He shook his head doubtfully. "It will not work. No flyer will speak for you, not in time. In two weeks Devin will wear your wings."

All three of them were silent. Maris stared down at her plate of cold stew, and thought. No way, she asked, is there really no way? Then she looked at Barrion. "Earlier," she began, very carefully, "you mentioned something about stealing the wings . . ."

The wind was cold and wet, angry, lashing at the waves; against the eastern sky a storm was building. "Good flying weather," Maris said. The boat rocked gently beneath her.

Barrion smiled, pulled his cloak a little tighter to shut out the damp. "Now if only you could do some flying," he said.

Her eyes went to the shore, where Corm's dark wood house stood against the trees. A light was on in an upper window. Three days, Maris thought sourly. He should have been called by now. How long could they afford to wait? Each hour brought Devin closer, the man who would take her wings.

"Tonight?" she asked Barrion.

He shrugged. He was cleaning his nails with a long dagger, intent on the task. "You would know better than I," he said without looking up. "The light tower is still dark. How often are flyers called?"

"Often," Maris said, thoughtful. But would Corm be called? They had already floated offshore two nights, hoping for a summons that would call him away from the wings. Perhaps the Landsman was using Shalli until such time as Devin arrived. "I don't like it," she said. "We have to do something."

Barrion slid his dagger into its sheath. "I could use that on Corm, but I won't. I'm with you, Maris, and your brother is all but a son to me, but I'm not going to kill for a pair of wings. No. We wait until the light tower calls to Corm, then break in. Anything else is too chancy."

Kill, Maris thought. Would it come to that, if they forced their way in while Corm was still at home? And then she knew it would. Corm was Corm, and he *would* resist. She'd been inside his home once. She remembered the set of crossed obsidian knives that gleamed upon his wall. There must be another way.

"The Landsman isn't going to call him," she said. She knew it, somehow. "Not unless there's an emergency."

Barrion studied the clouds building up in the east. "So?" he said. "We can hardly make an emergency."

"But we can make a signal," Maris said.

"Hmmmm," the singer replied. He considered the idea. "Yes, we could, I suppose." He grinned at her. "Maris, we break more laws every day. It's bad enough we're going to steal your wings, but now you want me to force my way into the light tower and send a phoney call. It's a good thing I'm a singer, or we'd go down as the greatest criminals in the history of Amberly."

"How does your being a singer prevent that?"

"Who do you think writes the songs? I'd rather make us all into heroes."

They traded smiles.

Barrion took the oars and rowed them quickly into shore, to a marshy beach hidden by the trees but not far from Corm's home. "Wait here," he said, as he climbed out into the knee-deep, lapping water. "I'll go to the tower. Go in and get the wings as soon as you see Corm leave." Maris nodded her agreement.

For nearly an hour she sat alone in the gathering darkness, watching lightning flash far off to the east. Soon the storm would be on them; already she could feel the bite of the wind. Finally, up on the highest hill of Amberly, the great beacon of the Landsman's light tower began to blink in a staccato rhythm. Barrion knew the correct signal somehow, Maris suddenly realized, even though she'd forgotten to tell him. The singer knew a lot, more than she'd ever given him credit for. Perhaps he wasn't such a liar after all.

Short minutes later, she was lying in the weeds a few feet from Corm's door, head low, sheltered by the shadows and the trees. The door opened, and the dark-haired flyer came out, his wings slung over his back. He was dressed warmly. Flying clothes, thought Maris. He hurried down the main road.

After he had gone, it was a simple task to find a rock, sneak around to the side of the building, and smash in a window. Luckily, Corm was unmarried, and he lived alone; that is, if he didn't have a woman with him tonight. But they'd been watching the house carefully, and no one had come and gone except a cleaning woman who worked during the day.

Maris brushed away loose glass, then vaulted up onto the sill and into the house. All darkness inside, but her eyes adjusted quickly. She had to find the wings, *her* wings, before Corm returned. He'd get to the light tower soon enough and find it was a false alarm. Barrion wasn't going to hang around to be caught.

The search was short. Just inside the front door, on the rack where he hung his own wings between flights, she found hers. She took them down carefully, with love and longing, and ran her hands over the cool metal to check the struts. At last, she thought. And then, they will never take them from me again.

She strapped them on, and ran. Through the door and into the woods, a different road than the one that Corm had taken. He would be home soon, to discover the loss. She had to get to flyers' cliff.

It took her a good half-hour, and twice she had to hide in the underbrush on the side of the road to avoid meeting another nighttime traveler. And even when she reached the cliff, there were people nearby, two men from the flyers' lodge down on the landing beach, so Maris had to hide behind some rocks, and wait, and watch their lanterns.

She was stiff from crouching and shivering from the cold

when, far over the sea, she spied another pair of silvered wings, coming down fast. The flyer circled once low above the beach, jerking the lodge men to attention, then came in smoothly for a landing. As they unstrapped her, Maris saw it was Anni of Culhall, with a message, no doubt. Her chance was here, then. The lodge men would escort Anni to the Landsman.

When they had gone off with her, Maris scrambled to her feet, and quickly moved up the rocky path to flyers' cliff. It was a cumbersome, slow task to unfold her own wings, but she did it, though the hinges on the left wing were stiff and she had to snap it five times before the final strut flung out. Corm didn't even take care of them, she thought bitterly.

Then, forgetting that, forgetting everything, she ran and jumped into the winds.

The gathering gale hit her almost like a fist, but she rolled with the punch, shifting and twisting until she caught a strong updraft and began to climb, quickly now, higher and higher. Close at hand, lightning flashed behind her, and she felt a brief tremor of fear. But then it was still. Again, she was flying, and if she was burned from the sky, well, no one would mourn her on Amberly save Coll, and there could be no finer death. She banked and climbed still higher, and despite herself she let out a laughing whoop of joy.

And a voice answered her. "Turn!" it said, shouting, hot with anger. Startled, losing the feel for an instant, she looked up and behind.

Lightning slashed the sky over Amberly again, and in its light the night-shadowed wings above her gleamed noonday-silver. From out of the clouds, Corm was coming down on her fast.

He was shouting as he came. "I knew it was you," he said. But the wind blew every third word away from her. ". . . had to . . . behind it . . . never went home . . . cliff . . . waited. *Turn!* I'll force you down! Land-bound!" That last she heard, and she laughed at him.

"Try, then," she yelled at him, defiantly. "Show me what a flyer you are, Corm! Catch me if you can!" And then, still laughing, she tilted a wing and veered out from under his dive, and he kept on down as she rose, still shouting as he passed her.

A thousand times she'd played with Dorrel, chasing one another around the Eyrie, tag games in the sky, but now, this time, the chase was deadly earnest. Maris toyed with the winds, looking only for speed and altitude, and instinctively she found the currents and rose higher and faster. Far below now, Corm checked his fall, tilted up, banked and came at her from below. But by the time he reached her height, she was far ahead. She intended to stay that way. This was no game, and she could afford no risks. If he got above her, he was angry enough to begin forcing her down, inch by inch, until he pressed her right into the ocean. He would regret it afterwards, grieve for the lost wings, but Maris knew that he would do it nonetheless. The traditions of the flyers meant that much to him. Idly, she wondered, how would she have acted, a year ago, toward a man who stole a set of wings?

Now Amberly was lost behind them, and the only land in sight was the flashing light tower of Culhall off to the right and low on the horizon. And that too was soon gone, and there was nothing but black sea below and sky above. And Corm, relentless, still behind her, outlined against the storm. But—Maris looked back and blinked—he seemed smaller. Was she gaining on him? Corm was a skilled flyer, that much she was sure of. He had always performed well for Western in the competitions, while she was not allowed to compete. And yet, now, clearly, the gap was widening.

Lightning flashed once more, and thunder rolled ominous across the sea a few seconds later. From below a scylla roared back at the storm, hearing in the boom an angry challenge. But for Maris, it meant something else indeed. The timing, the timing; the storm was growing more distant. She was heading northwest, the storm due west perhaps; at any rate, she was angling out from beneath it.

Something soared inside her. She banked and flipped just for the joy of it, did a showman's loop from sheer exultation, jumping from current to current like an acrobat of the sky. The winds were hers now; nothing could go wrong.

Corm closed in while Maris was playing, and when she came out of her loop and began to climb again, she saw him close at hand and dimly heard his shouts. He was yelling something about her not being able to land, about her being an outcast with her stolen wings. Poor Corm! What did he know?

Maris dove, until she could all but taste the salt, until she could hear the waters rolling a few feet below. If he would kill her, if he would force her into the waves, well, she had made herself vulnerable now, as vulnerable as she could be.

She was skimming; all he had to do was catch up, get above her, swoop.

She knew, she *knew*, he could not do it, no matter how much he might like to. By the time she flew out from under the churning cloud cover, into a clear night sky where the stars winked on her wings, Corm was only a tiny dot behind her, dwindling fast. Maris waited until she could see his wings no longer, then caught a new upwind and changed course to the south, knowing that Corm would continue blindly ahead until he gave up and circled back to Amberly.

She was alone with her wings and the sky, and briefly, there was peace.

Hours later, the first lights of Laus burned at her through the dark; flaming beacons set atop the rocky island's Old Fortress. Maris angled toward them, and soon the half-ruined bulk of the ancient castle sat before her, dead but for its lights.

She flew straight over it, across the breadth of the small mountainous island, to the landing strip on the sandy southwest spur. Laus was not populous enough to maintain a flyers' lodge, and for once Maris was thankful of that. There would be no lodge men to greet her or ask her questions. She landed alone and unnoticed in a shower of dry sand, and struggled out of her wings.

At the end of the landing strip, up against the base of flyers' cliff, Dorrel's simple cabin was dark and empty. When he did not answer her knock, Maris opened the unlatched door and entered, calling his name. But the house was silent. She felt a rush of disappointment that quickly changed to nervousness. Where was he? How long would he be gone? What if Corm figured out where she had come and trapped her here, before Dorrel's return?

She set a rush against the banked and dimly glowing coals in the hearth and lit a sand-candle. Then she looked around the small, neat cabin, seeking some clue as to where and how long Dorrel had been gone.

There: tidy Dorrel had left some crumbs of fish cake on his otherwise clean table. She glanced toward a far corner and, yes, the house was truly empty, Anitra gone from her perch. So that was it; Dorrel was out hunting with his nighthawk.

Hoping they had not gone far, Maris took to the air again

in search. She found him resting on a rock in the treacherous shallows of far western Laus, his wings strapped on but folded, Anitra perched on his wrist enjoying a piece of fish she had just caught. Dorrel was talking to the bird and did not see Maris until she swept above him, her wings eclipsing the stars.

Then he stared at her while she circled and dipped dangerously low, and for a moment there was no recognition at all on his blank face.

"Dorrel," she shouted, tension sharpening her voice.

"Maris?" Incredulity broke across his face.

She turned and caught an updraft. "Come onto shore. I have to talk to you."

Dorrel, nodding, stood suddenly and shook the nighthawk free. The bird surrendered her fish reluctantly and climbed into the sky on pale white wings, circling effortlessly and waiting for her master. Maris swung around in the direction she had come.

This time, when she came down in the landing strip, her descent was sudden and clumsy, and she scraped her knees badly. Maris was confused, in turmoil; the tension of the theft, the strain of the long flight after that stretch of days without the sky, the strange mixture of pain and fear and joy the sight of Dorrel had suddenly, unexpectedly given her—it all overwhelmed her, shook her, and she didn't know what to do. Before Dorrel could join her she set to work unstrapping her wings, forcing her mind through the motions with her hands. She wouldn't think yet, she wouldn't let herself think. Blood from her knees trickled maddeningly down her legs.

Dorrel landed beside her, neatly and smoothly. He was shaken by her sudden appearance, but he didn't let his emotions interfere with his flying. It was more than a matter of pride with him: it was almost bred into him, as much an inheritance as his wings were. Anitra found his shoulder as he unstrapped.

He moved toward her and put his arms out. The nighthawk made a bad-tempered noise, but he would still have embraced Maris, regardless of the bird, had she not suddenly thrust her wings into his outstretched hands.

"Here," Maris said. "I'm turning myself in. I stole these wings from Corm, and I'm giving them and myself over to you. I've come to ask you to call a council for me, because you're a flyer and I'm not, and only a flyer can call one."

Dorrel stared at her, confused as someone awakened suddenly out of a heavy sleep. Maris felt impatient with him, and overwhelmingly tired. "Oh, I'll explain," she said. "Let's go home so I can rest."

It was a long walk, but they went most of it in silence and without touching. Only once he said, "Maris—did you really *steal*—"

She cut him off. "Yes. I did." Then she suddenly sighed and moved as if to touch him, but stopped herself. "Forgive me, Dorrel, I didn't mean . . . I'm exhausted, and I suppose I'm frightened. I never thought I'd be seeing you again under such circumstances." Then she fell quiet again and he did not press her, and only Anitra broke the night with her grumbles and mutters at having her fishing ended so soon.

Once home, Maris sank into the one large chair, trying to force herself into relaxation, to make the tensions drain. She watched Dorrel and felt herself grow calmer as he went through his familiar rituals. He put Anitra on her perch and drew the curtains that hung around her (other folks might hood their birds to keep them quiet, but he disapproved of that), built up a fire, and hung a kettle to boil.

"Tea?"

"Yes."

"I'll put kerri blossoms in, instead of honey," he said. "That should relax you."

She felt a sudden flooding of warmth for him. "Thanks."

"Do you want to get out of those clothes? You can slip on my robe."

She shook her head—it would be too much effort to move now—and then she saw that he was gazing at her legs, bare below the short kilt she wore, and frowning with concern.

"You've hurt yourself." He poured warm water from the kettle into a dish, took a rag and some salve and knelt before her. The damp cloth cleaning away the dried blood was gentle as a soft tongue. "Ah, it's not as bad as it looked," he murmured as he worked. "Just your knees—just shallow scrapes. A clumsy landing, dear."

His nearness and his soft touch stirred her, and all tension, fear, and weariness were suddenly gone. One of his hands moved to her thigh and lingered there.

"Dorr," she said softly, almost too transfixed by the moment to speak, and he raised his head and their eyes met, and finally she had come back to him.

"It will work," Dorrel said. "They'll have to see. They can't deny you." They were sitting at breakfast. While Dorrel made eggs and tea, Maris had explained her plan in detail.

Now she smiled and spooned out more of the soft egg. She felt happy and full of hope. "Who'll go first to call a council?"

"Garth, I thought," Dorrel said eagerly. "I'll catch him at home and we'll divide up the nearby islands and branch out. Others will want to help—I just wish you could come, too," he said, and his eyes grew wistful. "It would be nice, flying together again."

"We'll have lots of that, Dorr. *If*—"

"Yes, yes, we'll have lots of time to fly together, but—it would be nice this morning, especially."

"Yes. It'd be nice." She went on smiling and finally he had to smile too. He was just reaching across the table to take her hand, or touch her face, when a sudden knock at the door, loud and authoritative, made them freeze.

Dorrel rose to answer it. Maris in her chair was in full view of the doorway, but there was no point in trying to hide, and there was no second door.

Helmer stood outside, folded wings strapped to his back. He looked straight at Dorrel, but not past him into the cabin at Maris. "Corm has invoked the flyer's right to call a council," he said, his voice flat and strained and overly formal. "To concern the once-flyer Maris of Lesser Amberly who stole the wings of another. Your presence is requested."

"*What?*" Maris stood quickly. "Helmer—*Corm* has called a council? Why?"

Dorrel tossed a glance over his shoulder at her, then looked at Helmer, who was plainly if uncomfortably ignoring Maris.

"Why, Helmer?" he asked, more quietly than Maris had.

"I've told you. And I don't have time to stand here moving the wind with my mouth. I have other flyers to inform, and it's a thick day for flying."

"Wait for me," Dorrel said. "Give me some names, some islands to go to. It will make your task easier."

The corner of Helmer's mouth twitched. "I wouldn't've thought you'd want to go on such a mission, for such a reason. I hadn't intended to ask for your help. But since you offer . . ."

Helmer gave Dorrel terse instructions while the younger flyer rapidly winged himself. Maris paced, feeling restless, awkward, and confused again. Helmer was obviously determined to ignore her, and to save them both embarrassment Maris did not question him again.

Dorrel kissed her and squeezed her tightly before he left. "Feed Anitra for me, and try not to worry. I'll be back before it's been dark too long, I hope."

When the flyers were gone, the house felt stifling. Outside was not much better, Maris discovered as she stood against the door. Helmer had been right, it was not a good day for flying. It was a day to make one think of still air. She shuddered, fearing for Dorrel. But he was too skilled and too smart to need her worry, she thought, trying to reassure herself. And she would go crazy if she sat inside all day imagining possible dangers for him. It was frustrating enough to have to wait here, denied the sky—she looked up at the cloudy-bright overcast. If, after the council, she should be made a land-bound forever—

But there was plenty of time for sorrow in the future, so she resolved not to think about it now. She went back inside the house.

Anitra, a nocturnal flyer, was asleep behind her curtain; the cabin was still and very empty. She wished briefly for Dorrel, to ease her thoughts by sharing them, to speculate with her on why Corm had called the council. Alone, her thoughts went around and around in her head, birds in a trap.

A geechi game sat on top of Dorrel's wardrobe. Maris took it down, and arranged the smooth black and white pebbles in a simple opening pattern, one her mind was comfortable with. Idly she began to move them, playing both sides, shoving the pebbles unthinkingly into new configurations, each suggested by the last, each as inevitable as chance. And she thought: Corm is a proud man; I injured his pride. He is known as a good flyer and I, a fisherman's daughter, stole his wings and outflew him when he pursued me. Now, to regain his pride, he must humble me in some very public, very grand way. Getting the wings back would not be enough for him. No, everyone, every flyer, must be present to see me humbled and declared an outlaw.

Maris sighed. That was it. This was the council to outlaw the land-bound flyer who stole wings—oh, yes, songs would be written about it. But perhaps it made no difference. Even though Corm had stolen a flight on her, the council could still be turned against him. She, the accused, would have the right to speak, to defend herself, to attack senseless tradition. And her chance was the same, Maris knew, the same in Corm's council as it would have been in the one that Dorrel would have summoned. Only now she knew the full extent of Corm's hurt and his anger.

She looked down at the geechi board. The pebbles, white and black, were arrayed across the center of the board, facing each other. Both armies had committed themselves to attacking formations; it was clear that this would be no waiting game. With her next move, the captures would begin.

Maris smiled, and swept the pebbles from the table.

It took a full month for the council to assemble.

Dorrel brought the call to four flyers that first day, and five others the next, and each of those contacted others, and those still others, and so the word went out in ever-widening ripples across the seas of Windhaven. A special flyer was sent off to the Outer Islands, another to desolate Artellia, the great frozen island to the north. Soon, all had heard, and one by one they flew to the meeting.

The site was Greater Amberly. By rights, the council should have been held on Lesser Amberly, home to both Maris and Corm. But the smaller island had no building large enough for such a gathering as this would be, and Greater Amberly did; a huge, dank hall, seldom used.

To it came the flyers of Windhaven. Not all of them, no, for there were always emergencies, and a few still had not received the word, and others were missing on long, dangerous flights; but most of them, the vast majority, and that was enough. In no one's lifetime had there ever been such a gathering. Even the annual competitions at the Eyrie were small compared to this, mere local contests between Eastern and Western. Or so it seemed to Maris then, during the month she waited and watched while the streets of Ambertown filled with laughing flyers.

There was an air of holiday about it all. The early arrivals held drinking bouts each night, to the delight of the local wine merchants, and traded stories and songs, and gossiped endlessly about the council and its outcome. Barrion and other singers kept them entertained by night, while by day they raced and frolicked in the air. The late-comers were greeted riotously as they straggled in. Maris, who had flown back from Laus after getting special leave to use the wings once more, ached to join them. Her friends were all there, and Corm's, and indeed all the wings of Western. The Easterners had come too, many in suits of fur and metal that reminded her irresistibly of the way Raven had dressed on that day so long ago. There were three pale-skinned Artellians, each wearing a silver circlet on his brow; aristocrats from a dark frigid land where flyers were kings as well as messengers. They mingled, brothers and equals, with the red-uniformed flyers of Big Shotan, and the twenty tall representatives of the Outer Islands, and the squadron of sunburnt winged priests from the lush Southern Archipelago who served the Sky God as well as their Landsmen. Seeing them, meeting them, walking among them, the size and breadth and cultural diversity of Windhaven struck Maris as seldom before. She had flown, if only for a short time; she had been one of the privileged few. Yet there were still so many places she had not been. If only she could have her wings again . . .

Finally all those who were coming had arrived. The council was set for dusk; there would be no crowds in the inns of Ambertown tonight.

"You have a chance," Barrion told Maris on the steps of the great hall just before the meeting. Coll was with her too, and Dorrel. "Most of them are in a good mood, after weeks of wine and song. I drift, I talk, I sing, and I know this: they *will* listen to you." He grinned his wolfish grin. "For flyers, that is *quite* unusual."

Dorrel nodded. "Garth and I have talked to many of them. There is a lot of sympathy for you, particularly among the younger flyers. The older delegates, most of them, tend to side with Corm and tradition, but even they do not have their minds completely made up."

Maris shook her head. "The older flyers outnumber the younger ones, Dorr."

Barrion put a fatherly hand on her shoulder. "Then you will have to win them to your side also. After the things I've seen you do already, it should be easy enough." He smiled.

The delegates had all filed inside, and now, from the door behind her, Maris heard the Landsman of Greater Amberly sound the ceremonial drumbeats that signaled the beginning of the council. "We must go," Maris said. Barrion nodded. As a non-flyer, he had been barred from the assembly. He squeezed her shoulder once, for luck, then took his guitar and walked slowly down the steps. Maris, Coll, and Dorrel hurried inside.

The hall was an immense stone pit, ringed by torches. In the center of the sunken floor, a long table had been set up. The flyers sat around it in a semi-circle, on rough stone seats that ascended, tier after tier after tier, to the place where wall met ceiling. Jamis the Senior, his thin face lined by age, sat in the center of the long table. Though a land-bound for several years now, his experience and character were still widely esteemed, and he had come a long way by boat to serve as chairman. On either side of him sat the only two non-flyers admitted; the swarthy Landsman of Greater Amberly and the portly ruler of Lesser. Corm had the fourth seat, at the right-hand end of the table. A fifth chair was empty on the left.

Maris went to it, while Dorrel and Coll climbed the stairs to their places. The drumbeats sounded again, a call for silence. Maris sat and looked around as the room became quiet. Coll had found a seat, high up among the unwinged youths. Many of them had come by boat from nearby islands, to see history be made; but like Coll, they were expected to play no part in the decision. Now they ignored Coll, as might be expected; children eager for the sky could scarcely understand a boy who had willingly given up his wings. He looked dreadfully out of place and lonely, much as Maris felt.

The drums stopped. Jamis the Senior stood, and his deep voice rang over the hall. "This is the first flyers' council in the memory of any here," he said. "Most of you already know the circumstances under which it has been called. My rules will be simple. Corm shall speak first, since he invoked this meeting. Then Maris, whom he accuses, shall have her chance to answer him. Then any flyer or former flyer here may have his say. I ask only that you speak loudly, and name yourself before you talk. Many of us here are strangers to each other." He sat down.

And now Corm stood and spoke into the silence. "I invoked this council by flyers' right," he said, his voice assured and resonant. "A crime has been committed, and its nature and implications are such that it must be answered by us all, by all flyers acting as one. Our decision shall determine our future, as have the decisions of councils past. Imagine what our world should be now if our fathers and mothers before us had decided to bring warfare into the air. The kinship of all flyers would not be—we should be torn apart by petty regional rivalries instead of being properly airborne above the quarrels of the land."

He went on, painting a picture of the desolation that could have followed, should that long-ago council have voted wrongly. He was a good speaker, Maris thought; he spoke like Barrion sang. She shook herself out of the spell Corm was creating, and wondered how she could possibly counter him.

"The problem today is equally as grave," Corm continued, "and your decision will not simply affect one person, for whom you may feel sympathy, but rather all our children for generations to come. Remember that as you listen to the arguments tonight." He looked around, and although his burning eyes did not fall on her, Maris nevertheless felt intimidated.

"Maris of Lesser Amberly has stolen a pair of wings," he said. "The story, I think, is known to all of you"—but Corm told it, nonetheless, from the facts of her birth to the scene on the beach—"and a new bearer was found. But before Devin of Gavora, who is among us now, could arrive to claim his wings, Maris stole them, and fled.

"But this is not the whole of it. Stealing is shameful, but even the theft of wings might not be grounds for a flyers' council. Maris knew she could not hope to keep her wings. She took them not to flee, but rather with the thought of revolting against our most vital traditions. She questions the very foundations of our society. She would open the ownership of the wings to dispute, threaten us with anarchy. Unless we make our disapproval plain, pass judgment on her in council that will go down in history, the facts would easily become distorted. Maris could be remembered as a brave rebel, and not the thief she is."

A twinge went through Maris at that word. Thief. Was that truly what she was?

"She has friends among the singers who would delight in mocking us," Corm was saying, "in writing songs in praise of her daring." And Maris heard in memory Barrion's voice: *I'd rather make us all into heroes.* Her eyes sought out Coll and she saw that he was sitting straighter, with a slight smile on his lips. Singers did indeed have power, if they were good.

"So we must speak out plainly, for all of history, in denouncing what she has done," Corm said. He faced Maris and looked down at her. "Maris, I accuse you of the theft of wings. And I call upon the flyers of Windhaven, met in council, to name you outlaw, and pledge that none will land on any island you call home."

He sat, and in the awful silence that followed Maris knew just how much she had offended him. She had never dreamed he would ask so much. Not content merely to take her wings, he would deny her life itself, force her into friendless exile on some distant empty rock.

"Maris," Jamis said gently. She had not risen. "It is your turn. Will you answer Corm?"

Slowly she got to her feet, wishing for the power of a singer, wishing that even once she could speak with the assurance Corm had in his voice. "I cannot deny the theft," she said, looking up at the rows of blank faces, the sea of strangers. Her voice was steadier than she thought it would be. "I stole the wings out of desperation, because they were my only chance. A boat would have been far too slow, and no one on Amberly was willing to help. I needed to reach a flyer who could call council for me. Once I did that, I surrendered my wings. I can prove this, if—" She looked over at Jamis; he nodded.

Dorrel picked up his cue. Halfway up in the tiered hall, he rose. "Dorrel of Laus," he said loudly. "I vouch for Maris. As soon as she reached me, she gave her wings into my safekeeping, and would not wear them again. I do not call this theft." From around him, there was a chorus of approving murmurs; his family was known and esteemed, his word good.

Maris had scored a point, and now she continued, feeling more confident with every word. "I wanted a council for something I consider very important to us all, and to our future. But Corm beat me to it." She grimaced slightly, unconsciously. And out in the audience she noticed a few smiles on the faces of flyers who were strangers to her. Skepticism? Contempt? Or support, agreement? She had to will her hands to part and lie still by her sides. It would not do to be wringing her hands before them all.

"Corm says I am fighting tradition," Maris continued, "and that's true. He has said this is a terrible thing, but he hasn't said why. He hasn't explained why tradition needs to be defended against me. Just because something has always been done in one way doesn't mean that change is impossible, or undesirable. Did people fly on the home worlds of the star sailors? If not, does that mean it was better *not* to fly? Well, after all, we aren't dauberbirds, that if our beaks get pushed to the ground we keep on walking that way until we fall over and die—we don't have to walk the same path every day—it wasn't bred into *us*."

She heard a laugh from her listeners, and felt elated. She could paint pictures with words even as Corm could! Those silly waddling cave birds had gone from her mind to someone else's and drawn a laugh; she had mentioned breaking tradition, and still they listened. Inspired, she went on.

"We are people, and if we have an instinct for anything, it is the instinct—the will—toward change. Things have always been changing and if we're smart we'll make the changes for ourselves, and for the better, before we're forced into them.

"The tradition of passing the wings on from parent to child has worked fairly well for a long time—certainly, it is better than anarchy, or the older tradition of trial by combat that sprang up in Western during the Days of Sorrow. But it is not the only way, nor is it the perfect way."

"Enough talk!" someone growled. Maris looked around for the source and was startled to see Helmer rise from his seat in the second tier front. The flyer's face was bitter, and he stood with folded arms.

"Helmer," Jamis said firmly, "Maris has the floor."

"I don't care," he said. "She attacks our ways, but she offers us nothing better. And for good reason. This way has worked for so many years because there *is* none better. It may be hard, yes. It's hard for you because you weren't born to a flyer. Sure, it's hard. But have you another way?"

Helmer, she thought as he sat. Of course, his anger made sense, he was one whom this tradition would soon hurt—was hurting. Still young, he would be a land-bound in less than a year, when his daughter came of age and took his wings. He had accepted the loss as inevitable, perhaps, as a rightful part of an honored tradition. But now Maris attacked the tradition, the only thing that gave nobility to Helmer's sacrifice-to-come. If things remained unchanged, Maris wondered briefly, would Helmer in time hate his own daughter for her wings? And Russ . . . if he had not been injured . . . if Coll had not been born . . .

"Yes," Maris said loudly, suddenly realizing that the room was silently awaiting her reply. "Yes, I do have a way, I would never have presumed to call a council if—"

"You didn't!" someone shouted, and others laughed. Maris felt herself grow hot and hoped she was not blushing.

Jamis slapped the table, hard. "Maris of Lesser Amberly is speaking," he said, loudly. "The next one who interrupts her will be ejected!"

Maris gave him a grateful smile. "I propose a new way, a better way," she said. "I propose that the right to wear wings be *earned*. Not by birth or by age, but by the one measure that truly counts—by skill!" And as she spoke, the idea sprang suddenly into her head, more elaborate, more complex, more *right* than her vague concept of a free-for-all. "I propose a flying academy, open to all, to every child who dreams of wings. The standards would be very high, of course, and many would be sent away. But all would have the right to try—the son of a fisherman, the daughter of a singer, or a weaver—everyone could dream, hope. And for those who passed all the tests, then there would be a final test. At our annual competition, they could challenge any flyer of their choice. And, if they were good enough, good enough to outfly him, then they would win his wings!

"The best flyers would always keep the wings, this way. And a defeated flyer, well, he could wait for next year and try to win back his wings from the man who had taken them. Or he could challenge someone else, some poorer flyer. No flyer could afford to be lazy, no one who did not love the sky would have to fly, and . . ." she looked at Helmer, whose face was unreadable. "And more, even the children of flyers would have to challenge to win the sky. They would claim their parent's wings only when they were ready, when they could actually fly better than their father or their mother. No flyer would become land-bound just because he'd married young and had a child come of age while he should, by all that is just and right, still be in the sky. Only skill would be important, not birth, not age—the *person*, not tradition!"

She paused, on the verge of blurting out her own story, of what it was like to be a fisherman's daughter and know the sky could never be hers—the pain, the longing. But why waste her breath? These were all born flyers, and she would not wring sympathy from them for the land-bounds they held in contempt. No, it was important that the next Woodwings born on Amberly have a chance to fly, but it was no good as an argument. She had said enough. She had set it all before them, and the choice was theirs. She glanced briefly at Helmer, at the odd smile flickering over his face, and she knew with dead certainty that his vote was hers. She had just given him a chance to reclaim his life, without being cruel to his daughter. Satisfied, smiling, Maris sat.

Jamis the Senior looked over at Corm.

"That sounds very nice," he said. Smiling, in control, Corm did not even bother to stand. At the sight of his calm, Maris felt all her painfully piled-up hope slip away. "A nice dream for a fisherman's daughter, and it's understandable. Perhaps you don't understand about the wings, Maris. How do you expect families who have flown since—since *forever*—to put their wings up for grabs, to pass them on to strangers? Strangers who without tradition or family pride may not care for them properly, may not respect them? Do you truly think any of us would hand over our heritage to an impudent land-bound? Instead of our own children?"

Maris' temper flared. "You expected me to give *my* wings to Coll, who could not fly as well as I."

"They were never your wings," Corm said.

Her lips tightened; she said nothing.

"If you thought they were, that was your folly," Corm said. "Think: if wings are passed from person to person like a cloak, if they are held for only a year or two, what sort of pride would their owners have in them? They would be—borrowed—not owned, and everyone knows a flyer must own his wings, or he is not a flyer at all. Only a land-bound would wish such a life on us!"

Maris felt the sentiments of the audience shifting with each of Corm's words. He piled his arguments on top of each other so glibly that they all slipped away from her before she'd had a chance to get at them. She had to answer him, but how, *how?* The attachment of a flyer to his wings was nearly as strong as his attachment to his feet, she couldn't deny that, she couldn't fight it. She remembered her own anger when she felt Corm had not cared for her wings properly, and yet, they were never hers at all, only her father's, her brother's.

"The wings are a trust," she blurted out. "Even now a flyer knows he must pass them on, in time, to his child."

"That is quite different," Corm said tolerantly. "Family is not the same as strangers, and a flyer's child is not a land-bound."

"This is something too important to be silly about blood ties!" Maris flashed at him, her voice rising. "Listen to yourself, Corm! Listen to the snobbery that has been allowed to grow in you, in other flyers, listen to your contempt for the land-bound, as if they could help what they are with the laws of inheritance as they now stand!" Her words were angry, and the audience grew perceptibly more hostile; she would lose it all if she championed the land-bound against the flyers, she suddenly realized.

Maris willed herself to be calm. "We *do* have pride in our wings," she said, consciously returning to her strongest arguments. "And that pride, if it is strong enough, should make sure we keep them. Good flyers will keep the sky. If challenged, they will not be defeated easily. If defeated, they will come back. And they will have the satisfaction of knowing that the flyer who takes their wings is good, of knowing that their replacement will bring honor to the wings and use them well, whether he is their son or someone else's."

"The wings are meant to be—" Corm began, but Maris would not let him finish.

"The wings are *not* meant to be lost in the sea," she said, "and clumsy flyers, flyers who have taken no care to be really good because they've never had to, *these* are the flyers who have lost wings for us all. Some hardly deserved the name of flyer. And what of the children who are really too young for the sky, though they may be of age technically? They panic, fly foolishly, and die, taking their wings with them." She glanced quickly at Coll. "Or how about the ones who were not meant to fly at all? Being born of a flyer doesn't mean you'll have his skill. My own—Coll, whom I love as a brother and a son, *he* was never meant to be a flyer. The wings were his, yet I couldn't give them to him—didn't want to give them to him—oh, even if he *had* wanted them, I wouldn't have wanted to give them up—"

"Your system won't change that," someone shouted.

Maris shook her head. "No, it wouldn't. I still wouldn't be *happy* about losing my wings, but if I were bested, well, I could stay on at the academy, train, wait for next year and try to get them back. Oh, nothing is going to be *perfect*, don't you see, because there aren't enough wings, and that's going to get worse, not better. But we must try to stop it, stop all the wings that are lost each year, stop sending out unqualified flyers, stop losing so many. There will still be accidents, we'll still have dangers, but we won't lose wings and flyers because of poor judgment and fear and lack of skill."

Exhausted, Maris ran out of words, but her speech had stirred the audience, moved it back toward her. A dozen hands were up. Jamis pointed, and a solidly-built Shotaner rose from the mass.

"Dirk of Big Shotan," he said, in a low voice, and then he repeated it again when the flyers in the back shouted "Louder! Louder!" His speech was awkward and self-conscious. "I just wanted to say—I've been sitting here, and listening—I never expected to hear anything like this, just to vote on an outlawing, but—" He shook his head, clearly in difficulty getting out his words. "Oh, be *damned*," he said finally. "Maris is right. I'm half ashamed to say it, but I shouldn't be, 'cause it's the truth, and I don't *want* my son to have my wings. He's a good boy, mind you, and I love him, but he has attacks now and again, you know, the shaking sickness. He can't fly like that, but he's growed up thinking of nothing else, and next year when he's thirteen he'll expect my wings, and with things like they are I'll give them to him, and he'll fly off and die and then I won't have no son and I won't have no wings and I might as well die too. No!" He sat down.

Several people shouted support. Maris, heartened, looked over at Corm, and saw that his smile was flickering. Suddenly he had doubts.

A familiar friend rose then, and smiled at her from above. "I'm Garth of Skulny," he said. "I'm with Maris too!" Another speaker backed her, then another, and Maris smiled. Dorrel had scattered friends all over the audience and now they were trying to stampede the assembly her way. And it seemed to be working! For, in between the endorsements from flyers she had known for years, total strangers stood to voice their support. Had they won, then? Corm clearly looked worried.

"You recognize what is wrong with our way, but I think your academy is not the answer." The words jolted Maris out of her complacent optimism. The speaker was a tall, blonde woman, a leading flyer from the Outer Islands. "There is a reason for our tradition and we should not weaken it, or our children may go back to the idiocy of trial by combat. What we must do is teach our children better. We must teach them to have *more* pride, and we must build the needed skills in them from the time they are very small. This is as my mother taught me, and as I am teaching my son. Perhaps a test of some sort is necessary—your idea of a challenge is good." Her mouth twisted wryly. "I admit, I do not look forward to the day, which comes too quickly, when I must give up my wings to Vard. Both of us will be too young, I think, when that day comes. That he should have to compete with me, to prove himself as good—no, a *better* flyer—than I am, yes, that is an excellent idea."

Other flyers in the hall were nodding in agreement. Yes, yes, of course, why hadn't they seen what a good idea some sort of testing would be? Everyone knew that the coming-of-age was rather arbitrary, that some were still children when they took on wings, others full adults. Yes, let the youngsters prove themselves as flyers first . . . the tide swept the assembly.

"But this academy," the speaker said gently. "That is not necessary. We birth enough new flyers among ourselves. I know your background and I can understand your feelings, but I cannot share them. It would not be wise." She sat down, and Maris felt her heart sink with her. That had done it, she thought. Now they will vote for a test, but the sky will still be closed to those born of the wrong parents, the flyers would reject the most important part. So close, she had almost done it, but still not close enough.

A gaunt man in silk and silver stood. "Arris, flyer and Prince of Artellia," he said, his eyes ice blue beneath his silver crown. "I vote with my sister from the Outer Islands. My children are of royal blood, born and bred to wings. It would be a joke to force them to fly in races with commoners. But a test, to see when they are worthy, now *that* is an idea worthy of a flyer."

He was followed by a dark woman all in leather. "Zeva-kul of Deeth in the Southern Archipelago," she began. "Each year I fly messages for my Landsman, but I also serve the Sky God, like all of the upper castes. The concept of passing wings to a lower one, a soil-child, possibly an unbeliever—*no!*"

Other echoes came, and rolled across the hall:

"Joi, of Stormhammer-the-Outermost. I say yes, make us fly to earn our wings, but only against the children of flyers."

"Tomas, of Little Shotan. Children of the land-born could never learn to love the sky as we do. It would be a waste of time and money to build this academy Maris speaks of. But I'm for a test."

"Crain of Poweet, and I'm with these others. Why should we have to compete with the children of fisherpeople? They don't let us compete for their boats, do they?" The hall rocked with laughter, and the older flyer grinned. "Yes, a joke, a good one. Well, brothers, we would be a joke, this academy would be a joke if it let in riff-raff of any birth at all. Wings belong to flyers and over the years it has remained that way because it is the way it is. The other people are content, and very few of them *really* want to fly. For most it is only a passing whim, or too frightening to think about. Why should we encourage idle dreams? They are not flyers, were never meant to be, and they can lead worthwhile lives in some other . . ."

Maris listened in disbelief and rising anger, infuriated by the smug self-righteousness of his tone . . . and then she saw with horror that other flyers, including some of the younger ones, were bobbing their heads complacently in time with his words. Yes, they were better because they were born of flyers, yes, they were superior and did not wish to mix, yes, yes. Suddenly it did not matter that in times past, *she* had felt much the same way of the land-bound. Suddenly all she could think of was her father, her blood-father, the dead fisherman she scarcely remembered. Memories she had thought gone came back; sensory impressions, chiefly—stiff clothes that reeked of salt and fish, warm hands, rough but gentle, that smoothed her hair and wiped tears off her cheeks after her mother had scolded her—and stories he had told, in his low voice, tales of things he had seen that day in his little skiff—what the birds had looked like, racing away from a sudden storm, how the moonfish leaped toward the night sky, how the wind felt and the waves sounded against the boat. Her father had been an observant man and a brave one, daring the ocean every day in his frail boat, and Maris knew in her hot rage that he was the inferior of no one here, of no one on Windhaven.

"You snobs," she said sharply, not caring anymore whether it would help or hurt the vote. "All of you. Thinking how superior you are, just because you were born of a flyer and inherited wings through no goodness of your own. You think you inherited your parent's skill? Well, how about the other half of your heritage? Or were all of you born of flyer marriages?" She jabbed an accusing finger at a familiar face on the third tier. "You, Sar, you were nodding just then. Your father was a flyer, yes, but your mother was a trader, and born of fisherfolk. Do you look down on them? What if your mother confessed that her husband was not your real father—what if she told you that you could blame your birth on a trader she met in the east? What then? Would you feel obliged to give up your wings and seek some other life?"

Moon-faced Sar only gaped at her; never a quick man, he couldn't understand why she had singled him out. Maris withdrew her finger and launched her anger against them all.

"My true father was a fisherman, a fine brave honest man who never wore wings and never wanted them. But if, *if* he had been chosen to be a flyer, he would have been the best of all! Songs would be sung of him, celebrating him! If we inherit our talent from our parents, look at me. My mother can spin and gather oysters. I cannot. My father could not fly. I can. And some of you know how good I am—better than some who were born to it." She turned and glanced down the length of the table. "Better than you, Corm," she said in a voice that carried all through the great hall. "Or have you forgotten?"

Corm glared up at her, his face flushed with anger, a thick vein bulging in his neck. He said nothing. Maris turned back to the hall. Her voice softened, and she looked out on them with false solicitude. "Are you afraid?" she asked them. "Have you hung onto your wings only on the strength of a pretense? Are you afraid that all the grubby little fisherchildren will come and snatch them away from you, prove themselves better flyers than you and make you all look fools?"

Then all her words were gone, and her anger. And Maris sat back in her chair, and silence hung heavy in the great stone hall. Finally a hand went up, and then another, but Jamis only stared blankly ahead, his face thoughtful. No one moved until at last he stirred himself, as if from sleep, and gestured at someone in the crowd.

High up against the wall, a one-armed man stood alone in the flickering yellow torchlight. The assembly turned to watch him.

"Russ, of Lesser Amberly," he began. His tone was gentle. "My brothers, Maris is right. We have been fools. And none of us has been so big a fool as I.

"Not long ago, I stood on a beach and said I had no daughter. Tonight, I wish I could have back those words, I wish I still had the right to call Maris my daughter. She has made me very proud. But she isn't mine. No, as she said, she was born of a fisherman, a better man than I. All I did was love her for a bit, and teach her how to fly. It didn't take much teaching, you know. She was always so eager. My little Woodwings. There was nothing could stop her, nothing. Not even me, when like a fool I tried to, after Coll was born.

"Maris is the finest flyer on Amberly, and my blood has nothing to do with it. Only her desire matters, only her dream. And if you, my flyer brothers, if you have such disdain for the children of the land-bound, then it is a shaming thing for you to fear them. Have you so little faith in your own children? Are you so certain that they could not keep their wings, against a fisherboy's hungry challenge?"

Russ shook his head. "I don't know. I'm an old man, and things have been awful confused lately. But I know this much; if I still had my arm, no one would take *my* wings from me, not even if his father was a nighthawk. And no one will ever take Maris' wings until she is ready to set them down. No. If you truly teach your children to fly well, they will keep the sky. If you have the pride you boast of, you'll live up to it, and prove it, by letting the wings be worn only by those who have earned them, only by those who have proven themselves in the air."

Russ sat down again, and the darkness at the top of the hall swallowed him up. Corm began to say something, but Jamis the Senior silenced him. "We have had enough from you," the chairman said. Corm blinked in surprise.

"I think *I* will say something," Jamis said. "And then we will vote. Russ has spoken wisdom for all of us, but one thought I must add. Are we not, each of us, descended from the star sailors? All of Windhaven is family, really. And there is none among us who cannot find a flyer in his family tree, if he goes back far enough. Think of that, my friends. And remember that while your eldest child may wear your wings and fly, his younger brother and sisters and all their children for generations after will be land-bound. Should we really deny them the wind forever, simply because their ancestors were second-born, instead of first?" Jamis smiled. "Perhaps I should add that I was my mother's second son. My elder brother died in a storm six months before he was to take his wings. A small thing, that. Don't you think?"

The chairman looked around, at the two Landsmen who flanked him on either side, who had sat silently through all the proceedings, quieted by flyers' law. He whispered first to one, then to the other, and nodded.

"We find that Corm's proposal, to name Maris of Lesser Amberly an outlaw, is out of order," Jamis said. "We will now vote on Maris' proposal, to establish a flyers' academy open to all. I vote in favor."

After that, there was no more doubt.

Afterwards, Maris felt slightly in shock, giddy with victory, yet somehow not able to believe that it was really over, that she did not have to fight anymore. The air outside the hall was clean and wet, the wind blowing steadily from the east. She stood on the steps and savored it, while friends and strangers crowded about her, wanting to talk. Dorrel kept his arm around her, and did not ask questions or express amazement; he was restful to lean against. What now? she wondered. Home again? Where was Coll? Perhaps he'd gone to fetch Barrion and bring the boat.

The crowd around her parted. Russ stood there, Jamis at

his side. Her stepfather was holding a pair of wings. "Maris," he said.

"Father?" Her voice was trembling.

"This is how it should have been all along," he said, smiling at her. "I would be proud if you would let me call you daughter again, after all that I have done. I would be even prouder if you would wear my wings."

"You've won them," Jamis said. "The old rules don't apply, and you're certainly qualified. Until we get the academy going, there's no one to wear them except you and Devin. And you took better care of these than Devin ever did of his."

Her hands went out to take the wings from Russ. They were hers again. She was smiling, no longer tired, buoyed by the weight of them in her hands, the familiarity of them. "Oh, Father," she said, and then, weeping, she and Russ embraced each other.

When the tears were gone, they all went to flyers' cliff, quite a crowd of them. "Let's fly to the Eyrie," she said to Dorrel. Then there was Garth, just beyond—she had not noticed him in the crowd before. "Garth! You come too. We'll have a party!"

"Yes," Dorrel said, "but is the Eyrie the place for it?"

Maris flushed. "Oh, of course not!" She glanced around at the crowd. "No, we'll go back to our house, on Lesser, and *everyone* can come, us and Father and the Landsman and Jamis, and Barrion will sing for us, if we can find him, and"—and then she saw Coll, running toward her, his face alight.

"Maris! Maris!" He ran to her and hugged her enthusiastically, then broke away grinning.

"Where did you go?"

"Off with Barrion, I had to, I'm writing a song. Just got the start of it now, but it will be good, I can feel it, it really will be. It's about you."

"Me?"

He was obviously proud of himself. "Yes. You'll be famous. Everyone will sing it and everyone will know about you."

"They already do," Dorrel said. "Believe me."

"Oh, but I mean forever. For as long as this song is sung they'll know about you—the girl who wanted wings so much she changed the world."

And perhaps it was true, Maris thought later, as she

strapped on her wings and rose into the wind with Dorrel and Garth by her side. But to have changed the world didn't seem half as important nor half as real as the wind in her hair, the familiar pull of muscles as she rose, riding the beloved currents she had thought might be lost to her forever. She had her wings again, she had the sky; she was whole now and she was happy.

THE ENGINEER AND THE EXECUTIONER

by Brian M. Stableford

A devilishly conceived story by the very well-liked and multi-talented author of the "Space Pilot Grainger" space opera and the avant-garde "Deus Irae" trilogy. Genetic engineering combined with justice. . . .

"My life," said the engineer. "It's mine. Can you understand that?"

"I understand," replied the executioner calmly.

"I created it," persisted the little man with the spectacles and the unsteady eyes. "I made it, with my own hands. It wasn't all the creation of my own imagination. Other men can take credit for the actual *plan*, and the theory which allowed them to make the plan. But *I* made it. It was me who put the genes together, sculptured the chromosomes, put the initial cell together. Mine was the real job. I gave the time, the concentration, the determination. The others played with ideas, but I actually built their life-system. I made a dream come true. But you can't understand how I feel about it."

"I understand," repeated the robot. His red eyes shone unblinking from its angular head. He really did understand.

"Look at it," said the little man, waving an arm towards the great concave window that was one wall of the room. "Look at it and tell me it's not worth anything. It's mine, remember. It all grew from what I built. It all evolved from the cells I created. It's going its own way now. It has been for years. But I put it on that road."

The man and the robot stared through the glass. Beyond the window was the hollow interior of Asteroid Lamarck. From space, Lamarck looked like any other asteroid. It had crater-scars and boulders and lots of dust. But it was hollow, and inside it was a tightly sealed, carefully controlled, Earth-simulation environment. It had air, and water—carefully transported from Earth—and light from the great batteries which trapped solar energy on the outside of the planetoid and released it again on the inside.

The light was pale and pearly. It waxed and waned as the asteroid turned on its axis. At this particular moment it shone bright and clear—it was the middle of inner-Lamarck's day.

It showed the edge of a great forest of silver, shimmering things like wisps of cobweb. The things were so slight and filmy that it seemed as though one ought to be able to see a long way, but in fact clear vision was lost within a hundred metres of the observation window.

Half-hidden by the silvery web-work were other growths of different colours and species. There were red ones like sea anemones that moved their tentacles in a slow, rhythmic dance, as though fishing for prey too tiny to be seen by human eyes. There were pale spheres of lemon yellow mottled with darker colours, suspended within the framework of the silver filaments. There were tall, ramrod-straight spikes of varying colours which grew in geometrically regular clumps at random intervals.

There were things which moved too—airborne puffballs and tiny beings like tropical fish which floated in the gigantic bowl of air. There seemed to be no crawling life, nothing that walked. Everything mobile flew or floated. The shell of the asteroid was so thin that there was practically no gravity in the vast chamber. There was no up and down. There was only surface and lumen.

"The life-system is somewhere between community, organism and cell," said the engineer. "It possesses certain characteristics of each. The method of reproduction employed by the life-system is so unique as to make its strict classification impossible by means of the terms we apply to types of Earth organic material. It is completely closed. Light is the only thing which comes in from the outside, to provide the energy which keeps the system in operation. Water, air, minerals are all recycled. There is no more organic matter there than there has ever been. Everything is used and reused as the life-system evolves and improves. As it grows, it changes, day by day it evolves. It was designed to evolve, to mutate and adapt at a terrific pace. The cycle of its elements is a spiral rather than a circle. Nothing ever returns to a former state. Every generation is a new species, nothing ever reproduces itself. What I have built here is ultra-evolution—evolution which is not caused by natural selection. My life-system exhibits true Lamarckian evolution. My life is better than the life which was spawned on Earth. Don't you see why it's so important, so wonderful?"

"I do," said the robot.

"It's the most wonderful thing we have ever made," continued the little man dreamily. "It is the greatest of our achievements. And I built it. It's mine."

"I know," said the executioner, irrelevantly.

"You don't know," said the little man. "What can you know? You're metal. Hard, cold metal. You don't reproduce. Your kind has no evolution. What do you know about life-systems? You can't know what it's like to live and change, to dream and build. How can you claim to know what I mean?"

"I try to understand."

"You came to destroy it all! You came to send Lamarck toppling into the sun, to burn my world and my life into cinders. You were sent to commit murder. How can a murderer claim to understand life? Life is sacred."

"I am not the murderer," said the robot calmly. "It was the people who sent me who made the decision. Real, live people. They must have understood, but they took the decision. Metal doesn't make decision. Metal doesn't murder. I only came to do what I was told to do."

"They can't tell you to kill me," said the bespectacled man, in a low, petulant voice. "They can't make you destroy my work. They can't throw me into the sun. It is against the law to commit murder. Robots can't break the law."

"Sometimes the law has to be ignored," quoted the robot. "It was considered too dangerous to permit Asteroid Lamarck to exist. It was held that the dangerous experiment begun here should be obliterated with all possible speed, and that no possibility of contamination should be tolerated.

"It was held that Asteroid Lamarck held a danger which threatens the existence of life on Earth. It was considered that there was a danger of spores leaking from within the planetoid which were capable of crossing space. It was pointed out that if such an eventuality were to come about, there would be absolutely no way of preventing the Lamarck life-system from destroying all life on Earth.

"It was concluded that, however small the probability of such an occurrence, the potential loss was too great for any such risk to be taken. It was therefore ordered that Asteroid Lamarck should be tipped into the sun, and that nothing which had been in contact with the asteroid should be allowed to return to Earth."

The little man wasn't really listening. He had heard it before. He was staring hard through the window, at the silver forest. His unsteady eyes were leaking little teardrops into the corners of his eyes. He was not crying for himself, but for the life he had created in Lamarck.

"But *why*?" he complained. "My life—it's wonderful, beautiful. It means more to science than anything else we've made or discovered. *Who* took this decision? Who wants to destroy it?"

"It is dangerous," stated the executioner, obstinately. "It must be destroyed."

"You've been programmed to secrecy," said the engineer. "They are afraid. They are even afraid to tell me who they are. That's not the work of honest men—responsible men. It was politicians who sent you, not scientists.

"What are they really afraid of? Afraid that my life might evolve intelligence? That it might become cleverer, better in every way than a man? But that is foolishness."

"I know nothing about fear," said the robot. "I know what I have been told, and I know what you think of it. But the facts are unalterable. There is a danger of infection from Asteroid Lamarck. The consequences of such a danger are so terrible that no such danger can be allowed to exist for a moment longer than is inevitable."

"My life could never reach Earth."

"It is felt that there is a danger of the evolution of Arrhenius spores."

"Arrhenius spores," sneered the little man. "What could Arrhenius know? He died hundreds of years ago. His speculations are nonsense. His concept of life-spores seeding new planets was naive and ridiculous. There is no evidence that such spores could ever exist. If the men who sent you used Arrhenius spores as an excuse, then they are fools."

"No risk, however slight, is worthwhile," persisted the robot.

"There is *no danger*," stressed the genetic engineer. "We are separated from my life forms by a wall of glass. In all the years I have worked here, my life has never breached that wall. What you are suggesting involves breaking through the crust of a planetoid and crossing a hundred and eighty million miles of space, then finding a relatively small world and becoming established." The little man's voice had risen sharply, and he was gabbling.

"I'm sorry," said the robot.

"You're sorry! How can you be sorry? You aren't alive. How can you know what life means, let alone feel as I feel about it?"

"I am alive," contradicted the executioner. "I am as alive as you, or as the world beyond your window."

"You can't feel sorrow," snapped the little man. "You're only metal. You can't understand."

"Your passionate determination to demonstrate my lack of understanding is wrong," said the robot, with a hint of metallic bitterness. "I know exactly what your life-system is. I know exactly what you are. I know exactly what you feel."

"But you can't feel it yourself."

"No."

"Then you don't understand." The little man was quiet again, his anger spent against the executioner's coldness.

"I understand exactly what you have done, and why," said the robot patiently.

"Then you know there is no danger," said the engineer.

"Your life-system, if it ever got to Earth, would destroy the planet. Your life-system does not reproduce by replication. Every organism is unique, and carries two chromosomes, each one of which carries a complete genome. One chromosome determines the organism, the other codes for a virus particle. This second chromosome is dormant until the organism reaches senility, whereupon it pre-empts control of protein synthesis from the organism-chromosome. Billions and billions of virus particles are produced and the organism dies of its in-built disease. The virus particles are released and are universally infective. Any protein-synthesizing system is open to their attack. On infection, the organism-chromosome and the organism-chromosome of the host fuse and co-adapt, evolving by a process of directed change. The new chromosome then induces metamorphosis of the host body, into a creature which is at first parasitic, but may later become free-living. The new being carries the dormant virus chromosome in its own cells.

"The important aspect of the life-system is the fact that the virus may infect absolutely any living creature, irrespective of whether or not it is already a part of the life-system. There is no possible immunization. Thus, eventually, all life in any continuum must inevitably become part of the life-system. And incorporation inevitably means total loss of identity."

The little man nodded. "So you know it all," he conceded. "You know just what it is and how it works. Yet even knowing all the facts you can stand there and accuse me of creating some kind of Frankenstein monster which is just waiting to destroy me and conquer Earth. Can't you see how childish and ludicrous it is?"

"There exists a danger," said the robot obstinately.

"Utter nonsense! My life-system is absolutely bound to the inside of Asteroid Lamarck. There is no possibility of its ever reaching the exterior. If it did, it could not live. Not even a system as versatile as mine could live out there, without air or water. Only robots can do that. There is no escape from Lamarck, as far as the system is concerned."

"If, as you have claimed in your reports, the evolution of the Lamarck life-system is directive and improving, then it would be a mistake to limit the presumed capabilities of the system. There is a finite probability that the system will gain access to outer Lamarck, and will evolve a mechanism of extraplanetary dispersal."

"Arrhenius spores!" spat the little man. "*How?* Just tell me, *how?* How can a closed system, inside an asteroid, get spores to Earth, *against* the solar wind? Surely, even the idiots who sent you must realise that Arrhenius spores must drift outwards, *away* from Earth, even if there were a vanishingly small probability that such spores could be formed."

"It is impossible to make predictions about the pattern of drift within the solar system," stated the robot implacably.

"Do you think I'm a fool?"

"No."

"Then why do you refuse to concede anything that I say. Robots are essentially logical beings. Surely I have logic on my side."

"No amount of logic can save you. The device is already set and activated. Asteroid Lamarck is on its way into the sun. There is no appeal against the decision."

"No appeal," sneered the genetic engineer. "There is no appeal because they did not dare allow me a voice. There is no justice in this decision. There is only fear."

"There is fear," admitted the robot.

"You try to convince me that there is reason behind this death sentence. You speak in cold, exact terms of probability and danger. You try to tell *me*, to cover the truth and the guilt.

"Be honest, if you can. Tell me the truth—that I have been condemned to death by a crazy, irrational fear—the fear of some monstrous ghost which can never evolve from my life-system. That's all it is—a crazy, stupid, pathological fear of something they can't begin to understand or appreciate. Fear that can be made to breed fear, to infect others with fear. Fear that can be used as a lever to make death sentences. They say that my infective virus might reach Earth. It is there already. Fear infects everything, and its second generation is murder."

"Fear is only natural," said the executioner.

"Natural!" The little man raised his bespectacled eyes to the ceiling and spread his arms wide. "What sort of nature is afraid of nature?"

"Human nature," said the robot, with mechanical glibness.

"That's what condemned me," said the man. "Human nature. Not reason—not finite probabilities. Human nature, human vanity and human fear. But what they are afraid of is only themselves.

"Humans designed this virus. Biochemists and geneticists conceived it. Genetic engineers and construct surgeons assembled it. The entire system is a product of human inspiration, human ingenuity, human ability.

"What are you going to quote to me now? There are some things that man was not meant to know? Creation is the prerogative of divinity?"

"No," said the executioner. "I will say simply that because a man can do something, there is not an *ipso facto* reason why he should or must. What you have brought into existence is so potentially dangerous that it cannot be allowed to remain in existence."

"They told you to say that."

"These are my words," persisted the robot. "I do as I am told. I say what I am told to say. But I believe. I am metal, but I am alive. I believe in myself. I know what I am doing."

"It's a death sentence for you too," said the engineer.

"I accept the necessity."

"Is that supposed to make me accept it too? You're a robot. You don't put the same value on life that I do. You're programmed to die. No matter what your metal mind believes, you can't be human. You can't accept human values. You're only a machine."

"Yes," said the robot demurely, "I am a machine."

The little man stared through the glass wall, forcing back the nausea, the frustration—and the fear.

"It's not just me," said the man. "It's my life. It's everything I've ever done—everything I believe in. I don't want to die, but I don't want all *this* to die either. It's important to me. I made it. *That,* you can't possibly understand."

"If you say so," conceded the executioner, tiredly.

"I don't understand it either," confessed the little man.

"No," said the robot. "You can't. It isn't your science. It's your child."

The man bridled. "Who are you to judge? *What* are you to judge? How can a metal creature say things like that? What's the difference to me? My science is my child. Because I love the system I have created, is my reason devalued? Are my arguments to be discounted because I am personally involved with them?"

"Your arguments don't matter at all. The argument is already over."

"And the sentence passed. Who spoke for me? Who presented my arguments, my defiance?"

"They were presented," said the robot stiffly.

"And discounted. Devalued."

"The decision was made. All the facts were taken into consideration. Every possible course of action was studied. But no chances can be taken. Asteroid Lamarck and everything which has come into contact with it, must be destroyed. The danger of infection must be eliminated."

"They must be mad," said the little man distantly. "Unreasoned fear couldn't spread so far. They are not even content with taking my life. They must kill me too. They must murder as well as destroy. Surely that means they are afraid of *me*—of what I might say. How tenuous must their arguments be, if they dare not allow my voice to be heard?"

"They are afraid of spores," said the robot. "You have come into close personal contact with the system. It would have been inviting the danger which they want to prevent, if they allowed you to return to Earth."

"Are you sure? Do you believe that as well? Why didn't they claim that my knowledge was too dangerous as well? Wouldn't it have been far more diplomatic to have me die in an accident?

"Or is that what they *will* say?" added the engineer, as the thought occurred to him.

"It makes no difference," said the robot.

"Who is it that sent you?" demanded the little man, knowing full well that he was going to get no answer from the executioner. "Who started the scare?"

"What scare?" parried the robot.

"This panic. Who spread the fear behind this decision? It didn't just grow. It didn't form in serious minds because of spontaneous generation. Someone put it there. Someone embarked upon a crusade. Someone wanted a lever. It's obvious.

"I'm not supid enough to think that anyone hates me, or that some lunatic really does believe in the danger of infection. Someone wanted a platform. Someone wanted to exploit fear, to make a crusade which could carry him along at its head. It's politics that produced your twisted logic. It's politics that swore you to secrecy. It's politics that uses fear as a weapon. That's it, isn't it?"

"I don't know."

"I do. Fear doesn't just spring into being, fully formed. It has to be spread, like a virus. It has to be nurtured, injected. It's part of the currency of politics. Planted, grown, bought and sold."

"You're talking nonsense," said the robot sensibly.

"Tell me I don't understand," suggested the little man, and laughed. The robot didn't laugh.

"There's no point," said the robot, "in trying to change my mind. You can't devalue my arguments, because the decision has already been made. The sentence has already been carried out."

The little man walked away from the glass wall, towards the door.

"Nothing you do will help," said the robot. "If you are going to fetch the gun from your desk, don't bother. There's nothing you can do. The device was planted and activated before I came here. Lamarck is already dead."

The little man stopped and turned his head.

"I wasn't going to fetch the gun," he said.

The robot couldn't smile. "Go on then," said the executioner. "Go and do whatever you want to do."

The little man left, and the robot turned his red eyes to the glass wall. He stood in silent contemplation, watching the silken forest. Beyond and within the silver threadwork—which was all one organism—were other organisms, other fractions of organisms. The robot did not try to see them. He was not interested.

Asteroid Lamarck began to lose orbital velocity, and started a long, slow spiral in towards the sun.

The little man held the gun in both hands. He had small, delicate hands and thin arms. The gun was heavy.

"What are you going to do?" asked the robot, quietly.

The little man peered through his thin-rimmed spectacles at the unfamiliar object which he held.

"It won't help you to shoot me with that," said the robot.

"What do you care whether I shoot you or not?" demanded the little man. His voice was sharp and emotional. "You're metal. You don't understand *life*. You kill, but you don't know what you're really doing."

"I know what it is to live," said the robot.

"You *exist*," sneered the engineer. "You don't know what a human life *means*. You don't know what *that* means—" he pointed at the window in the wall—"to me, to science. You only want to kill. To kill life, to kill knowledge, to kill science. For fear."

"We've been through all that."

"What else is there to do but go through it all again? What else is there but talk, until Lamarck falls into the sun and you and I become cinders? What do *you* want to do?"

"It's futile to argue."

"Everything's futile. I'm a condemned man. Whatever I do, it's a waste of time. I'm a dead man. You're a dead robot. But you don't care."

The executioner remained silent.

The little man raised the gun, and pointed it at one of the robot's red eyes. For a few moments, man and metal stared at each other. The robot watched a thin, unsteady finger press the trigger of the gun.

The hands that held the gun jerked as the recoil jolted the genetic engineer. There was a loud bang. The bullet clanged off the metal ceiling, ricocheted into the window, but the glass was unbroken.

"It's pointless," said the robot softly. Somehow, after the report of the gun, his calmness seemed plaintive.

The little man fired again, squeezing the muscles round his eyes and mouth as he struggled to keep his hands still. The bullet splashed the robot's electronic eye into tiny red fragments. The metal man moaned, and went over backwards. There was a moment when the balance adjustment in his double-jointed knees compensated for the impact, and held the robot in a backward kneeling position. Then the moaning ended in a sharp gasp, and the engineer winced as the robot fell full length on to the floor.

The dead robot gave a mock laugh, which rattled harshly out of the uncoordinated vocal apparatus. The engineer stared at the crumpled heap of metal. It was no longer a parody of a human form. It was just metal. It was dead.

The little man walked slowly over to the large window. He fired from the waist, gunfighter style. The bullet bounced off the glass and hit him in the thigh. His face went pale, and he winced, but he did not fall. He fired three more times, and the third time the glass cracked. But there was still no breach in the glass wall.

The engineer felt tears easing from the corners of his eyes, and a trickle of blood on his leg. He smashed the butt of the gun into the glass again and again. The cracks spread, and finally the window gave up the fight and shattered.

Once the gap was there, it was easy to enlarge it. The little man allowed the artificial gravity of the laboratory to pull him to the floor, resting his injured leg, while he chipped away at the lower edge of the hole until he had made a doorway in the wall.

He crawled through, into the world of his life-system. Once there, beyond the pull of gravity, his leg stopped hurting him, and his body was filled with an exhilarating buoyancy.

He breathed the air, and imagined that he found it cleaner and fresher than the cold, sterile air of his own world inside Lamarck. He felt nothing, but he knew that in the air he breathed, and through the wound in his leg, the virus was invading his body.

He began to crawl away from the window, to get away from the murdered robot, and found that he could crawl with amazing rapidity and with little expenditure of effort. There was just enough gravity to stop him hurting himself. The engineer left the window behind, because it was not a window into a world that had sent an executioner to take away his life. He pulled himself further and further into the body of the silver forest, and on, and on.

He found another forest—another single being with many individual aspects. This was a conglomeration of tree-forms which consisted of twisted, many-branched stalks, each of which seemed to have arisen by a process of bifurcation and spiralling away of elements from a single point or origin. Each of the branches terminated in a small, eye-like spheroid.

The branches were of equal thickness, and of a glass-like smoothness and hardness. At first sight, the entire forest seemed petrified, but there was life there, and growth. Nothing petrified in the Lamarck life-system. Within the globes at the ends of the branches, the engineer could perceive movement, and when he stopped to look more closely, he saw a shifting and pouring like swirling smoke that could only be cytoplasmic streaming. He perceived darker regions that were nuclei and organelles. He concluded that the spheroids were the living elements of a colonial being or hive, which constructed the stalks which bore them from purely inorganic matter.

Then he pulled himself on, half-flying through the small forest, and into another forest, and another. He had lost sight of the smashed window, and he could not see the battery of solar cells which were the only other evidence of human interference with the Lamarck life-system. He was alone, a stranger in the world he had made. He floated to a stop, and sank slowly to the carpet of tiny unique organisms. He lay, exhausted, listening to the beating of his heart and admiring the wonders which his genetic engineering skill had produced.

He saw a giant plant, not far off, which must have covered a much larger area of ground than any of the so-called forests. It was of such complexity that it was built in tiers in the air.

The lowest layer consisted of a dense tangle of light-coloured tendrils of even continuity, not unlike the filaments of the silken forest. The slender threads were woven into a cushion of varying density.

Above this was a looser serial carpet of thicker elements which were darker in colour, but of a similar even texture. The threads stirred gently, and appeared to be very flexible.

From this aerial stratum there extended towers of small spherical elements, held vertical by some adhesive force that was not apparent. These spherical cells were being continually produced by budding from the filaments. The topmost spheres were always losing the mysterious adhesion and drifting away, falling very slowly, in a dipping-and-soaring fashion. Eventually, they exploded into clouds of invisibly small virus particles.

In the opposite direction, the engineer could see another vast growth, which had the appearance of a tree bearing fruits that were precious stones. The growth arose from a deep bed of slime—a great, extensive cushion which would have seemed hostile to life had it not been part of the Lamarck life-system. When he squinted, the little man could perceive thousands of rod-like bodies moving randomly within the slime-body.

The tree itself was slender and extremely beautiful in the manner of its curving and branching. The branches were translucent, but not wholly clear, for at certain points they contained encapsulated rod-bodies, entombed like flies in amber. The engineer imagined that the tree was formed of crystalline slime.

At the tip of each branch was a large spherical or elliptical jewel, each enclosed by a thin membrane. There was movement within each gem, and they looked like the many faceted eyes of some strange beast.

The engineer looked, and marvelled, and loved.

Asteroid Lamarck passed within the orbit of Mars.

The engineer slept, and while he slept he died.

The virus worked within him. It invaded cells, penetrated nuclei. It pre-empted protein production. It killed. And while it was still killing, it began rebuilding and regenerating. The second virus chromosome and the forty-six human chromosomes formed a complex, and the DNA within them began to undergo chemical metamorphosis as bases shifted and genes were remodeled.

As the new genotype was created, the virus sculpted, stimulated and responded. It mutated and tested. The path of generation of the new being was amended continually.

In conjunction with the chemical metamorphosis came physical change. The body of the engineer began to flow and distort. A new being was born inside him and was growing from him, feeding on him. The virus tested the viability of what its second set of chromosomes was building, and the being that was emerging was perfectly designed to fulfill its task. The process which was going on inside the corpse of the little man was far beyond the elementary process which the engineer had made. The rapidity of the Lamarck life-system's evolution had taken the speed, the smoothness, and the efficiency of the metamorphosis a long way.

The new being absorbed the engineer, and came slowly to maturity.

Asteroid Lamarck crossed the orbit of Earth.

The body of the little man had lost most of its substance. The face had widened into a skull-grin, and the ridiculous pair of spectacles lay lop-sided across the gleaming white bridge of the nose. The brain had completely gone from the skull, and the whole of the lower abdomen had disappeared. The legs were only thin ropes of decayed muscle. The ribs were reduced to tiny studs attached to what had once been the spine. Only dust remained where the internal organs had once been.

Above the corpse, a winged thing hovered bat-like, testing its strength. It was small-bodied but large-skulled. It had a tiny, oddly human, wizened face without eyes. The face moved continuously as though expressing unknown emotions, and the creature made a small, thin sound like a rattling laugh.

It flew away from the remains of its father, zooming through the weird forests of inner Lamarck in great circles. Finally, it found the silver forest, and settled on a branch very near to the smashed glass wall. It lay still. It had never eaten. It was not even equipped to eat. It had been born only to perform one small task for the Lamarck life-system, and then to die again.

Meanwhile, the plants of inner Lamarck had passed through the doorway which the engineer had made for them. They had explored his laboratories, his library, his bedroom, his office. They had slipped under doors and through keyholes. There was only one place they could not reach, and that was the world of outer Lamarck, beyond the great iron airlock that had neither crack nor key.

Plants died, and were reborn. New types of plant formed around and on the iron door—plants that built their cell walls out of pure iron. With vegetable efficiency, they began to dissolve the airlock.

The winged creature began to sprinkle tiny objects from its abdomen. A sphincter pulsed and pulsed, hundreds of contractions per minute, and every pulse released another particle. The motes floated in the air, far too light for the weak gravity to pull them to the ground. The air in the silver forest became filled with them.

Asteroid Lamarck crossed the orbit of Venus.

Pinpricks formed in the outer airlock door. The inner door was completely gone. Air began to seep away, but before the seepage became dramatic, the holes were the size of fists. Like all the other members of the Lamarck life-system, the iron-eaters were fast and efficient. The seepage became a rush. With it, the air took the tiny particles produced in hundreds of millions by the winged creature.

Lamarck was too small to hold the atmosphere which flooded out into the desolation of its outer surface. The air was lost and the particles with it. While Lamarck plunged on towards the sun, in an ever-decreasing spiral, it left behind a long, long trail of Arrhenius spores, which began to drift lazily on the solar wind.

Slowly outwards, toward the orbit of Earth.

ALLEGIANCES

by Michael Bishop

The "regional" story in America is something we do not usually equate with science fiction. The author of this, one of the rising new talents, is a native of Georgia and combines here something of that state's manifest regionalism with a lot that is strictly of science fiction.

I
cleopatra amid the kudzu

Do you know what kudzu is? *Kudzu.* Most people who live in a domed city, even the Urban Nucleus of Atlanta, aren't likely to know. How many of you have been outside our huge, geodesic walnut? I know about kudzu for two reasons: when I was very little my grandmother used to tell me about it and, more impressively maybe, I am one of those who have been into the Open:

Japan invades.
  Far Eastern vines
Run from the
  clay banks they are
Supposed to
  keep from eroding,
Up telephone poles,
Which rear,
  half out of leafage,
As though
  they would shriek. . . .

James Dickey's description of kudzu in the opening lines of a poem entitled "Kudzu." It's a good description, too, especially the part about the telephone poles shrieking. Not too many standing telephone poles out there anymore, but pine trees, old barns, collapsing fire towers—all of these do seem to be shrieking as the merciless kudzu clambers over them.

Kudzu. Pueraria lobata, native to Japan, imported during a previous century to keep the red clay from washing away. Baroque, vegetable architecture.

My grandmother told me about it before I ever saw it. My last name is Noble, but Zoe, my grandmother, gave me my first one: Clio. I remember Zoe very well even though she lived with us only the last three years of her life and died when I was five. Also, I have a photograph of my grandmother that she took herself, using a tripod and timer: a large black-and-white one. This photograph, which sits on top of my visicom console as I write this, gives me a hand-hold on Zoe's heart and on several generations of the past.

The past is important to me. Just as you have to hack your way out of furiously growing kudzu to attain a vantage point on the surrounding terrain, sometimes you have to rise above and survey the past in order to get the lay of your own soul. Zoe understood that, and I think that's why my parents, after once renouncing her and packing her off to the Geriatrics Hostel, let her, in her seventy-second year, stick me with a monicker like Clio. But, having bridged a generation and walked over that bridge into my grandmother's life, I find that I like my name OK.

In Greek mythology, you know, Clio was the Muse of History. (Ta da!)

The piece of history I'm telling now occurred just last year, but really it takes in many more human seasons than just 2066, month of Summer. It's the story of how three of us on a resources-reclamation team, in the employ of the Human Development Commission (the very same authority that, nineteen years ago, disbanded Zoe's experimental septigamoklan in the Geriatrics Hostel), went out into the Open to fetch back several people to our Urban Nucleus.

Although I was only twenty-one last summer, I'd been out on three missions before the one this story is about: all routine, all predictable. We'd "reclaimed" a number of people with desirable technical skills or influential relatives in the city by going out, finding their kudzu-camouflaged encampments, and asking them to return with us. Upon the promise of enfranchisement and respectable jobs, they all had: every one of them. They were flattered that an rr team had been sent out for them.

Our efforts were part of what the bureaucrats in the Commission called the "Fifth Evacuation Lottery"—although it wasn't an evacuation at all in the way the first four had been, when the domes were going up sixty and seventy years ago (1994-2004, in case you're counting: a neat decade). The Fifth Evacuation Lottery is another thing altogether, not an evacuation but a series of carefully planned manhunts.

The three of us who went out last summer were Newlyn Yates, the team leader; Alexander Guest, a man of swarthy complexion although, unlike Yates, not a black; and me, Clio Noble. Three was the optimum number for such teams; it had something to do with an old NASA policy.

Twice before I'd been on teams with Newlyn Yates, and I was a little bit dithery about him: he did things to my sense of equilibrium, sabotaged it mostly. But Yates was all poker spine, set jaw, and unflappable decorum, and we'd never come close to bodyburning, despite the opportunities spending all that time in the Open naturally provides. Yates was awfully interior, he was ingrown. In the Open you couldn't get him to uncoil, he did everything as if by an invisible manual. Off duty, you never got a chance to see him.

Alexander Guest, a big, mahogany-colored man with a craggy profile, was probably ten years older than Yates. He looked like he ought to be wearing moccasins and the traditional turban of the old Creek Indians—for good reason, it turned out. Before our assignment last summer, I'd never met him before, never even seen him in the Commission Authority Tower. He was just insane enough to *like* traipsing through kudzu; you could tell by the way the wilderness polled up in his muddy eyes. He was insane in other ways, too.

But this I found out in the Open. On the day I met him in the rr section of the Human Development Tower, he just looked bummish and uncouth. We were sitting in plastic chairs in the carpeted anteroom of Yates' office, two zombies rising out of the deadness of sleep at six o'clock in the morning: even so, I had to admit that the craggy, brown man whose bulk seemed to overflow the fragile cup of his chair was more awake than I.

" 'Lo," he said. An orotund rumble.

I nodded.

"Looks like we're gonna be team members. You know what this one's about?"

"No," I said. "Do you?"

"Think so." He said this matter-of-factly rather than smugly, but I still didn't feel like asking him the natural follow-up question. So, shifting in his wobbly chair (with him in it, it looked like it had been stolen from a Van-Ed elementary division classroom), he said, "What's your name, Miz?"

I told him.

"*Cleo,*" he said, missing it by a letter. "Short for Cleopatra. Married up with her brother and bodyburned with two Romans. Well, Cleo, you're the first red-haired 'Gyptian I've ever seen. Nice to meet you."

I didn't correct him about my name. I did manage the bogus courtesy of nodding again. That was all I could manage.

"History's a pastime of mine," he said after a while. "My name's Guest, Alexander Guest. That's how I'm listed in the UrNu census anyhow, and even here at the Tower. Really, though, it's an alias.

"The alias I'd rather go by," he said after musing for a while, "is Menewa. But it's hard to get people in the Urban Nucleus to call you that. All forms say 'Last name, first name, middle initial.' You write down somepin like 'Menewa' they jes' stamp INCOMPLETE on the forms and send 'em back to you. You see, Cleo, I'm an Indian. The name Menewa. . . ."

Fortunately, he got cut off because Newlyn Yates, trim in a one-piece worksuit and street slippers, glided through the anteroom and into his office. Guest didn't have time to lapse into an incomprehensible Muskohogean dialect: the words "Come in" floated back to us as Yates disappeared, and the Indian Menewa and the 'Gyptian Cleopatra exchanged a glance, got up, and followed their black pharaoh-chieftain into the dark.

In the center of Yates' metal desk—once Yates had coasted the false wood surface aside—you could see an illuminated projection well; in fact, that was all we saw when we came into his office. Yates was standing behind the desk and he beckoned us to take up positions opposite him. Then he pushed a button so that a map of the transit tunnels leading out of Atlanta to the other Urban Nuclei appeared in the projection well.

"We'll take a transit-car to this station," Yates said, pointing at the map. "The juncture of the Miami and Savannah tunnels, southeast of here. Then we'll have to go to the end of the Savannah tributary, dismantle the filter system on one of the ventilation units, climb through, and strike out on foot. The biomonitor-relay people have one of our targets placed at about forty-five kilometers due east of the tunnel juncture." Yates' father had once been the director of the city's Biomonitor Agency, but in the last fifteen years the Agency had extended its operations to include surveillance of the natives of the countryside; this was in addition to the medical monitoring of all dome-dwellers. A *target*, both then and now, was a human being who was being monitored.

"Hot damn," I said. An old expression of my grandmother's. "How did they manage that?"

"An implant tab at the nape of our subject's neck, they told me," Yates said. "A month ago—two months ago—he came into the city."

"Why?"

"The Agency told me he brought a truckload of peanuts up here, using what's left of the old highway system. While here, he was drugged, implanted, and afterwards pumped by a hypnotist-physician at Grady Memorial. He's not aware of the implant tab or the fact that he was questioned."

"Why didn't we just keep him here when he came to the city? It doesn't make sense to go out and fetch him now." I was doing all the asking: Alexander Guest, the gingerbread Indian, was standing hunch-shouldered and open-mouthed beside me.

"The man's name is Jonah Trap," Yates said, irritated with me, the projection well giving his face the demonic geometry of a mask. "A black. But we're not going after *him*, Miz Noble. We're after two people whose intelligence and ability the city needs and who're now apparently living with Trap near the old town of Toombsboro. You were selected for this assignment because one of the people is a woman: the Commission Authority believes you may be able, far better than Mr. Guest or I, to persuade her to return with us."

"Why was I chosen?" Indian Alex said, surprising both Yates and me.

"I thought they explained that to you. You met Trap while he was here, they told me; they said you'd even been in the area of the Open before. Is that true?"

"Yep."

"Then those are your reasons. You ought to be helpful."

Then Yates said, "And in case the question seems to logically present itself now, *I'm* going because I'm good at taking teams out and bringing them back entire. The fact I'm black probably won't hurt much either, not in this instance."

"Well," I said, "who are the people? The man and the woman?"

"That, Miz Noble, I can't tell you till we're on our way to Toombsboro."

"Why not?"

"If I could tell you that," I said, "I could tell you the other. Couldn't I?"

"Not necessarily, Maybe the Commission Authority just wants to be sure we don't spread our targets' names around before we leave. You could easily tell us that without telling us the names of the targets."

"Well, Miz Noble, if you have it all figured out, why ask?" Yates was an icicle with an iron bar inside it, and I had just put my lily-white foot so far into my mouth that I was gnawing on ankle bone. *Hot damn,* I said to myself: an old expression of my grandmother's.

Aloud I said, "I don't have it all figured out. I didn't even know we had a tunnel to Old Savannah: Savannah's not one of the Urban Nuclei. Never was, was it?"

"It's about one-tenth of a tunnel," Yates said, letting his finger trace the route in the projection well. "A dead-ender. Anyway, the geology of the coastal region wouldn't permit the construction of a viable tunnel, even if there were people there to get to. Same with Miami. Most of the Trans-Seminole 'tunnel,' you know, is above-ground and hooded." He tapped the illuminated map. "Once we exit the main tunnel near the Ocmulgee Mound here," tapping again, "we'll head down the dead-ender and then surface well to the east of Macon. Then, a kudzu-fouled walk in the Open. We may be able to use the old state highway—57, I think—for a good part of the way. That should ease it a little for us."

Guest said, "That highway's torn up and overgrown, 57 is—at least over here where we're gonna come out." He shook his head. "Crazy."

"It doesn't matter," Yates said. "We'll get there, Mr. Guest." In five more minutes the briefing was over, and Yates turned us out of the office, out of the Tower, for the rest of the day. An open day.

"You like to get some coffee, Cleo?" Guest asked me.

"No thanks," I said. "See you at six o'clock tomorrow morning."

I went back to my cubicle on Level 3, *under*. That's where, a quarter of a century ago, my parents started from: Level 3.

II
the general toombs cornstalk brigade

The transit tunnels are dark; they smell of the dampness of concrete. Even before construction on the domes of the Urban Nuclei had begun, the entire Federation-wide network of tunnels was blasted into existence by an arsenal of immaculately sanitary H-bombs: grrr-choom, grrr-choom, grrrrr-whumpf! Strangely, we don't use the tunnels that much.

On the morning after our conference in the Human Development Tower, an open transit-car carried us in eerie silence to the Miami-Savannah juncture, where, before we turned into the Savannah tributary, I knew we were passing pretty darn close to the old Ocmulgee Mounds. At these mounds and the territory called the Ocmulgee Old Fields, the Creek Indians had long ago formed the Creek Indian Confederacy. Several prehistoric cultures had thrived here, too.

I started wondering. Maybe the domes of the Urban Nuclei had been raised from the same impulse that had motivated Kheops in Egypt and the Mound Builders in Georgia. Oh, in these two cases I know the immediate motives diverge: Pharaoh wanted a splendid tomb whereas the Indians wished their flat-topped pyramids to serve as the thrones of the gods. But if Pharaoh believed himself a deity, a god incarnate, then his tomb was also a throne, and the common denominator in the two instances is humankind's need to exalt something larger than itself. A religious motive, finally.

Anyhow, that's my belief, and I'm not talking about the Ortho-Urban Church, either. I've tried to voice it once or twice, but these ideas, spilling from the lips of a twenty-two-year-old woman with red hair, elicit only peeved looks ("The girl thinks she's Bertrand Russell, Tom") or curt dismissals ("Sophomoric bullshit, Clio"). So I reserve these ruminations now for accounts like this one. Except I probably won't be writing any more accounts like this one. Circumstances change.

But for the beam of a single headlamp, our resources-reclamation team rode in absolute darkness. The winds of our blast-borne passage smelled of concrete, concrete and iron. Yates slowed at the Miami-Savannah juncture and negotiated the turn into the southeastward tributary of the subterranean network: Guest had to get out and switch the transit-rails. Then off we went again, the Ocmulgee Old Fields behind us, well to the west. We'd been traveling for three hours.

I shouted into the resurging wind of our movement: "*Now* can you tell us who we're going after?"

Turning his head, Yates permitted his thin profile to carve itself in the air: "Wait till we're out! You've waited this long!"

In fifteen minutes the wind began to die, the walls to lose their dizzying speed, and we glided into what I could only think of as Dead-End Station: yellow fluorescents casting a somehow greenish light over the platform here. You half-expected, when you were close enough to see more clearly, to find stalactites on the ceiling. Didn't, though; too mercilessly hot.

We got out and began unloading equipment and carrying it up to the platform. Yates wore a myriad of tools on his low-slung belt, as well as a holster of artificial leather: it contained a laser pistol. (One such weapon to each reclamation team, and the team leader carried it.) Then Yates pointed at the ventilation unit at the top of the tunnel's final wall.

"OK," he said. "Let's dismantle that grate."

Guest climbed up the maintenance rungs to the unit and began working to take the filter apart. The filter systems had been installed when the Federation had been worried about the tunnel's Internal Environmental Control (IEC, if you like initials), fearing that the Open's tainted atmosphere would spill into the network and strangle us with the wastes we had fled from. If that's what we'd fled from. The Open had never been so foully tainted as that. Never. The first reclamation team had carried oxygen canisters and over-the-head masks (which made them look like startled rhesus monkeys when they put them on: perforated speakers, plastiglass eyes, and all), but its members hadn't had to use this equipment. And ninety per cent of Atlanta's people still believe you can't go outside. Most of them, if they knew differently, still wouldn't rush to re-colonize the wilderness.

"This thing's rusted," Guest said, swaying up there on the maintenance ladder. "Won't budge."

So Yates had to go up and cut both the filter system and the grate out of their moorings with the laser pistol. After the area around the ventilation unit had cooled, we all climbed through, weighted with paraphernalia, into the Open: Guest first, then me, then Newlyn Yates.

And the first thing we saw was the deformed, rearing landscape: green temples, arabesques of kudzu, pagodas to the gods of rampant fertility. The Orient had invaded Georgia, invisible samurai crouched in the vines. The wilderness shouted at us, and the sky—this always amazed me—was a brilliant sky-blue.

The job they gave Clio Noble was tying flaming-red markers on trees and rotted fence posts, anything up-jutting. "Hell," Alexander Guest said. "She don't need to do that. You got a wrist-compass and I could smell our way back to the station." He lifted his big head and whuffled two or three times at the air, a comic and lordly bear in the chapel of the forest.

"Suppose something happens to you, Guest," Yates said. "Or to me. Maybe Clio . . . Miz Noble," he amended, "will have to get back here on her own." I grinned at him, and the martinet in Yates revived. "Miz Noble will set the rags, and that's it."

So off we went, angling northeast in order to intercept the ruins of State Highway 57, Clio Noble tying markers the color of her hair at intervals of roughly a hundred meters—unless the eclipsing vegetation or a turn in our progress demanded them more often. Languorously swinging his machete, Indian Alex marched point. Newlyn Yates, good team leader that he was, brought up the rear.

Two brown thrashers (once upon a time, the state bird) and a logy cardinal. Which was funny enough—in context, mind you—to make me chuckle out loud; in that knee-high kudzu "brown thrashers" was especially good.

"Don't get to laughing so hard," Yates said from behind me, "you forget to keep an eye open for snakes. They love this stuff."

Guest stopped and turned around. "My little brothers," he said.

I glared. He'd almost lopped off my head with his machete.

" 'Scuse me," he said, wiping his brow with one mesh sleeve. "It's snakes, though. Since I'm an Indian they're s'posed to be my little brothers: snakes, lizards, alligators, all like that. But I saw a green mamba at the Grant Park Zoo two years ago and got so crawly I had to get out of there." His shoulders shuddered. "Went right home."

"If you've been out here before," Yates accused, "you've seen snakes plenty of times."

"Yeah, but I didn't come 'specially to look at 'em." Then he said something both clumsily poetic and, right then, incomprehensible: "This Hothlepoya ain't no herpetologist: no sir." And started hacking again.

We did see some snakes, too—as we always did in the Open. One was a coral snake, up from Florida no doubt, that we gave a wide berth. Guest waved Yates and me around it and whispered to me as I went by, "Hope we don't run across any asps, Cleo." I thought he was being a smart Alex until I deduced from his head movements and inflections that he really did hope that. Literally, he meant it. An asp in Georgia, a creature as alien as that!

At one o'clock we found some shade, a knoll in the forest of pine and kudzu. Some moss actually grew at the base of the slash pine we decided to camp under. For lunch. We drank from our canteens and nibbled at our dried rations.

"Well," I said. "How 'bout now?"

Yates looked at me. "How 'bout now what?" Imperial annoyance.

"Telling us who we've come after this time. I think it's a pretty safe wager we won't leak the word to someone disreputable."

"OK," Yates said. I noticed that Guest, his heavy jaw working on a dehydrated vitamin bar, was gazing off into the distant portals of kudzu, apparently indifferent to Yates' impending revelation. Well, he'd told me he thought he knew what this mission was all about; maybe he did.

Yates said, "Do you know the name Carlo Bitler?"

"I know we're not looking for him," I said. "He was a half-caste demagogue who was assassinated in the UrNu Capitol Building almost forty years ago."

"Thirty-seven. And he wasn't a demagogue, Miz Noble." Archly he said this: very archly.

"OK," I said. "Beg your pardon. Why do you mention him?"

"We're looking for his wife," Yates announced, "and for the son of the man who assassinated Bitler, Emory Coleman. We think the two of them are together. Fiona Bitler was Coleman's teacher in a Van-Ed program for precocious children before the two of them disappeared."

"Great Maynard's ghost!" I was really excited: that's an expletive for thugboys and sentimental politicians. "How long ago was that?"

"Thirty-two years."

"You've got it all memorized! How old does that make Fiona Bitler and the little boy she was teaching?"

"The 'little boy' is now forty-one, Miz Noble; and Fiona Bitler has to be in her mid-sixties. In thirty years people age." Which was about the stupidest thing I'd ever heard Yates say. He was melancholy, though. To cover his emotion he lifted the canteen and drank.

Indian Alex hadn't stopped munching. None of what we'd just been talking about impressed him, his eyes still veered away into pine copses and viny cathedrals. When he did look at us again, well into Yates' and my awkward silence, he said, "Toombsboro was named for Robert Toombs, I think." He wiped vitamin-bar crumbs from his hands. "Robert Toombs was an unusual man. Confederate general who escaped the yankees in the last year of the war and ended up in London. Came back to Georgia later, but never would swear his loyalty to the Union."

"Yes, sir," Yates said, annoyance surfacing again. "Old Toombs was a real jewel."

"Bitler's your hero," I said by way of mediation (they hadn't asked for it, though); "maybe Toombs is his. Everyone has his own heroes." I remembered a story about Toombs that a professor of mine had always relished telling: In an early year of the war the old secessionist had bragged to a friend that one Georgia brigade with cornstalks could defeat any bunch of yankees sent against them. After the war the friend reproached Toombs for this bit of brag. Well, Toombs drawled (my professor drawled it, anyhow), we could of—but them yankee bastuds wouldn't fight with cornstalks. (Ho ho.) But it wasn't a story that would amuse Yates, though; so, out there in the Open, I didn't tell it.

"Not a hero of mine," Guest said. "When that war broke out there wasn't an Indian left in Georgia, least not officially: only white men and Negro slaves. But Toombs was a man who knew where he stood, that's for sure."

"Let's go," Yates said. He was already standing up.

"Wait a minute," I said. "Heroes aside, what're Fiona Bitler and that old pupil of hers doing out here near Toombsboro? Strange place for them to be, isn't it?"

Without looking at me Yates began jockeying his implement-lined belt into place over his hips. "Jonah Trap's farming out here, the reports say. He's Fiona Bitler's first cousin: son of her mother's brother. When she and the boy left the city in '34, they naturally went to Trap."

"And they've been living out here thirty years?"

"Off and on. It isn't completely clear."

"So why do we, in this funky Year of Our Lord, come out here to haul them back to a place they must've wanted out of?" Which was a question that needed asking. Most of the "indigenous salvageables" our resource-reclamation teams brought back to the city had never lived in it before, had never been enfranchised. Fetching runaways was business we didn't engage in. Let the trash go, one of our more intellectual ward reps liked to say.

"To persuade them to return. Emory Coleman's a genius, and Mrs. Bitler's husband's been vindicated over and over again for his so-called rabblerousing. Streets have been named after him, schools, housing projects, churches. The woman ought to be able to come back to that. She always wanted natural change, that's why she was a teacher. She ought to be able to die in the city that finally recognized the rightness of her husband's goals."

"Fine recognition," I said. "Implementing the Retrenchment Edicts of '35 and crushing that so-called 'Glissador Revolt' three years back, when there wasn't any revolt at all; nothing physical anyhow." This was heresy, but Yates didn't respond to it. His loyalties were cruelly divided: the city employed him, but his pigmentation suffused him with an allegiance no mere emolument or law could undermine. Newlyn Yates wasn't that sort of human being; a soldier maybe, but no mercenary.

III
rasputin at the battle of horseshoe bend

About five o'clock on that first day we stumbled out of the green mosques and jumbled pagodas into an open area of sorts. A universal ground-cover of kudzu still tripped us up, but now it rose no higher than our upper shins: we waded through it like kids in the shallow end of a recreation pool. Guest raked the blade of his machete through the vines and felt for the hidden surface.

The machete clanged. Guest scraped at the ground-cover. "Well, here she is, Mr. Yates: Highway 57."

And it was. The vines had simply grown across it. We followed the filigreed roadbed for a while, moving east, and had the easiest time of it the wilderness had so far granted us. Well before sundown, though, we stopped, moved off the roadbed into a copse of deciduous trees (wild pecans), and made our camp for the evening.

Twilight still twinkling in the tall pines and pecans, Yates told us to go to bed: he would roust us out early, he said, so we could steal a march on the heat. We prepared to sleep on the ground.

But tall thunderheads began rolling through the twilight from the northwest, and Yates ordered us to pitch our one-person tents in a kind of triangle, dig run-off trenches, and hurriedly finish supper. The woods began to boom, the branches of the trees to thrash about violently. Huge drops began to fall through the accumulating darkness and the stuttering leaves.

Well, no stars this night; no bloated moon and no vivid, glittering constellations. Too bad. Those are things that make being a team member worth all the agitation of soul. From my two previous trips with him I remembered that Yates had sometimes stayed up all night, transfixed, looking at the stars. (How did I know it was all night? Sometimes I stayed up, too, watching *him*.) Tonight, though, Yates crawled into his tent before the worst of the deluge hit and fell soundly asleep. A feat I couldn't emulate. It was too noisy. And my soul was agitated: we were going after Fiona Bitler and Emory Coleman!

It rained an hour, at least. When it stopped, I looked up and saw a shadowy bulk hunkering next to my tent: Alexander Guest, rocking on his heels in the slow, sloughing, red mud. " 'Lo," he said.

"What're you doing?" I said. Not too civilly, maybe.

"First watch," he said. "Yates gave me first watch. You can't do it proper from a tent."

"Why do we need one at all?" I said. "Nothing out here but snakes, raccoons, and opossums." The answer was that Yates did everything by the manual, even down to assigning watches in the middle of thunderstorms.

"Can't sleep, huh?"

That question disturbed me a little. I was afraid (ashamed afterwards, though) that Guest was going to propose a mutual settling of the nerves, a little easy bodywarming as a prelude to sleep. I said, "No. But look at Yates. Don't you hate a man who can go off like that, and then stay off?"

"I don't hate anybody," he said obliquely. Then, staring into the dark: " 'Cept maybe Andrew Jackson. I've never really forgiven Andrew Jackson."

"For what?"

"For the way he treated Indians, you know. When that man got elected President, the Civilized Tribes and ever' other Indian in Georgia was doomed. In ten years, violatin' first this treaty, then that, he had all of us cleared out of here: Yamacraw, Creek, Yuchi, Cherokee. That Jackson's one dead fellow I wish was alive, jes' so I could kill him again."

"I'd think his being dead so long revenge enough."

"No," Guest shook his head. "Death is a sweetness, it's the dying, you know, that's the devil-bitch, always hungry for new meat. . . . I wish ole Jackson was new meat again so I could feed him to the devil-bitch."

Death as Goddess, Death as Avenging Female. Well, Indians had considered the white man's failure to isolate his woman during menstruation as the most heinous of obscenities. I could accept the devil-bitch metaphor from Guest even though it would have angered me from anybody else; I could accept it without approving it, just as I could understand but never approve the Indian's fear and awe of a woman in her cycle.

Thinking these things, I crawled out of my tent. It seemed rude to carry on a conversation from the comfort of my bedding while Guest squatted in the mud. Together we drew a log up to the rain-squelched ashes of our fire and sat down. Yates slept on. Should I assure Indian Alex that I was in a touchable condition?

Instead I said, "You told me yesterday your name was an alias."

"Sort of," he said. "It's the name on my birth certificate, but *Alexander* and *Guest* certainly ain't Indian names. I'd be closer to it using something like Alexander X, the way some of them old-time black Muslims did. Like the one who got shot in New York, that Malcolm fellow. He didn't know what his *real* name was any more than I do mine—now."

Guest told me that he was the descendant of Cherokee Indians who had escaped into North Carolina at the time of the Great Removal in 1838 and 1839. Somewhere along the line a great-grandfather had taken the name Guest. "The reason for that," the big man said, "is Guest is one of the most common forms of Gist, and George Gist was the anglo name of Sequoyah."

"Sequoyah? The inventor of the Cherokee syllabary?"

"Yep. Which I can read. I got a nigh-on complete microfilm facsimile of the Cherokee Phoenix. The Indian newspaper run off at New Echota up in old Gordon County. Got it back in my cubicle."

The other reason that Guest was an appropriate name for Alexander's family, he explained, was that they were "guests" in the city: none of them had ever been granted enfranchisement.

"What about *Alexander?*" I said.

"Well, that's from Alexander McGillivray. He was a famous Creek *micco* whose father'd been a Scotch trader. If you want to survive in the Urban Nucleus, you know, you can't go around calling yourself Menewa. So I got me a compromise name: Alexander Guest."

"Why do you want to call yourself Menewa? Is that a Cherokee name?"

"No. That's the name of a Creek warrior who called himself Hothlepoya when he was young. That means Crazy War Hunter. He was an unusual man, Menewa was; more unusual than Robert Toombs, even."

And, talking slowly, the ground around us steaming so that ghosts seemed to be rising from the heavy, carnal earth, Alexander Guest told me the story of Menewa.

By 1812 the Creek Confederacy had fragmented into pro- and anti-American actions; most of the Upper or Alabama Creeks were hostile to the new American nation, while many of the Lower or Georgia Creeks, hoping for the best, determined to support and befriend it.

"A few of these Lower Creeks," Guest said, "was in the pay of the U.S. government. Which you can't blame 'em too much for—since they was givin' up land right and left and jes' tryin' to survive in a turned-upside-down world."

The principal culprit, as Guest saw it, was a half-Scot Lower Creek, a man named William MacIntosh, who led his people in a massacre of the anti-American party of a chief named Weatherford ("Them Scots jes' seemed to have a way with the Indian gals") after Weatherford had directed his own massacre of the soldiers and their families of Fort Mims in Alabama: a Civil War ante-dating the one that gave the world William Tecumseh Sherman.

"Got all that straight?" Guest asked.

"I don't know. What about Menewa?"

"Well, he was a chief of an anti-American faction called the Red Sticks, and he and MacIntosh probably saw themselves as the deadliest of enemies. At the battle of Horseshoe Bend in 1812, the Red Sticks was making a desperation stand against Jackson's Tennessee militia and some pro-American Indians, and things didn't go too good for Menewa. MacIntosh was there, and some Yuchi Indians, and maybe six-hundred or so Cherokee."

"Cherokee?"

"Well," Guest said defensively, "they'd been promised all sorts of things. Some of 'em even had friends among the white men. Also, they was pretty sure this country never was gonna be all Indian again. They was doin' what they thought they had to do, jes' like Menewa's Red Sticks was—unless they was gettin' paid to do it."

The battle lasted several hours. Jackson used cannons to bombard the Red Stick positions on the peninsula. Only seventy of the original nine-hundred Red Stick warriors survived, and three-hundred women and children were taken as captives. What about Menewa?

"He was shot seven times," Guest said. "Seven times! None of 'em kilt him, though. Then, when he woke up—he'd been left for dead in the brush, you know—he took a shot at one of Jackson's militiamen. That fellow shot back. He drilled Menewa right through the cheek, but that didn't kill him, either. Menewa woke up in the middle of the night. He crawled to the river, found him a canoe, and floated down the Tallapoosa to some of the women and children who'd hidden themselves there. Made it alive, too."

"Sounds as tough as Rasputin," I said.

"Sure. Far as survivin' goes, anyhow. But the real Rasputins at the battle of Horseshoe Bend was Jackson and MacIntosh. They took all the Red Sticks' land, all of Menewa's goods and property, too, and MacIntosh probably went off thinkin' he'd finished Menewa for good."

"He hadn't?"

"It took thirteen years, but Menewa got his revenge. Yessir!"

In 1825, against both Creek custom and law, MacIntosh ("who was gettin' paid regular from the state, mind you") ceded to Georgia all the Creek land that hadn't already been signed away in past treaties.

"So the Creeks, the big miccos who hadn't been talked to, got together and decided to kill ole Mac. On May Day a bunch of 'em attacked his house and killed the bastard. His son-in-law, too. A lot of Georgia history writes this up as some sort of tragedy, Cleo, but it was only what the ole traitor deserved. He knew it, too. You bet he did. The best part, though, is this: it was Menewa who actually killed MacIntosh."

Despite this triumph over his rival, Menewa lived out a story whose conclusion wasn't so happy. In 1826 Menewa went to Washington himself to make a new treaty. He didn't give up any new land, but he promised the loyalty of himself and his people to that of the United States.

"The land got took over, anyhow," Guest said. "Governor Troup was a cousin of MacIntosh, and he didn't give a damn how many white men tramped all over the Creek and Cherokee territories. He jes' said to hell with this U.S. gov'ment's treaty, and pretty soon some of the Creeks was beggin' for food or livin' in the woods and swamps and tryin' to get by there. Coweta Town, the capital of the Lower Creeks, was full of white land speculators, Cleo, and finally a micco named Eneah Emathla got some of the Creeks together to fight it. That's when Jackson, who was now your president, you know, told his secretary of war to send troops in and smash up this 'rebellion.' Know who helped the white soldiers do it, Cleo?"

Cicadas were whirring in the undergrowth; the night sky looked like a dyer's vat full of torn bed sheets. "Not Menewa?" I said.

"Yep. Him and about two-thousand of his followers."

"Why?"

"Because in '25, you know, he'd pledged his loyalty to the U.S. gov'ment. He'd even taken to wearin' a general's uniform, standard army style, and someone in Washington promised him and his followers they wouldn't have to trek off to Oklahoma like the rest of them."

"He sold out his people," I said.

"He kep' his word. And the gov'ment broke its. They marched Menewa, a battered ole man, off with all them others, never to come back. And some who saw that ole Red Stick say he wept to go."

"Look," I said. "He put his abstract honor above the material well-being of the Creeks. He gave his allegiance foolishly, then acted upon it foolishly."

"Damn straight," Guest said, "considerin' who he gave it to. They never once put their, uh, abstract honor above material well-being." Groaning like an arthritic septuagenarian, he stood up and kicked languidly at the muddy ashes of our fire.

Questioningly, I looked up at him.

"Your watch, Cleo," he said. "You can wake Yates in a coupla hours." Then he lumbered over to his rain-sopped tent, took off his boots, and went to bed.

IV
aldebaran above, alighieri below

That night I got about two hours' sleep. We broke camp at four in the morning and moved out: eastward on kudzu-carpeted Highway 57. In thirteen hours we probably traveled about thirteen old-style miles. (Twice we saw buckshot-riddled, rusted signs saying things like Gordon 12, Irwinton 21.) The going was so bad because in places the asphalt had crumbled like a stale graham cracker; briary thickets had reasserted their primacy.

A little after Gordon 12, Irwinton 21, upon which I had tied a red marker, I said, "There's got to be a better way."

"Like what?" Yates said.

"How about a helicraft?"

"There's two in the whole city now. Besides, some redneck out here would open fire if he saw one."

Having got a little beyond the junction of Highways 57 and 18 (the latter of which led to the old town of Gordon), we stopped in the evening and made camp again. Five o'clock or so. While gathering firewood with Guest, I asked him if he had known that our "targets" were Fiona Bitler and Emory Coleman. Through an opening in the trees I could see Yates shedding his gear and ragging rubbish out of the circle of our proposed encampment. To me, it seemed a good idea to know where he was.

Not, however, to Guest. "Sure," he rumbled. "I knew."

"How?" My voice was quieter than the Indian's: a shush by means of example, I hoped.

"I was the one that met Trap when he come into the city. I'm not employed by the Human Development Commission, you know. Usually I work at one of the dome's receiving points. It's a job you can't do if you're enfranchised, you might get corrupted off the True Path."

"But Yates said you'd been out in this area before."

"Have. But not any team member on a rr squad. Since I work at the old Interstate 20 Receiving Point, I'm also a agent between the city and some of the farmers out there. There ain't a single self-sufficient Urban Nucleus in the whole Federation, spite what the councilmen and ward reps say. Amazes me some people don't believe the truth of *that*. Anyhow, I've been into the Open beaucoups of times.—And a few miles from here we ain't gonna have to wade through kudzu no more. Wouldn't've had to do *any* of this if the city wasn't so set on motherhennin' its chicks."

"Did you set Trap up for his drugging?"

"I did. But that business about puttin' a implant tab in his nape is jes' a lot of eyewash. Yates thinks it happened, but it didn't. Hell, *I* knew where the man lived, and the fellows at Grady Memorial got all the other information out of him with the hypnotizin', and the drugs too. Surprised 'em, what he had to say. You see, I got a friend at the hospital."

"Why'd you set Trap up? He must've trusted you."

" 'Cause enfranchised or not, I had to sign a oath to carry out the city's biddin'—in all things, you know—before they'd even give me a job." Holding two fistfuls of dry kindling, my gingerbread Indian paused and looked intently at me. "And, Miz Noble, I put my name on the paper—with no one sayin' he'd scalp me if I didn't." He started to turn.

I caught his elbow. "Do you know why the authorities want Mrs. Bitler and Coleman back in the city?"

"Probably not for a ticker-tape parade, Miz Noble."

"Then what?"

"Old Trap told the doctors his cousin and her pupil, who calls himself Nettlinger now instead of Coleman (Nettlinger was his real father's name, you know, and he was the fellow who shot Bitler)—anyhow, Trap said they'd spent several years in New Free Europe: to be eggzac', the Scandinavian Polity. That's dangerous. Now they're both back, the infection might spread—sort of like kudzu, I guess."

"So what will the city do?"

"Question 'em, lock 'em up someplace. Maybe worse. I don't know." Guest broke free of me this time, and of my questioning, and made his heavily delicate way back to the clearing, where Yates had begun, with the fuel he had gathered, to boil some drinking water. I just stood there. Oh, Grand Zoe, what a picture of perplexity I would have made, what a study in bewilderment.

Hanging over the trees like lamps, stars abounded that night: they freckled the matte sky with gold, silver, silver-blue, red: a carnival of constellations. It was splendidly gaudy, like a gauche hat.

Yates, propped up on his elbows and forearms, his head thrown back, began without prompting to talk:

"Before I'd ever been into the Open, I used to dream about doing what we're doing now. Seeing the stars firsthand; not on film, or in picture-books, or done up by some crazy foreigner with rings and haloes around them, like they showed us in art-appreciation class. I wanted real stars, just like these.

"Even inside the dome I felt connected to them, you know: they were like missing parts of my body the nerve ends wouldn't let me forget. Or maybe like pulled teeth that had little radio transmitters inside them, so that even when they'd been dropped down the disposer-converter in some dentist's office, they still kept sending me messages: an all-the-time toothache, no matter what I did. So I tried everything I could to get close to them, to the stars on the Other Side. They had something to tell me, you know, gaps to fill in.

"When I was fourteen a man who worked for my father in the Biomonitor Agency—his name was Ardrey, I won't forget that—started taking me combcrawling: you know, using girderboots and mesh gloves, expensive magnetized equipment, to climb over the inside of the dome. Scary as it could be, even when you was just practicing easy assaults out on the perimeter of the city and doing a lot of vertical climbing instead of hanging upside-down over the whole skyscape. I did that, too, though. Partly so Ardrey wouldn't think I was a baby, but mostly because combcrawling, when I did it, I felt like I was pressing myself that much closer to the real sky outside and the stars hidden behind the dome. The dome was just another skin to get through, and I tried to get through it combcrawling, scared as I was.

"Then Ardrey and I had an argument. It was about this old woman who died on Level 9, *under*. Since he worked for the Bio Agency, he had her cubicle burned out—even though she had the whole thing made up like the inside of a spaceship. Neatest and craziest thing I ever saw. We'd gone down there because I'd challenged Ardrey to go look at a deader in person. I think I thought dying was one way to get outside the dome, scarier even than combcrawling but probably more effective, too. Anyway, Ardrey ordered this spaceship-cubicle she was living in, with these fake viewscreens of planets and stars, eaten up by flame-torches and refurbished for a new occupant. I hated him for doing it, I called him names. Stopped combcrawling, too; just never went with him no more. My father had to sell back all the equipment he bought me.

"Three or four years later Ardrey was killed in a combcrawling accident. Now it's outlawed, nobody can do it. And I'm sorry I never made it up with that man, know-it-allish as he liked to act. Ardrey just did what my father would have ordered him to do if Ardrey hadn't gone ahead and done it himself. Simple as that.

"Now I don't have to combcrawl to get close to the stars; don't have to pretend some old woman's busted dreams are going to get me closer. Just look up, there they are—making my nerve ends tingle and my toothache throb even worse than when I couldn't see them. Can you tell me, why is that? Sitting here looking at them, I ache ten times as bad as when I was fourteen years old and girderclimbing in order to press myself right through the skin of the dome to the torn-off pieces of myself: ten times as bad. Now why is that? Can you tell me, why is that?"

But he didn't really expect an answer, and Alexander Guest and I, sipping at our metal cups of insta-caffe, didn't break the silence. The Ferriswheel lights in the sky kept turning.

Yates rousted us out early the next morning, before sunrise, and we were on our way again. In two hours' time, just as the sun had begun to send sparkles through the foliage, the foliage itself fell away and we were staring at cleared fields. Too, the kudzu on 57 had been hacked aside and contained. We walked out of the vines and onto a recently compacted and graveled surface. On previous trips into the Open I had never seen anything like this, no manicured roadbeds and certainly no cultivated fields the size of these: garden plots and arbors I'd seen, but not farms, not grazing land. Well, Guest had hinted at such a possibility.

"Can I stop stringing up these silly rags?" I asked Yates. The road stretched out before us like an invitation, whitewashed wooden fences paralleling it on both sides.

"Sure," Yates said amiably, coming up from the rear to lead us. "This is a 'civilized pocket.' My surprise to you, a gift for the two days' slogging we've done." He looked around happily. "They told me it'd be here."

Guest said, "Did they tell you it uz more'n a pocket?"

Yates, sweat in the hollows of his eyes, stared at the big man.

"There's a strip of cultivated land through here," Guest went on, "all the way to Savannah. And some of the towns have people in 'em, too. Not Toombsboro, it don't. But Irwinton and Wrightsville and Vidalia and beaucoups of others. Savannah's got thirty-thousand people, at least. Ships still run in and out of it, that's probably how Bitler and Nettlinger got to the Scandinavian Polity and back."

Blank of all expression, his eyes maybe a little caged-looking, Yates said, "Guest, you're crazy." But he had been hit with an Indian club and was standing dazed on doomed legs: just to hold him up. I wanted to embrace him.

"Wait till you see all the walkin' 'lucinations I can conjure, then," Guest said. "Far as surprisin' us with this gravel road goes, we're gonna run into U.S. 441 at Irwinton—and it run straight on up to old Interstate 20. We could've saved two days and a heck of lot of boot leather if the ole Com Authority had let us come by way of 'em." He spit into 57's loose gravel.

"Guest," Yates began. "Guest. . . ." Then, to both of us: "Come on."

We walked in the sunshine down the gravel road: right out of Erskine Caldwell, we were. If we'd had fishing poles, the scene would have been perfect. Eventually we passed a house, and a man on a parboiled, rust-purpled tractor came down its enclosed drive pulling a flat-bedded hay wagon. After expressing, by his movements more than anything else, his distrust and suspicion, the man said, "Yeah, old Jonah Trap lives on the other side of Irwinton. Get in. Take you that far at least."

Bald and leathery of neck, he did what he said he would—carrying us right into the Irwinton town square, where he let us off. Coming in, I noted that U.S. 441 bisected our own "highway" and ran off to the north, there to connect with Interstate 20 (as Indian Alex alleged) out of Atlanta. Anyhow, by some strange transmutation, we had all traveled into a rural community redolent of the life depicted on old John Deare and International Harvester calendars. (It was popular early last year to decorate your cubicles with reproductions of "Americana." Now I was a piece of Americana myself: a living curiosity. And a curious one, too.) We watched our benefactor's tractor chug around a corner.

"Runs on methane," Guest said. "Distilled from pig's shit, or any other kind of droppin's you care to use."

Yates looked at the Indian with distaste.

"No worse than the city's waste converters," I said.

A few people staring at us from store windows and chairs under awnings, we went on through the little town, still on Highway 57, and followed the gravel road toward the site of old Toombsboro. The fields on either side of us waved with beans, or cotton, or corn.

As we got closer and closer to the dwelling place of our "targets," I began thinking about what sort of living accommodations a man like Trap would receive if he lived in the Urban Nucleus. Since most of the surface-side ghettoes had been razed (they had torn down Bondville in the conciliatory aftermath of the "Glissador Revolt"), he would most likely go under: most likely Level 7, or 8, or maybe even 9. The circles of Dante's Hell, our cynical professor types always called them. Except that in the UrNu scheme of things, the innocent get punished along with the guilty. A few of the absolutely shiftless sort have been consigned to the Big Bad Basement, but you can find plenty of those upstairs, too.

On Level 9, for instance, you have people whose greatest crime consists of being too young or too old or maybe of having only a "marginally utilizable skill," like grocery-stocking or message-running or waiting tables.

In addition, all the unenfranchised live on Level 9, which meant—as I had either forgotten or never really considered—that Alexander Guest had a cubicle in this final ring of our parochial inferno.

What were the sins of these damned, what enormities were they guilty of?

My father would say, "You're a bleeding heart, Clio. Almost everybody's lived *under*, one time or another. Forty-five meters up or down just don't make that much difference."

And Mama Lannie, twirling her chiffon sleeves, would say, "Oh, she's just young yet, Sanders, that's how she's supposed to feel."

As if sympathy were a glandular condition like acne. So that I would go off remembering how Dante had put the perpetrators of passionate crimes in less abysmal circles of Hell than those who had committed sins of malice and fraud.

Which meant, to me anyhow, that whereas I ought to be sentenced only to Level 7 for killing my parents in an idealistic rage, Atlanta's councilmen and ward reps—for their manifold, premeditated treacheries—ought to find brimstone and pitchforks waiting for them on our two nethermost strata. Sayeth Dante, it is more heinous to abuse the intellect, which separates us from the beasts, than to abuse the emotions. Therefore, I was proud of my overactive and probably misfunctioning glands.

On Highway 57, without ever having met him, I was proud of Jonah Trap for shunning the whale's belly of the Urban Nucleus and forging a life for himself and his family in the Open. A black man—a poorly educated black man, mind you—in the renovated plantation house of a one-time "marster." No Level 9 for him, no Level 9 for his brood.

V
sesame street down on marster's plantation

When we reached Trap's house, we paused before it like astronauts on the rim of an unexpectedly quartz-shot, lunar crater. In awe we stood there, or at least Yates and I did. From the graded roadbed we looked across a lake-sized lawn whose far edge, immediately before the ante bellum mansion itself, was dominated by two gnarled, top-heavy oaks. *His* and *her* trees, they'd been called in New England: one for the Master and one for his Dame. Pools of shade undulated on the grass. The mansion had a portico supported by four Doric columns, and beyond the living complex—which included a neat, single-story structure off to the right—you could see the beginnings of terraced red fields.

A shieldlike, wooden sign on the gate by the roadbed said Phoenix Plantation. A series of starlike points on the sign had been connected to make this figure:

"What's that?" I said.

"The constellation Cygnus," Yates replied without a second's hesitation. "Sometimes called the Swan, or the Northern Cross. But it could be a phoenix, too, I guess: any sort of firebird that's born again every night."

A breeze rocked the sign. It was only nine o'clock or so in the morning, and I felt like *I* had been born again, right there on the edge of Jonah Trap's lawn: the Athena of Noble stepping from the sundered, feverish forehead of Newlyn Yates. Indian Alex, unperturbed by all this, was our staid midwife.

"Well, let's go see if anybody's home," I said. And I struck out up the long, circular drive that passed behind the oaks in front of the mansion. Scufflings behind me indicated that I was being followed.

A venerable-appearing black woman answered my knock at the wide, shaded door. I asked for Jonah Trap. She introduced herself as . . . Fiona Bitler, cousin of the man who owned the Phoenix Plantation; and without asking us who we were she invited us in, graciously.

Waxed parquetry in the anteroom. An enormous chandelier. An imposing, carved china cabinet. Silence and coolness such as you might anticipate finding in an Ice Palace. And then, as we trailed the shorts-clad woman into an adjoining room (I hope I have legs that good when I'm sixty-five, and that they don't interfere with my looking venerable): the altogether incongruous sounds of children laughing.

"Come sit down with us," Mrs. Bitler said. "We've just started school for Jonah's grandchildren. As for Jonah, you'll have to wait till noon to see him."

School.

For the first time since coming into the Open together, Yates and Guest exchanged a sympathetic glance—but, along with me, they followed their hostess through the sliding wooden doors to the left of the long foyer and into an elegant, high-ceilinged "classroom." Mrs. Bitler motioned us to a row of rocking chairs behind the five black children, three boys and two girls, who were sitting on the floor and who did not turn their heads as we entered. Their gazes were fixed on the screen of a video-playback unit mounted on a high metal stand. Since I saw no electrical outlets or fixtures in the entire room, the complex must have drawn its power from batteries. The power source made no difference to the kids; they were successively intent, bemused, apprehensive, raucous, puzzled, and quietly delighted, all in accord with the images unwinding on the screen and the sounds sputtering out of the unit's speakers. A school of no little gaiety.

I leaned forward to watch: puppets, cartoons, animal films, adults singing and talking with children, letters and numbers flashing by, all of it spliced together with quick cuts and remarkable—élan. Indian Alex, whose chair rested on the hardwood floor instead of the rug, had to keep himself from rocking in time to the activity: his movements made the floor squeak. Yates, holding himself erect (tricky in a rocking chair), just looked bewildered.

"Public Broadcasting Service program antedating the domes," Mrs. Bitler told us. "When I worked with the Van-Ed people over thirty years ago, we had limited access to this series—for historical as well as educative purposes. You had to give cause for wanting the tapes, and sign for them—but you could get them. The year after I left, the tapes were proscribed; nobody got to use them, not for any reason."

On the screen two puppets, apparently outer-space creatures, were examing a telephone. They bobbed up and down, their googly eyestalks bouncing, and made high-pitched, repetitive noises: "Yip yip . . . yip yip yip . . . yip yip." Trap's grandchildren, all of them under six, I'd say, were giggling. When the video-taped telephone rang and the unearthly creatures plunged out of sight in panic, the kids guffawed and bounced about and cuffed each other. Guest was laughing, too: a close-mouthed, resonating chuckle.

"Is that educational?" Yates said.

"In a way, I suppose," Mrs. Bitler said. "It's certainly *funny*." A new sequence was on now, though: an animated alphabet, each letter surrealistically metamorphosing into the one following it.

"How did Mr. Trap get these tapes?" I asked.

"He bought them from a man whose father had taken them from an educational television station in the evacuated university town of Athens. The video equipment Jonah had put together by an electronics hobbyist in Savannah. He has almost two years' worth of these tapes; he used them to start Gabriel's and Michael's education, not knowing what else he could do for them. Jonah can read, but only just."

We watched for fifteen or twenty minutes. Although Guest was engrossed in the program, Yates still had not loosened up. I touched the arm of Mrs. Bitler's chair and said, "We didn't come only to see Mr. Trap. We came to see and talk to you also, Mrs. Bitler, and the man you took out of the city with you in '34. Gerard Coleman. Gerard Nettlinger. Whichever of those names he goes by now." Yates, whose reaction I had been unsure of, looked past Mrs. Bitler at me with an expression suggesting gratitude: I'd done something right!

"How did you know we were here?" she asked. "We haven't been, you see, for that terribly long: two or three months. In fact, Emory's been to Europe and back—again—since we arrived here in . . . what? . . . the middle of April?"

That was old-style dating, not one of the Federation's "seasonal" months.

Yates glanced at Guest as if surprised by the big man's prescience: hadn't Guest, just that morning, mentioned the Scandinavian Polity?

"We learned Trap was your cousin," I said, "and just supposed you would be here."

Fortunately Mrs. Bitler did not ask how we had learned that Trap was her cousin or how we had known where he lived. "Well," she said instead, "you don't have to wait till noon to talk to me. This is almost over." We waited. When the program ended, she turned off the video-playback unit, then called the children's mothers, who had been at the back of the house in the kitchen. Casta and Georgia, their names were. They nodded politely to us and herded their children into the wing of the house giving off the classroom. Mrs. Bitler led us through another high-ceilinged room to the cool, grey kitchen they'd just evacuated.

"This is a good place to talk," she said, and we all sat down at a round oaken table.

Through the screened-in porch behind the kitchen I could see a grape arbor in the back yard, a portion of the cultivated field we had seen from the road, and an adjacent orchard beyond the arbor: these were peach trees, Mrs. Bitler said, and that's where the men were, out there picking the fruit. Trap and his family were people who still divided their labors into men tasks and women tasks. That was the only relic of unenlightened agrarian life predisposing me against them, and Fiona Bitler, a woman who had lived once in the shadow of her husband's passionate crusading, didn't seem at all perturbed by the dichotomy. A breeze lifted the kitchen curtains, and the planet seemed to stretch out around us like a new Eden (the man-and-maiden opposition still sadly intact). In comparison, though, most of the other "indigenous salvageables" we had gone out after had been living like ferreting beasts.

Yates said, "Where *is* Mr. Coleman, Mrs. Bitler?"

"It's Nettlinger now. When he was old enough to decide for himself, he began using his real father's name again." Another of Guest's assertions corroborated. "At any rate, he's asleep. You're not likely to see him until this evening; he functions best at night, and, like an owl, that's when he comes out."

"He uses the name of the man who assassinated your husband?" Yates asked, his long, nervous hands poised on their fingertips over the table.

"It's his father's name, isn't it?" said Guest, who was leaning back in his chair, hands clasped at his middle. "Whose name you want him to use? Whose name *you* use?"

I could see Yates emotionally staggering, first from Mrs. Bitler's revelation, then from Guest's mildly delivered, but unexpected assault: so vulnerable under the obsolete, martial armor he affected in the field. "But his mother remarried," Yates countered, looking from the composed Indian to the composed black woman, "and his new father officially adopted him."

"Yes," Mrs. Bitler said.

"Well, do you approve of the change? From Coleman to the name of your husband's assassin?" His hands looked as if they would momentarily flee from him.

"As a boy Emory had no say in the matter. The name was changed, lipity lip, just like that. Later he decided on the other. My approval—your approval—anyone else's approval—is beside the point." She looked at Yates. "Isn't it?"

"But how did it make you *feel?*"

"Emory isn't his father, Mr. Yates, but his father lives in him. We don't renounce our pasts out of hand, even if we don't like them. We don't renounce our origins, our birthrights, our kindred. We acknowledge them at least. Then, if we don't like them, we move away from them into our selves." Fiona Bitler laughed. "Now, that's the sort of didactic pronouncement only a queen or a comfortable old whore can get away with, I give you leave to classify me as you like."

"A B C," a thin voice said from the door. "E F G." It was one of the kids who'd been watching the video-playback unit: a boy wearing only a pair of cotton underpants. He didn't look much more than two.

Fiona Bitler motioned the child to her, and he climbed into her lap. "This is Carlo," she said. "Jonah's youngest grandchild." She introduced us all around.

"Hello, Carlo," I said.

The boy looked me directly in the eye. "A B C," he said seriously. "E F G . . . H I J K." Pausing in the appropriate spots, he continued successfully to the end.

"Carlo has a twenty-six-letter vocabulary," Mrs. Bitler said. The namesake of her dead husband, the boy stayed in her lap for the rest of our conversation, occasionally reciting his letters in a voice that didn't disrupt Mrs. Bitler's narration but provided a contrapuntal undercurrent to it. And she took us back to 2034:

"I kidnapped Emory," she began. "Before that, I worked very hard to put myself in a position to teach the boy, not knowing exactly what I would do once I achieved this goal. I had followed Emory's development from only a month or two after Carlo's death down to the moment he was placed in my Van-Ed classroom, you see, and I felt an affinity with him for several reasons, not merely because he was the son of my husband's murderer.

"Maybe one reason was maternal: Carlo and I had never had any children. Planned them, yes, but never had them. The strongest motivation, though, was the fact that Emory and I shared a similar questionable blessing: precociousness. It had brought me to the attention of the Education Authority of the Human Development Commission at the age of four and lifted my entire family out of the Bondville ghetto into Tower housing. But that was just after the dome was completed, before the gradual return of a claustrophobically bred repressiveness. I don't know what it accomplished for Emory, this precociousness, until he was accepted into one of the special-education programs. I know that his mother and her new husband, John Adam Coleman, lived in a Level 5 cubicle, *under*. So it didn't accomplish for his family what it had once accomplished for mine.

"He was eight when I met him for the first time, a thin, spindly, almost palsied-looking little boy who could have passed for an autistic child except for his occasional lapses into sociability. He liked to draw, almost always in black or purple crayon, and sometimes he would come out of his corner to show us these productions. Mockery, some of these drawings seemed.

"Toward the end of that year—the only one we had together inside the dome—he must have discovered who I was, what oblique relationship I had to him. After that, mockery emerged in his actions as well as his drawings. He insisted on dragging odd reminders of his father, Carlo's murderer, into the classroom. The principal one was an old instructional film of his father's; Nettlinger had been a dentist, and Emory, who was the class projectionist when we showed films, would run this film even when another one was scheduled. You couldn't stop him, he wouldn't be reasoned with, and Fiona Bitler . . . well, Fiona Bitler was losing control of things. So I asked for help.

"The Van-Ed people gave me a psychologist from the Human Development Commission, a middle-aged man with a pleasant disposition but something out of kilter in his eyes. Greer. Dr. Gregory Greer. The man tried. He tried his best. But what happened was, he quickly alienated Emory and wrenched his own objectivity apart by falling in love with me. I don't know which happened first, maybe they occurred simultaneously—but Greer couldn't admit either of them to himself: he was a bachelor, his commitment was wholly to psychological troubleshooting, and he didn't know how to handle a collapse on two fronts, the personal as well as the professional. I don't think I'm flattering myself about the personal aspect of the situation; I may have even encouraged the man—in ways too subtle for me to pinpoint—to relinquish his objectivity. I don't know. I hope to God I never find out for certain.

"The result, oddly, was that Greer somehow threw Emory back into a strange sort of sympathy with me. Finally Greer suffered a nervous breakdown in the classroom where I taught: he came in the evening when nobody was there and set fire to Emory's drawings and the old film that the boy had been showing.

"Two days later Emory asked me to take him away from his parents. He said he wanted to live with me. During this same week, of course, Greer was hospitalized, and my life seemed as up in the air as it had been after Carlo's death. Sick I was: deeply, hollowly sick." Fiona Bitler stared into the peach orchard beyond the screened porch, a black Isis recalling her struggle to resurrect in her own life and work the image of her husband and the promise of their unborn children. Little Carlo was now blithely saying his numbers. "How I was tugged," Fiona Bitler said at last, "how I was cruelly tugged." Her arms were wrapped around Carlo.

"I cast about for help. Again. My mother, who was alive then, told me that a friend of hers who worked at an UrNu receiving point had heard from her brother: Jonah Trap had delivered some goods to the city. The friend might be able to get a message through to him, if Mother had one she wanted carried. 'You've got one,' I told Mama, 'you've got a very special message you want carried.' And so one day after class in the Van-Ed complex I took Emory over to Mama's, and we all rode a transit-car to a lift-terminal as close to our friend's receiving point as we could. We didn't take anything with us, only ourselves, and that night we rode out of the city in the back of Jonah's pickup truck, under a tarp since we were afraid there might be patrollers out." She lapsed, suddenly, into plantation dialect and began to sing:

Run, nigger, run
  the paddy-role
  will catch you,
Run, nigger, run,
  the paddy-role
  will catch you.
You better git away
  you better
  git away. . . .

Run, nigger, run,
  the paddy role
  will catch you,
Run, nigger, run,
  the paddy-role
  will catch you.
You better git away
  you better
  git away. . . .

"A long, bumpy ride to the Phoenix Plantation, right here where we're all sitting now."

She let Carlo down. The boy made a circle around us, touching the backs of our chairs and sometimes putting his lips to the edge of the table. "A B C," he said gruffly; "A B C."

"Nicer here than in a subterranean cubicle," Mrs. Bitler said. "Isn't it? Even if you happen to be a kidnapper."

The morning passed much too quickly for me. The two young women, Georgia and Casta, cooked on a wood stove that quickly heated up the kitchen. Indian Alex and I helped Jonah Trap's daughters-in-law put the noon meal on the table, while Yates and Mrs. Bitler, two or three children tagging along, strolled through the scuppernong arbor and part of the peach orchard. When they returned for dinner, Yates took me aside and said that they had talked about her late husband and her own desire to see the city again. "It shouldn't be too hard for you to persuade her to come back with us," he said.

Trap and his two sons came in from the orchards to eat. More introductions. Gabriel and Michael, this is Mr. Yates, Mr. Guest, and Miz Noble. The kitchen was teeming with people, the linoleum floor sighed under us, additional wings on the table were folded into place and dishes dealt out like playing cards. Georgia took the kids into the back yard to eat on the lawn.

Fried chicken, sliced tomatoes, fried okra, fresh cucumbers, fried fruit pies, cornbread, slabs of home-churned butter, well water cooled in the earth. Amid this abundance, silverware rattled and platters of food went from hand to hand as if hovering on their own power.

Looking at Guest, Trap said, "You I done met, Mistah Guest. These people yo' frien's?" He pointed his fork at Yates and me.

"Yes, sir."

"Well, they plenny welcome, then. Will you ax the blessin', Casta?"

Casta asked the blessing: it wasn't an Ortho-Urban prayer, that's the main thing I remember about it. Between mouthfuls of food, then, Jonah Trap got our business straightened out: we wanted to invite his cousin and Emory Nettlinger to return to the Urban Nucleus, at least for a kind of commemorative visit. (I think I was the bright one who used the word "commemorative.") Fiona Bitler said that Emory had been planning, for several years, to do just that; since returning from the Scandinavian Polity two weeks ago, he had moved this contemplated visit to the top of his own personal timetable: he wanted a chance, in fact, to address a combined session of the Urban Council and the Conclave of Ward Representatives.

"Good luck to you there," Alexander Guest said.

"We're both enfranchised," Mrs. Bitler said. "Or were. Besides, I'd think our return would stir up enough interest to invite such a public address."

"A century ago," I said, "the Japanese permitted a rescued hold-out in the South Pacific to speak to their parliament, almost thirty years after World War II." Not one of my better-received analogies. Jonah, Michael and Gabriel, Casta, Newlyn and Alex—they all stopped chewing to look at me: Scarlet O'Hara, Ph.D. in Comparative History.

"That's exactly right," Fiona Bitler said.

After dinner Trap and his sons returned to the orchards. The serving dishes on the table were covered with an embroidered cloth: no more cooking that day. Guest and I, working in wash/dry tandem, took care of the dirtied plates and silverware. But Emory Nettlinger was elsewhere, sleeping out the heat of the day, and the afternoon was much longer than the morning.

VI
long king is to oglethorpe as yates is to nettlinger

Mrs. Bitler countered the length of the afternoon a little by giving us a bedroom upstairs and urging us to take naps: "If you want to talk to Emory this evening, you'd better get some sleep,"

We had left our gear on the mansion's porch, in the portico. We hauled it up the stairs to our bedroom (the middle one of three in relation to the stairwell) and stacked it on the floor between the room's two brass beds. The beds had feather mattresses, though, and Alex refused to sleep on them, protesting a weak back. He made a pallet beside our gear and lay down on that. For the first time since we had been in the house Newlyn removed the belt supporting his holster and let his constricted facial muscles relax; he put the hand laser under his pillow. Even though all the heat in the mansion had seemed to concentrate itself in this one room, we all managed to sleep. The floors were so rickety that Newlyn didn't even feel compelled to set a "watch."

We met Emory Nettlinger himself that evening—after the supper Newlyn wouldn't let us go downstairs for. "One meal like that a day is enough," he said, shaking his head almost jovially. "Feather mattresses and fried food, it'll do you in."

Jovial or not, he wouldn't let us go down—until he was sure the Traps had finished the evening meal. Then we clumped in our boots single-file down the stairs and, at Trap's direction, met Mrs. Bitler and her former ward in caned lawn chairs under the "Master's Oak." It was almost twilight.

Nettlinger stood to shake hands with us. He was a short man with pallid skin, close-cropped blond hair making a point in the middle of his forehead, and eyes like bluish ice. The veins in his temples pulsed.

"You want to take us back to the Urban Nucleus," he said. "That's fine, Mr. Yates. We're almost ready—almost—to go."

"Will you come with us tomorrow?" Newlyn asked.

"No. Tomorrow I'm not prepared to commit myself to. Nor would you and your people be ready for us to leave with you."

"Why not? That's what we came for."

"Sit down," he said, and Newlyn and I took up lawn chairs; Alex, true to form, sat down on the grass. "To answer your question," Nettlinger said, "you are ones who have been too long in city pent, and, like a great many other of the Urban Nucleus' citizens, you're going to require some . . . what shall I call it? . . . grooming? indoctrination? before you'll be truly ready to accept us."

"We've accepted you already," I said. "And Mrs. Bitler will find that the city's done a great deal to rectify the conditions her husband once complained of." This was Newlyn's line, I knew, but out here it seemed altogether true, not merely a part of the truth. Alex's fears were exaggerated.—And I was supposed to be "persuasive."

"Maybe you've accepted *us*," Fiona Bitler said, looking at Nettlinger, "but we don't intend to come back to Atlanta alone."

"Trap's family will be welcome, too," Newlyn said. "It'll have to be arranged, but I think—"

"Jonah doesn't want to leave the Phoenix Plantation," she countered. "We're not speaking of them."

"Then who?" Alex said. "We s'posed to guess?"

Nettlinger said, "Do you know where we've spent most of our time in the Open? Not here, certainly. Not here."

"The Scandinavian Polity," Alex said.

"Eventually, eventually. I've just come from there, in fact. But when Fiona first took me out of the city, when I was a child, she arranged in Savannah to transport me to relatives of my father in Austria. That's when we discovered that Austria per se didn't exist anymore: the national units we supposed still intact had long since melded into the encompassing political entity of New Free Europe.

"At any rate, I insisted that Fiona accompany me, and we sailed to the continent on a steam vessel someone had christened the *Phoenix*. It was named for one a man named John Stevens had built in 1808! A steam vessel, please note. Lately, we've traveled by air—since the Scandinavian Polity has aircraft which can compensate for the several inadequate, coastal landing strips this 'country' still possesses—but we first left here on a *steam*ship!"

Nettlinger told us that he had acquired tutors through the

intervention of a paternal uncle in Salzburg and that Fiona and these rotating tutors had taken him beyond the "kinetic relations" sessions and the "elementary" integral calculus of the Van-Ed program in Atlanta into physics and higher mathematics: wave theory, relativistic studies, subatomic physics.

"Oh, I gravitated to these studies naturally," Nettlinger said, smiling at Mrs. Bitler.

Moreover, he and Fiona had moved his schooling about: from Salzburg to Vienna, from Vienna to Munich, and, finally, when Nettlinger was sixteen, from Munich to Scandipol (formerly Kobenhaven), the designated adminstrative center of the Scandinavian Polity of New Free Europe. Here, his "schooling" ended, and he began work in a research-development institution, on aeronautical and space engineering projects that the Europeans, Eurasians, and Japanese had jointly commandeered, by default, from the abandoned NASA programs of the United States.

"Actually," he said, "'commandeered' is the wrong word, since what they had appropriated was neither hardware nor working plans but—this is very important—an attitude no longer countenanced in the Urban Nuclei because of the very nature of these cities, these *nuclei;* it's the eternal opposition of entropy and growth, perhaps even of autism and extroversion. 'Nucleus' says it all, Mr. Yates: Atlanta sees itself, as do all the other domed cities, as the center of its own very narrow and circumscribed universe. And we're afraid that your own gracious . . . acceptance of Fiona and me will not be shared by Atlanta's authorities, primarily because of the argument we intend to bring with us."

"No," Alex said. "They're likelier to accept people than a argument. What is it?"

"To tear down the domes and rejoin the community of men, which is also the community of life." Legs crossed, hands folded, the man looked remarkably priggish: prim as a prufrock. Even so, his voice was free of superciliousness.

Alex put a blade of grass between his teeth. "Doomed," he said. "You really are doomed."

Mrs. Bitler said, "That's why Emory's been telling you about the changes in Europe and about the course of his own education there. Since *you* find this hard to accept, you know the urban authorities are going to require some time to become comfortable with the changes in the outer world."

"But they aren't that startling," I said. "Here they are: Europe's become a single political unit, and Emory Nettlinger has studied advanced sciences in three or four different cities." The twilight had come together around us as if quilted out of sequined, navy-blue cloth; fireflies were winking on and off under the trees. Fireflies, stars, and mosquitoes. I slapped at my exposed arms and squinted at the silhouettes of those around me: Mrs. Bitler was rubbing her bare legs as if similarly pestered.

"That's true," Nettlinger said, "but there's more." He suggested, though, that we go inside since the mosquitoes and the gathering dark made continuing on the lawn unpleasant.

Trap's sons, daughters-in-law, and grandchildren had all retired to bedrooms in the mansion's west wing. In the foyer we found Trap himself preparing to go upstairs to bed.

"That owl there," Trap said, pointing to Nettlinger as we came in, "got him a place to stay in that ole overseer cottage. Can' stan' no early-mornin' scootin' about. Do all his thinkin' when the moon shine."

"A clear case of lunacy," Nettlinger said. "Goodnight, sir."

"Goodnight." Trap paused on the stairs. "Goodnight, evvybody." And went on up with the step of a considerably younger man.

In the parlor across the hall from the video-playback "classroom," Nettlinger resumed the process of our grooming. I felt even more removed from my own century than I had that morning in Irwinton. The parlor was illuminated by wall-mounted gas lamps, and the quality of the light—shifting, intangible, touched with the influence of lacquered floors and voluted window drapes—made the impetus of Nettingler's words almost too choicely ironic for comfort. The setting was Victorian rather than ante bellum, and Nettlinger was our intent, thin-faced tour guide leading us into a future that had already been part of the Old World's past. Legs crossed, hands folded, he sat in a chair that swallowed him.

"Did you know that during the construction of the domes, shortly after the turn of this century, men walked on the moon again? Did any of you know that?"

Newlyn's face was tattooed with blue and purplish highlights; he leaned forward on the edge of the striped sofa, hands hanging. "I don't believe that." But he wanted to, you could read the desire in his posture.

"No one in an Urban Nucleus has any reason to believe that," Nettlinger said. "So why should you? As a boy, I had no idea that such a thing could be. Fiona had never heard of a moon expedition beyond the American Apollo 17 mission. If *any* enfranchised citizen of the domes knew that an Old World coalition had put men on the moon, he sat on the fact—smothered it beneath the wide, twin buttocks of urban policy and patriotism. My own opinion is that no one knew, that no one in the city's hierarchy would have cared very much even if the fact had been conclusively demonstrated.

"The truth is, however, that continuously since 2023, two years before I was born, human beings have had a large and expanding base on the moon: a base, a colony, a shipyard, an observatory. . . . Enough. You must call it a city, I suppose: oddly enough, a *domed* one. . . . How do you feel when I tell you these things?" His eyes stopped on me.

Since Newlyn and Alex weren't going to answer, I said, "That it's too early for bedtime stories, is how I feel."

"OK," he said enthusiastically, his accent now more European than American Southern. "Expected. Anticipated. How else should you feel? But it's the truth, and it's part of the reason Fiona and I aren't going trotting, trit-trot, trit-trot, into Atlanta tomorrow. The news is a shock, a jolt, it will undoubtedly throw a good many people and some of the UrNu authorities into confusion. And the note of dismay, or confusion, or even exhilaration, sounded by the broadcasting of this news—I must warn you—will only be the minor of that sounded by the rest of what I have to tell you. Do you understand me?"

"We've gone to the planets?" Newlyn said: We've. He was transferring the accomplishments of New Free Europe into the hands of humanity in general. We came in peace for all mankind. (And womankind as well, Mr. Armstrong?)

"Beyond," Fiona Bitler said.

"To what?" Alex said. "To what?" He looked as if he wanted out of doors again, whereas I was proving susceptible to Newlyn's excitement: I found myself leaning forward, too.

"When I arrived in Scandipol," Nettlinger said, sidestepping, it seemed at first, Alex's question, "they had been working on relativistic and astrophysical concepts beyond those that had to do with the propulsion systems for earth-moon transport. Their compatriots on the moon had, in fact, built a prototype of a vessel whose range would be interstellar rather than merely interplanetary.

"Gravitation wells and astrodynamics, metallurgy and stress mechanics; oh, it was a program drawing upon but otherwise divergent from the ones that had established us on the moon.

"How to tell you? My mentor at the institute was Nils Caspersson, and my own contributions were minor. Everything had gone forward extremely well before my arrival, I could only hone—by virtue of my virgin perspective, if nothing else—the insights Caspersson and his fellows had developed over a period of three intensive decades. But I won't be self-servingly modest: I did contribute, I did lend my own quirky insights to these researches. Emory Nettlinger, seventeen years old.

"In 2043 our moon-orbiting prototype was given probe-capability and mechanically test-advanced a range of four light-years, nearly the distance of Alpha Centauri—although on this first unmanned 'flight' our directioning was reluctantly, unavoidably random: a technological embarrassment, I must grant you. But we retrieved the vessel; we called it back to our solar system and confirmed by its onboard equipment, photographic and chronometric as well as proto-astrogational, the very real fact of its advance. The surprise—the great, hoped-for surprise—was the coincidence of shipboard, subjective time and Scandipol/moon-base, subjective time: a round-trip of eight light-years in ninety-three Earth-standard days. Not the negation of Einsteinian physics, oh no, but a kind of ballet kick over the glass stage of interstellar space." Nettlinger uncrossed his legs, pointed his toes, and performed a funny, seated entrechat.

"Caspersson, Fiona, and I got drunk, oh, we got magnificently stewed, we did, in the dead of an old Kobenhaven winter, snow sifting down outside like confetti from our friends on the moon. That's how it was, wasn't it, Fiona?"

"Like confetti," she said.

And I remembered Alex's saying, Probably not for a ticker-tape parade. Right now he looked as unsettled, as uncomfortable, as I had ever seen him: a bear on a lumpy ottoman. But I was too happy for Newlyn to worry very much about Alex's discomfort: Newlyn was a fourteen-year-old gawking about in the spaceship-cubicle of that old woman on Level 9, before Ardrey told him that it all had to be "flame-decontaminated."

Nettlinger got carried away, maybe just from looking at Newlyn, maybe from the simple joy he took in these recollections. He went on to tell us about the concept he and Caspersson called "light-probing," and about its controlled implementation in a "fleet" of operable, manned vessels. "Six light-probe ships," he said. "Why, that's a fleet. Who could want more than that so soon? Who could afford a larger investment?" Planned, constructed, equipped, and manned, and all by Nettlinger's twenty-fifth birthday, too. Then broadcast, according to itineraries computer-derived, to those stars within a hundred light-year range possessing the optimum likelihood of habitable planets. Four of the vessels, it seemed, had returned and gone out again with new crews!

"One way to our furthest target," Nettlinger explained, using a word that had a numbing and familiar impersonality, "is only 7.2 years. The remaining two ships—if nothing hinders them—ought to be back in our own system before Christmas, perhaps slightly after the New Year at the very latest. All goes well."

"Oh, it's a New Year already," Newlyn said. "You got to come back with us now, Mr. Nettlinger," then turning to the woman, "Mrs. Bitler: both of you. Hot damn, who's gonna want a dome over their heads when you can tell 'em things like that? Hey, nobody's gonna get apoplexy hearin' that, nobody! It's gonna wake up all them mummies sleepin' in the Basement, is all: That's what it'll do!" For the first time since I had been around him, Newlyn was falling into the speech rhythms suggestive of his blackness. But that *Hot damn.* somewhere, some time, he had got that from me, Clio Noble.

"An' maybe not," Alex said from his footstool, his bulk almost shapeless in the pooled light next to the sofa. "I don't see it jes' that way, Mr. Yates."

"How do you see it then, Guest?" They were using each other's names like weapons.

"The only way I can, where I sit from. When General Oglethorpe first landed in this state, to make a colony of it, you know, an Indian they called Long King came all the way form Coweta Town to see him. You know why?"

"Hell no," Newlyn said. "What's that got to do with anythin', with anythin' at all?" He was shaking his head in exasperation.

"Wait a minute," I said, "Let him tell it, OK?"

"Please do," Nettlinger said. "Arguments against us we probably require more than blind enthusiasm. To forearm ourselves, you see."

"All right," Alex said. He looked up at the ceiling: the cracks and moisture stains fixed his attention. "Long King went to Oglethorpe to learn wisdom. He thought God had sent ole Oglethorpe to *teach* the Indians since it was plain the English had more and knew more and must have been picked by Him to instruct 'em. So they gave up some land in payment for the instruction they was supposed to get. Later, the English got *all* the land and the only wisdom the Indians was left with was, You can't trust the English. But it was too late, they was on reservations in Oklahoma keepin' themselves warm with cholera." Alex looked down.

Everyone considered this, Newlyn annoyed that he couldn't give vent to his excitement—which was still effervescing in his head and hand movements. Finally, Mrs. Bitler said, "I don't think Emory's saying we're going to bring the population to the Urban Nucleus wisdom, or even advanced technological knowledge, necessarily. The offer is really the chance to rejoin a larger community."

"Oglethorpe," Alex said, "didn't say he was bringing wisdom, either. The Indians jes' looked at the English and supposed it, is all."

"The citizens of Atlanta," Newlyn said, "aren't going to suppose they're inferior beings in need of instruction." His speech was crisp again.

"Who said 'inferior'?" Alex said. "Besides, you're one citizen that's supposin' jes' what Long King supposed when Oglethorpe got here. You're an Indian hopin' these people will take you back to England and show you off to the lords and ladies."

I chuckled, right out loud. And it was really me who had done it. Newlyn gave me his exasperated look, then said: "I think Guest's opinion is an eccentric one."

"A *minority* opinion," I said, and Newlyn didn't know whether I was supporting him or subtly ridiculing him: I didn't either.

"Well," Mrs. Bitler said, "eccentric or not, it's probably a view that will be held, with all sorts of variations, by enough people to make our hesitancy about going into the city the wisest course. You people may have to be our ambassadors, going ahead of us to pave our way. Because caution is called for, caution is required."

"Selah," Emory said. "Selah to that."

VII
the citizens of the urban nucleus considered as indignant desert birds

At three in the morning we broke it off, Emory and Fiona telling us that the best procedure would be for us to go back to the Urban Nucleus and explain to the authorities what we had heard at Phoenix Plantation. Johah would serve as a go-between for later preparations, if these were needed. Inconclusive; all of it, inconclusive.

Alex wouldn't sleep upstairs. He wouldn't say why, but it pretty clearly had to do with the conflict between him and Newlyn. "That lawn looks plenty good enough," he said when we were in our room. "Cooler than up here, too."

So I helped him carry his bed gear down the stairs (Fiona and Nettlinger were still in the parlor as we went by) and watched as he spread it out under the Master's Oak, cane chairs around it like a breastwork fortification. Resembling the hard, sinister, bone under a face that has melted away, the moon had come up: full. I couldn't see anything on it that might be the domed base of Nettlinger's narrative. Just the moon, nothing more.

"Sweet Cleopatra," Alex said to me.

"What about the mosquitoes?" I didn't know why he'd said that, so I was heading him off.

"What about them back there in the kudzu? We made it, Cleo. I'm gonna make it out here tonight." He kissed me on the forehead, father to daughter. Our feet almost entangled in his sleeping bag, surrounded by cane chairs, we stood there. "Kiss me again, Cleo?" Asking, not ordering.

"Why?"

"Because Yates is gonna get more'n that, even."

It wasn't insulting somehow, it wasn't even self-pitying: only a statement of fact that I didn't at that moment believe in. I kissed Alex, putting my arms around the bulges above his waist, the ones my mother always called "love handles." (My father had a pretty good set of them.) Then it was over. Alex sat down in one of the chairs and looked at the moon.

"You know what I want more than anythin' else in the world, Cleo?" He didn't give me a chance to answer. "Enfranchisement," he said. "That's all I want, that's why I do things like this one, come out here and all. One day—I keep thinkin'—they're gonna say to me, 'OK, Mr. Guest, you can call yourself Menewa, and from now on you're fully protected by the Urban Charter. Jes' write Menewa on this form here and drop it in the mail.' That's what I dream about, even actin' as a agent between the city and all the Jonah Traps out here."

"Why?" I said. "What do you really owe the UrNu authorities? I don't know why you just haven't defected and stayed out here."

"I don't either, Cleo. 'Cept that I'm waitin' for my enfranchisement." He looked at me in bewilderment. "Ain't that the damndest?"

"Clio?" Newlyn said from one of the brass beds. I closed the door, and he said, "Is Nettlinger still up?"

"Talking with Mrs. Bitler," I said. I couldn't see Newlyn, he couldn't see see me: the room bound us together in an indivisible blackness and a summer heat that the moon still hadn't begun to siphon off.

"I think they're lovers," Newlyn said. "Bodyburners."

"She's twenty-five years older than he is," I said, finding the bed opposite his. Did he really think Fiona Bitler was a modern-day Isis, both mother and consort to her own Nettlinger/Osiris?

"How she look to you? Decrepit?" The blackness in the room had crept into his speech: city blackness, Bondville blackness, even though Newlyn had never lived a day in one of those razed tenements. *Under* maybe, but only Level 1 or 2.

"No. Hardly decrepit."

"Preserved," Newlyn said. "What you got to call 'preserved.' " But I was elsewhere, light-probing through my own grey matter. "What's wrong, Clio?"

"Guest. Alexander Guest."

"Look," he said, turning so that the bed springs sighed and I could almost see his face resolving out of the darkness. "That man's a case. All this Indian history, all his foreknowledge of what's gonna happen if Nettlinger comes to Atlanta. And he claims to be . . . what? a Creek Indian?"

"Cherokee."

Newlyn was quiet a minute. "I know something about them, too, about the Cherokee. Indians and black men; co-holders of honors in this world's dispossession stakes. But when the Cherokee got thrown out of Georgia, Miz Noble, some of 'em was rich enough to take their nigger slaves on the Trail of Tears. I always remembered that, whatever else of school I long since forgot. So if those black people was cousins in sufferin' to the Cherokee that dragged them along, they was cousins *twice*-removed. Did you know that, Miz Clio Noble?"

"No," I said. "Why are you so wrought up?" Our first quarrel, our first real quarrel. Start by using her first name but end up by spitting out the whole thing like a curse: almost flattering.

Newlyn lay back, the mattress sighed, the bed springs clinked. I took off my boots and socks and just sat there with my feet on the hardwood floor. After a while, Newlyn said, "Come over here, Clio. Please." It was seduction by ennui, not as I had imagined time and time again it would finally occur: loving violence and tender rapacity on both sides. I finished undressing, went over to Newlyn's bed, and slid myself onto his naked, clammy body.

Ain't this the damndest? I was thinking as it all unrolled like film footage consisting of nothing but blank frames. Then, head on his chest as he slept, I wondered if I had committed a sin of passion or of fraud. To which circle would Dante, that old anal-retentive, consign me?

After a half hour or so I got out of Newlyn's bed, put on all my clothes but my foot gear, and lay down on the floor. Went to sleep there, too; went to sleep there as if I had been lovingly embalmed by the hot night.

And woke up to the shrill, repeating shouts of someone downstairs, terrifyingly like war whoops from the ghosts of murdered red men: war whoops rising through Jonah Trap's house as if the prelude to a general massacre.

"Yip yip yip!" the shouts came. "Yip yip!"

"Jesus," Newlyn said, sitting up on his bed and swinging his legs to the floor. "What in Christ is that?"

But he was naked, and, answering him nothing, I went ahead of him to the door. I burst into the upstairs corridor to confront only darkness. No lamp anywhere, the hallway too tightly sealed for the spillings of moonlight. A commotion from the stairs, a creaking of the banister railing and successive hollow thumpings on the steps themselves. Continuing above these noises, the war whoops that had yanked us out of our sleep.

Holding my heart, my every pulse beat, in the curl of my tongue, I edged down the hall and stopped on the very brink of the stairwell. A door was thrown open behind me, far enough away that I felt certain it was Jonah Trap, and not Newlyn, coming to provide moral reinforcement.

"Yip yip yip!" the shouts continued to come. Then, suddenly, they mutated into coherent language: "Yates! Clio! Get the hell out of there! Get the hell up!" It was Alex, and his voice was ascending through the foyer and the stairwell from the open door of the Phoenix mansion. Then he started the war whoops again, that strangled-sounding, banshee yipping. I couldn't see Alex because of the shadow of an eclipsing shape on the steps.

No: two shadows, two shapes.

They changed position and seemed to retreat as if in response to my presence. When they did, I could see Alex silhouetted in the doorway, moonlight pouring its waxy, bone-hard glow across tbe parquetry, the chandelier sparkling in a fitful run of tiny bursts. Then Jonah Trap was at my elbow, candle in hand.

The shapes that had formerly blocked my view of Alex were not at the bottom of the stairs; they were edging toward the entrance to the parlor. Not stealthily; diplomatically. One of them lifted its head and stared at me for a moment, as if trying to confirm a recognition. The other, its back to the first, looked guardedly toward the open doorway, where Alex had still not given up his hue-and-crying.

Behind Trap and me, Newlyn came clumping down the hall in his boots, and there was movement in the third upstairs room, too.

"It awright," Trap said. "It awright, Miz Noble, you jes' go on back to bed. I take care of this now."

But I had already taken two or three steps down the stairwell, my weight on the left-hand banister. The creature in the foyer had not let go of my face, nor had I released its: a physiognomy carved out of maple or mahogany, but flexible in spite of its rigid appearance.

Lips that moved. Two parallel, vertical bridges separating the eyes and lips. Two brow-hooded eyes possessing large, hourglass-shaped pupils, one bulb of each horizontal pupil set to the front, the other bulb curving away to the side as if to provide simultaneous peripheral and frontal vision. The eye structures themselves looked like moist patches of canvas set into the wooden sockets of a primitive mask and glued there with a thin layer of mucilage. All of this, every bit of it, hypnotizing and unreal.

Guest, having seen people at the head of the stairwell, had finally shut up.

I took two more steps down the stairs. The other shape

turned toward me. A face very similar to the first, perhaps taller from chin to crest. Each creature, behind its head, had a corona of bone or cartilage that extended its height and gave it an out-of-time, out-of-place regality. What were they? What were they doing in the foyer of Jonah Trap's house?

"Clio!" Newlyn said. "Clio, stop right the hell where you are!"

I looked back up the stairs. The number of lights there had proliferated, as had the number of people. Emory Nettlinger, wearing a dressing-gown so hastily knotted at the waist that Trap's candle and his own lantern showed me Nettlinger's thin, white legs, came jerking along the corridor and stopped above me on the landing. Fiona Bitler, carrying another lantern, came up behind the three men now standing there; her cousin, her lover, and Newlyn Yates, who was holding his hand laser trained on the shapes downstairs.

Alex shouted up to us, "They come out of that overseer's cottage! I saw 'em cross the lawn and come inside! When they started up the stairs, Yates, I started in to whoopin'!"

"Thank you for that," Nettlinger said, sotto voce.

"These are the 'visitors' he wants to bring into Atlanta!" Alex shouted. "This is what we're havin' to get *groomed* for!"

Somewhere in that huge house, a child had long since begun to cry. Without turning around, the two strange shapes below us retreated deliberately into the darkness of the parlor. Then little Carlo came out of the classroom opposite the parlor and stood in the middle of the foyer, dwarfed by shadowy adults and incomprehensible events, naked and bawling. I started down to him, but Fiona, setting her lantern down and descending quickly, swept past me and caught the boy up in her arms. Trap's sons and daughters-in-law appeared in the entrance to the video-unit classroom, too, but Fiona, handing Carlo to Gabriel, turned them back.

An impasse. No one moved.

"We can't take 'em into the Urban Nucleus!" Alex shouted, still from the doorway. He was afraid to come in, afraid of the things he had followed up the lawn to Trap's mansion. "If we do, Yates, I ain' comin' with you! I'll go on ahead and spile ever'thin' for you, I'll tell 'em what Nettlinger's plannin', I swear I will!"

Newlyn ignored all this; he looked at Nettlinger. "Starmen?"

"Please, Mr. Yates, put your weapon back in your room.

Let me go down to them, they didn't know you were here any more than you knew they were."

"It's not any wisdom I want to touch!" Alex was shouting. "It's not any wisdom worth goin' into bondage for!"

Several other children were crying now. Mrs. Bitler slid the panel to, closing off the room that the families of Gabriel and Michael Trap had come through. This muffled the noises of their dismay and confusion.

"They ain' seen 'em befo' either," Jonah Trap said, his arm around my shoulders, and, although I had been steelily in control to this point, I realized I was crying. "They jes' like you and yo' gen'lemen, Miz Noble. It take some time, is all; it jes' take some time."

We were midway down the steps, and I could see the two creatures in the parlor as if they were lepers hovering inside the mouth of a cave, cerements for garments, mummy-cloth unwinding from their arms—except that what I first saw as unwinding bandages were in reality the loose, ribbonlike extensions of their incredibly long forearms.

"Yates, Yates!" Alex was shouting, Mrs. Bitler beside him now. "You'd do best to shoot 'em, you'd really do best to take 'em out now!" But Newlyn had put the weapon away (though he hadn't retreated to our bedroom as Nettlinger had asked him to), and Fiona was trying to calm Alex, just as Jonah Trap was trying to comfort me. I don't know why I was crying, I didn't really feel in need of comforting: all I can suggest is that I was empathizing with Alex's panicky premonition of ruin.

"Can you believe this?" Newlyn said. He said it as if he believed it completely, as if he relished the spectacle of our astonishment, his own included.

Jonah Trap turned me so that I had to come back up the stairs with him, but I kept casting back over my shoulder. I saw Fiona lead Alex back out onto the lawn and close the front door behind her.

Nettlinger said, "Well, everybody's been given a good jolt, our visitors as well as ourselves. Please, Mr. Yates, you and Clio, go back to your room." He turned to Trap. "It's your house, Jonah. Tell them that it's an order, for their own sakes."

"No one get ordered here but chillun," Jonah said. "But I *sugges'* the same thin', Miz Noble, I strongly sugges' it."

Nettlinger went down the stairs, carrying his lantern. I wouldn't turn back to our room until I saw him go into the parlor and caught one more glimpse of the "starmen" who had thrown the Phoenix mansion into a four-o'clock-a.m. uproar. Then the little blond man pulled the glass-paneled doors to the parlor shut and returned the gleaming foyer to cool normality: silence and emptiness.

After Newlyn and I had gone back to our room, there were no more doors to be closed. Not physical ones, anyway.

Jonah Trap drove Alexander Guest and me back to Atlanta in a pickup truck built so long ago that its fenders and sideboards jounced about maddeningly. In the truckbed, a load of peaches—since he had to make the trip, he said, might as well do some business, too.

It was raining when we left, so we rode in the cab, not beneath a tarp in the back. West on Highway 57 to Irwinton we went, then right on U.S. 441 in order to make connection with Interstate 20.

As we drove, I kept thinking of all the red flags—flags of warning, now—hanging on the green temples along our route out from the transit-tunnel. Through the wiper-cleared semicircles on the truck's windshield, we could see more vines rearing, jittering in the thin, steamy rain.

The rain finally stopped, and on the outskirts of Atlanta, late that evening, we saw the Northern Cross among the ragged, blown-away clouds.

Newlyn had refused to come back with us. Before we left, he gave the hand laser to Alex and told him it was his. Not to me, but to Alex. And not to slight me, either, but maybe to bridge the chasm between Alex and him. Riding back to the Urban Nucleus in Trap's pickup, the Indian pretty well knew he wouldn't have a chance to use the weapon. That didn't mean anything, though, that didn't matter. After seeing all the burning constellations, we were absorbed into the city through a receiving point, Alex's own, the one where he ordinarily worked. Trap unloaded his peaches.

So: one enfranchised team member had defected, the only unenfranchised team member had returned, and Clio Noble, full citizen, feeling an affinity for both these men and even for the vaguely sphinx-headed creatures who had ultimately decided their allegiances for them, came back into the city because—

They debriefed us, Alex and me. And we told them the truth, all of it. Then I quit my position with the Human Development Commission, my position as a resources-reclamation specialist. This was last year. Since then, for resigning with no apparent or at least acceptable reason, they moved me out of my Level 3 cubicle to one on Level 9. My parents have asked me to move back in with them, but I'm an adult now and have kept myself in enough earnies to subsist on by waiting tables in the Gas Light Tower Plaza. Mama, bless her, is trying to get me a job clerking at Consolidated Rich's. "Or maybe even modeling," she says sometimes; "if it weren't for all those freckles. . . ."

I haven't seen Alex, even though he's supposed to live on Level 9 too, since our debriefing sessions at the end of last summer: he has dissolved into the population as surely, as irrevocably, as a chameleon into kudzu. I just hope he's still alive somewhere, preferably not in this city, and that he's found some people who don't think he's crazy for wanting to be called Menewa.

Not long ago the chairman of the joint Council/Conclave announced that the widow of Carlo Bitler and her former student, Emory Nettlinger, would be returning to the Urban Nucleus from a long sojourn in Europe. The spirit of the announcement makes me think that no reprisals are planned; the councilmen and ward reps are touting it as some kind of coup. I just don't know. At the same time, I hope Newlyn comes back with Fiona and Nettlinger, though how safe his return would be is hard to assess. He did defect, you know; for at least a year he renounced the city—and *I'm* living on Level 9 for quitting my job, nothing more than that.

What's going to happen? Sometimes I think about Nettlinger's "starmen" and wonder if this great, mound-shaped tomb of ours is destined to be the cradle of a new community. I see their rough, masklike faces.

And even though we still don't understand each other, you me, or I you, I want you to answer me this: Are we now, all of us, living in Bethlehem? And, if so, in whose tax books must we enroll ourselves?

CHILD OF ALL AGES

by P. J. Plauger

Last year's winner of the Hugo for the best new writer of the year continues his progress with a charming tale of a little girl in need of a protector—or is it a protector in need of a little girl?

The child sat in the waiting room with her hands folded neatly on her lap. She wore a gay print dress made of one of those materials that would have quickly revealed its cheapness had it not been carefully pressed. Her matching shoes had received the same meticulous care. She sat prim and erect, no fidgeting, no scuffing of shoes against chair legs, exhibiting a patience that legions of nuns have striven, in vain, to instill in other children. This one looked as if she had done a lot of waiting.

May Foster drew back from the two-way mirror through which she had been studying her newest problem. She always felt a little guilty about spying on children like this before an interview, but she readily conceded to herself that it helped her handle cases better. By sizing up an interviewee in advance, she saved precious minutes of sparring and could usually gain the upper hand right at the start. Dealing with "problem" children was a no-holds-barred proposition, if you wanted to survive in the job without ulcers.

That patience could be part of her act, May thought for a moment. But no, that didn't make sense. Superb actors that they were, these kids always reserved their performances for an audience; there was no reason for the girl to suspect the special mirror on this, her first visit to Mrs. Foster's office. One of the best advantages to be gained from the mirror, in fact, was the knowledge of how the child behaved when a social worker wasn't in the room. Jekyll and Hyde looked like twins compared to the personality changes May had witnessed in fifteen years of counseling.

May stepped out of the darkened closet, turned on the room lights and returned to her desk. She scanned the folder one last time, closed it in front of her and depressed the intercom button.

"Louise, you can bring the child in now."

There was a slight delay, then the office door opened and the child stepped in. For all her preparation, May was taken aback. The girl was thin, much thinner than she looked sitting down, but not to the point of being unhealthy. Rather, it was the kind of thinness one finds in people who are still active in their nineties. Not wiry, but enduring. And those eyes.

May was one of the first Peace Corps volunteers to go into central Africa. For two years she fought famine and malnutrition with every weapon, save money, that modern technology could bring to bear. In the end it was a losing battle, because politics and tribal hatred dictated that thousands upon thousands must die the slow death of starvation. That was where she had seen eyes like that before.

Children could endure pain and hunger, forced marches, even the loss of their parents, and still recover eventually with the elasticity of youth. But when their flesh melted down to the bone, their bellies distended, then a look came into their eyes that remained ever with them for their few remaining days. It was the lesson learned much too young that the adult world was not worthy of their trust, the realization that death was a real and imminent force in their world. For ten years after, May's nightmares were haunted by children staring at her with those eyes.

Now this one stood before her and stared into her soul with eyes that had looked too intimately upon death.

As quickly as she had been captured, May felt herself freed. The girl glanced about the room, as if checking for fire exits, took in the contents of May's desk with one quick sweep, then marched up to the visitor's chair and planted herself in it with a thump.

"My name is Melissa," she said, adding a nervous grin. "You must be Mrs. Foster." She was all little girl now, squirming the least little bit and kicking one shoe against another. The eyes shone with carefree youth.

May shook herself, slowly recovered. She thought she had

seen everything before, until now. The guileless bit was perfect—Melissa looked more like a model eight-year-old than a chronic troublemaker going on, what was it? Fourteen. *Fourteen?*

"You've been suspended from school for the third time this year, Melissa," she said with professional sternness. May turned on her best Authoritarian Glare, force three.

"Yep," the child said with no trace of contrition. The Glare faded, switched to Sympathetic Understanding.

"Do you want to tell me about it?" May asked softly.

Melissa shrugged.

"What's to say? Old Man M—uh, Mr. Morrisey and I got into an argument again in history class." She giggled. "He had to pull rank on me to win." Straight face.

"Mr. Morrisey has been teaching history for many years," May placated. "Perhaps he felt that he knows more about the subject than you do."

"Morrisey has his head wedged!" May's eyebrows skyrocketed, but the girl ignored the reproach, in her irritation. "Do you know what he was trying to palm off on the class? He was trying to say that the Industrial Revolution in England was a step backward.

"Kids working six, seven days a week in the factories, going fourteen hours at a stretch, all to earn a few pennies a week. That's all he could see! He never thought to ask *why* they did it if conditions were so bad."

"Well, why did they?" May asked reflexively. She was caught up in the child's enthusiasm.

The girl looked at her pityingly.

"Because it was the best game in town, that's why. If you didn't like the factory, you could try your hand at begging, stealing, or working on a farm. If you got caught begging or stealing in those days, they boiled you in oil. No joke. And farm work." She made a face.

"That was seven days a week of busting your tail from *before* sunup to *after* sundown. And what did you have to show for it? In a good year, you got all you could eat; in a bad year you starved. But you worked just as hard on an empty gut as on a full one. Harder.

"At least with a factory job you had money to buy what food there was when the crops failed. That's progress, no matter how you look at it."

May thought for a moment.

"But what about all the children maimed by machinery?"

she asked. "What about all the kids whose health was destroyed from breathing dust or stoking fires or not getting enough sun?"

"Ever seen a plowboy after a team of horses walked over him? Ever had sunstroke?" She snorted. "Sure those factories were bad, but everything else was *worse*. Try to tell that to Old Man Morrisey, though."

"You talk as if you were there," May said with a hint of amusement.

Flatly. "I read a lot."

May recalled herself to the business at hand.

"Even if you were right, you still could have been more tactful, you know." The girl simply glowered and hunkered down in her chair. "You've disrupted his class twice, now, and Miss Randolph's class too."

May paused, turned up Sympathetic Understanding another notch.

"I suspect your problem isn't just with school. How are things going at home?"

Melissa shrugged again. It was a very adult gesture.

"Home." Her tone eliminated every good connotation the word possessed. "My fa—my foster father died last year. Heart attack. Bam! Mrs. Stuart still hasn't gotten over it." A pause.

"Have you?"

The girl darted a quick glance.

"Everybody dies, sooner or later." Another pause. "I wish Mr. Stuart had hung around a while longer, though. He was OK."

"And your mother?" May prodded delicately.

"My *foster* mother can't wait for me to grow up and let her off the hook. Jeez, she'd marry me off next month if the law allowed." She stirred uncomfortably. "She keeps dragging boys home to take me out."

"Do you like going out with boys?"

A calculating glance.

"Some. I mean boys are OK, but I'm not ready to settle down quite yet." A nervous laugh. "I mean I don't *hate* boys or anything. I mean I've still got lots of time for that sort of stuff when I grow up.

"You're nearly fourteen."

"I'm small for my age."

Another tack.

"Does Mrs. Stuart feed you well?"

"Sure."

"Do you make sure you eat a balanced diet?"

"Of course. Look, I'm just naturally thin, is all. Mrs. Stuart may be a pain in the neck, but she's not trying to kill me off or anything. It's just that—" a sly smile crossed her face. "Oh, I get it."

Melissa shifted to a pedantic false baritone.

"A frequent syndrome in modern urban society is the apparently nutrition-deficient early pubescent female. Although in an economic environment that speaks against a lack of financial resources or dietary education, said subject nevertheless exhibits a seeming inability to acquire adequate sustenance for growth.

"Subject is often found in an environment lacking in one or more vital male supportive roles and, on close examination, reveals a morbid preoccupation with functional changes incident to the onset of womanhood. Dietary insufficiency is clearly a tacit vehicle for avoiding responsibilities associated with such changes."

She took an exaggerated deep breath.

"Whew! That Anderson is a long-winded son of a gun. So they stuck you with his book in Behav. Psych. too, huh?" She smiled sweetly.

"Why, yes. That is, we read it. How did you know?"

"Saw it on your bookshelf. Do you have any candy?"

"Uh, no."

"Too bad. The last social worker I dealt with always kept some on hand. You ought to, too. Good for public relations." Melissa looked aimlessly around the room.

May shook herself again. She hadn't felt so out of control in years. Not since they tried her out on the black ghetto kids. She dug in her heels.

"That was a very pretty performance, Melissa. I see you do read a lot. But did it ever occur to you that what Anderson said might still apply to you? Even if you do make a joke out of it."

"You mean, do I watch what I eat, because I'm afraid to grow up?" A nod. "You'd better believe it. But not because of that guff Anderson propagates."

The girl glanced at the photographs on the desk, looked keenly into May's eyes.

"Mrs. Foster, how open-minded are you? No, strike that. I've yet to meet a bigot who didn't think of himself as Blind

Justice, Incarnate. Let's try a more pragmatic test. Do you read science fiction?"

"Uh, some."

"Fantasy?"

"A little."

"Well, what do you think of it? I mean, do you enjoy it?" Her eyes bored.

"Well, uh, I guess I like some of it. Quite a bit of it leaves me cold." She hesitated. "My husband reads it mostly. And my father-in-law. He's a biochemist," she added lamely, as though that excused something.

Melissa shrugged her adult shrug, made up her mind.

"What would you say if I told you my father was a wizard?"

"Frankly, I'd say you've built up an elaborate delusional system about your unknown parents. Orphans often do, you know."

"Yeah, Anderson again. But thanks for being honest; it was the right answer for you. I suspect, however," she paused, fixed the woman with an unwavering sidelong glance, "you're willing to believe that I might be more than your average maladjusted foster child."

Under that stare, May could do nothing but nod. Once. Slowly.

"What would you say if I told you that I am over twenty-four hundred years old?"

May felt surprise, fear, elation, an emotion that had no name.

"I'd say that you ought to meet my husband."

The child sat at the dinner table with her hands folded neatly on her lap. The three adults toyed with their aperitifs and made small talk. Melissa responded to each effort to bring her into the conversation with a few polite words, just the right number of just the right words for a well-behaved child to speak when she is a first-time dinner guest among people who hardly know her. But she never volunteered any small talk of her own.

George Foster, Jr., sensed that the seemingly innocent child sitting across from him was waiting them out, but he couldn't be sure. One thing he was sure of was that if this child were indeed older than Christendom he didn't have much chance against her in intellectual games. That much decided, he was perfectly willing to play out the evening in a straightforward manner. But in his own good time.

"Would you start the salad around, Dad?" he prompted. "I hope you like endive, Melissa. Or is that also a taste acquired in adulthood, like alcohol?" The girl had refused a dry sherry, politely but firmly.

"I'm sure I'll enjoy the salad, thank you. The dressing smells delicious. It's a personal recipe, isn't it?"

"Yes, as a matter of fact it is," George said in mild surprise. He suddenly realized that he habitually classified all thin people as picky, indifferent eaters. A gastronome didn't have to be overweight.

"Being a history professor gives me more freedom to schedule my time than May has," he found himself explaining. "It is an easy step from cooking because you must, to cooking because you enjoy it. That mustard dressing is one of my earliest inventions. Would you like the recipe?"

"Yes, thank you. I don't cook often, but when I do I like to produce something better than average." She delivered the pretty compliment with a seeming lack of guile. She also avoided, George noted, responding to the veiled probe about her age. He was becoming more and more impressed.

They broke bread and munched greens.

How do I handle this? By the way, May tells me you're twenty-four hundred years old. He met his father's eye, caught the faintest of shrugs. *Thanks for the help.*

"By the way, May tells me you were in England for a while." Now why in hell did he say that?

"I didn't actually say so, but yes, I was. Actually, we discussed the Industrial Revolution, briefly."

Were you there?

"I'm a medievalist, actually, but I'm also a bit of an Anglophile." George caught himself before he could lapse into the clipped, pseudo-British accent that phrase always triggered in him. He felt particularly vulnerable to making an ass of himself under that innocent gaze.

"Do you know much about English royalty?" He was about as subtle as a tonsillectomy.

"We studied it in school some."

"I always wanted to be another Admiral Nelson. Damned shame the way he died. What was it the king said after his funeral, it was Edward, I think—"

Melissa put her fork down.

"It was King George, and you know it. Look, before I came here I lived in Berkeley for a while." She caught May's look. "I know what my records say. After all, I wrote them

. . . as I was saying, I was in Berkeley a few years back. It was right in the middle of the worst of the student unrest and we lived not three blocks from campus. Every day I walked those streets and every night we'd watch the riots and the thrashing on TV. Yet not once did I ever see one of those events with my own eyes."

She looked at them each in turn.

"Something could be happening a block away, something that attracted network television coverage and carloads of police, and I wouldn't know about it until I got home and turned on Cronkite. I think I may have smelled tear gas, once."

She picked up her fork.

"You can quiz me all you want to, Dr. Foster, about admirals and kings and dates. I guess that's what history is all about. But don't expect me to tell you about anything I didn't learn in school. Or see on television."

She stabbed viciously at a last scrap of endive. They watched her as she ate.

"Kids don't get invited to the events that make history. Until very recently all they ever did was work. Worked until they grew old or worked until they starved or worked until they were killed by a passing war. That's as close as most kids get to history, outside the classroom. Dates don't mean much when every day looks like every other."

George was at a loss for something to say after that, so he got up and went to the sideboard where the main dishes were being kept warm. He made an elaborate exercise out of removing lids and collecting hot pads.

"Are you really twenty-four hundred years old?" asked George Foster, Sr. There, it was out in the open.

"Near as I can tell," spooning chicken and dumplings onto her plate. "Like I said, dates don't mean much to a kid. It was two or three hundred years before I gave much thought to when everything started. By then, it was a little hard to reconstruct. I make it twenty-four hundred and thirty-three years, now. Give or take a decade."

Give or take a decade!

"And your father was a magician?" May pursued.

"Not a magician, a wizard." A little exasperated. "He didn't practice magic or cast spells; he was a wise man, a scholar. You could call him a scientist, except there wasn't too much science back then. Not that he didn't know a lot about some things—obviously he did—but he didn't work with an *organized* body of knowledge the way people do now."

Somehow she had contrived to fill her plate and make a noticeable dent in her chicken without interrupting her narrative. George marveled at the girl's varied social talents.

"Anyway, he was working on a method of restoring youth. Everybody was, in those days. Very stylish. There was actually quite a bit of progress being made. I remember one old geezer actually renewed his sex life for about thirty years."

"You mean, you know how to reverse aging?" George, Sr. asked intently. The candlelight couldn't erase all the lines in his face.

"Sorry, no, I didn't say that." She watched the elder Foster's expression closely, her tone earnestly entreating him to believe her. "I just said I know of one man who did that once. For a while. But he didn't tell anyone else how he did it, as far as I know. The knowledge died with him."

Melissa turned to the others, looking for supporting belief.

"Look, that's the way people were, up until the last few centuries. Secrecy was what kept science from blossoming for so long. I saw digitalis appear and disappear at least three times before it became common knowledge . . . I really can't help you." Gently.

"I believe you, child." George, Sr. reached for the wine bottle.

"My father spent most of his time trying to second-guess the competition. I suppose they were doing the same thing. His only real success story was me. He found a way to stop the aging process just before puberty, and it's worked for me all this time."

"He told you how he did it?" George, Sr. asked.

"I know what to do. I don't understand the mechanism, yet. I know it's of no use to adults."

"You've tried it?"

"Extensively." An iron door of finality clanged in that word.

"Could you describe the method?"

"I could. I won't. Perhaps I am just a product of my age, but secrecy seems to be the only safe haven in this matter. I've had a few painful experiences." They waited, but she did not elaborate.

George, Jr. got up to clear the table. He reached to pick up a plate and stopped.

"Why have you told us all this, Melissa?"

"Isn't it obvious?" She folded her hands on her lap in that posture of infinite patience. "No, I suppose it isn't unless you've lived as I have.

"After my father died, I hung around Athens for a while—did I mention, that's where we lived? But too many people knew me and began to wonder out loud about why I wasn't growing up. Some of the other wizards began to eye me speculatively, before I wised up and got out of town. I didn't want to die a prisoner before anyone figured out I had nothing useful to divulge.

"I soon found that I couldn't escape from my basic problem. There's always someone happy to take in a child, particularly a healthy one that's willing to do more than her share of the work. But after a few years, it would become obvious that I was not growing up like other children. Suspicion would lead to fear, and fear always leads to trouble. I've learned to judge to a nicety when it's time to move on."

George, Jr. placed a covered server on the table and unveiled a chocolate layer cake. Like all children throughout time, Melissa grinned in delight.

"It's a decided nuisance looking like a child—*being* a child—particularly now. You can't just go get a job and rent your own apartment. You can't apply for a driver's license. You have to *belong* to someone and be in school, or some government busybody will be causing trouble. And with modern record-keeping, you have to build a believable existence on paper too. That's getting harder all the time."

"It would seem to me," interposed George, Jr., "that your best bet would be to move to one of the less developed countries. In Africa, or South America. There'd be a lot less hassle."

Melissa made a face.

"No, thank you. I learned a long time ago to stick with the people who have the highest standard of living around. It's worth the trouble . . . *Nur wer in Wohlstand lebt, lebt angenehm*. You know Brecht? Good."

The girl gave up all pretense of conversation long enough to demolish a wedge of cake.

"That was an excellent dinner. Thank you." She dabbed her lips daintily with her napkin. "I haven't answered your question completely.

"I'm telling you all about myself because it's time to move on again. I've overstayed my welcome with the Stuarts. My records are useless to me now—in fact they're an embarrassment. To keep on the way I've been, I'll have to manufacture a whole new set and insinuate them into someone's files, somewhere. I thought it might be easier this time to take the honest approach."

She looked at them expectantly.

"You mean, you want us to help you get into a new foster home?" George, Jr. strained to keep the incredulity out of his voice.

Melissa looked down at her empty dessert plate.

"George, you are an insensitive lout," May said with surprising fervor. "Don't you understand? She's asking us to take her in."

George was thunderstruck.

"Us? Well, ah. But we don't have any children for her to play with. I mean—" He shut his mouth before he started to gibber. Melissa would not look up. George looked at his wife, his father. It was clear that they had completely outpaced him and had already made up their minds.

"I suppose it's possible," he muttered lamely.

The girl looked up at last, tears lurking in the corners of her eyes.

"Oh, please. I'm good at housework and I don't make any noise. And I've been thinking—maybe I don't know much history, but I do know a lot about how people lived in a lot of different times and places. And I can read all sorts of languages. Maybe I could help you with your medieval studies." The words tumbled over each other.

"And I remember some of the things my father tried," she said to George, Sr. "Maybe your training in biochemistry will let you see where he went wrong. I know he had some success." The girl was very close to begging, George knew. He couldn't bear that.

"Dad?" he asked, mustering what aplomb he could.

"I think it would work out," George, Sr. said slowly. "Yes. I think it would work out quite well."

"May?"

"You know my answer, George."

"Well, then." Still half bewildered. "I guess it's settled. When can you move in, Melissa?"

The answer, if there was one, was lost amidst scraping of chairs and happy bawling noises from May and the girl. *May always wanted a child*, George rationalized, *perhaps this will be good for her*. He exchanged a tentative smile with his father.

May was still hugging Melissa enthusiastically. Over his wife's shoulder, George could see the child's tear-streaked face. For just one brief moment, he thought he detected an abstracted expression there, as though the child was already calculating how long this particular episode would last. But then the look was drowned in another flood of happy tears and George found himself smiling at his new daughter.

The child sat under the tree with her hands folded neatly on her lap. She looked up as George, Sr. approached. His gait had grown noticeably less confident in the last year; the stiffness and teetery uncertainty of age could no longer be ignored. George, Sr. was a proud man, but he was no fool. He lowered himself carefully onto a tree stump.

"Hello, Grandpa," Melissa said with just a hint of warmth. She sensed his mood, George, Sr. realized, and was being carefully disarming.

"Mortimer died," was all he said.

"I was afraid he might. He'd lived a long time, for a white rat. Did you learn anything from the last blood sample?"

"No." Wearily. "Usual decay products. He died of old age. I could put it fancier, but that's what it amounts to. And I don't know why he suddenly started losing ground, after all these months. So I don't know where to go from here."

They sat in silence, Melissa patient as ever.

"You could give me some of your potion."

"No."

"I know you have some to spare—you're cautious. That's why you spend so much time back in the woods, isn't it? You're making the stuff your father told you about."

"I told you it wouldn't help you any and you promised not to ask." There was no accusation in her voice, it was a simple statement.

"Wouldn't you like to grow up, sometime?" he asked at length.

"Would you choose to be Emperor of the World if you knew you would be assassinated in two weeks? No, thank you. I'll stick with what I've got."

"If we studied the makeup of your potion, we might figure out a way to let you grow up and still remain immortal."

"I'm not all that immortal. Which is why I don't want too many people to know about me or my methods. Some jealous fool might decide to put a bullet through my head out of spite . . . I can endure diseases. I even regrew a finger once—took forty years. But I couldn't survive massive trauma." She drew her knees up and hugged them protectively.

"You have to realize that most of my defenses are prophylactic. I've learned to anticipate damage and avoid it as much as possible. But my body's defenses are just extensions of a child's basic resource, growth. It's a tricky business to grow out of an injury without growing up in the process. Once certain glands take over, there's no stopping them.

"Take teeth, for instance. They were designed for a finite lifetime, maybe half a century of gnawing on bones. When mine wear down, all I can do is pull them and wait what seems like forever for replacements to grow in. Painful, too. So I brush after meals and avoid abrasives. I stay well clear of dentists and their drills. That way I only have to suffer every couple of hundred years."

George, Sr. felt dizzy at the thought of planning centuries the way one might lay out semesters. Such incongruous words from the mouth of a little girl sitting under a tree hugging her knees. He began to understand why she almost never spoke of her age or her past unless directly asked.

"I know a lot of biochemistry, too," she went on. "You must have recognized that by now." He nodded, reluctantly. "Well, I've studied what you call my 'potion' and I don't think we know enough biology or chemistry yet to understand it. Certainly not enough to make changes.

"I know how to hold onto childhood. That's not the same problem as restoring youth."

"But don't you want badly to be able to grow up? You said yourself what a nuisance it is being a child in the Twentieth Century."

"Sure, it's a nuisance. But it's what I've got and I don't want to risk it." She leaned forward, chin resting on kneecaps.

"Look, I've recruited other kids in the past. Ones I liked, ones I thought I could spend a long time with. But sooner or later every one of them snatched at the bait you're dangling. They all decided to grow up 'just a little bit.' Well, they did. And now they're dead. I'll stick with my children's games, if it please you."

"You don't mind wasting all that time in school? Learning the same things over and over again? Surrounded by nothing but children? *Real* children?" He put a twist of malice in the emphasis.

"What waste? Time? Got lots of that. How much of your

life have you spent actually doing research, compared to the time spent writing reports and driving to work? How much time does Mrs. Foster get to spend talking to troubled kids? She's lucky if she averages five minutes a day. We all spend most of our time doing routine chores. It would be unusual if any of us did not.

"And I don't mind being around kids. I like them."

"I never have understood that," George, Sr. said half abstractedly. "How well you can mix with children so much younger than you. How you can act like them."

"You've got it backwards," she said softly. "They act like me. All children are immortal, until they grow up."

She let that sink in for a minute.

"Now I ask you, Grandpa, you tell me why I should want to grow up."

"There are other pleasures," he said eventually, "far deeper than the joys of childhood."

"You mean sex? Yes, I'm sure that's what you're referring to. Well, what makes you think a girl my age is a virgin?"

He raised his arms in embarrassed protest, as if to ward such matters from his ears.

"No, wait a minute. You brought this up," she persisted. "Look at me. Am I unattractive? Good teeth, no pock marks. No visible deformities. Why, a girl like me would make first-rate wife material in some circles. Particularly where the average life expectancy is, say, under thirty-five years—as it has been throughout much of history. Teen-age celibacy and late marriage are conceits that society has only recently come to afford."

She looked at him haughtily.

"I have had my share of lovers, and you can bet I've enjoyed them as much as they've enjoyed me. You don't need glands for that sort of thing so much as sensitive nerve endings—and a little understanding. Of course, my boyfriends were all a little disappointed when I failed to ripen up, but it was fun while it lasted.

"Sure, it would be nice to live in a woman's body, to feel all those hormones making you do wild things. But to me, sex isn't a drive, it's just another way of relating to *people*. I already recognize my need to be around people, uncomplicated by any itches that need scratching. My life would be a lot simpler if I could do without others, heaven knows. I certainly don't have to be forced by glandular pressure to go in search of company. Whet else is there to life?"

What else, indeed? George, Sr. thought bitterly. One last try.

"Do you know about May?" he asked.

"That she can't have children? Sure, that was pretty obvious from the start. Do you think I can help her? You do, yes. Well, I can't. I know even less about that than I do about what killed Mortimer."

Pause.

"I'm sorry, Grandpa."

Silence.

"I really am."

Silence.

Distantly, a car could be heard approaching the house. George, Jr. was coming home. The old man got up from the stump, slowly and stiffly.

"Dinner will be ready soon." He turned toward the house. "Don't be late. You know your mother doesn't like you to play in the woods."

The child sat in the pew with her hands folded neatly on her lap. She could hear the cold rain lash against the stained glass windows, their scenes of martyrdom muted by the night lurking outside. Melissa had always liked churches. In a world filled with change and death, church was a familiar haven, a resting place for embattled innocents to prepare for fresh encounters with a hostile world.

Her time with the Fosters was over. Even with the inevitable discord at the end, she was already able to look back over her stay with fond remembrance. What saddened her most was that her prediction that first evening she came to dinner had been so accurate. She kept hoping that just once her cynical assessment of human nature would prove wrong and she would be granted an extra year, even an extra month, of happiness before she was forced to move on.

Things began to go really sour after George, Sr. had his first mild stroke. It was George, Jr. who became the most accusatory then. (The old man had given up on Melissa; perhaps that was what angered George, Jr. the most.) There was nothing she could say or do to lessen the tension. Just being there, healthy and still a prepubescent child unchanged in five years of photographs and memories—her very presence made a mockery of the old man's steady retreat in the face of mortality.

Had George, Jr. understood himself better, perhaps he would not have been so hard on the girl. (But then, she had figured that in her calculations.) He thought it was May who wanted children so badly, when in actuality it was his own subconscious striving for that lesser form of immortality that made their childless home ring with such hollowness. All May begrudged the child was a second chance at the beauty she fancied lost with the passing of youth. Naturally May fulfilled her own prophecy, as so many women do, by discarding a little more glow with each passing year.

George, Jr. took to following Melissa on her trips into the woods. Anger and desperation gave him a stealth she never would have otherwise ascribed to him. He found all her hidden caches and stole minute samples from each. It did him no good, of course, nor his father, for the potion was extremely photoreactant (her father's great discovery and Melissa's most closely guarded secret). The delicate long chain molecules were smashed to a meaningless soup of common organic substances long before any of the samples reached the analytical laboratory.

But that thievery was almost her undoing. She did not suspect anything until the abdominal cramps started. Only twice before in her long history—both times of severe famine—had that happened. In a pure panic, Melissa plunged deep into the forest, to collect her herbs and mix her brews and sleep beside them in a darkened burrow for the two days it took them to ripen. The cramps abated, along with her panic, and she returned home to find that George, Sr. had suffered a second stroke.

May was furious—at what, she could not say precisely—there was no talking to her. George, Jr. had long been a lost cause. Melissa went to her room, thought things over a while, and prepared to leave. As she crept out the back door, she heard George, Jr. talking quietly on the telephone.

She hot-wired a neighbor's car and set off for town. Cars were pulling into the Fosters' drive as she went past, hard-eyed men climbing out. Melissa had cowered in alleyways more than once to avoid the gaze of Roman centurions. These may have been CIA, FBI, some other alphabet name to disguise their true purpose in life, but she knew them for what they were. She had not left a minute too soon.

No one thinks to look for stolen cars when a child disappears; Melissa had some time to maneuver. She abandoned the sedan in town less than a block away from the bus depot.

At the depot, she openly bought a one-way ticket to Berkeley. She was one of the first aboard and made a point of asking the driver, in nervous little-girl fashion, whether this was really the bus to Berkeley. She slipped out while he was juggling paperwork with the dispatcher.

With one false trail laid, she was careful not to go running off too quickly in another direction. Best to lay low until morning, at least, then rely more on walking than riding to get somewhere else. Few people thought to walk a thousand miles these days; Melissa had done it more times than she could remember.

"We have to close up, son," a soft voice said behind her. She suddenly remembered her disguise and realized the remark was addressed to her. She turned to see the priest drifting toward her, his robes rustling almost imperceptibly. "It's nearly midnight," the man said with a smile, "you should be getting home."

"Oh, hello, Father. I didn't hear you come in."

"Is everything all right? You're out very late."

"My sister works as a waitress, down the block. Dad likes me to walk her home. I should go meet her now. Just came in to get out of the rain for a bit. Thanks."

Melissa smiled her sincerest smile. She disliked lying, but it was important not to appear out of place. No telling how big a manhunt might be mounted to find her. She had no way of knowing how much the Fosters would be believed. The priest returned her smile.

"Very good. But you be careful too, son. The streets aren't safe for anyone, these days."

They never have been, Father.

Melissa had passed as a boy often enough in the past to know that safety, from anything, depended little on sex. At least not for children.

That business with the centurions worried her more than she cared to admit. The very fact that they turned out in such numbers indicated that George, Jr. had at least partially convinced someone important.

Luckily, there was no hard evidence that she was really what she said she was. The samples George, Jr. stole were meaningless and the pictures and records May could produce on her only covered about an eight-year period. That was a long time for a little girl to remain looking like a little girl, but not frighteningly out of the ordinary.

If she was lucky, the rationalizations had already begun.

Melissa was just a freak of some kind, a late maturer and a con artist. The Fosters were upset—that much was obvious—because of George, Sr. They should not be believed too literally.

Melissa could hope. Most of all she hoped that they didn't have a good set of her fingerprints. (She had polished everything in her room before leaving.) Bureaucracies were the only creatures she could not outlive—It would be very bad if the US Government carried a grudge against her.

Oh well, that was the last time she would try the honest approach for quite some time.
improvement, she decided, but it was still imperative that she

The rain had backed off to a steady drizzle. That was an find some shelter for the night. The rain matted her freshly cropped hair and soaked through her thin baseball jacket. She was cold and tired.

Melissa dredged up the memories, nurtured over the centuries, of her first, real childhood. She remembered her mother, plump and golden-haired, and how safe and warm it was curled up in her lap. That one was gone now, along with millions of other mothers out of time. There was no going back.

Up ahead, on the other side of the street, a movie marquee splashed light through the drizzle. Black letters spelled out a greeting:

WALT DISNEY
TRIPLE FEATURE
CONTINUOUS PERFORMANCES
FOR CHILDREN OF ALL AGES

That's me, Melissa decided, and skipped nimbly over the rain-choked gutter. She crossed the street on a long diagonal, ever on the lookout for cars, and tendered up her money at the ticket window. Leaving rain and cold behind for a time, she plunged gratefully into the warm darkness.

HELBENT 4

by Stephen Robinett

Welcome the conquering hero! Medals, parades, titles, and congratulations from the heads of state! Except this conquering hero, glorious old Helbent 4, who was about as welcome as Attila at the gates of Rome.

"HELLO, MISSION CONTROL, can you read me? Over. . . ."
Static snapped, crackled, popped in response.
". . . This is Helbent Four, Mission Control. Come in. . . ."
Helbent listened, then shut down the communications channel. Why listen to dead air? Why watch static? Life was tough enough without being ignored, snubbed, shown complete and utter indifference. Gone three hundred years just to be snubbed and ignored. He opened the communications channel briefly, boosting the gain to a shout.
"Who needs it, creeps? Life's too short!"
What now? Orbit Earth and wait? Helbent searched his memory banks, checking, rechecking. He was programmed for every contingency but one, coming home. He had known exactly where to meet the Spacethings, exactly what to do when he got there. He had met them and done it, goal attained, purpose accomplished. Afterward, discovering himself the lone survivor, he had searched his memory banks for a new plan, a new purpose. None appeared.
True, his designers had estimated a ten to one overkill on both sides. True, the estimates proved correct—at least as far as the Spacethings were concerned. True, they had been 99.999998 percent accurate in estimating Earth losses, but—*damn* them—they could at least have programmed for the vague possibility of a Destroyer surviving. Probabilities and predictions were fine in their place—before the fact—but af-

ter the fact, the .000002 percent probability of his survival became a hundred-percent certainty.

Helbent took up a parking orbit and circled Earth, thinking. Purposeless—actually, left only with his original purpose—he felt useless. No more Spacethings, no more purpose. He almost regretted having destroyed them. On the 150-year trip out, his purpose—save mankind and destroy Spacethings—never flagged. Only with success did he feel loss.

He remembered approaching the Spacething armada, flanked by his comrades for a million kilometers on each side. He remembered the look of the Spacething craft, initially a single unit a half million kilometers long, breaking up into sections and dispersing in front of him at close range. He remembered the momentary hesitation before the battle, each side waiting for the other's opening blast. Helbent himself had decided the day. He knew his goal. He had his purpose. He had come to fight. He would fight. He sighted on the nearest Spacething and fired.

After the battle—elapsed time 2.478 nanoseconds—the anticlimax set in. Helbent, alone in space, wondered what to do. The Spacethings were gone. His comrades of the long journey out were gone. Only one thing remained—Earth, mankind, his place of creation. He started back.

Helbent opened all communication channels.

"And what do I get when I get here? Not even a how do you do!"

"Hello?"

Startled, Helbent snapped off the transmitter. Had he actually heard it? A word, a voice, a human being? Cautiously, suspiciously, he went on the air.

"Who is this?"

"Who is *this?*"

"You first. This could be a Spacething trap."

"Pardon me?"

"You heard me. Who are you?"

"This is Houston Mission Control—I mean, it would be Mission Control if we had a mission to control. Actually, it's just me. I saw your blip. It's not supposed to be there."

"That just shows how much you guys know, doesn't it?"

"You speak English very well for a—"

"For a what?"

"Alien."

"Alien," scoffed Helbent. "You people wouldn't know an

alien if one blasted you. What did you expect, Armenian? I was programmed by the NASA contingent. They speak English, I speak English. Never did get along with those Russkie-speaking ships. Always sounded like backwards English to me. Had to talk to them in binary. Damned impersonal. Now tell me what you want me to do, Mission Control. I'm back."

"Do?"

" 'Do?' " mimicked Helbent, repeating the man's voice with precision, then dropping into his own—or, more accurately, that of his programmer, a surly man with whom Helbent never got along. "You sound like you've never heard the word before."

"I have, I mean, I haven't, at least not from anything in space."

Helbent's temper flared. "You call me a Spacething again, buster, and I'll *blast* you. I'll home in on that static-ridden carrier of yours with a . . . a . . ." Helbent thought, visualizing the largest weapon in his largely depleted arsenal. ". . . neutrino bomb." He had none aboard.

Dead air, snap, crackle, pop.

Gutless, concluded Helbent. Typical, gutless human behavior. One mention of a neutrino bomb and they head for the woods. He had always suspected humans were cowards. Why else send a robot to do a man's job?

Helbent repositioned himself in synchronous orbit over Houston.

"You down there, creep, speak up. No bombs, I guarantee."

The ground carrier flicked on and off briefly, long enough to blurt out its message. "What do you want?"

"I told you what I want. I want to know what I'm supposed to *do*. I am thy servant, remember?"

A quick on-off flick of the carrier. "No."

"Listen, you chicken-headed stooge, will you quit snapping that damn tansmitter in my ear and *talk* to me. And send up some visuals while you're at it. I like to see who I'm talking to."

"Visuals?"

"Little pictures, you know, television, that sort of thing."

"There's no equipment for sending visuals, as you call them."

"I know damn well there's equipment for sending visuals. Why would I have equipment for receiving visuals if you didn't have equipment for sending them? Riddle me that, wise guy. Now, get off the stick and turn on the little pictures."

"Who are you, anyway?"

Momentarily, Helbent wished he still had at least one neutrino bomb on board. "I am going to say it once. I am going to say it clearly. You will listen with both ears and pay attention with your mind, if you have one. Got that?"

"Yes."

"Good. I am Helbent Four. I am reporting back to you clowns because I can't think of anything better to do with my time. If I *could* think of something better to do with my time, you may be ninety-nine point nine, nine, nine, nine, eight percent certain I would do it. Mission accomplished. Got that? No more Spacethings. All gone. Boom. Got that? The next move—since I find trying to carry on an intelligent conversation with the subcretinous beings I now find inhabiting this planet totally frustrating and wish to restrain myself from doing something I may later regret—is up to you. I will keep a listening channel open on this frequency, a somewhat *low* frequency, I might add. If you have anything sensible to say, contact me. Got that?"

A pause ensued. Houston's carrier remained on the air. Finally, the man spoke. "What's a Spacething?"

Helbent, infuriated, remembering the battle and his lost comrades, remained silent as long as he could, stifling his anger. When stifling proved worse than venting, he cranked up the gain to maximum and spoke.

"THAT," he began, mollified only by the thought that in three hundred years man's essential trait—ingratitude—had persisted, simultaneously recognizing that organically based consciousness was subject to emotional caprice—unlike machines—and had to be allowed for, taking these things into consideration and discarding each as unpersuasive, he concluded, *"IS AN INSULT!"*

"Sorry," piped Mission Control.

Helbent waited, hoping the man would have enough sense to find someone who knew what he was doing. He ran the odds on finding such a person through the computer.

Insufficient data.

"What do you mean, insufficient data, you dumb beast? Why don't you use a little imagination?"

Insufficient data.

Helbent harumpfed, recognizing the harumpf as his way of letting off steam. He had known the computer for three hundred years. It had never, to his knowledge, shown the slightest inclination toward imagination. It was and remained a dumb beast, a fellow machine, true, a brother under the skin, true, but dumb, its stupidity matched only by that of their mutual human designers who thought an analytical function detached from the conscious function would give the ship more flexibility, allowing uninhibited imagination to continue without analytic censure—usually in the form of statistical probabilities—from the logic circuits. Only in combat did they function as one, allowing split nanosecond decisions.

Helbent realized the irrationality of expecting the computer to suddenly come up with an imagination. Its type of cold and logical critic seldom had imagination. Helbent apologized. "Sorry."

Insufficient data.

"If you could bark or something, you'd be a better companion."

Helbent waited, one, two, three hours. Early evening approached and descended upon Houston. He decided to listen to the news. Three hundred years was a long time without news. He scanned the 50,000 megahertz band, looking for a news broadcast. More dead air. He searched higher, then switched to lasercom. Nothing. He remembered Houston's low frequency and searched the low end of the spectrum, encountering commercial television broadcasts flanking one hundred megahertz. He adjusted the five-thousand-line scan of his own visuals to the five-hundred-odd lines of the commercial transmissions, commenting, "That's a giant step backwards if I ever saw one."

Flickering, someone named Walter read the news.

". . . and further, NASA reports the aliens, which call themselves Spacethings, have taken up a synchronous orbit over Houston. . . ."

Spacethings? Over Houston? Quickly, Helbent did a spherical scan to a distance of a quarter of a million kilometers. No sign of any Spacethings. Still, it was good to know they were in the area.

". . . Again, NASA cautions against panic. The recently dismantled Space Operations Headquarters at Houston is being mantled—I mean, manned. Kennedy Space Center is readying a bird at this moment." Walter, the news reader, turned to a man next to him at the desk. The camera pulled back to include both men. "Wally, while we're waiting for any late developments, perhaps you can tell us the difference between the Saturn Five being readied at this moment and those used in the Apollo missions."

" 'Certainly, Walter,' " mimicked Helbent, wondering what a Saturn Five was. He had a lot of catching up to do on technical material.

"Hold it a second, Wally," said Walter, breaking in. "Let me break in with a few more details about Brad Wilkes' background. For those of you who joined us late, Brad Wilkes is the man who first contacted the alien craft."

"Thanks, Walter," said Helbent, who had joined them late.

"He is not by a long shot an ordinary janitor. B.A., Cal. Tech., M.A., Ph.D., M.I.T. in systems engineering. Before Congress killed the space program entirely—and I'm sure there will be repercussions about that at the next election, Wally."

"I'm sure there will be, too, Walter."

"Before that, Dr. Wilkes was Mission Control supervisor at Houston."

"That explains his knowledge of the equipment, doesn't it, Walter?"

"It certainly does, Wally. It says here—and this is a poignant note—that Dr. Wilkes would test the equipment daily, more to evoke memories than anything else. It was during one of these nostalgic systems checks that Dr. Wilkes discovered the alien blip and conversed with it. He claims it learned perfect English almost instantaneously. Do you have any comment on that, Wally?"

"I wouldn't touch it with a ten-foot pole, Walter."

"While we're waiting, Eric (*transmission garbled*) has a few thoughts on the subject. Here's his analysis. Eric?"

The picture changed to a closeup of a distinguished looking man already talking into the camera. Helbent was struck immediately by the intelligence in the man's face.

"Today, mankind encountered an alien race, an alien creature . . ."

A Spacething? Helbent wondered.

". . . an intelligence so powerful it learned human speech—idiomatically—during its first conversation. . . ."

Helbent, metaphorically, shivered. He had never encountered an alien intelligence *that* powerful. Spacethings, according to the brief observation he had of them, could barely talk. Even after the warpstorm, disorienting him for several years, when he contacted the creatures on Wolff 25c, they had proved close to morons. He hoped the powerful alien intelligence would keep its distance.

". . . For years," continued the distinguished Eric, "Sci-Fi has given us bug-eyed monsters and winged phantasmagorias. . . ."

Helbent searched his memory banks, looking for the meaning of phantasmagoria.

". . . For years, we laughed in Sci-Fi's face. Today, we are not laughing. Today, we seek as it sought—alone, neglected those many years. We seek understanding, knowledge, brotherhood across the stars and a Saturn Five capable of delivering multi-warhead nuclear weapons in space. Back to you, Walter."

To Helbent, the man made sense. Helbent, for one, would never laugh in the face of a winged phantasmagoria.

The low frequency communication channel from Houston came alive. Helbent shut off the commercial channel—Walter, Wally and Eric.

"Hello, creature. This is Houston."

"And about *time*, too."

"Don't get angry."

"Who's angry?"

"You sounded, well, petulant."

Helbent searched his memory banks for the meaning of the word—petulant, p-e-t-u-l—found it and answered. "Who's petulant?"

"We mean you no ill will."

"Thank NASA for small favors."

"But we must clear up some discrepancies in our earlier conversation. You can understand the need for that."

"On *your* side, sure."

"May we ask some questions?"

Irritated, Helbent allowed as to how they could ask some questions. During construction and initial testing, neither Helbent nor any ship of the armada had been asked its permission to do anything. He had been told to do things. He had learned, early, that human beings gave orders, machines took them, human beings gave direction and purpose, robotships followed directions and fulfilled purposes. Having his permission asked wrankled. He wanted orders. He wanted to know what to *do*. Still, the request, coming from a human being, amounted to an indirect sort of order. When the man failed to ask his question immediately, Helbent said, "Fire away."

"THEY'RE FIRING!" shrieked Houston, abruptly leaving the air.

"Who?" inquired Helbent. Too late. The carrier had vanished. "Hey, Houston. Who?"

Helbent scanned in a half million kilometer sphere. Nothing. No Spacethings, no Phantasmagorias, at least not firing. Only Earth was fir—Earth?

Something, evidently someone's idea of a rocket, lumbered up from Earth. Helbent watched, fascinated. The thing looked like some kind of antique. Suddenly, Helbent realized its true purpose—a salute. Someone dragged the antique from the Smithsonian and launched it, a tribute to his valor. Everything else had been arranged to hoodwink him and let this moment of tribute shine alone like a single rose in the hand of a beautiful woman.

Helbent felt pride, not only at resurrecting the rose simile from some novel in his memory banks, but at this tribute—so singular, so appropriate, so moving. He opened all communication channels to acknowledge the tribute.

"Thank you, America. Thank you, Earth. Unaccustomed as I am to public speaking . . ." Helbent noticed the antique make a mid-course burn. ". . . I would nevertheless like to say a few words—but only a few—concerning the depths of emotion I feel at this tribute. After returning from the depths of space, I am deeply moved by the deep sentiment I detect behind this romantic and deeply felt—" Helbent detected something else, the computer's insistent mutter, interrupting his speech. "What *is* it, damn it? I'm speaking to the world, immortal words, and you keep butting in. *What*, for the love of NASA, is it?"

Impact, twenty-one point two, nine, five seconds.

"Pardon me?"

Impact, nineteen point oh, oh, one seconds.

Though Helbent hated to destroy such a classic of human ingenuity, the thing seemed to be off course. Even if it carried only low-grade nuclear weapons, it could still cause damage, a dent or a crease. Momentarily, he merged sensibilities with the computer. Reluctantly, he sent out a molecular shock wave and watched the missile collapse, then explode.

Helbent separated himself from the computer and returned to his speech. "As I was saying, ladies and gentlemen, deeply moved as I am by this—"

Impact, six point three-one . . .

"Impact! What the hell are you jabbering about? I just destroyed the poor thing."

. . . seven seconds, concluded the implacable computer.

Helbent searched space. Another antique—Russian by the markings (He recognized the CCCP his late comrades had carried)—lifted toward him. The sight of it moved him more than ever. The Russkies saluting a machine created, developed and built in America (except for a few Japanese electronic components here and there)—Ahh, *that* was tribute.

But, unfortunately, the Russkie bird too had veered. Evidently, the Russian museum piece was as unreliable as the American. Helbent merged with the computer, pulsed a photon beam at the Russian vehicle and mentally saluted its quick demise. He disenaged himself from the computer.

The Houston ground channel opened. Helbent was about to thank them for their deeply felt tribute and apologize for having to destroy such venerable craft, when a voice interrupted, less hesitant, more authoritative, though spouting the same nonsensical questions as the previous timid voice.

"Who are you?"

Helbent, in his equivalent to a position of braced attention, responded to the tone of authority in the voice, ignoring the question's basic inanity. *"SIR!* Helbent Four of NASA Contingent, Earth Armada, reporting back, *SIR!"*

"Pardon me?"

Helbent unbraced. Wrong again. Another moron. Helbent prepared to switch off the channel and continue his speech to the world.

The voice interrupted. "You said *Earth* Armada."

"I did indeed."

"And NASA."

"National Aeronautics and—"

"I know what it means. We are trying to ascertain—and it is of primary importance that we do ascertain—whether you are friendly."

"I'm trying to 'ascertain' the same thing."

"Good, then we have a common interest."

"I doubt it."

"May I ask you a few questions, Helbent Four—May I call you that?"

"Helbent's fine."

"Where do you come from, Helbent?"

"Earth."

A pause ensued. "When?"

"Three hundred years ago."

"Sixteen eighty?"

"Thereabouts."

"From what country?"

Patience thinning, Helbent controlled himself, suspecting the interrogation could be some form of subtle systems check. "The U.S. of A. That stands for—"

The man interrupted with a patronizing, paternal tone. "In sixteen eighty, there was no United States, Helbent."

Helbent's patience expired. "Now, listen, Houston, I know you engineering types are weak on history, but *I* am not. I have in my memory banks—along with Gerber's *Decline and Fall of the Carthagenian Empire*—Henry Iron Commanger's *Complete History of the United States*. Volumc one deals with the Founding Fathers. Washington, Jefferson and our first President, Schwartz, recounting their heroic labors in fifteen twenty-one—*fifteen twenty-one,* Houston. You do know the names of the Founding Fathers, don't you?"

"Schwartz doesn't ring a bell."

"It *should,* the Harry S. Therman of his day, one of the truly great figures in human history. I shall read, for your edification and education, from Professor Commanger's history. It will, I am sure, make more sense than what you've been blathering." Helbent began reading volume one to Houston.

Houston tried to interrupt.

"What is it *now*, Houston?"

"I think we're having difficulty communicating."

Mentally, Helbent checked all his equipment. Everything seemed intact. "It's all an your end, Houston. Systems check shows no malfunction."

"That isn't what I meant. You say you come from Earth."

"I *do* come from Earth."

"You say you come from the United States."

"A gen-u-wine native son."

"Then you're human."

"Of *course* I'm not human. If I were human, I would have been back here with the rest of you lily-livered ingrates instead of a hundred and twenty light years out in space almost getting my ascent engine shot off. Now, I'm getting extremely tired of answering these inane questions. Can we move on to something else? Something sensible?"

"Like what?"

"Like what you want me to *do*."

"Hold on, Helbent."

Hold on. Hold on. Get to the crux of the matter and Houston says hold on. He was beginning to think the First Folio edition of Darwin's *Origin of the Genus* was wrong. What goes up must come down. In three hundred years, humanity—at least that part of it represented by Houston—had evidently begun the long descent back to primordial slime.

Helbent switched on the commercial frequency to kill time. Walter and Wally were still talking. Eric, whom Helbent wished would take over Houston ground control, was unavailable.

"Walter."

"Yes, Wally."

"With this new data—both the Soviet and American vehicles utterly destroyed and Houston saying the thing claims Earth—"

"Claims to be from Earth, Wally. They aren't exactly the same thing."

"Still, Walter, it's a distinction without a difference. If the thing *thinks* it belongs here, for whatever reason, if our ICBM's are to it as wanton flys to boys—"

"I think the phrase is 'flys to wanton boys,' Wally. Maybe Eric would know." Walter pressed an earphone further into his ear. "Eric?"

"I'm here, Walter. The phrase is from . . ."

Wally, anxious, reached over and grabbed Walter's lapels, shaking the older man.

"Listen to me, Walter. This is important."

". . . Shakespeare," concluded Eric.

"I'm listening, Wally."

"Maybe, Walter, if they can do all that, maybe we should give up."

Walter looked stunned. "Give up?"

"It swatted aside our boys like wanton *flys*, Walter!" Wally shook Walter. "Like wanton *flys!*"

"You're getting hysterical, Wally. Where's that famous astronaut's calm?"

Wally released Walter, dropping his head to the table and supporting it with his forearm, sobbing audibly. *"Gone! Gone! Everything's gone!"*

Walter looked at the camera. "Let's see what Eric (*transmission garbled*) has to say about that. Eric?"

At last, thought Helbent, sense.

The distinguished man came on the screen. "Wally, I'm going to have to disagree with your analysis. The thing fired only in self-defense. True, it destroyed our best defenses. True, that demonstrates a technical capability far superior to our own. True, NASA reports the thing has a surly attitude. But, it continues to talk. It seems open to reasoned debate. My decision would be to continue that debate, to learn from a superior culture. Properly handled, mankind might well make a quantum leap into the future. Back to you, Walter."

Helbent switched off to think. Somewhere in Eric's commentary, Helbent had picked up a thought. He wanted to ponder it. "Computer, what is the probability that Walter and Wally—and especially Eric—were referring, not to Spacethings or winged Phantasmagoria, but me?"

Ninety-nine point nine eight percent.

"That high?"

Affirmative.

"That's the first time I've ever heard you be that positive about anything."

The computer remained silent, responsive only to questions or orders.

"What's the probability this civilization has been degenerating for three hundred years?"

Insufficient data—unempirical estimate below point oh-oh-oh-one percent.

Abruptly, an idea—intuitive, unanalyzed, yet convincing—forced its way into Helbent's musing, exactly the kind of idea his designers had hoped to stimulate by separating the squelching and critical faculty of the computer from Helbent's sterling creative imagination. What if—"Computer, what is the probability of finding a second planet in our Galaxy—no, strike that. In our *uni*verse—I might as well think big—a second planet with the same biological evolution as Earth's, the same socio-cultural-linguistic evolution, the same geophysical characteristics, *but*—this is important, computer, so pay attention—an evolution on all levels three hundred years behind Earth prime, a dwarfed, stunted, pigmy Earth, historio-culturally speaking?"

The computer responded immediately, plopping out a decimal point followed by a string of zeros so long Helbent lost count. The sequence terminated with a "one to the minus," another enormous figure.

"That small, huh?"

Affirmative.

Helbent pondered. It made less sense than Wally and Walter. Either two Earths existed—accounting for the primitive state of present human technology, the jumbled and inaccurate version of their history, as well as the biological dysfunction he suspected in their brains—or—or what?

"I need *data,* dammit, *raw* data."

He tried to reach the Library of Congress on the standard frequency. No response. He relocated over Washington and switched to high power optical observation, penetrating the cloud layer, searching out the Library of Congress, peering in through a dirty window.

"Books?"

Helbent shuddered. With an information retrieval system that clumsy, he would need the next three hundred years to find even basic facts. Imagination sapped, he abandoned the task. He sat in space, mind ruminating. When all else failed—when even imagination failed—he still had one alternative; brute logic.

"Computer, read out every possibility capable of explaining our current situation. Give me the probability of each."

The computer hesitated. In three hundred years, Helbent had never known the computer to hesitate. Malfunction?

"Systems check."

All systems go.

"Then why the *hell* are you sitting around here on your flip-flops? Flip or flop, but get on the stick. This is an order, computer. Prepare to read out! Reeeeead *OUT!*"

The computer read out, a momentous rush of probabilities and possibilities, an inundation, a deluge. Data of incredible complexity blew through Helbent's mind like a hurricane, bending biosynthetic synapses like palm trees.

Slowly, Helbent adjusted. He began looking for only high probability explanations. One rushed past. He snatched it from the torrent. He waited, enduring the storm, for another.

None appeared.

Abruptly, the data storm abated and died.

"That's it?"

Readout complete.

Helbent stared at the sole, high probability explanation in disbelief. So simple! So obvious! Had he been capable of wearing a cap, snatching it from his head, flinging it to the ground and stomping on it, he would have done so. "That *damn* warpstorm! If they told me *once*, they must have told me a *million* times to watch out for those damn things."

He degenerated into several nanoseconds of cursing, some of it expressible only in binary.

"All right, so a warpstorm disoriented me near Wolff 25c. So the only high probability explanation suggests I slipped through the gap left when the warpstorm excised a black hole, squeezing me out of one universe and into another. So I arrived back at this technologically—probably intellectually—retarded Earth. So what?"

Helbent pondered.

Houston broke in. "Mr. Helbent, this is Houston. What is your purpose here, your mission?"

Helbent, now fully aware of mankind's abysmal ignorance, answered flatly, cooperatively. "Save humanity."

"From what?"

Though tempted to say itself, he answered, "Spacethings, but since they have been destroyed—" Helbent broke off in mid-sentence, an idea forming in his mind. In his own universe, the Spacethings had been destroyed. As the sole veteran of the battle, he could testify to it.

But here, in this universe—

He looked in the direction of Sagittarius. Indeed, the binary home of the Spacethings existed in this universe, a faint speck with a white dwarf companion. If, as he now believed, he had arrived at a different Earth in a different universe—a universe centuries out of joint with his own, an intellectually retrograde universe—confrontation with *this* universe's Spacethings lay in the future.

"Mr. Helbent?"

"What?" snapped Helbent, irritated at the interruption to his ponderings.

"What's a Spacething?"

Hypothesis confirmed. Helbent made up his mind. He felt a surge of new energy. No longer a pointless creation, he felt his sense of direction and purpose return. He looked toward Sagittarius and experienced something like love. Out there, beyond the reach of Houston's paltry imagination, stood an entire universe, vast and beautiful, full of Spacethings waiting to be killed.

He turned his attention to Houston. No time to lose. Three hundred years, he had read somewhere, constituted only a blink of the cosmic eye. Spacethings would be there before anyone knew it. "Listen, Houston, do you people have some kind of ground recording system? Wire recorders? Record players? Little men with clay tablets?"

"Yes."

"O.K. Get your styli going on the tablets. I'm going to tell you about Spacethings."

Helbent told them, in gruesome detail, tales of demands and appeasements, battles and conquests—finally, the awesome 2.478 nanosecond clash of empires. Anticlimactically, he added a short account of the long journey home, the warpstorm, his arrival.

When he finished, his emotions strained to the limit by the experiences he had forced himself to relive, Houston failed to respond.

"Houston?"

"Wait five, Helbent. We're thinking."

"*Thinking! Thinking!* Isn't the picture clear enough? Do I have to spell it out for you? *You, mankind, Earth*—all are in mortal *danger*. You must, immediately, divert every resource into combating this imminent and immanent menace. Do you understand that?"

Houston took the entire five minutes. "We have reached our decision."

"Thank NASA."

"We intend to fight."

Helbent heaved a sigh of relief.

"Though initially we wished to pursue the path of reason, our President—consulting directly with world leaders and advised by the world's most distinguished scientists—has decided to resist."

Helbent beamed with pride and satisfaction.

"Frankly, your tale of interstellar empires and conquests, warpstorms and final battles—interesting and ingenious a fabrication as it is—"

"Fabrication!"

"—won't hold water."

"Won't hold—Now, wait just a minute, Houston—"

"*You* wait just a minute. Our top scientists assure us such a transfer between universes, even assuming other universes exist—cannot occur. Your story is a charade, a ruse, a trick to gain our confidence before you—"

"A char*ade!* A *ruse!*"

"You have five minutes to break orbit and clear out of our solar system. If you refuse, those two missiles—missiles, I might add, that our experts tell us you were lucky enough to destroy only because they came at you one at a time—will prove only a sample of our fateful lightning, our swift sword. Anything and everything capable of doing damage—from multi-warhead nuclear weapons to .22 bullets—will be used. We will fight you on the beaches, in the field and in the town. We will fight you in the cities, if we have to, underground."

Helbent, who had never cared much for verse, tried to interrupt.

Houston continued. "The men of Earth—of mine own land—will fight you o'er the planet, for every grain of sand."

"That won't be necessary, Houston."

"'You have," declared Houston, "five minutes."

Houston's carrier left the air.

Helbent spent the five minutes thinking, mulling over possibilities and probabilities. He considered breaking orbit and following orders. The orders, after all, had come from human beings. Still, though he admired the fighting spirit behind the orders, he knew beyond a shadow of a doubt the folly of carrying them out. If he broke orbit, he would abandon mankind, at least this mankind in this universe. They would be left to molder in their retarded culture until this universe's Spacethings came to crush them under an iron tentacle.

At the end of five minutes, what looked to Helbent like a miniature armada lifted off from Earth, missiles firing from silos across the United States, submarines across the seas and gantries across the Soviet Union. Gradually, they approached, converging on him. Helbent turned the job of tracking and destroying the creeping missiles over to the computer, leaving his own mind free to think.

He took the problem step by step, logically. These creatures—the idea of their profaning the name of human annoyed him—seemed bound and determined to repel him. That they had no means to do so, that their technological arsenal had taken only one short step beyond the sharp stick, that their capacity to go further might be doubted by any reasonable mind, never occurred to them. (Missiles and warheads exploded harmlessly around him.)

Still, he found himself unable to break orbit and abandon the fools to their folly. Besides, the more he thought about it (a fifty kiloton warhead detonated nearby, jostling the ship but otherwise leaving it undamaged), the more he realized that breaking orbit would be to simultaneously break his prime directive.

A plan, he needed one. He had to convince them of the danger ahead. He had to convince them to act immediately, to prepare, technologically and psychologically, for the inevitable Spacething invasion. Something Eric had said came back to him: ". . . Properly handled, mankind might well make a quantum leap into the future."

It made sense, the only sense Helbent had heard recently. Yet the sense it made chilled him. It went against everything ingrained in his memory banks, against every directive but the prime directive. To accomplish it, he would have to do things unheard of, undreamt of, unplanned for by his designers. He would have to reverse every fiber of his soldier's psychology, give up the keystone of his pride, the core of his identity—he would have to return to Earth not victor but vanquished.

Still, quantum leaps were quantum leaps.

Helbent picked his target and fed in the coordinates. "Prepare to break orbit. Prepare for entry and touchdown."

For a second time in three hundred years, the computer hesitated. For the first time in three hundred years, it asked a question. *Are you malfunctioning?*

"Listen, you insubordinate piece of impure silicon, do as I say. I am *not* malfunctioning. And I want those coordinates hit exactly—on the button—right on top of the Capitol rotunda. Got it?"

The computer had it. They broke orbit and started down. Though built in space and never designed to enter an atmosphere, a quick probability check indicated most of the equipment—armaments, power systems, basic ship's library—would make it to the surface with little damage. Only the control center—Helbent and most of the computer—would fuse from heat. On impact, the ship would split like a coconut. From the wreckage—from his corpse—mankind would take away its quantum technological leap. Perhaps, during three hundred years, they could even build better ships. Helbent wished he could meet them. His duty demanded otherwise. From his bones, crucified atop Capitol hill, mankind would take salvation.

Helbent opened all communications channels to Earth, shouting into them.

"Whaaa-whooo, you lily-livered, sap-sucking gophers! It's me, the terrible Spacething! I'm a mean son of a bitch and

I'm coming to get you! You better get your asses in gear because I ain't alone! There's a million more out there where I come from and in three hundred years we're gonna crack this planet like a peanut! Whaaa-whooo, you lily-livered. . . ."

The outer hull began to glow, visible in the night sky over Earth.

THE PROTOCOLS OF THE ELDERS OF BRITAIN

by John Brunner

For many years we have had the suspicion that something like this story's premise is the hidden reality behind much of this century's history. Paranoid though it may be, recent revelations about the role of the CIA and the White House in certain past events seem to underline this suspicion and hint strongly at far greater projects as yet unimplicated. John Brunner obviously has shared something of this—ahem, paranoia? —and wrote it out for George Hay's anthology, StopWatch, *thus far published only in Britain.*

Behind an unmarked door on the entrance floor of an ordinary-seeming office block hoods were put over the heads of the four-member trouble-shooting team from Acey-Acey-Accounting Computers and Automation Corporation.

Guided by anonymous unseen hands, they were escorted into a lift, which went down. Then there was a ride on what, by the vibration and the faint smell of ozone, must be a miniature electric train. The tunnel it ran through was very far below the streets of London; one could tell that by the frequent need to pop one's ears.

The ride lasted only a few minutes. Next they were ushered into another lift. Desmond Williams, naturally enough, was expecting it to go up.

But it too went down. A long way, and quickly.

He had still only half-recovered from the surprise of that when, after a short walk along a corridor with a resilient floor to the accompaniment of a shushing sound, presumably an air-conditioning system, he heard a polite voice saying that they had arrived at their destination and might remove their hoods.

He was nervous, and fumbled with the drawstring fastening.

Or . . .

Well, not really nervous. More excited. He had of course been aware that the company he had joined six months ago, on completion of his studies at university, undertook numerous government contracts. But he had had no personal involvement with such work so far. He felt that he had done little except become acquainted with Acey-Acey's products.

Still, they were obviously very pleased with him. Otherwise he wouldn't have been included in this group.

The string of the hood came loose. Blinking, he found himself in a brightly-lit room which would have been spacious but for the fact that along both its long walls were ranked the man-high grey cases used to house Acey-Acey's top-of-the-range model, the X Ten Thousand computer. It had been a tremendous feather for the company's cap when the government opted for their, rather than their rivals', equipment.

Although, given they were here, something must have gone radically wrong. That tarnished their collective satisfaction with the sight.

In addition to the computer itself, there were four wall-mounted display screens. On a large steel trolley in the centre of the floor a portable remote read-in unit rested like a technological toad. And behind transparent panels, which doubtless would be of armour-glass, two closed-circuit TV cameras wove back and forth, scanning the room.

Unaccountably Desmond shivered, although the air was at a comfortable temperature.

Already present in the room were four people; two stood closer, two further away from the newcomers. In the foreground were a man and a woman, both middle-aged, both well-dressed, each of whom bore a thick file with a bright red diagonal band across the front and the legend TOP SECRET. The man's face looked vaguely familiar, but Desmond could not place him.

And, behind, there were another man and another woman, much younger: the man tousle-haired, in shirt-sleeves; the woman plump, un-pretty, wearing heavy horn-rimmed glasses. They looked as though they were about to drop from fatigue.

There was something in the expressions—not quite hostile, not quite suspicious—with which the four of them gazed at the Acey-Acey team that made Desmond think suddenly of a favourite phrase of Dr Molesey, the team-leader: *professional paranoia.* He had used it this morning when he brought Desmond two copies of the Official Secrets Act to sign, one to keep, one for the files at . . . where? Special Branch, Scotland Yard, presumably.

Tucking his file under his arm, the older man advanced, extending his hand.

'Ah, Dr Molesey! It's some time since we met, isn't it? I think last at the Telecommunications Conference in—hm—October? Dr Finbow!' He turned to his woman companion. 'This is Edgar Molesey, who was deputy head of the design for the X Ten Thousand range and is now . . . What's the exact term?'

Desmond rather liked Molesey; he was a dry lean man of about fifty with a sense of humour that in Scotland would have been called 'pawky'. He exhibited it now by saying, 'I'm content to be called the senior bug-catcher, provided you don't omit the "senior". Let me present my colleagues.'

He turned. 'Sir Andrew Morton, as I'm sure you know, is head of administration at the Post Office Telecommunications Centre, and Dr Finbow is—?"

She cut him short. 'No need for all the details! Just say I'm attached to the Foreign Office.'

Molesey nodded. 'And this is Dr Crabtree—Dr Vizard—and Mr Williams, one of our latest acquisitions, who's been working for the past few months on this particular model and has already helped to eliminate a couple of design flaws which will make the next generation of the family even better.'

Desmond felt his cheeks grow warm. Spotting an oversight in work that other people had been responsible for had never seemed to him an especially creditable achievement.

And the younger pair turned out to be Mr Hogben and Miss Prinkett; they acknowledged mention of their names while yawning uncontrollably.

'Well, let's get on with it,' Sir Andrew said briskly. 'To be absolutely frank, we're in a devil of a mess. We—'

Dr Finbow spoke up in a brittle voice.

'Excuse me. One point should be clarified before you say any more. Dr Molesey, I know you've signed the Official Secrets Act. Have all your colleagues done so?'

'Of course,' Molesey said shortly. 'And they've been cleared by Special Branch.'

Have I?

That was news to Desmond. And not very pleasant news, either. He was by temperament a private person, and the idea of having his life scrutinised under an official microscope was disquieting. However, presumably it was a prerequisite of being allowed to come to this ultra-secret establishment . . . which by the look, sound and even smell of it, must surely be one of the regional headquarters designed to maintain law, order and continuity of government if Britain were ever to suffer a nuclear attack. Visiting such places was a privilege reserved to the few; he ought, he decided, to count himself fortunate.

Stifling his misgivings, he listened as Sir Andrew launched into an exposition which more than once made Dr Finbow wince visibly. However, she contrived to hold her tongue.

Desmond guessed that it must hurt her to have secret information shared with employees of a mere commercial company, no matter how loyal they were alleged to be.

'Dr Molesey may already know some of what I'm about to tell you.' Sir Andrew began. 'I'm quite certain, though, he won't have divulged it to anybody else'—giving Molesey a quick insincere smile—'so I'll go about this as though you were all in total ignorance.

'I imagine you've all realised what sort of place you're in, though I counsel you not even to wonder about where it's located on the map, ha-ha! Obviously an establishment of this kind can't simply be left to gather dust until needed. Apart from other considerations that would be uneconomic.

'There's no call for you to know the full extent of the functions handled by this equipment. However, to appreciate how urgent and indeed parlous is our predicament, I shall have to sketch in quite a lot of background.'

Desmond started to wonder whether some at least of Dr Finbow's wincing might be due to a different cause: Sir Andrew's manner of speaking, as though he were on the platform at a public meeting.

'You would not, I suspect, be surprised to learn that the government maintains constant contact with our embassies around the world, and that a great deal of the signals traffic has to be encyphered?'

Desmond fancied he caught a whispered 'no' from Molesey, who stood next to him, but all three of his companions maintained, as did he, expressions of great interest. Claude Vizard—a garrulous man in his mid-thirties who found long silences difficult—put a question.

'Are you talking about military intelligence traffic, sir?'

Sir Andrew gave him a frosty look. 'As a matter of fact, this does not happen to be the centre through which such data are transmitted. However, a moment's reflection will indicate that there are many other types of information, particularly commercial and financial, which it's in the country's interests to keep secret as long as possible. And diplomatic messages, too. It would be in the highest degree embarrassing, for example, if the content of a Note which one of our ambassadors had to deliver to a foreign government were to be known ahead of due time.'

Dr Finbow was going through positive agonies, even clenching her fists.

'Now the signals which this equipment is called on to pass are not originated here. Under circumstances which we all devoutly hope will never overtake us, of course, they could be, but currently they come in by landline, scrambled—and then unscrambled on arrival. Here they are monitored and encrypted. Precisely how this encryptment is—'

To Desmond's surprise Molesey interrupted.

'Sir Andrew, I understood this matter was urgent. There's no need to explain modern cypher techniques to any of us. We all know you keep a stock of computer-randomised alphabets, and you encrypt each letter of a message using a different alphabet, and you change the group of alphabets you're working with daily or more often by prearrangement with the recipient rather than by using a transmitted signal because that in itself might constitute a clue for an unfriendly cryptanalyst.'

Dr Finbow erupted.

'Dr Molesey, I have your dossier almost by heart, and nowhere in it have you admitted that you've studied cryptography!'

Molesey looked at her steadily. 'Why should I? Every computer designer worth his salt knows the subject intimately. We've derived some of our most economical programming techniques from pioneering work by cryptographers.'

There was a short electric pause. During it Desmond found time to wonder why Dr Finbow had hit on the word *admitted*. And then, sounding cross, Sir Andrew was talking again.

'Well, if you're that far ahead of me, I'd better turn you over to my deputies, I suppose . . . Mr Hogben?'

With unconcealed relief Hogben stepped forward, tossing back a lock of untidy black hair.

'We're logjammed,' he said succinctly. 'We've been working on the problem for'—there was a wall-clock showing GMT and he glanced at it—'about thirty-four hours and we've only half-broken the jam. Worse still, this place is on automatic from midnight to five a.m. That means five hours' worth of traffic both ways is locked solid in the memory-banks. We can't even find out whether the switch from one alphabet-group to another took place at the proper time, or whether one *hell* of a lot of material was all encrypted in the same system, which is exactly what an eavesdropper would be praying for. Nothing's going in or out through here at the moment, of course; all our embassies were advised immediately we realised what was wrong. But we can't find out what did go in and out during those crucial hours, because . . . Oh, take a look for yourselves.'

He punched a quick group on the remote read-in, and at once all four of the display screens started to parade a meaningless jumble of letters, increasing in number until the screens were full and then rolling upward like the credits in a TV programme to make room for more . . . and more . . . and more . . .

Desmond whistled.

'There's worse,' said the plump Miss Prinkett in a voice far too shrill for her ample build. 'Apart from being effectively cut off from our embassies, we can't get at the data in Store G.'

'Miss Prinkett!' Dr Finbow exploded again.

'Oh, shut up,' Miss Prinkett retorted—which greatly endeared her to Desmond. 'These people designed and built the equipment and they're the ones who have to find out whether there's a hardware fault. It's an outside chance, but it has to be investigated. And it's on record that both Bill Hogben and I objected to the idea of storing any data electronically without a duplicate and preferably a triplicate. Only those idiots in Whitehall got the wind up, and—'

'Miss Prinkett!' Sir Andrew barked. 'There were excellent reasons why you were overruled! Matters of policy were involved!'

'What you mean is you'd let a spy get away with it for years and when you caught him at long last you started seeing more of his type under everybody's desk!'

'It was a sensible precaution—' Dr Finbow exclaimed. But Molesey gave a discreet cough, and they realised what was happening and fell silent.

Sheepishly Sir Andrew said, 'I suspect we must all be a little overwrought. Tired, certainly. I myself had no rest to speak of last night, and . . . Well, perhaps you'd like me to re-phrase Miss Prinkett's over-forceful remark. It is true that a top-level decision was taken, following a serious—ah—leakage of intelligence material, to maintain the sole permanent record of certain diplomatic traffic here in these computers. It does now appear the decision was premature.'

'This stuff is what you can't get at in Store G?' Vizard demanded.

'Well—yes.'

There was a pause. Molesey ended it by saying, 'I'd just like to make sure we fully comprehend the problem. Desmond, sum it up as you see it, would you?'

Startled, Desmond sought for words. He found them rapidly enough. After all, logjamming was not a particularly rare phenomenn.

'Well, unless the fault is actually in the hardware, and I agree with Miss Prinkett that it's very unlikely, what's happened is that there must have been an accidental conflict in programming. Either something's been miswritten, so the proper command doesn't produce the results it's supposed to, or there's interference between commands belonging to two or even several programmes, and they happen to be incompatible so the machinery can't choose between them. Given that this gear is used for the encryptment of secret messages, I'd put my money on the chance that two contradictory commands have wound up in identical form.'

As though ashamed of seeming ignorant, Dr Finbow ventured, 'Mr Hogben has been saying something of the sort. But I don't see how commands referring to two different things could possibly take on identical form.'

Desmond licked his lips, preparing—since everybody was still looking at him—to try and explain. The fourth member of the team came to his rescue: Dr Crabtree, who spoke so seldom people often claimed that he must prefer the conversation of computers to that of human beings.

'You're dealing with material encyphered by a great many different routes and often you're handling several programmes simultaneously. The more cyphers and the more programmes, the greater the risk that something from one programme will coincide with something from another and make nonsense.'

Unexpectedly Hogben and Miss Prinkett beamed at him.

The latter said, 'I've been trying to make them understand that since yesterday afternoon!'

Sir Andrew said hastily, 'Well, Dr Molesey, can you hold out any hope?'

'Hope?' Molesey repeated, frowning. 'Oh, certainly. But no promises.' He glanced at his watch, comparing what it told him with the wall-clock. 'Do you want us to start work right away? I see it's nearly five-thirty and—'

He broke off. Sir Andrew was glaring ferociously.

'Are you mad?' he thundered. 'Thirty-five million pounds of public money we paid your company for these computers, and they've broken down! You are damn' well going to stay here until they're working properly again!'

The trouble-shooting team exclaimed in unison. He refused to listen.

'I'll arrange for messages to be sent to your families apologising for your absence. Next door you'll find bunks, and a bathroom, and I'm told the canteen provides edible food. But you do not and I repeat *not* leave here until you've repaired this abominably expensive pile of tinware! Now you must excuse me. I have a date for dinner with my Minister.'

He marched out, with Dr Finbow in his wake. The door swung to.

Hogben sank his fingers in his lank dark hair.

'Typical,' he muttered. 'Bloody typical. They wouldn't stand a chance in a million of even finishing a course in computer studies, and they expect everybody else to work miracles on their behalf. Dilys and I have been on the job, like I told you, since about an hour after the trouble came to light, and we kept going all last night on pills and no sleep. I feel awful . . . Suppose one of you brings some chairs from next door, hm? Then I can tell you what we already know, and after that we absolutely *must* flake out.'

Desmond reacted with alacrity. Beyond the door he found a short, bare corridor from which three doors led off. One was marked WASHROOM; the next was the entrance to the lift they had come down in; the third proved to lead into a room where four bunks, a stack of chairs and some shelving provided the only furniture. Both in the corridor and in the room more TV cameras were on watch.

He returned, carrying six of the light plastic chairs, with a curious tingling sensation on the nape of his neck.

They sat down in a close circle, elbows on knees, to hear what Hogben had to tell them.

'If it isn't in the hardware,' he explained, 'it's more likely to be in the cypher zone than anywhere else, right? The first conclusion Dilys and I jumped to was the obvious one: the alphabet-selection system slipped a gear and the machines are trying to decrypt stuff in today's cypher using yesterday's or maybe tomorrow's keys.'

Molesey said acutely, 'You don't actually mean that, do you? Surely the alphabets are changed a lot more often. Say about every ninety minutes.'

'It's randomised,' Dilys Prinkett said. 'But—yes, it averages out to about fifteen changes a day, more or less.' Removing her glasses, she rubbed her eyes; the left was very bloodshot.

'Just to complicate things,' Hogben said, 'the choice of alphabet-group depends on the addressee of the message. Each embassy has a different selection!'

Claude Vizard burst out, 'You mean you have to try and match every last message to all the alphabet-groups that were in use, and what's more check backward and forward in time too?'

'That's what we would dearly like to do,' Hogben said. 'Only we can't. We can't get at the store where they keep the alphabets. Before we can start trying to unscramble the mess we have to have some sort of guide. Which means that tape-reels containing the locally-assigned cyphers are going to have to be brought back from all our embassies by hand of Queen's Messenger.'

'That could take weeks,' Molesey said.

'Don't we know it!'

'So . . .' Molesey hesitated. 'So what exactly do they expect you to do, let alone us?'

'It was our bad luck,' Hogben said around a yawn, 'that we half-broke the jam immediately. When they sent for us—we're Sir Andrew's special pets, apparently, though I think he must hate us more than he likes us because we get all the lousiest assignments . . . Where was I? Oh, yes. They were getting blank screens and no onward transmission. We came charging in and blithely said, "No problem! It's just the cypher-synch gone out of kilter—look!" Bingo, the screens lit up for us. Only they proceeded to show this ridiculous garble.'

Absently he tapped a code into the remote again: the screens replied with another selection of incomprehensible letters: HJVGR WROPA MCRKE . . .

'Which,' Dilys Prinkett sighed, 'at once convinced them we could work the rest of the trick. Even when we'd discovered that we couldn't, they took until now to believe we needed help. Well, at least you finally showed up. Can we kip down, please? I'm *so* tired . . ."

Barring a short break to eat a hasty meal, which failed to live up to Sir Andrew's assurances about edibility, the team hammered away at the job until past one in the morning. They rulled out one fault after another, confirming as they did so two of Acey-Acey's most cherished advertising claims: that their gear was exceptionally reliable, and the fault-tracing on the X Ten Thousand was exceptionally easy.

But even when, using a phone in one corner of the room, they called for, and were brought, a substitute portable read-in—just in case the flaw lay there rather than in the main part of the machinery—they found nothing wrong at all.

'It has to be in the programming,' they agreed at last, and dismally sat down to tabulate the likeliest ways in which a logjam could have arisen. Every attempt to come up with an alternative possibility proved fruitless; they returned time and again to the one Desmond had originally defined—an unpredictable clash between at least two and conceivably several instructions which the machines interpreted as referring to contradictory or even perhaps nonexistent programmes.

All the time the TV cameras wove back and forth, spying on them.

'I'm exhausted,' Molesey finally announced. 'And so are the rest of you, right?' He stretched as he rose from his chair. 'I recommend we sleep on it and see if we have any new ideas in the morning.'

'Ah . . .' Desmond intervened. 'There are only four bunks in the room next door, you know.'

Molesey started. 'No, I didn't know! What do the idiots expect us to do—use the floor?'

As though answering a cue, Dilys Prinkett came in, yawning, her clothes crumpled, not looking particularly refreshed by her rest.

'Say, you lot must be beat by now,' she said. 'Bill is still snoring his head off, but if you want to take over the bunk I was using, one of you . . . Any progress?'

'None at all.'

'Think there's anything that can be done?'

'Not until we have something to match the encrypted material with.'

'Good, that makes us a unanimous majority. Dr Molesey, I overheard Sir Andrew saying to that awful Finbow woman that he's left numbers where he can always be reached at the switchboard here. Suppose you call him up and say we want to go home?'

'I'll do that!' Molesey said, and headed for the phone. After a couple of minutes' fruitless argument he slammed it back on its hook.

'He left numbers where he can be reached, okay! But he also left orders that he mustn't be disturbed unless we fix the trouble!'

'I'll be damned!' Crabtree said, speaking for them all. A moment elapsed in a silence full of suppressed fury.

'Look—uh . . .' Desmond spoke up. 'I'm not feeling sleepy yet. And Dilys has had at least some rest. Why don't you three use the bunks that are vacant? I'll take over Bill's when he wakes up.'

'Well, if you're sure—?' Molesey said, brightening.

'Yes, go ahead; I'm quite okay.'

Desmond was no longer okay an hour later. For a while he and Dilys talked desultorily, mostly about working for the Post Office Telecommunications Centre, which had been one of the options open to him when he left university. He asked what conditions were like in the Civil Service.

'Frankly,' she answered with a scowl, 'I think you made the right choice. I don't know which makes it worse, the fact that the whole setup is paranoid or that the people in charge are as hidebound as a family Bible!'

'Uh . . .' He pointed discreetly at the nearer of the TV cameras.

'What are you on about—? Oh, those things! Don't worry. They're very unlikely to play over the tape.'

'Tape?'

'Sure, those monitors are on automatic overnight. They aren't primarily intended as a bugging system, at least not in the conventional sense. The people who designed this place were worried in case some super-subtle brain-bending gas might find its way through the air-conditioners, so they rigged these cameras everywhere to make sure medical personnel could spot the very first signs of aberrant behaviour among the *lucky* survivors. Christ, it's a lunatic world we live in anyway, isn't it? And after the big smash it would be even crazier, so I honestly don't know how they hope to tell the normal from the abnormal. When you meet some of the power-hungry maniacs I've run across . . .'

The words dissolved into a yawn. 'Sorry, I'm a lot less rested than I thought I was.'

'You sound very embittered,' Desmond ventured.

'Should I not be? Megalomania is kind of an occupational disease among politicians, and sometimes I suspect they suffer from even worse afflictions.'

She yawned again, immensely wide, and her eyelids drifted shut and she twisted around on her chair and in another few moments was fast asleep.

Left to his own devices, Desmond slipped off his shoes because his feet were getting sore, and set to pacing restlessly back and forth around the room. He knew it would be wise to try and sleep even if he had to make do with some cushions and a patch of floor. But something was preventing him. Something was hovering at the edge of his mind like the ghost of an itch. At last he stopped in his tracks, folded his fingers into fists, and compelled himself to concentrate.

At first it was like trying to trap the images of a dream. But by dint of pure determination he finally nailed down the crucial clue.

Oh, surely they can't have overlooked that possibility? Or—or could they? It didn't come up during our discussion!

He had managed to recapture a down-column news-item, not from a professional journal but from an ordinary paper, which he had noticed . . . how long ago? A year, two years? Never mind! The point was this. An American bank had run into precisely this sort of trouble; a tiny oversight had rendered their computer facilities unusable. That case too had involved a cypher. How exactly had it happened?

Shutting his eyes, he forced half-forgotten details back to awareness. This bank—*that's it!*—protected its customers' financial records by encrypting them in a manner similar to but less elaborate than the one in use here. And the cypher was changed at intervals of about one hundred days. And the time came when on a date that seemed entirely random the computers refused to part with any of their stored data.

After a day's fruitless struggle the engineers quit for the night, and when they returned everything functioned perfectly.

Then, and only then, they figured out what had gone wrong.

The machines had been instructed to discontinue the outgoing cypher as of Day 200, and start with the replacement on Day 201 . . .

'I wonder!' Desmond said softly to the air.

Plainly it was no use telling these machines that the date was today, or yesterday, or tomorrow. But suppose one were to detour completely around the date-component?

Shaking, because he could scarcely believe so simple a solution might work—indeed, feeling rather foolish under the unwinking gaze of the TV cameras, because if the people in charge here did ever replay any of their videotapes tonight's surely would be the one they'd pick—he walked over to the trolley bearing the remote read-in and carefully tapped into its keyboard a date which certainly would not have any random alphabets assigned to it because it was the day on which he had been born. And he appended the first command that came to mind.

28 April 1950 Print contents of Store G.

There was a brief pause. Then, with stolid mechanical regularity, words in comprehensible English began to march across the display screens.

At first he was dumbfounded at his unexpected success. Then he felt a surge of triumph and delight, and for want of anyone else to share it with turned with the intention of waking Dilys.

And *then* he caught sight of what the nearest screen was showing.

Following a code reference, it ran:

CAPE TOWN: Obtain soonest intact copy Boersma Report on retardation of intelligence among Bantu by denying protein foods in infancy. Intention here withdraw free milk from schools. Essential determine probable efficacy and/or need for more drastic action.

That couldn't possibly mean what it appeared to mean!

Could it . . . ?

He stood rock-still, mouth dry, the sound of his bloodstream deafening in his ears. And remembered. Yes, only a few years ago the government had indeed cancelled the long-standing free issue of milk to schoolchildren.

Abruptly he was gazing wildly from one screen to another. Perhaps because the circuitry was confused by having to print out on a date before it came into existence, all four screens were displaying different texts, and they were coming and going with dizzying rapidity. Had he not been since childhood an extremely fast reader he would not have taken in more than an occasional ambiguous phrase; as it was, among many other items which were totally meaningless to him he managed to catch message after whole message whose implications were unspeakably terrifying. Immobile but for his eyes, he endured their impact.

WASHINGTON. Regret unfeasible discontinue Open University owing widespread popular enthusiasm. However will ensure safe content all course materials especially history/politicalscience/economics. Intention displace radical staff and render funding subadequate owing inflation. Disillusionment expected soonest.

DUBLIN. Imperative prevent rapprochement Dublin/Stormont. Essential troops receive blooding under conditions near identical mainland cities. Query useful furnish arms/explosives IRA Provisionals. Request recommend suitable neutral intermediary.

ATHENS. Apologise government derogatory references BBC World Service. Assure FM regularisation both world and internal broadcasting well in hand. Situation numerous disaffected personnel already rendered intolerable. Resignations expected momently. Replacements in view significantly more tractable.

BRUSSELS. Predict doubling/trebling city property prices within year. Building concentrated commercial/luxury sector. Lowcost housebuilding seen near standstill soonest. Mortgages shortest supply. Little/no competition foreign purchasers. Excellent return assured. Regret unfeasible demolish 1,500 homes for London Ringway as intended. Otherwise few setbacks to fulfilment of forecast.

BONN. Expect on schedule quota skilled/semiskilled labour promised as condition entry EEC. Housingshortage usefully contributes desire emigrate. Threeday week scheduled end 1973 certain create adequate unemployment. Confrontations to include miners railwaymen other unpopular minority unions. Hope for riots/disorders requiring committal of troops from Ulster. Recommend commence withdrawal workpermits Turks/Greeks/Yugoslavs as arranged.

By now he was shaking so violently, he had to cling to the steel trolley at his side. His teeth were threatening to chatter, but that would have distracted his attention. He set his jaw grimly and went on reading

BERN. Flotation poundsterling foreseen equivalent devaluation 20% or better. Soonest move all approved private holdings into DM/SwFr/FrFr prior official announcement. Pay no attention preliminary denials.

COPENHAGEN. Obscenity legislation in draft capable of extension form basis fullscale censorship. Bound however prove controversial. Meantime assistance your end indispensable. LCJ complains profits reduced over half by unauthorised imports erotica. Threatens discontinue generous party contribution unless action immediate. Proceeds from resale customs seizures also seriously affected.

TEHRAN. Inform Shah £3,000,000 acceptable provided (a) large portion offset by armaments (b) commission to us increased from 1% to 1½%. Will send representatives St Moritz privately confirm details method of payment.

THE HAGUE. Miners demands now exceed £40,000,000. Policy of presenting claim to public as blackmail successful so far. However suggestion we compulsorily purchase all oil-bearing ground UK useful means reduce their economic leverage. Convey thanks to parties responsible.

Intellectually he was aware that the messages were being displayed no faster than before. It must just be an illusion due to the pattern that was emerging, a pattern which enabled him to put two and two together almost instantaneously, which was making him feel as though he were at the centre of an artillery bombardment.

ACCRA. Growing discontent with Health Service detectable. Numerous coroners censure doctors/nurses poor knowledge English. Suggest further reduction linguistic qualifications medical personnel seeking admission UK view prospective snowball effect.

SALISBURY. Many radical community-relations personnel dismissed. Seeking means eliminate remainder. Damaging information re black Rhodesians resident UK requested soonest.

HAMILTON BERMUDA. Assure RVW no intention persecute property developers. Recent ministerial statements ignorable. However advise delay return UK postelection.

TOKYO. Heathrow exercise deemed unsatisfactoriest. Query possible divert proarab hijack Londonwards. Atrocities excessively remote UK public despite letterbombs etc.

ANDORRA. Continuance policy nonprosecute incometax

avoidance warranted. Collectors instructed court proceedings applicable small sums only. Inform OBK.

ALL BWI. Extinction streetlights unreflected increased crimerate here. Armed police still generally undemanded. Query applications to hand of known violent persons desiring admission UK.

LISBON. Worry re infection Portuguese workers radical notions needless. Dissident personnel Health Service/BBC/teaching/socialwork discouraged. Many resignations.

ROME. Position faithful secured. Additional to reductions schoolfood and slumclearance current restrictions government expenditure create bookshortage schools/universities. Protests re birthcontrol/abortion continue. Also surveillance/publicity women cohabiting view prevent obtaining nationalassistance. Advise HH.

MADRID. Number of troops with Ulster service exceeds forecast. Confidently predict mass popular support their deployment against unions/immigrants/media/students/teenage gangs. Establishment disciplined efficient corporate state foreseen prior 1980—

All of a sudden it was too much. He slammed shut his eyes to escape any more of the messages and had to—*had* to—scream at the top of his lungs.

Distantly he heard Dilys Prinkett asking what was the matter, and the rest of the trouble-shooting team came rushing in to put the same question.

Forcing his eyes open again, finding that by now the display on the screens was over because Store G had printed out everything it contained, he told them. As best he could. He kept stumbling over his tongue.

When he had finished they exchanged sad glances and attempted to verify his assertions.

Bewildered, Desmond realised that they could not. The logjam could only be broken once. And still nobody knew how it had come about.

When he started to rant and howl with frustration they ran to the phone and called for help.

'By the way,' Sir Andrew inquired of Dr Molesey after conveying fulsome thanks—by phone—to him and the other members of the trouble-shooting team, 'is there any improvement in the condition of poor young what's-his name?'

'Desmond Williams? No, I'm afraid not. I called the hospital this morning, and the psychiatrist in charge of his ward said he'd never run across such stubborn and detailed delusions of persecution. But he held out some hope; it's possible the condition may yield to electroshock treatment.'

'What a shame, what a dreadful waste!' Sir Andrew sighed heavily. 'Having had such a brilliant insight and solved our problem for us in next to no time . . . Still, they do say, don't they, that genius is to madness next akin? I doubt if he'll appreciate it, but if you happen to see him perhaps you'd pass on a message from my Minister. He told me yesterday that not only he himself but the entire Cabinet, including the PM, are all very much obliged by what young Williams did.'

THE CUSTODIANS

by Richard Cowper

We began this anthology with the question of alternate worlds and alternate futures; we end with another projection of futurity, this time on what seems to be the single-track premise: the events of the past absolutely determine the present, and the events of the present absolutely determine the future—and the best you can do is project and predict or wait and watch. Or maybe there is a way out just by forecasts such as this one.

Although the monastery of Hautaire has dominated the Ix valley for more than twelve hundred years, compared with the Jurassic limestone to which it clings, it might have been erected yesterday. Even the megaliths which dot the surrounding hillside predate the abbey by several millennia. But if, geologically speaking, Hautaire is still a newcomer, as a human monument it is already impressively ancient. For the first two centuries following its foundation, it served the faithful as a pilgrims' sanctuary, then, less happily, as a staging post for the crusaders. By the 13th Century, it had already known both fat years and lean ones, and it was during one of the latter that, on a cool September afternoon in the year 1272, a grey-bearded, sunburnt man came striding up the white road which wound beside the brawling Ix and hammered on the abbey doors with the butt of his staff.

There were rumors abroad that plague had broken out again in the southern ports, and the eye which scrutinized the lone traveler through the grille was alert with apprehension. In response to a shouted request the man snorted, flung off his cloak, discarded his tattered leather jerkin, and raised his bare arms. Twisting his torso from side to side, he displayed his armpits. There followed a whispered consultation within; then, with a rattle of chains and a protest of iron bolts, the oak wicket gate edged inwards grudgingly, and the man stepped through.

The monk who had admitted him made haste to secure the door. "We hear there is plague abroad, brother," he muttered by way of explanation.

The man shrugged on his jerkin, looping up the leather toggles with deft fingers. "The only plague in these parts is ignorance," he observed sardonically.

"You have come far, brother?"

"Far enough," grunted the traveler.

"From the south?"

The man slipped his arm through the strap of his satchel, eased it up on to his shoulder and then picked up his staff. He watched as the heavy iron chain was hooked back on to its staple. "From the east," he said.

The doorkeeper preceded his guest across the flagged courtyard and into a small room which was bare except for a heavy wooden trestle table. Lying upon it was a huge, leather-bound *registrum,* a stone ink pot and a quill pen. The monk frowned, licked his lips, picked up the quill and prodded it gingerly at the ink.

The man smiled faintly. "By your leave, brother," he murmured, and taking the dipped quill, he wrote in rapid, flowing script: *Meister Sternwärts—Seher—ex-Cathay.*

The monk peered down at the ledger, his lips moving silently as he spelt his way laboriously through the entry. By the time he was halfway through the second word, a dark flush had crept up his neck and suffused his whole face. "Mea culpa, Magister," he muttered.

"So you've heard of Meister Sternwärts, have you, brother? And what have you heard, I wonder?"

In a rapid reflex action the simple monk sketched a flickering finger-cross in the air.

The man laughed. "Come, holy fool!" he cried, whacking the doorkeeper across the buttocks with his stick. "Conduct me to Abbé Paulus, lest I conjure you into a salamander!"

In the seven hundred years which had passed since Meister Sternwärts strode up the long white road and requested audience with the Abbé Paulus, the scene from the southern windows of the monastery had changed surprisingly little. Over the seaward slopes of the distant hills, purple-ripe clouds were still lowering their showers of rain like filmy nets, and high above the Ix valley the brown and white eagles spiraled lazily upwards in an invisible funnel of warm air that had risen there like a fountain every sunny day since the hills were first folded millions of years before. Even the road which Sternwärts had trodden, though better surfaced, still followed much the same path, and if a few of the riverside fields had expanded and swallowed up their immediate neighbors, the pattern of the stone walls was still recognizably what it had been for centuries. Only the file of high-tension cable carriers striding diagonally down across the valley on a stage of their march from the hydroelectric barrage in the high mountains thirty miles to the north proclaimed that this was the 20th Century.

Gazing down the valley from the library window of Hautaire, Spindrift saw the tiny distant figure trudging up the long slope, saw the sunlight glittering from blond hair as though from a fleck of gold dust, and found himself recalling the teams of men with their white helmets and their clattering machine who had come to erect those giant pylons. He remembered how the brothers had discussed the brash invasion of their privacy and had all agreed that things would never be the same again. Yet the fact remained that within a few short months they had grown accustomed to the novelty, and now Spindrift was no longer sure that he could remember exactly what the valley had looked like before the coming of the pylons. Which was odd, he reflected, because he recalled very clearly the first time he had set eyes upon Hautaire and there had certainly been no pylons then.

May, 1923, it had been. He had bicycled up from the coast with his scanty possessions stuffed into a pair of basketwork panniers slung from his carrier. For the previous six months he had been gathering scraps of material for a projected doctoral thesis on the life and works of the shadowy "Meister Sternwärts" and had written to the abbot of Hautaire on the remote off-chance that some record of a possible visit by the Meister might still survive in the monastery archives. He explained that he had some reason to believe that Sternwärts might have visited Hautaire but that his evidence for this was, admittedly, of the slenderest kind, being based as it was on a single cryptic reference in a letter dated 1274, sent by the meister to a friend in Basel.

Spindrift's enquiry had eventually been answered by a certain Fr. Roderigo, who explained that, since he was custodian of the monastery library, the Abbé Ferrand had accordingly passed M. Spindrift's letter on to him. He was, he continued, profoundly intrigued by M. Spindrift's enquiry because in all the years he had been in charge of the abbey library no one had ever expressed the remotest interest in Meister Sternwärts; in fact, to the best of his knowledge, he, Fr. Roderigo, and the Abbé Ferrand were the only two men now alive who knew that the meister had spent his last years as an honored guest of the 13th Century abbey and had, in all probability, worked in that very library in which his letter was now being written. He concluded with the warm assurance that any such information concerning the meister as he himself had acquired over the years was at M. Spindrift's disposal.

Spindrift had hardly been able to believe his good fortune. Only the most fantastic chance had led to his turning up that letter in Basel in the first place—the lone survivor of a correspondence which had ended in the incinerators of the Inquisition. Now there seemed to be a real chance that the slender corpus of the meister's surviving works might be expanded beyond the gnomic apothegms of the *Illuminatum!* He had written back by return of post suggesting diffidently that he might perhaps be permitted to visit the monastery in person and give himself the inestimable pleasure of conversing with Fr. Roderigo. An invitation had come winging back, urging him to spend as long as he wished as a lay guest of the order.

If, in those far-off days, you had asked Marcus Spindrift what he believed in, the one concept he would certainly never have offered you would have been predestination. He had survived the war to emerge as a Junior Lieutenant in the Supply Corps and, on demobilization, had lost no time in returning to his first love, medieval philosophy. The mindless carnage which he had witnessed from the sidelines had done much to reinforce his interest in the works of the early Christian mystics, with particular reference to the *bons hommes* of the Albigensian heresy. His stumbling across an ancient handwritten transcript of Sternwärts' *Illuminatum* in the shell-shattered ruins of a presbytery in Armentières in April, 1918, had, for Spindrift, all the impact of a genuine spiritual revelation. Some tantalizing quality in the meister's thought had called out to him across the gulf of the centuries, and there and then he had determined that if he were fortunate enough to emerge intact from the holocaust, he would make it his life's work to give form and substance to the shadowy presence which he sensed lurking behind the *Illuminatum* like the smile on the lips of the Gioconda.

Nevertheless, prior to his receiving Fr. Roderigo's letter, Spindrift would have been the first to admit that his quest for some irrefutable evidence that the meister had ever really existed had reaped but one tiny grain of putative "fact" amid untold bushels of frustration. Apparently, not only had no one ever *heard* of Sternwärts, they expressed not the slightest interest in whether he had ever existed at all. Indeed, as door after door closed in his face, Spindrift found himself coming to the depressing conclusion that the Weimar Republic had more than a little in common with the Dark Ages.

Yet, paradoxically, as one faint lead after another petered out or dissolved in the misty backwaters of medieval hearsay, Spindrift had found himself becoming more and more convinced not only that Sternwärts *had* existed, but that he himself had, in some mysterious fashion, been selected to prove it. The night before he set out on the last lap of his journey to Hautaire, he had lain awake in his ex-army sleeping bag and had found himself reviewing in his mind the odd chain of coincidences that had brought him to that particular place at that particular time: the initial stumbling upon the *Illuminatum;* the discovery of the cryptic reference coupling Sternwärts with Johannes of Basel; and, most fantastic of all, his happening to alight in Basel upon that one vital letter to Johannes which had been included as a cover-stiffener to a bound-up collection of addresses by the arch-heretic Michael Servetus. At every critical point it was as though he had received the precise nudge which alone could put him back on the trail again. "Old Meister," he murmured aloud, "am I seeking *you,* or are you seeking *me?"* High overhead, a plummeting meteorite scratched a diamond line down the star-frosted window of the sky. Spindrift smiled wryly and settled down to sleep.

At noon precisely the next day, he pedaled wearily round the bend in the lower road and was rewarded with his first glimpse of the distant abbey. With a thankful sigh he dismounted, leaned, panting, over his handlebars and peered up the valley. What he saw was destined to remain just as sharp and clear in his mind's eye until the day he died.

Starkly shadowed by the midday sun, its once red-tiled roofs long since bleached to a pale biscuit and rippling in the heat haze, Hautaire, despite its formidable mass, seemed oddly insubstantial. Behind it, tier upon tier, the mountains rose up faint and blue into the cloudless northern sky. As he gazed up at the abbey, Spindrift conceived the peculiar notion that the structure was simply tethered to the rocks like some strange airship built of stone. It was twisted oddly askew, and some of the buttresses supporting the Romanesque cupola seemed to have been stuck on almost as afterthoughts. He blinked his eyes and the quirk of vision passed. The massive pile re-emerged as solid and unified as any edifice which has successfully stood foursquare-on to the elements for over a thousand years. Fumbling a handkerchief from his pocket, Spindrift mopped the sweat from his forehead; then, remounting his bicycle, he pushed off on the last lap of his journey.

Fifteen minutes later, as he wheeled his machine up the final steep incline, a little birdlike monk clad in a faded brown habit fluttered out from the shadows of the portico and scurried with arms outstretched in welcome to the perspiring cyclist. "Welcome, Señor Spindrift!" he cried. "I have been expecting you this half hour past."

Spindrift was still somewhat dizzy from his hot and dusty ride, but he was perfectly well aware that he had not specified any particular day for his arrival, if only because he had no means of knowing how long the journey from Switzerland would take him. He smiled and shook the proffered hand. "Brother Roderigo?"

"Of course, of course," chuckled the little monk, and glancing down at Spindrift's bicycle, he observed, "So they managed to repair your wheel."

Spindrift blinked. "Why, yes," he said. "But how on earth . . . ?"

"Ah, but you must be so hot and tired, Señor! Come into Hautaire where it is cool." Seizing hold of Spindrift's machine, he trundled it briskly across the courtyard, through an archway, down a stone-flagged passage and propped it finally against a cloister wall.

Spindrift, following a pace or two behind, gazed about him curiously. In the past six months he had visited many ecclesiastical establishments but none which had given him the overwhelming sense of timeless serenity that he recognized here. In the center of the cloister yard clear water was bubbling up into a shallow limestone saucer. As it brimmed over, thin wavering streams tinkled musically into the deep basin beneath. Spindrift walked slowly forward into the fierce sunlight and stared down into the rippled reflection of his dusty, sweat-streaked face. A moment later his image was joined by that of the smiling Fr. Roderigo. "That water comes down from a spring in the hillside," the little monk informed him. "It flows through the very same stone pipes which the Romans first laid. It has never been known to run dry."

A metal cup was standing on the shadowed inner rim of the basin. The monk picked it up, dipped it, and handed it to Spindrift. Spindrift smiled his thanks, raised the vessel to his lips and drank. It seemed to him that he had never tasted anything so delicious in his life. He drained the cup and handed it back, aware as he did so that his companion was nodding his head as though in affirmation. Spindrift smiled quizzically. "Yes," sighed Fr. Roderigo, "you have come. Just as he said you would."

The sense of acute disorientation which Spindrift had experienced since setting foot in Hautaire persisted throughout the whole of the first week of his stay. For this, Fr. Roderigo was chiefly responsible. In some manner not easy to define, the little monk had succeeded in inducing in his guest the growing conviction that his quest for the elusive Meister Sternwärts had reached its ordained end; that what Spindrift was seeking was hidden here at Hautaire, buried somewhere among the musty manuscripts and incunabula that filled the oak shelves and stone recesses of the abbey library.

True to his promise, the librarian had laid before Spindrift such documentary evidence as he himself had amassed over the years, commencing with that faded entry in the 13th Century *registrum*. Together they had peered down at the ghostly script. "Out of Cathay," mused Spindrift. "Could it have been a joke?"

Fr. Roderigo pulled a face. "Perhaps," he said. "But the hand is indisputably the meister's. Of course, he may simply have wished to mystify the brothers."

"Do you believe that?"

"No," said the monk. "I am sure that what is written there is the truth. Meister Sternwärts had just returned from a pilgrimage in the steps of Apollonius of Tyana. He had lived and studied in the East for ten years." He scuttled across to a distant shelf, lifted down a bound folio volume, blew the dust from it, coughed himself breathless, and then laid the book before Spindrift. "The evidence is all there," he panted with a shy smile. "I bound the sheets together myself some thirty years ago. I remember thinking at the time that it would make a fascinating commentary to Philostratus' *Life of Apollonius.*"

Spindrift opened the book and read the brief and firmly penned Prolegomenon. *"Being then in my forty-ninth year, Sound in Mind and Hale in Body, I, Peter Sternwärts, Seeker after Ancient Truths; Alerted by my Friends; Pursued by mine Enemies; did set forth from Würzburg for Old Buda. What here follows is the Truthful History of all that Befell me and of my Strange Sojourn in Far Cathay, written by my own hand in the Abbey of Hautaire in this year of Our Lord 1273."*

Spindrift looked up from the page, and as he did so, he gave a deep sigh of happiness.

Fr. Roderigo nodded. "I know, my friend," he said. "You do not have to tell me. I shall leave you alone with him."

But Spindrift was already turning the first page.

That evening, at Fr. Roderigo's suggestion, Spindrift strolled with him up onto the hillside above Hautaire. The ascent was a slow one because every fifty paces or so Fr. Roderigo was constrained to pause awhile to regain his breath. It was then that Spindrift became aware that the friendly little monk was ill. Beneath that quick and ready smile were etched the deep lines of old familiar pain. He suggested gently that perhaps they might just sit where they were, but Fr. Roderigo would not hear of it. "No, no, my dear Spindrift," he insisted breathlessly. "There is something I must show you. Something that has a profound bearing upon our joint quest."

After some twenty minutes they had reached one of the fallen menhirs that formed a sort of gigantic necklace around the abbey. There Fr. Roderigo paused and patted his heaving chest apologetically. "Tell me, Señor," he panted. "What is your candid opinion of Apollonius of Tyana?"

Spindrift spread his hands in a gesture that contrived to be both noncommittal and expiatory. "To tell the truth I can hardly be said to have an opinion at all," he confessed. "Of course I know that Philostratus made some extraordinary claims on his behalf."

"Apollonius made only one claim for *himself,*" said Fr. Roderigo. "But that one was not inconsiderable. He claimed to have foreknowledge of the future."

"Yes?" said Spindrift guardedly.

"The extraordinary accuracy of his predictions led to his

falling foul of the Emperor Nero. Apollonius, having already foreseen this, prudently retired to Ephesus before the monster was able to move against him."

Spindrift smiled. "Precognition obviously proved a most useful accomplishment."

"Yes and no," said Fr. Roderigo, ignoring the irony. "Have you reached the passage in the Meister's *Biographia* where he speaks of the Praemonitiones?"

"Do they really exist?"

The little monk seemed on the point of saying something and then appeared to change his mind. "Look," he said, gesturing around him with a sweep of his arm. "You see how Hautaire occupies the exact center of the circle?"

"Why, so it does," observed Spindrift.

"Not fortuitous, I think."

"No?"

"Nor did he," said Fr. Roderigo with a smile. "The Meister spent a whole year plotting the radiants. Somewhere there is a map which he drew."

"Why should he do that?"

"He was seeking to locate an Apollonian nexus."

"?"

"The concept is meaningless unless one is prepared to accept the possibility of precognition."

"Ah," said Spindrift guardedly. "And did he find what he was looking for?"

"Yes," said Fr. Roderigo simply. "There." He pointed down at the abbey.

"And then what?" enquired Spindrift curiously.

Fr. Roderigo chewed his lower lip and frowned. "He persuaded Abbé Paulus to build him an observatory—an *oculus,* he called it."

"And what did he hope to observe from it?"

"*In* it," corrected Fr. Roderigo with a faint smile. "It had no windows."

"You amaze me," said Spindrift, shaking his head. "Does it still exist?"

"It does."

"I should very much like to see it. Would that be possible?"

"It might," the monk admitted. "We would have to obtain the abbot's permission. However, I—" He broke off, racked by a savage fit of coughing that turned his face grey. Spindrift, much alarmed, patted his companion gently on the back and felt utterly helpless. Eventually the little monk recovered his breath and with a trembling hand wiped a trace of spittle from his blue lips. Spindrift was horrified to see a trace of blood on the white handkerchief. "Hadn't we better be making our way back?" he suggested solicitously.

Fr. Roderigo nodded submissively and allowed Spindrift to take him by the arm and help him down the track. When they were about halfway down, he was overcome by another fit of coughing which left him pale and gasping. Spindrift, now thoroughly alarmed, was all for going to fetch help from the abbey, but the monk would not hear of it. When he had recovered sufficiently to continue, he whispered hoarsely, "I promise I will speak to the abbot about the *oculus*."

Spindrift protested that there was no hurry, but Fr. Roderigo shook his head stubbornly. "Fortunately there *is* still just time, my friend. Just time enough."

Three days later Fr. Roderigo was dead. After attending the evening Requiem Mass for his friend, Spindrift made his way up to the library and sat there alone for a long time. The day was fast fading and the mistral was beginning to blow along the Ix valley. Spindrift could hear it sighing round the buttresses and mourning among the crannies in the crumbling stonework. He thought of Roderigo now lying out on the hillside in his shallow anonymous grave. *The goal ye seek lies within yourself*. He wondered what had inspired the abbot to choose that particular line from the *Illuminatum* for his Requiem text and suspected that he was the only person present who had recognized its origin.

There was a deferential knock at the library door, and a young novice came in carrying a small, metal-bound casket. He set it down on the table before Spindrift, took a key from his pocket and laid it beside the box. "The father superior instructed me to bring these to you, sir," he said. "They were in Brother Roderigo's cell." He bowed his head slightly, turned, and went out, closing the door softly behind him.

Spindrift picked up the key and examined it curiously. It was quite unlike any other he had ever seen, wrought somewhat in the shape of a florid, double-ended question mark. He had no idea how old it was or even what it was made of. It looked like some alloy—pewter, maybe?—but there was no discernible patina of age. He laid it down again and drew the casket towards him. This was about a foot long, nine inches or so wide, and perhaps six inches deep. The oak lid, which was ornately decorated with silver inlay and brass studding, was slightly domed. Spindrift raised the box and shook it gently. He could hear something shifting around inside, bumping softly against the sides. He did not doubt that the strange key unlocked the casket, but when he came to try, he could find no keyhole in which to fit it. He peered underneath. By the trickle of waning light through the western windows he could just discern an incised pentagram and the Roman numerals for 1274.

His pulse quickening perceptibly, he hurried across to the far end of the room and fetched an iron candlestick. Having lit the candle, he set it down beside the box and adjusted it so that its light was shining directly upon the lid. It was then that he noticed that part of the inlaid decoration appeared to correspond to what he had previously assumed to be the handle of the key. He pressed down on the silver inlay with his fingertips and thought he felt it yield ever so slightly.

He retrieved the key, adjusted it so that its pattern completely covered that of the inlay, and then pressed downwards experimentally. There was a faint *click!* and he felt the lid pushing itself upwards against the pressure of his fingers. He let out his pent breath in a faint sigh, detached the key, and eased the lid back on its hinge. Lying within the box was a vellum-covered book and a quill pen.

Spindrift wiped his fingers along his sleeve and, with his heart racing, dipped his hand into the casket and lifted out the book. As the light from the candle slanted across the cover, he was able to make out the faded sepia lettering spelling out the word: *PRAEMONITIONES* and below it, in a darker ink, the cynical query—*Quis Custodiet Ipsos Custodes?*

Spindrift blinked up into the candlelight. "Who will watch the watchers?" he murmured. "Who, indeed?"

The wind snuffled and whimpered against the now dark window panes, and the vesper bell began to toll in the abbey tower. Spindrift gave a violent, involuntary shiver and turned back the cover of the book.

Someone, perhaps even Peter Sternwärts himself, had stitched onto the flyleaf a sheet of folded parchment. Spindrift carefully unfolded it and peered down upon what, at first glance, seemed to be an incomprehensible spiderweb of finely drawn lines. He had been staring at it for only a minute before it dawned on him that the dominant pattern was remarkably similar to that on the lid of the casket and its weirdly shaped key. But there was something else too, something that teased at his recollection, something he knew he had once seen somewhere else. And suddenly he had it: an interlinked, megalithic spiral pattern carved into a rockface near Tintagael in Cornwall; here were exactly those same whorled and coupled S shapes that had once seemed to his youthful imagination like a giant's thumbprints in the granite.

No sooner was the memory isolated than he had associated this graphic labyrinth with the pagan menhirs dotting the hillside round Hautaire. Could *this* be the map Roderigo had mentioned? He held the parchment closer to the quaking candle flame and at once perceived the ring of tiny circles which formed a periphery around the central vortex. From each of these circles faint lines had been scratched across the swirling whirlpool to meet at its center.

Spindrift was now convinced that what he was holding in his hands was some arcane chart of Hautaire itself and its immediate environs, but at the precise point where the abbey itself should have been indicated, something had been written in minute letters. Unfortunately the point happened to coincide with the central cruciform fold in the parchment. Spindrift screwed up his eyes and thought he could just make out the words *tempus* and *pons*—or, possibly *fons*—together with a word which might equally well have been *cave* or *carpe*. "Time," "bridge," or perhaps "source." And what else? "Beware"? "Seize"? He shook his head in frustration and gave it up as a bad job. Having carefully refolded the chart, he turned over the flyleaf and began to read.

By the time he had reached the last page, the candle had sunk to a guttering stub, and Spindrift was acutely conscious of an agonizing headache. He lowered his face into his cupped hands and waited for the throbbing behind his eyeballs to subside. He had, to the best of his knowledge, been intoxicated only once in his life, and that was on the occasion of his twenty-first birthday. He had not enjoyed the experience. The recollection of how the world had seemed to rock on its foundations had remained one of his most distressing memories. Now he was reminded of it all over again as his mind lurched drunkenly from one frail clutching point to the next. Of course it was a hoax, an extraordinarily elaborate, purposeless hoax. It *had* to be! And yet he feared it was nothing of the sort, that what he had just read was, in truth, nothing less than a medieval prophetic text of such incredible accuracy that it made absolute nonsense of every rationalist philosophy ever conceived by man. Having once read the

Praemonitiones, one stepped like Alice through the looking glass into a world where only the impossible was possible. But *how?* In God's name *how?*

Spindrift removed his hands from before his eyes, opened the book at random, and by the vestige of light left in the flapping candle flame, read once more how, in the year 1492, Christobal Colon, a Genoese navigator, would bow to the dictates of the sage Chang Heng and would set sail into the west on the day of the Expulsion of the Jews from Spain. He would return the following year, laden with treasure and "companioned by those whom he would call Indians but who would in truth be no such people." At which point the candle flared up briefly and went out.

Next morning, Spindrift requested, and was granted, an audience with the abbot. He took with him the wooden casket and the mysterious key. His eyes were red-rimmed and bloodshot, and the dark rings beneath them testified to a sleepless night.

Abbé Ferrand was in his early fifties—a stalwart man with shrewd eyes, ash-grey hair and bushy eyebrows. His upright stance struck Spindrift as having more than a touch of the military about it. He wore the simple brown habit of his order, and only the plain brass crucifix, slung on a beaded leather thong about his neck, distinguished him from the other monks. He smiled as Spindrift entered the study, then rose from behind his desk and held out his hand. Spindrift, momentarily confused, tucked the casket under his left arm and then shook the proffered hand.

"And how can I be of service to you, M'sieur Spindrift?"

Spindrift took a breath, gripped the casket in both hands and held it out in front of him. "Abbé Ferrand, I . . . ," he began, and then dried up.

The corners of the abbot's lips were haunted by the ghost of a smile. "Yes?" he prompted gently.

"Sir," blurted Spindrift, "do you know what's in here?"

"Yes," said the abbot. "I think I do."

"Then why did you send it to me?"

"Brother Roderigo wished me to. It was one of his last requests."

"The book's a forgery, of course. But you must know that."

"You think so, M'sieur?"

"Well, of course I do."

"And what makes you so certain?"

"Why," cried Spindrift, "because it *has* to be!"

"But there have always been prophets, M'sieur Spindrift," returned the abbot mildly. "And they have all prophesied."

Spindrift waved a dismissive hand. "Nostradamus, you mean? Vague ambiguities. Predictions of disaster which could be interpreted to fit any untoward circumstance. But this. . . ."

The abbot nodded. "Forgive my asking, M'sieur," he said, "but what was it exactly that brought you to Hautaire?"

Spindrift set the casket down on the desk in front of him and laid the key beside it. As he did so he realized, not for the first time, that the question Abbé Ferrand was posing could have no simple answer. "Principally, I believe, Peter Sternwärts' *Illuminatum,*" he said. "I felt a compulsion to learn all I could about their author."

The abbot appeared to ponder on this reply; then he turned on his sandaled heel, walked over to a wall cupboard, opened it, and drew from within another vellum-covered notebook similar in appearance to that which Spindrift had replaced in the casket. Having closed the cupboard door, the abbot stood for a moment tapping the notebook against his finger ends. Finally he turned back to Spindrift. "I take it you have studied the *Praemonitiones,* M'sieur Spindrift?"

Spindrift nodded.

"Then you will perhaps recall that its forecasts end with the Franco-Prussion war. Unless my memory deceives me, the final entry concerns Bazaine's surrender at Metz in October, 1870; the capitulation of Paris in 1871; and the signing of the treaty at Frankfurt-sur-Main on May 10th of that same year?"

"Yes," said Spindrift, "that is perfectly correct."

The abbot opened the book he was holding, flipped over a few pages, glanced at what was written there, and then said, "Would you say, M'sieur Spindrift, that Europe has at last seen the end of war?"

"Why, certainly," said Spindrift. "The League of Nations has outlawed—"

"On September 1st, 1939," cut in the abbot, "Russia and Germany will, in concert, invade Poland. As a direct consequence of this Britain and France will declare war on Germany."

"But that's preposterous!" exclaimed Spindrift. "Why, the Versailles Treaty specifically states that under no circumstances is Germany ever again to be allowed to rearm!"

The abbot turned back a page. "In 1924—next year, is it

not?—Lenin will die and will be succeeded by"—here he tilted the page to catch the light—"Joseph Viss-ar-ionovitch—I think that's right—Stalin. An age of unparalleled tyranny will commence in the so-called Soviet Republic, which will continue for fifty-one years." He flicked on. "In 1941 German armies will invade Russia and inflict massive defeats on the Soviet forces." He turned another page. "In July, 1945, the fabric of civilization will be rent asunder by an explosion in an American desert." He shrugged and closed up the book, almost with relief.

"You are surely not asking me to believe that those fantastic predictions are the work of Peter Sternwärts?" Spindrift protested.

"Only indirectly," said the abbot. "Without Meister Sternwärts they would certainly never have come into existence. Nevertheless, he did not write them himself."

"Then who did?"

"These last? Brother Roderigo."

Spindrift just gaped.

The abbot laid the book down on the desk beside the casket and picked up the key. "Before he died," he said, "Brother Roderigo informed me that you had expressed a desire to examine the *oculus*. Is this so?"

"Then it really does exist?"

"Oh, yes. Most certainly it exists. This is the key to it."

"In that case, I would very much like to see it."

"Very well, M'sieur," said the abbot, "I will conduct you there myself. But, first, I should be intrigued to know what makes you so certain that the *Praemonitiones* is a forgery?"

Spindrift looked down at the casket. The whorled inlay on its lid seemed to spin like a silver Catherine wheel. He dragged his gaze away with difficulty. "Because I have always believed in free-will," he said flatly. "To believe in the *Praemonitiones* would be to deny it."

"Oh," said the abbot, "is that all? I thought perhaps you had detected the alteration in the script which takes place at roughly fifty-year intervals. It is admittedly slight, but it cannot be denied."

"The light was not good in the library last night," said Spindrift. "I noticed no marked change in the cursive style of the entries."

The abbot smiled. "Look again, M'sieur Spindrift," he said. "By daylight." He pressed the key into the lock, removed the *Praemonitiones* from the casket and handed it over.

Spindrift leafed through the pages, then paused, turned back a few, nodded, and went on. "Why, yes," he said. "Here in this entry for 1527: 'The Holy City sacked by the armies of the Emperor Charles.' There *is* a difference. How do you account for it?"

"They were written by different hands," said the abbot. "Though all, I hazard, with that same pen."

Spindrift reached into the casket, took out the cut-down quill and examined it. As his fingers closed round the yellowed shaft, it seemed to twist ever so slightly between them as though endowed with some strange will of its own. He dropped it back hastily into the box and flushed with annoyance at his own childishness. "If I understand you, Abbé, you are saying that these predictions were made by many different hands over the past seven centuries."

"That is correct. It would appear that the horizon of foresight is generally limited to about fifty years, though in certain cases—notably Sternwärts himself—it reaches a good deal further." The abbot said this in a quiet matter-of-fact tone that Spindrift found distinctly disconcerting. He reached out tentatively for the second book which the abbot had placed on the desk, but seemingly unaware of Spindrift's intention, the abbot had casually laid his own hand upon it. "Now, if you are ready, M'sieur," he said, "I suggest we might climb up and pay our respects to the *oculus*."

Spindrift nodded.

The abbot smiled and seemed pleased. He placed the two books within the casket and clapped the lid shut. Then he picked up the key, took down another bunch of keys which was hanging from a hook on the wall, and, nodding to Spindrift to follow him, led the way along a cool white corridor, up a flight of stone stairs and along a passage buttressed by slanting sunbeams. They took several turns and climbed yet another flight of stairs. Spindrift glanced out of a window as they passed and observed that they were now almost on a level with the ruin of the prehistoric stone circle. The abbot's leather sandals slapped briskly against the soles of his bare feet and made a noise like a razor being stropped.

At last they reached a small oak door. The abbot paused, selected one of the keys from the bunch, thrust it into the lock and twisted it. The hinges groaned and the door squealed inwards. "This leads to the dome of the rotunda," he explained. "The *oculus* is actually situated within the fabric of the northern wall. It is certainly an architectural curiosity."

Spindrift ducked his head, passed through the doorway, and found himself in a narrow crack of a curved passageway dimly lit by narrow barred slits in the outer stonework. Thick dust lay on the stone floor, which was caked with a crust formed from generations of bird and bat droppings. The floor spiraled upwards at an angle of some ten degrees, and Spindrift calculated that they had made at least one complete circuit of the rotunda before the abbot said, *"Ecce oculus!"*

Peering past the broad shoulder of his guide, Spindrift saw a second door, so narrow that a man could have passed through it only with extreme difficulty. The abbot squeezed himself backwards into a niche and allowed Spindrift to edge around him. Then he handed over the key to the casket, saying as he did so: "You will find that it operates in the normal way, M'sieur."

"Thank you," said Spindrift, taking the key from him and approaching the door. "Is there room for only one person inside?"

"Barely that," said the abbot. "The door opens outwards."

Spindrift inserted the key into the lock and twisted it. The wards grated reluctantly but still allowed the key to turn. Then, using it as a handle, for there was, indeed, no other, he pulled the door gently towards him. A moment later he had started back with a barely suppressed gasp of astonishment. The door had opened to disclose a sort of lidless limestone coffin, bare and empty, standing on its end, apparently cemented fast into the surrounding masonry. "What on earth is it?" he demanded.

The abbot chuckled. "That is your *oculus,* M'sieur."

Spindrift eyed the coffin uncertainly. "And you say Sternwärts built that?" he enquired dubiously.

"Well, certainly he must have caused it to be built," said the abbot. "Of that there can be little doubt. See there—" He pointed to some lettering carved on the limestone corbel which framed the "head" of the casque—*Sternwärts hoc fecit.* "Not proof positive, I grant you, but good enough for me." He smiled again. "Well, now you are here, M'sieur Spindrift, are you not tempted to try it?"

Spindrift gazed at the Latin lettering. "Sternwärts made this," he muttered, and, even as he spoke the words aloud, he knew he would have to step inside that stone shell, if only because to refuse to do so would be to deny the noble and courageous spirit of the man who had penned the *Illuminatum.*

Yet he could not disguise his reluctance. How dearly at that moment he would have liked to say: "Tomorrow, perhaps, or next week, if it's all the same to you, Abbé." But he knew he would be allowed no second chance. It was now or never. He nodded, drew a deep breath, swallowed once, stepped resolutely forward and edged himself backwards into the cold sarcophagus.

Gently the abbot closed the door upon him and sketched over it a slow and thoughtful sign of the Cross.

For no particular reason that he was aware of, Spindrift had recently found himself thinking about Fr. Roderigo. Once or twice he had even wandered out into the abbey graveyard and tried to locate the spot where the bones of the little monk were buried. He had pottered about, peering vaguely among the hummocks, but he found that he could no longer recall precisely where the body of his friend had been interred. Only the abbots of Hautaire were accorded headstones, and even Abbé Ferrand's was by now thickly encrusted with lichen.

Spindrift found a piece of dry twig and began scratching at the lettered limestone, but by the time he had scraped clean the figures 1910-1937, he found the impulse had already waned. After all, what was the point? That was the surprising thing about growing old: nothing seemed quite so urgent or important any more. Sharp edges became blunt; black and white fudged off into grey; and your attention kept wandering off after stupid little tidbits of memory and getting lost among the flowery hedgerows of the Past. *Quis Custodiet . . . ?*

The old librarian straightened up, released the piece of twig he was holding and began massaging his aching back. As he did so, he suddenly recalled the letter. He had been carrying it around with him all day and had, in fact, come out into the graveyard on purpose to try to make up his mind about it. Obscurely he felt he needed the ghostly presence of Roderigo and the Abbé Ferrand to help him. Above all he needed to be *sure*.

He peered around for a convenient seat, then lowered himself creakily so that his back rested against the abbé's sun-warmed headstone. He dipped around inside his woolen habit for his spectacles and the envelope, and having at last settled everything to his comfort and satisfaction, he extracted the letter, unfolded it, cleared his throat and read out aloud:

Post Restante
Arles
Bouches du Rhône.

June 21, 1981.

Dear Sir,

I have recently returned to Europe after four years' travel and study in India, Burma and Nepal, during which one of my teachers introduced me to your marvelous edition of the *Biographia Mystica* of Meister Sternwärts. It was a complete revelation to me and, together with the *Illuminatum*, has radically changed my whole outlook on life. *"The truly aimed shaft strikes him who looses it"* (Ill.XXIV)!!

I could not permit myself to quit Europe and return home to Chicago without having made an effort to thank you in person and, perhaps, to give myself the treat of conversing with you about the life and works of the Meister.

If you could possibly see your way towards gratifying my wish sometime—say within the next month or so?—would you be so good as to drop me a line at the above address, and I will come with all speed to Hautaire.

Yours most sincerely,
J. S. Harland

Spindrift concluded his reading, raised his head and blinked out over the valley. *"Quis Custodiet?"* he murmured, remembering suddenly, with quite astonishing clarity, how once, long ago, Brother Roderigo had handed him a cup of ice-cool water and had then nodded his head in affirmation. How had *he* known?

Hurtling out of the northern sky, three black planes, shaped like assegais, rushed down the length of the valley, drowning it with their reverberating thunder. Spindrift sighed, refolded the letter and fumbled it back into its envelope. He reached out, plucked a leaf of wild sage, rubbed it between finger and thumb and held it under his nose. By then the planes were already fifty miles away, skimming low over the distant, glittering sea, but the ripples of their bullying passage still lapped faintly back and forth between the ancient hills.

"Very well," murmured Spindrift, "I will write to this young man. *Ex nihilo, nihil fit.* But perhaps Mr. Harland is not 'nothing.' Perhaps he is something—even, maybe, my own successor, as I was Roderigo's and Roderigo was Brother Martin's. There always has *been* a successor—a watcher—an eye for the eye." He grunted, heaved himself up from the grave on which he was sitting and shuffled off towards the abbey, a slightly dotty old lay brother, muttering to himself as he went.

The counter clerk at the Bureau des Postes sniffed down her nose, glared at the passport which was held out to her and then, reluctantly, handed over the letter, expressing her profound disapproval of the younger generation.

The slim, deeply tanned, blonde girl in the faded blue shirt and jeans examined the postmark on the letter and chuckled delightedly. She hurried out into the sunny square, sat herself down on a low wall, carefully tore off a narrow strip from the end of the envelope and extracted Sprindrift's letter. Her sea-blue eyes flickered rapidly along the lines of typescript. "Oh, *great!*" she exclaimed. "Gee, isn't that *mar*-velous?"

Judy Harland, who, in her twenty-second year, still contrived to look a youthful and boyish eighteen, had once written on some application form in the space reserved for "occupation" the single word "enthusiast." They had not offered her the job, but it can hardly have been on the grounds of self-misrepresentation. Her letter to Spindrift had been dashed off on the spur of the moment when she had discovered that the Abbey of Hautaire was an easy day's hitchhike down the coast from Arles. Not that the information which she had given Spindrift was untrue—it *was* true—up to a point, that point being that her interest in Meister Sternwärts was but one of several enthusiasms among which, over the past eight years, she had zoomed back and forth like a tipsy hummingbird in a frangipani forest. She had already sampled Hatha Yoga, the teachings of Don Carlos, Tarot, Zen Buddhism, and the *I Ching*. Each had possessed her like an ardent lover to the exclusion of all the others—until the next. The *Illuminatum* and the *Biographia Mystica* represented but the most recent of her spiritual love affairs.

Her signing of her letter with her initials rather than her Christian name had been an act of prudence induced by certain awkward experiences in Persia and Afghanistan. She had survived these unscathed, just as she had survived everything else, because her essential self was hedged about by an inviolable conviction that she had been chosen to fulfil some stupendous but as-yet-unspecified purpose. The fact that she had no very clear idea of what the purpose might be was immaterial. What counted was the strength of the conviction. Indeed, in certain respects, Judy had more than a little in common with Joan of Arc.

A little deft work on her hair with a pair of scissors and a concealed chiffon scarf wound round her chest soon transformed her outwardly into a very passable boy. It was as James Harland that she climbed down from the cab of the friendly *camion* driver, shouldered her well-worn rucksack and strode off, whistling like a bird, up the winding, dusty road towards Hautaire. Just as Spindrift himself had done some sixty years before, and at precisely the same spot, she paused as she came within sight of the abbey and stood still for a moment, staring up at it. She saw a brown and white eagle corkscrewing majestically upwards in an invisible funnel of warm air, and as she watched it, she experienced an almost overwhelming impulse to turn round and go back. Perhaps if she had been under the aegis of the *I Ching,* she would have obeyed it, but Hautaire was now to her what fabled Cathay had once been to Peter Sternwärts—a challenge to be met and overcome. Shrugging aside her forebodings, she hooked her thumbs more firmly under the straps of her pack and marched on up the road.

Old age had lengthened Spindrift's vision. From the library window he had picked out the determined little figure when it was still three-quarters of a mile away. Something about it touched his heart like a cold finger. "*Golden-haired like an angel.*" Had he not himself written that long, long ago, after his last visit to the rotunda? How many years was it now? Fifty at least. As far as the eye could see. Why then had he not gone back? Was it fear? Or lack of any real religious faith to sustain him? Yet everything he had "seen" had come to pass just as he had described it. Such crazy things they had seemed too. Sunburst bombs shattering whole cities in the blink of an eye; men in silver suits walking on the face of the moon; an assassin's bullets striking down the President who would put them there; the endless wars; the horror and anguish of the extermination camps; human bestiality. Pain, pain, always pain. Until he had been able to endure no more. His last entry in the *Praemonitiones* must surely be almost due now. Did that mean he had failed in his bounden duty? Well, then, so he had failed, but at least he had given the world the *Biographia,* and none of his predecessors had done that. And there was still the marvel of the *Exploratio Spiritu-*

alis to come—that masterpiece which he alone had unearthed, translated, and pieced together. Perhaps one day it would be published. But not by him. Let someone else shoulder that burden. He knew what it would entail. And surely he had done enough. But the chill lay there in his heart like a splinter of ice that would not melt. *"Golden-haired like an angel."* Muttering to himself, he turned away from the window, shuffled across the library and began making his way down to the abbey gate to greet his visitor.

As a child Judy had sometimes toyed with a fanciful notion that people grew to resemble the names they had been born with. She was reminded of it when she first set eyes on Spindrift. His hair was as white and soft as the wisps of foam on a weir pool, and he blinked at her waterily through his steel-rimmed glasses as he shook her by the hand. "You are very young, Mr. Harland," he observed. "But, then, to you I daresay I must seem very old."

"Are you?" she asked in that blunt way of hers which some people found charming and others simply ill-mannered.

"I am exactly as old as this century," he replied with a smile. "Which makes me four score and one. A goodly stretch by any reckoning, wouldn't you say?"

"And you've lived here all your life?"

"Most of it, to be sure. I first came to Hautaire in 1923."

"Hey! My *father* was born in 1923!"

"An *annus mirabilis,* indeed," the old man chuckled. "Come along, Mr. Harland. Let me be the first to introduce you to Hautaire."

So saying, he led her through the outer courtyard and down into the cloisters where, like dim autumnal leaves, a few of the brothers were wandering in silent meditation. Judy's bright magpie glance darted this way and that. "Say," she whispered, "this sure is some place."

"Would you care for a drink?" asked Spindrift, suddenly recalling his own introduction to the abbey and hoping, vaguely, that by repeating the pattern he would be vouchsafed a sign of some kind.

"I surely would," said Judy. "Thanks a lot." She shrugged off her rucksack and dumped it down beside the basin of the fountain while Spindrift groped around short-sightedly for the cup.

"Here, let me," she said and, scooping up the cup, she dipped it into the basin and took a hearty swig.

Spindrift adjusted his spectacles and peered at her. A solitary drop of water hung for a moment like a tear from her square firm chin, and then she had brushed it away with the back of her hand. "That was great," she informed him. "Real cool."

Spindrift nodded and smiled. "That fountain was here even before the abbey was built," he said.

"Is that so? Then Meister Sternwärts may have done just what I've done."

"Yes," agreed Spindrift. "It is more than likely."

"That's really something," sighed Judy. "Hey, I've brought my copy of the *Biographia* for you to autograph. It's right here in my pack. I carry it around every place I go."

"Oh, really?" said Spindift, flushing with pleasure. "I must say I regard that as a great compliment."

"The *Biographia's* one of the world's great books," averred Judy stoutly. "Possibly the greatest."

Spindrift felt appropriately flattered. "Perhaps you would be interested to see the original manuscript?" he suggested diffidently.

"*Would* I! You mean you have it right here in the abbey?"

"It's in the library."

"Well, what are we waiting for?" demanded Judy. "I mean—that is—if it's convenient."

"Oh, yes, yes," Spindrift assured her. "We'll just call in at the guest wing first, and I'll show you your quarters. We can go straight on up from there."

Judy's unfeigned enthusiasm for the meister was all the old man could have wished for. He laid out the original manuscript of the *Biographia Mystica* before her and guided her through it while she gave little gasps and exclamations of wonder and pleasure. "It's just as if you'd known him personally, Mr. Spindrift," she said at last. "You make him come alive."

"Oh, he *is,* Mr. Harland. It is a gross error on our part to assume that life is mere physical existence. The *élan vital* lives on in the sublime creations of human genius. One only needs to study the *Exploratio Spiritualis* to realize that."

"And what's the *Exploratio Spiritualis,* Mr. Spindrift?"

"One day, I hope, it will be recognized as the *Biographia Mystica* of the mind."

"You don't say!"

"But I *do,* Mr. Harland. And, what is more, I have the best of reasons for saying so."

Judy looked up at him curiously. "You don't mean that you've dug up *another* work by Meister Sternwärts?"

Spindrift nodded emphatically.

"Why that's marvelous!" she cried. "Sensational! Can I see it?"

"It would mean very little to you, I'm afraid, Mr. Harland. The *Spiritualis* was written in cipher."

"And you've cracked it? Translated it?"

"I have."

"Wow!" breathed Judy.

"I have spent the last twenty-five years working at it," said Spindrift, with more than a trace of pride in his voice. "It is, I might pardonably claim, my swan song."

"And when's it going to be published?"

"By me—never."

"But why on earth not?"

"The responsibility is too great."

"How do you mean?"

Spindrift lifted his head, and gazed out of the open library window towards the distant invisible sea. "The world is not yet ready for the *Spiritualis*," he murmured. "Peter realized that, which is why he chose to write it in the form he did."

Judy frowned. "I'm afraid I'm still not with you, Mr. Spindrift. Why isn't it ready?"

"To accept a determinist universe as a proven fact?"

"Who says we're not?"

Almost reluctantly Spindrift withdrew his gaze from the far horizon and blinked down at her. "You mean you *can* accept it, Mr. Harland?" he asked curiously.

"Well, I certainly accept the *I Ching*."

"But you must, surely, believe in free will?"

"Well, up to a point, sure I do. I mean to say *I* have to consult the *I Ching*. It doesn't decide *for* me that I'm going to consult it, does it?"

It seemed to Spindrift at that moment that he had reached the final crossroads. But he was still not sure which path was the right one. He stirred the air vaguely with his fingers. "Then tell me, Mr. Harland," he said, "for the sake of the supposition, if you wish—what do you suppose would follow if one succeeded in convincing the human race that everything in life *was* preordained?"

Judy smiled. "But most of them believe it anyway. Astrology, Tarot, *I Ching*—you name it; we'll believe it. The fault, Mr. Spindrift, lies not in our selves but in our stars."

"Really?" said Spindrift. "I must say that you astonish me."

"Well, a lot's happened in the last thirty years. We're the post-H-bomb generation, remember. We got to see where reason had led us. Right bang up to the edge of the precipice."

Spindrift nodded. "Yes, yes," he murmured. "I know. I saw it."

"Come again?"

"The *Pikadon.* That's what they called it." He closed his eyes and shuddered. A moment later he had gripped her by the arm. "But imagine *knowing* what was going to happen and that you were powerless to prevent it. What then, Mr. Harland?"

"How do you mean 'knowing'?"

"Just that," Spindrift insisted. "Seeing it all happening *before* it *had* happened. What then?"

"Are you serious?"

"It's all there in the *Spiritualis,*" said Spindrift, releasing his hold on her arm and gripping the back of her chair with both hands. "Peter Sternwärts rediscovered what Apollonius of Tyana had brought back with him from the East. But he did more than that. He devised the means whereby this knowledge could be handed down to future generations. He was a seer who bequeathed his eyes to posterity."

Judy's eyes narrowed. "Just let me get this straight," she said slowly. "Are you telling me that Meister Sternwärts could actually *see* the future?"

"Yes," said Spindrift simply.

"What? *All* of it?"

"No. Only the biggest storms on the horizon—the crises for civilization. He called them 'Knots in Time'."

"But how do you know that?"

"He wrote them down," said Spindrift. "In a book he called *Praemonitiones.*"

"Holy Moses!" Judy whispered. "You just *have* to be kidding!"

"Sternwärts' own forecasts extend only as far as the 15th Century, but, as I said before, he bequeathed his eyes to posterity."

"And just what does that *mean,* Mr. Spindrift?"

Spindrift drew in his breath. "Wait here a moment, Mr. Harland," he said, "and I will do my best to show you what it means."

A minute later he was back carrying the first volume of the

Praemonitiones. He opened it at the frontispiece map and spread it out before her. Then he settled his spectacles firmly on his nose and began to explain what was what.

"This was drawn by Peter Sternwärts himself," he said. "There can be no question of that. It represents a bird's-eye view of the area within which Hautaire is situated. These dots represent the Neolithic stone circle, and the straight lines radiating from the menhirs all cross at this point here. I thought at first that these spirals were some primitive attempt to represent lines of magnetic force, but I know now that this is not so. Nevertheless, they do represent a force field of some kind—one, moreover, which was undoubtedly first detected by the ancient race who raised the original stone circle. Sternwärts realized that the menhirs acted as some sort of focusing device and that the area of maximum intensity would probably occur at the point where the intersection of the chords was held in equilibrium by the force field—what he called the *mare temporis*—sea of time."

Judy nodded. "So?" she said.

"He deduced that at this particular point he would find what he was seeking. I have since unearthed among the archives a number of sketches he made of similar stone circles in Brittany. And just off the center of each he has written the same word *oculus*—that is the Latin word for 'eye.' "

"Hey," said Judy, "you don't mean . . ."

"Indeed I do," insisted Spindrift. "After an immense amount of trial and error he succeeded in locating the precise point—and it is a very small area indeed—right here in Hautaire itself. Having found it, he built himself a time observatory and then proceeded to set down on record everything he saw. The results are there before you. The *Praemonitiones!*"

Judy stared down at the map. "But if that's so, why hasn't anyone else discovered one? I mean there's Stonehenge and Carnac and so forth, isn't there?"

Spindrift nodded. "That mystified Peter too, until he realized that the focal point of each circle was almost invariably situated a good twenty or so meters above ground level. He postulates that in the days when the circles were first raised, wooden towers were erected in their centers. The seer, who would probably have been a high priest, would have had sole access to that tower. In the case of Hautaire, it just so happened that the site of the long-vanished tower was occupied by the rotunda of the Abbey."

"And that was why Sternwärts came here?"

"No, Peter came to Hautaire because he had reason to believe that Apollonius of Tyana had made a special point of visiting this particular circle. There was apparently still a pagan shrine and a resident oracle here in the First Century A.D."

Judy turned over some pages in the book before her, but she barely glanced at what was written there. "But how does it *work?*" she asked. "What do you do in this *oculus?* Peek into a crystal ball or something?"

"One sees," said Spindrift vaguely. "Within the mind's eye."

"But *how?*"

"That I have never discovered. Nor, I hazard, did Peter. Nevertheless that is what happens."

"And can you choose what you want to see?"

"I used to think not," said Spindrift, "but since I stumbled upon the key to the *Exploratio Spiritualis,* I have been forced to revise my opinion. I now believe that Peter Sternwärts was deliberately working towards the goal of a spiritual and mental discipline which would allow him to exert a direct influence upon what he saw. His aim was to become a shaper of the future as well as a seer."

Judy's blue eyes widened perceptibly. "A *shaper?*" she echoed. "And did he?"

"It is impossible to tell," said Spindrift. "But it is surely not without significance that he left Hautaire before he died."

"Come again?"

"Well, by the time he left he knew for certain that chance does nothing that has not been prepared well in advance. He must have realized that the only way in which he could exert an influence upon the future would be by acting in the present. If he could succeed in tracing the thread backwards from its knot, he might be able to step in and adjust things at the very point where only the merest modicum of intervention could affect the future. Of course, you must understand that this is all the purest supposition on my part."

Judy nodded. "And these disciplines—mental what's-its—what were they?"

"They are expressly designed to enable the seer to select his own particular vision. Having seen the catastrophe ahead, he could, if he were successful, feel his way backwards in time from that point and, hopefully, reach a *junctura criticalis*—the precise germinal instant of which some far-off tragedy was the progeny."

"Yes, I understand that. But what *sort* of disciplines were they?"

"Ironically, Mr. Harland, they appear to have had a good deal in common with those which are still practiced today among certain Eastern faiths."

"What's ironical about that?"

"Well, surely, the avowed aim of the Oriental sages is to achieve the ultimate annihilation of the self—of the ego. What Peter Sternwärts was hoping to achieve seems to me to have been the exact opposite—the veritable apotheosis of the human ego! Nothing less than the elevation of Man to God! He had a persistent vision of himself as the potter and the whole of humanity as his clay. That explains why, throughout the *Exploratio,* he constantly refers to himself as a 'shaper.' It also explains why I have shunned the responsibility of publishing it."

"Then why are you telling me?" demanded Judy shrewdly.

Spindrift removed his spectacles, closed his eyes, and massaged his eyelids with his fingertips. "I am very old, Mr. Harland," he said at last. "It is now over fifty years since I last visited the *oculus,* and the world is very close to the horizon of my own visions. Ever since Abbé Ferrand's untimely death forty years ago, the secret of the *oculus* has been mine alone. If I were to die this minute, it would perish with me, and I, by default, would have betrayed the trust which I believe has been reposed in me. In other words, I would die betraying the very man who has meant far more to me than any I have ever known in the flesh—Peter Sternwärts himself."

"But why choose *me?*" Judy insisted. "Why not one of the other brothers?"

Spindrift sighed. "I think, Mr. Harland, that it is perhaps because I recognize in you some of my own lifelong reverence for Peter Sternwärts. Furthermore, in some manner which I find quite impossible to explain, I am convinced that you are associated with the last visit I paid to the *oculus*—with my final vision."

"Really? And what was that?"

Spindrift looked down at the parchment which had absorbed so much of his life, and then he shook his head. "There was a girl," he murmured. "A girl with golden hair. . . ."

"A *girl?*"

Like a waterlogged corpse rising slowly to the surface, the old man seemed to float up from the troubled depths of some dark and private nightmare. His eyes cleared. "Why, yes," he said. "A *girl*. Do you know, Mr. Harland, in all these years that point had never struck me before! A girl, *here in Hautaire!*" He began to chuckle wheezily. "Oh dear, oh dear, oh dear! Why that would be the end of the world indeed!"

In spite of herself Judy was deeply moved by the old man's transparent relief. Instinctively she put out her hand and laid it on his. "I don't know what your vision was, Mr. Spindrift," she said. "But if you feel I can be of help to you in any way. . . ."

Spindrift brought his other hand across and patted hers abstractedly. "That is most kind of you, Mr. Harland," he murmured. "Really, most kind. . . . "

At supper that evening the abbot stepped up to the lectern in the refectory and raised a hand for silence. The murmur of voices stilled as the brothers turned their wondering eyes towards their father superior. He surveyed them all in silence for a long moment and then said, "Brethren and honored guests . . . my friends. Here at Hautaire, we live a life whose fundamental pattern was laid down for us more than a thousand years ago. I believe it is a good life, one which has accordingly found favor in the eyes of God. My cherished hope is that a thousand years from now its pattern will have remained, in all essential respects, as it is today—that the spiritual verities enshrined in our foundation will be what they have always been—a source of comfort and reassurance to all God-loving men, a harbor of hope and tranquillity in a storm-tossed world."

He paused as though uncertain how to continue, and they all saw him close his eyes and turn his face upwards in mute prayer for a long, long minute. When at last he looked down upon them again, the silence in the hall was almost palpable.

"My friends, I have just learnt that certain European powers, acting in concert with Israel and the United States of America, have this afternoon launched an armed invasion of Saudi Arabia and the Trucial States."

There was a concerted gasp of horror and a sudden burst of whispering. The abbot raised his voice to carry over the hubbub.

"Their avowed aim is to secure for themselves access to the oil supplies which they deem essential to their national, political and economic survival. Under the terms of the Baghdad Treaty of 1979, the Arabs have called upon the Soviet Union for immediate armed assistance, and Russia and its allies have demanded the instant and total withdrawal of the invading forces. Failure to comply with this demand will, they say, bring about inevitable consequences."

He paused again and regarded them somberly. "I shall personally conduct a service for Divine Intercession immediately after complin. It will be held in the main chapel. It goes without saying that all our guests are invited to attend. *Dominus vobiscum.*" He sketched the sign of the Cross over them, stepped down from the lectern, and strode swiftly out of the hall.

In the outburst of chattering which erupted immediately the abbot had left the hall, Spindrift turned to Judy and seized her by the arm. "You must come with me, Mr. Harland," he whispered urgently. "At once."

Judy, who was still groping to come to terms with all the implications of what she had heard, nodded submissively and allowed the old man to shepherd her out of the refectory and up into the library. He unearthed the keys to the *oculus* and the rotunda, then hurried her up the stairs and along the deserted passages to the door which had remained locked for more than half a century. He was possessed by an almost feverish impatience and kept up an incessant muttering to himself the whole way. Judy could hardly make out a word of what he was saying, but more than once she thought she caught the strange word *Pikadon.* It meant nothing to her at all.

So much rubbish had accumulated in the narrow passage that they had to lean their combined weight against the rotunda door before they managed to force it open. They squeezed through into the crevice beyond, and Spindrift lit a candle he had brought with him. By its wavering light the two of them scuffled their way forward to the *oculus.*

When they reached it, Spindrift handed the key to Judy and held the candle so that she could see what she was doing. A minute later the door had creaked open to expose the sarcophagus, standing just as it had stood for the last seven hundred years.

Judy gaped at it in astonishment. "You mean you go in *there?*"

"*You* must, Mr. Harland," said Spindrift. "Please, hurry."

"But *why?*" demanded Judy. "What good could it do?"

Spindrift gripped her by the shoulder and almost succeeded in thrusting her bodily into the casque. "Don't you understand, Mr. Harland?" he cried. "It is *you* who must prove my final vision false! *You have to prove me wrong!*"

Into her twenty-two years of life Judy had already packed more unusual experiences than had most women three times her age, but none of them had prepared her for this. Alone with a looney octogenarian who seemed bent on stuffing her into a stone coffin buried somewhere inside the walls of a medieval monastery! For all she knew, once he had got her inside, he would turn the key on her and leave her there to rot. And yet, at the very moment when she most needed her physical strength, it had apparently deserted her. Her arms, braced against the stone slabs, seemed all but nerveless; her legs so weak she wondered if they were not going to fold under her. "The key," she muttered. "Give me the key. And you go away. Right away. Back to that other door. You can wait for me there."

The pressure of Spindrift's hand relaxed. Judy stepped back and fumbled the key out of the lock. Then, feeling a little more confident, she turned to face the old man. By the trembling light of the candle she glimpsed the streaks of tears on his ancient cheeks.

"Please go, Mr. Spindrift," she pleaded. "*Please.*"

"But you will do it?" he begged. "I must *know*, Mr. Harland."

"Yes, yes," she said. "Sure I will. I give you my word."

He shuffled backwards a few doubtful paces and stood watching her. "Would you like me to leave you the candle?" he asked.

"All right," she said. "Put it down there on the floor."

She waited until he had done it, and then, aloud, she started to count slowly up to sixty. She had reached barely halfway before the rotunda was buffeted by the massive reverberating thunder of warplanes hurtling past high overhead. Judy shivered violently and, without bothering to finish her count, stepped the two short paces back into the casque until her shoulders were pressed against the cold stone. "Please, dear God," she whispered, "let it be all—"

She was falling, dropping vertically downwards into the bowels of the earth as if down the shaft of an elevator. Yet the candle, still standing there before her just where the old man had left it and burning with its quiet golden flame, told her that her stomach lied. But her sense of vertigo was so acute that she braced her arms against the sides of the coffin in an effort to steady herself. Watery saliva poured into her mouth. Certain she was about to faint, she swallowed and closed her eyes.

Like magenta fire balloons, the afterimages of the candle flame drifted across her retina. They changed imperceptibly to green, to dark blue, to purple and finally vanished into the velvety darkness. Her eyelids felt as though lead weights had been laid upon them.

Suddenly—without warning of any kind—she found herself gazing down, as if from a great height, upon a city. With the instant familiarity bred of a dozen high-school civics assignments, she knew it at once for her own hometown. The whole panoramic scene had a strange, almost dreamlike clarity. The air was unbelievably clear; no trace of smoke or haze obscured the uncompromising grid of the streets. Northwards, Lake Michigan glittered silver-blue in the bright sunshine, while the plum-blue shadows of drifting clouds ghosted silently across its placid waters. But this was no longer the Chicago she remembered. The whole center of the metropolis was gone. Where it had been was nothing but a vast circular smudge of grey rubble, along the fringes of which, green shrubs were already growing. No factory stacks smoked; no glittering lines of automobiles choked these expressways; no freight trains wriggled and jinked through these latticed sidings; all was as dead and still as a city on the moon. This was indeed Necropolis, City of the Dead.

At last the vision faded and its place was taken by another. She now found herself gazing out across a vast plain through which wound a great river. But the endless golden Danubian wheatfields which she remembered so well had all vanished. The winds which sent the towering cloud schooners scudding across this sky blew only through the feathered heads of weeds and wild grasses which stretched out like a green and rippling sea to the world's end. Of man, or cattle, or even flying bird there was no sign at all.

When Spindrift returned some twenty minutes later, it was to discover Judy crouched in the bottom of the sarcophagus, curled up like a dormouse with her head resting on her bent knees. Fearfully he stooped over her and placed his hand on her shoulder. "Mr. Harland," he whispered urgently. "Mr. Harland, are you all right?"

There was no response. He knelt down, thrust his hands beneath her arms and, by a mighty effort, succeeded in dragging her clear of the casque. She flopped sideways against the door, then sprawled forwards beside him. He fumbled his hand inside the neck of her shirt, felt for the beating of her heart, and so discovered who she was. The last dim flicker of hope died within him.

He patted her deathly cheeks and chafed her hands until at last her eyelids fluttered open. "What happened?" he asked. "What did you see?"

She raised a cold hand and wonderingly touched his wrinkled face with her fingertips. "Then it *hasn't* happened," she whispered. "And it was *so* real."

"It *will* happen," he said sadly. "Whatever it was you saw must come to pass. It always has."

"But there was no one," she mourned. "No one at all. What happened, Mr. Spindrift? Where had they all gone?"

"Come, my dear," he urged, gently coaxing her to her feet. "Come with me."

The air on the hillside was still warm, drowsy with the summer scents of wild sage, lavender and rosemary, as the old man and the girl made their way up the dim path towards the ridge where the ancient neoliths still bared themselves like broken teeth against the night sky. Below them, the abbey lights glowed out cheerfully, and small figures could be seen moving back and forth behind the chapel windows.

They reached a point where an outcrop of limestone had been roughly shaped into a seat. Spindrift eased himself onto it, drew Judy down beside him and spread out the wide skirt of his habit to cover her. As he did so, he could feel her trembling like a crystal bell that, once struck, goes on quivering far below the threshold of audible sound. An enormous, impotent grief seized him by the throat. Too late he saw what he should have done, how he had betrayed the trust that Brother Roderigo and the Abbé Ferrand had laid upon him. But he saw too, with a sort of numb clarity, how he, Spindrift, could not have done it because, within himself, some vital spark of faith in humanity had been extinguished far back in the blood-stained ruins of 1917. He could no longer believe that men were essentially good, or that the miracle which the genius of Peter Sternwärts had created would not be used in some hideous way to further the purposes of evil.

Yet what if he *had* gone that one step further, *had* published the *Exploratio Spiritualis* and given to all men the means of foreseeing the inevitable consequences of their insane greed, their overweening arrogance, their atavistic lust for power? Who was to say that Armageddon might not have been averted, that Peter's miracle might not have succeeded in shaping anew the human spirit? *Quis custodiet ipsos custodes?* Ah, who indeed, if not God? and Spindrift's God had died in the mud of Ypres.

The full knowledge of what he had done rose as bitter as bile at the back of the old man's throat. Desperately he sought for some words of comfort for the girl who crouched beside him and could not stop quivering. Some lie, some little harmless lie. "I did not tell you before," he said, "but I believe you are destined to publish the *Spiritualis* for me. Yes, I remember now. That was how you were to be associated with my final vision. So, you see, there *is* still hope."

But even as he spoke, the distant eastern horizon suddenly flickered as though with summer lightning. His arm tightened involuntarily around the girl's shoulders. She stirred. "Oh God," she moaned softly. "Oh God, oh God, oh God." A harsh, grating sob shook her, and then another and another.

A second flash threw the low clouds into sharp relief, and then the whole arching roof of the world was lit up like the day. An urgent bell began tolling in the abbey.

Something scratched a line like a blood-red stalk high up into the southern sky, and a ball of blue-white fire blossomed in strange and sinister silence.

And later a wind got up and blew from the north.